For Tom and Paula

Philip Kerr was born in Edinburgh in 1956, and now lives in London with his wife and family. He is the author of *March Violets*, *The Pale Criminal*, *A German Requiem*, *A Philosophical Investigation* (which is shortly to be filmed), and *Dead Meat* (shown on television as Grushko). His last two novels, *Gridiron* and *Esau* have been sold for film development, along with *A Five Year Plan*.

A FIVE YEAR PLAN

Philip Kerr

ARROW

Published in the United Kingdom in 1998 by
Arrow Books

3 5 7 9 10 8 6 4

First published in the United Kingdom in 1997 by Hutchinson

Arrow Books Limited
Random House UK Ltd
20 Vauxhall Bridge Road, London SW1V 2SA

Random House Australia (Pty) Limited
20 Alfred Street, Milsons Point, Sydney
New South Wales 2061, Australia

Random House New Zealand Limited
18 Poland Road, Glenfield, Auckland 10, New Zealand

Random House South Africa (Pty) Limited
Endulini, 5a Jubilee Road, Parktown 2193, South Africa

Random House UK Limited Reg. No. 954009

A CIP catalogue record for this book
is available from the British Library

Papers used by Random House UK Limited
are natural, recyclable products made from wood grown in
sustainable forests. The manufacturing processes conform to
the environmental regulations of the country of origin

Printed and bound in Great Britain by
Cox & Wyman Ltd, Reading, Berkshire

ISBN 0 09 925718 1

ACKNOWLEDGMENTS

Special thanks are due to Ben Gunn for supplying me with much of the information about merchant shipping; to Robert Bookman, for doing the business, as always; and to Marian Wood, my editor, and Michael Naumann, my publisher, for their faith. I should also like to thank Nicholas Bognor, Graham Saltmarsh, Frances Coady, Linda Shaughnessy, Caradoc King, Terry Burke, Deborah Hayward, Nick Marston, and my wife, Jane Thynne for all their help and encouragement.

CHAPTER ONE

'Ah-choooo!'

The sneeze reverberated like a gunshot.

Jimmy Figaro glanced around his well-appointed office to check nothing was damaged.

'Fuckin' hay fever,' sniffed Rizzoli from behind a napkin-sized handkerchief. 'According to the fuckin' *Herald*, the pollen index is 129. That's on a scale of 201. On account of all the fuckin' mango trees we got down here in Florida.'

Rizzoli sneezed again, a great explosion of noise that was half growl, half whoop, like the yahooing sound a rodeo-rider might make on exiting the ring aboard a bucking horse. He said, 'It was up to me? I'd burn every fuckin' mango tree in Miami.'

Figaro nodded vaguely. He liked mangoes. He'd never given the trees much thought, but now that he did, his mind's eye saw Ursula Andress in *Doctor No*, singing a song about mango trees as she wiggled her ass out of the Caribbean sea with a conch in her hand. Why couldn't he have a client like that for once instead of a minor mobster like Tommy Rizzoli?

'Every fuckin' one of them. Bonfire of the mango trees.' Rizzoli chuckled. 'Just like that fuckin' movie, huh?'

'Which movie is that, Tommy?'

'Bonfire of the mango trees.'

Figaro felt himself frown. He was uncertain if Rizzoli was making a joke, or if he really did think that was what the movie was called.

'You mean Tom Wolfe?'

Rizzoli rubbed his nose furiously and shrugged.

'Yeah, right.'

But it was plain to Figaro that Tommy Rizzoli knew as much about Tom Wolfe as he did about fine porcelain. Figaro turned his attention back to the notes he'd been making. The facts were as clear as Tommy Rizzoli's guilt. He and an unnamed associate – but most probably it had been Rizzoli's half-brother, Willy Barizon – had taken extortionate control of most of Dade County's ice-trucking. There was that and the assault on one of the arresting police officers that had left the man with a broken nose.

'Ah-chooo!'

The trooper's nose. It was almost ironic in view of the allergic condition of Rizzoli's own Durante-sized hooter. But Rizzoli was adamant that the trooper had slipped and fallen.

'How do you feel about a plea, Tommy?'

'As in guilty plea, or plea for mercy?' He took hold of his nose and bent it one way and then the other, almost as if it had been broken. 'No fuckin' way.'

'As in plea bargain. I figure they'll drop the assault if we put our hands up to the extortion. Meanwhile I suggest you sell your interests in the ice and trucking business and get ready to pay some kind of fine.'

Both men flinched as outside the office door, a woman screamed. Figaro tried to ignore it.

'The People's evidence is at best not much more than hearsay,' he continued. 'Just a couple of undercover cops. I can make them look like Swiss cheese.'

'That's the cheese with the holes in, right?'

'Precisely. The DA knows it too. I don't see that you have to go to jail for this.'

'You don't?' Rizzoli snorted like he had been fast asleep. 'You don't? Well, that's great Jimmy. You know, I never much liked ice anyway.'

There was a knock at the door.

'It's a bitch to handle. On account of the interesting crystalline structure.'

'Come.'

'Somethin' I read about. S'got a laminar structure. Which means it deforms by gliding. That's why ice kind of falls apart the way it does. Like a deck of cards.'

Figaro's secretary peered round the door.

'And I ask you, Jimmy, what kind of business can you build on a crystalline structure like that?'

'I don't know, Tommy. Yes, Carol?'

'Mister Figaro? I wonder, could you spare a minute please?'

Figaro glanced at his client.

'I think we're about through here,' he said, standing up. 'I'll speak to the DA's office. Give me a week to structure a deal, Tommy. OK?'

Rizzoli stood up, automatically straightening the cuffs and the creases on his shiny sharkskin suit.

'Thanks Jimmy. 'Preciate it a lot, man. Naked Tony was right. You're one of us.'

Buttoning his own jacket and ushering Rizzoli toward the open door, Figaro looked pained.

'No, don't make that mistake, Tommy. Y'know, Tony means well by that remark, but it's not true. I'm your priest, is nearer to it. Priestly intercession before judgment on your behalf. Only don't ever fuckin' confess to me. I don't want to know. If you're guilty I don't give a shit any more than I would if you were as innocent as a walk round a church on a Sunday afternoon. All I care about is whether we can make a better case than the other guy.' He grinned. 'It's a lawyer thing.'

'I got ya.'

The two men shook hands, which served to remind Figaro of how tough and strong the other smaller man really was.

'So long Jimmy, and thanks again.'

Figaro waved Rizzoli through the reception area and beyond the doors of Figaro & August, and then glanced questioningly at Carol.

'I think you'd better come and see this for yourself,' she

said and led the way through the suite of offices to the boardroom.

'When we saw what it was, we thought we'd better have it put in here,' Carol explained nervously. 'Gina's in the Ladies' room with Smithy. It was Smithy who unpacked it. I think she had a bit of a shock.'

'It was Smithy who screamed?'

'She's sort of a nervous individual, Mister Figaro. Nervous, but loyal. Smithy cares about you. We all do. That's why an incident like this is so upsetting. I suppose, with our client list, it's understandable. But this – this is like something out of the movies.'

'Now I really am intrigued,' said Figaro and followed her into the boardroom.

Smithy was now lying on the sofa beneath the window, and Gina was fanning her pale-looking face with a copy of the *New Yorker*.

Figaro recognized the cover. It was the issue that included the profile of himself. He glanced around the room, his dark, quick eyes serving a usefully photographic memory, taking in the probable chain of causation. The *New Yorker* piece. The dismantled packing case. The pubic clumps of straw. The delivery item itself.

Free standing, about five feet high, and looking like something that had met the stony gaze of a Gorgon, was a topcoat made of stone.

'What kind of sick person?' Carol bleated. 'No, wait just a minute. I know what kind of person. There's a name on the delivery note.'

She handed him a sheet of pink paper and placed a tentative hand on her boss's shoulder. It was the first time in three years of working for Figaro that she had ever touched him and she was surprised to find hard muscle underneath the jacket of his expensive Armani suit. He was a tall, attractive man, in good shape for someone who spent most of his time in the office and the rest of it in court. Kind of like Roy Scheider, she thought. The same long nose. The same high forehead. The same glasses. Only paler. Almost as pale as the woman lying on the couch.

'Do you feel all right, Mister Figaro? You look a little pale.'

Figaro, who was rarely in the sun, looked away from the stone topcoat and met her eye. For a moment he said nothing. Then he laughed.

'I'm fine, Carol,' he replied, and started to laugh again, only this time it really took hold of him until he had taken off his glasses and was leaning with both hands on the boardroom table, tears streaming down both cheeks.

CHAPTER TWO

Two things happened on the morning of Dave Delano's release from the Miami Correctional Center at Homestead.

One was that Benford Halls, recently transferred from Homestead to the State Penitentiary at Stark, was executed. Although Stark was many hundreds of miles upstate, the circumstances of Halls's final hours – meticulously reported on almost all of Florida's TV and radio stations – caused a lot of anger and resentment among the cons at Homestead. Not only had Halls been kept waiting for several hours after his scheduled 11 p.m. execution because of a problem with the ancient electric chair, but it had also been reported that movie actor Calgary Stanford had been allowed to attend the execution in order to research a death-row role he was soon to play.

Dave Delano had good reason to remember Benford Halls. They had both been sentenced in the same Miami courthouse on the same day, exactly five years before. That Dave should have served the full term – since 1987, parole for federal prisoners had been more or less eliminated – didn't seem so bad when he compared it with waiting around for five years to be put to death in front of some movie actor. If that didn't rank as cruel and unusual, then Torquemada must have been one of the world's great humanitarians.

The second thing that happened was that Dave received an airmail letter. It was from Russia and written in the unmistakably clear hand and cryptic style of Einstein Gergiev. Gergiev had been released from Homestead some six months before Dave, after serving eight years on a racketeering charge. Released and then deported as an undesirable alien.

Undesirable he may have been, but it was mostly down to Gergiev that Dave had used his time inside so well. It had been Gergiev who had persuaded the younger man that he had a real flair for foreign languages and that the peculiarities of the federal penal system would give him the opportunity for study and self-improvement people with liberty could only dream about. Just a few months before an amendment to the 1994 Crime Bill had banned federal grants to prisoners for post-secondary education, Dave had obtained a diploma in Russian. He had always had good Spanish. Growing up on Miami's South Beach, it might as well have been Cuba for all the good English did you. And on a fine day when he had a tan to complement his dark hair and brown eyes, Dave could just about pass for one of the *marielitos* who helped make Miami the sometime crime capital of America. Dave's potential as a Russian scholar might have come from the fact he was the son of a Russian-Jewish immigrant who had fled the Soviet Union after the war. His father's real name was Delanotov, which he had changed to Delano upon arrival in America, choosing the middle name of the previous American president in order to enhance his future prospects, such as they were. When he wasn't drunk, he spent the next thirty years installing air-conditioning systems in luxury yachts. Out of love and gratitude for his adopted country and hatred of the one he had left behind, Dave's father never again spoke his own native language.

Dave looked at the postmark and shook his head. It was four weeks since it had been sent. Another day and it would have missed him.

'Fuckin' Aeroflot,' he muttered before carefully reading the letter, written in Russian. Prices, crime and the incompetence of government – things did not sound so very different from what was happening at home. Dave read the letter several times, making certain of some of the more difficult words with the aid of a Russian dictionary. Speaking Russian was a lot easier than reading it. The Cyrillic alphabet was a whole different ball-game to the western writing system. For a start there were six more letters than English used.

By the time the guard came to escort Dave to freedom he had memorized the letter's contents and flushed the pieces down the toilet under the eyes of his cellmate, Angel, who had been lying silently on the top bunk. It was always tough when the guy you roomed with got his freedom. His departure brought home the fact that you were still in prison. Equally troublesome was the prospect of a new cellmate. Suppose he was queer?

'Man gets a letter and gets hisself released all on the same day,' grumbled Angel. 'Somehow it don't seem fair.'

Dave picked up the cardboard carton containing his books, notebooks, correspondence, art reproductions and photographs, tucked it under one well-muscled arm and then tugged at the Uncle Sam beard that helped to disguise his boyish face.

'OK man, I'm outta here.'

Angel, a tall Hispanic with a gold tooth, descended, embraced Dave fondly, and tried not to cry. Tamargo, the truck-sized guard, loitered patiently on the landing outside the cell door.

'I left you everything that was in the cabinet. All my shit. Candy, vitamins, cigarettes. Smoke 'em soon, though.' Dave laughed. 'Smoke 'em or trade 'em. They'll be turning this into a No Smoking prison like everywhere else, and they won't be worth shit.'

'Thanks man. 'Preciate it.'

'You take care of yourself. You'll be out in no time.'

'Yeah. Right.'

Without another word Dave turned and followed Tamargo along the ground-floor tier, shouting his goodbyes to the other prisoners and trying not to look too damn pleased with himself. He felt vaguely nauseous, the same feeling he used to have when he'd been about to sit a test, or face a courtroom. But it was nothing to what Benford Halls must have felt. Dave shivered.

'Fuck that,' he muttered.

'Say something?' returned Tamargo.

'No, sir.'

They exited the two-tier modern building and, crossing the neat lawn, Dave realized that this was the first time he had ever been allowed to walk on the grass. It was in the small things that freedom was to be discovered.

In the laundry and supply building he submitted meekly to the last indignity the system had to inflict upon him: the strip search. It was a palindrome of the way he had entered the system. He took off his prison clothes and bending over spread the cheeks of his buttocks so that one of the other guards who were waiting there for him could inspect his ass. Then they returned his own clothes and he started to get dressed in the sports coat, shirt and pants he had worn to the last day of his trial. To his surprise, the coat was too small and the pants were too big.

'Wish I had a dollar for every time I seen that happen,' guffawed the man searching the box containing Dave's personals. He glanced around at his equally amused colleagues. 'Spend five years pumping iron like you was Arnie fuckin' Schwarzenegger and then you wonder why your clothes don't fit.'

Dave gave himself up to their amusement.

'Look at these pants,' he grinned, holding the waistband away from his stomach. 'I must have lost twenty pounds. You know, you could market this place as a fat farm. The Homestead Plan diet. Safe serious weight loss through lifestyle change. Personalized care from corrective professionals.'

'You're lucky you did your time here, Slicker,' said one guard. 'In Arizona they'd have had you in a chain gang. You'd have lost a heck of a lot more weight out there.'

The guard searching Dave's personals riffled through the pages of a book and then regarded its cover with mild distaste.

'What is this shit, anyway?' he grumbled.

'*Crime and Punishment*, by Dostoevsky,' said Dave. 'Russia's greatest writer. In my opinion.'

'You some kind of communist, or something?'

Dave thought it over for a second.

'Well, I believe in the redistribution of wealth,' he said. 'Just about everyone in here believes in that, don't they?'

'Chain gangs aren't the answer,' said Tamargo. 'Nor anything else that keeps a man in shape. Prison shouldn't make guys who are comin' out more of a threat to law-abiding citizens than when they went in. You ask me, when guys come in here, we should give 'em all lots of fatty food. Cheeseburgers, ice-cream, Coca-Cola, French fries, much as they want, whenever they want. No exercise and plenty of TV. Phil Gramm wants the system to stop turning out hardened criminals, then that's the way to do it. Plenty of fuckin' junk food and easy chairs. That way when these fuckers eventually hit the streets they're regular couch potatoes like the rest of us, instead of muscle-bound bad-asses.'

Dave straightened his tie as best he could on a shirt collar that he could no longer button and grinned affably at Tamargo and his cushion-sized stomach.

'You're an enlightened man,' he said. 'At least you would be if you could get on the Homestead Plan.'

'Not even out yet and you're talkin' like a wiseguy,' observed Tamargo. 'Your mission, should you decide to accept it, Slicker, is to stay the fuck out of trouble and this place. Got that?'

'Is that your rehabilitation speech?'

'Yeah.'

'Your lawyer's here,' said the guard who had asked him if he was a communist. ''Magine that. Wants to give you a ride back into the city. Must be your witty conversation, Slicker.'

'You've noticed it too, huh?'

The guard waved him toward a door.

'See ya, Commie.'

Dave shrugged. Now that he had thought about it some

more, communism just seemed like a different kind of theft, that was all. And what was happening to the whole corrections system, to people like Benford Halls, made him realize that the government didn't really give a shit about releasing human beings from prisons. All it cared about was the next election. He remembered a scene in his favorite movie, *The Third Man*. Orson Welles's famous cuckoo clock speech. The one where Harry Lime meets his old friend Holly Martins on the Ferris wheel. Dave had seen the movie so many times he could remember the speech word for word.

'These days, old man, nobody thinks in terms of human beings. Governments don't, so why should we? They talk of the people and the proletariat and I talk of the mugs. It's the same thing. They have their five year plans and so have I.'

He took a last look around and nodded.

'Come on,' urged Tamargo. 'I want to get out of here too, y'know? I'm going off duty now. I got some plans.'

'So have I,' said Dave. 'So have I.'

CHAPTER THREE

'So what's the plan?'

'The plan?'

'Your schedule for the first day of the rest of your life?'

Dave was sitting in Jimmy Figaro's seven-series BMW appreciating all the leather and woodwork and thinking that it looked and felt like a small Rolls-Royce. Not that he had ever been in a Rolls. But this was what he imagined when he thought of one. Adjusting his seat electronically, he glanced through the tinted window as they drove away from Homestead onto Highway 1. There wasn't much to look at. Just broad fertile fields where, for a few dollars, you could 'pick your own' crop of whatever was growing out there – peas, tomatoes, corn, strawberries, they had all kinds of shit. Only Dave had a different kind of crop in mind.

'I dunno, Jimmy. I mean, you're driving the car. And what a car it is.'

'Like it?'

'You got room service on this?' said Dave, inspecting the phone in the armrest. 'And I've never seen a car with a TV in front.'

'Trip computer. Only picks up TV when the engine is off.'

'What about the Feds? Does it pick them up too?'

Figaro grinned.

'You've been reading the *New Yorker*.'

'I read all kinds of shit these days.'

'So I hear. As a matter of fact I sweep the car every morning. And I don't mean the fucking rugs. I got this little handheld bug detector in the glovebox there.' Then he jerked his head back on his shoulders and allowed a big smirk to climb up onto his face. 'But just in case they decide to get on my tail with one of those directional mikes, we have double glazing on the side and rear windows of the automobile.'

'Double glazing, on a car? You're joking.'

'A joke is not an option on a BMW. Can you hear any traffic noise?'

'Now you come to mention it, no I can't.'

'No more can anyone hear what you're saying. Not that you're saying much. As usual.'

'It's what's kept me alive until now.' Dave shrugged, and then flipped open the glovebox. The bug detector was a black box about the size of a cigarette packet, with a short aerial. 'Neat. You're pretty serious about this surveillance shit, aren't you?'

'With my client list, I have to be.'

'House counsel to Naked Tony Nudelli. Yeah, you've sure come a long way since you defended the likes of me, Jimmy. What puzzles me is why you came all the way out here to fetch me back into the city. I could have got the bus.'

'Tony asked me to make sure you were all right. And house counsel's putting it a little strongly, Dave. That fucking article made me sound like Bobby Duvall. However, unlike the name of that character he played in *The Godfather* — '

'Tom Hagen.'

'Yeah, Hagen. Unlike him I have more than one client. You, for instance. Should you ever need my advice on anything — '

'Well, thanks Jimmy, I appreciate that.'

'OK, if you have no particular plans for the day, then here's what we'll do. Like I say, Tony wanted me to make sure you were OK. We'll drop by the office where I'll show you a balance sheet I've prepared. What I've done with your money, that kind of thing. Then, if you'll allow me to, I'll make a few suggestions as to what you can do with it. After that we can maybe take an early lunch. Only I have to be in court at 2.30.'

'Sounds fine, Jimmy. I've got nothing but appetite.'

'You're hungry? For what? Just tell me. I know this little Haitian place on Second Avenue. We could stop there for some breakfast if you wanted.'

'I've had breakfast, thanks. And it isn't food I'm hungry for, Jimmy. Sounds a little cheesy, but it's life I'm hungry for. Y'know? It's life.'

They drove along North Bay Shore Drive, round the side of the modern building where Figaro & August had its suite of offices, and into the underground parking lot. Figaro led the way toward the elevator.

'So,' he said, 'yesterday morning, our office receptionist takes a delivery addressed to me while I'm stuck in a client meeting.' Figaro started to chuckle as they rode the car upstairs. 'This is apropos of what we were just talking about? She and my secretary unwrap the item and nearly pass out with fright when they see what it is. Because people in jail aren't the only ones who read the *New Yorker*. Anyway, to them, the delivery item looks like a concrete topcoat. And the delivery docket says it's from someone called Salvatore Galeria. So they think this is a Mafia message along the lines of Luca Brazzi sleeps with the fishes, etceteras etceteras. Only it's not a Mafia message at all. It's this piece of sculpture I bought in a gallery on South Beach last week. Salvatore Galeria, on Lincoln Avenue. Cost me $10,000. I bought it as a kind of conversation piece. Something I thought the types on my client list might appreciate. To keep wise guys like you amused while I was taking a leak.'

'That's some black sense of humor you have there, Jimmy.'

'Smithy – she's our receptionist – we had to send her home in a cab, she was so upset by the sight of what she perceived to be a threat upon my life. Kind of touching when you think about it. I mean, it's like she really gives a shit what happens to me.'

'When you put it like that, it is kind of hard to believe.'

The two men stepped out of the elevator and went along the quiet corridor into the suite. Figaro's office occupied a corner of the building with a wrap-around window affording a panoramic view of Brickell Bridge and the bookshelf shapes of the Downtown skyline. As an apartment it would have seemed generous; but as an office for one man it was awesome. Dave's eyes took in the lime-oak panelling, the cream leather sofas, the Humvee-sized desk, the crummy art and the concrete overcoat, and he found himself admiring everything except maybe the man's sense of humor and taste in paintings. After the confines of his cell in Homestead, Figaro's office made him feel almost agoraphobic. He glanced down at his feet. He was standing on a parquet floor at the corner of an enormous sand-colored rug. In the parquet was a brass plate inscribed with some sentiment that Dave did not bother to bend down and read.

'What's this? First base? Jesus, Jimmy, you could play ball in here.'

'Of course,' remarked the lawyer. 'You haven't been in these offices, have you?'

'Business must be good.'

'When you're a lawyer, Dave, business is always good.'

Figaro motioned Dave towards a sofa, checked through the notes that were stuck to the edge of his walnut partner's desk, and waited for Carol to hike across the floor with the file she was carrying.

'Is that Mister Delano's file?' asked Figaro.

'Yes, it is,' she said and, laying it neatly on the desk in front of him, glanced at the man sitting down on the sofa. Carol was used to seeing all kinds of characters – that was the politest word for who and what they were – appearing in her boss's office. Mostly they were walking mugshots, blunt faces in sharp suits, knuckle-draggers with silk shirts and ties as loud as Mardi Gras. This particular character appeared to be a little different from the rest. With his matching gold earrings, Laughing Cavalier beard and mustache, and Elvis-sized quiff he looked like a pirate who had borrowed some clothes after swimming to shore. But he had a nice even smile and even nicer eyes.

'Would you like coffee?' she asked Figaro.

'Dave?'

'No thanks.'

Smiling back at him as she went out of the office, Carol decided that with a haircut and a shave and a change of clothes he might look younger and a little less like someone who was on his way to the gas chamber. Cute was what he would look. The door closed behind her and she knew that the feeling she had got on her tightly skirted butt had been from those big brown eyes.

Figaro sat down opposite Dave and flipped a sheet of paper across the glass coffee table towards him. His eyes still on the room, Dave made no move to look at the paper.

'Cigar?'

Dave shook his head.

'They give me a throat. Could use a cigarette, though.'

Figaro helped himself from the box of Cohibas on the table – a present from Tony – and then fetched Dave a cigarette from a silver cigarette box on his desk.

'It was the smart move, Dave,' he said through a speech bubble of blue smoke. 'Keeping your mouth shut.'

Dave smoked his cigarette silently. He figured it had been Figaro's advice and Figaro's mistake, so let him do the talking now.

'It was too bad the Grand Jury decided to construe your silence as complicity in what happened. I guess maybe the judge was taking your previous conviction into account. But even so, five years, for something you had nothing to do with. It seemed excessive.'

'And if they pinch you for something, Jimmy? Even if it's something you had nothing to do with. And they want you

16

to finger one of your clients. Maybe your biggest client. What
will you do?'

'Keep my mouth shut, I guess.'

'Right. It's not like you really have a choice, you know?
You're dead for a lot longer than five years, let me tell you.
It's a big consolation when you're in the joint. There's not a
day passes when you don't say to yourself: this is hell, but
it could be worse. I could be doing time at the bottom of
the ocean wearing Jimmy's $10,000 overcoat.' Dave jerked
his head at the work of art occupying a corner of Figaro's
office and grinned coolly. 'It *is* a conversation piece, just like
you said it would be. Yes sir, I can see how that is going to
come in very handy. But more object lesson than *objet d'art*,
I'd say. Keep your mouth shut, or else.'

'You're a talented guy, Dave.'

'Sure. Look where it got me. A lifetime achievement
award at Homestead. Talent's for people who play the
piano, not the angles, Jimmy. It's not something I can
afford to indulge.'

'You can afford,' said Figaro, and tapped the sheet of paper
meaningfully. 'Just look at this balance sheet. In consideration
for your time and inconvenience — '

'That's a nice way of icing a five-year slice of cake.'

'Two hundred and fifty thousand dollars, like we agreed.
Paid into an offshore account and then invested at 5 percent
per annum. I know. Five percent. That's not much. But I
figured that under the circumstances, you'd want zero risk
on an investment like this. So that comes to $319,060, tax
free. Less 10 percent for my own management services, which
comes to $31,906. Leaves you with $287,154.'

'Which works out at $57,430 a year,' said Dave.

Figaro thought for a moment and then said, 'Is the right
answer. There's no end to your talents. Math too.'

'In case you ever wondered, that's how I got started in the
rackets. I used to do numbers for a living. When I was a kid.
Harvard Business School was not an option. I was the only

heebie in our neighborhood and the Italian kids thought it would be cool if they had a Jewish banker.'

'It figures.'

'Well figure me this, Figaro. I never charged more than 5 percent for my financial services. Ten percent seems more like vig than commission.'

'Most clients who pay five percent will also pay tax. And they'll usually take a cheque.'

'Point taken.'

Figaro stood up and went behind the desk. When he returned to the sofa he was carrying a sports bag. He dropped it beside Dave and sat down again.

'You do prefer cash, don't you?'

'Doesn't everyone?'

'Not these days. Cash can be hard to explain. Anyway, have you thought what you're going to do with it?'

'This isn't exactly fuck-off money, Jimmy. Three hundred grand minus the change doesn't buy you a lifestyle.'

'I could recommend some things. Some investments maybe.'

'Thanks Jimmy, but I don't think I can afford the green fee.'

'Consider it waived. You know, now is a perfect opportunity to get onto the property-owning ladder. There's plenty of good value real estate throughout the county. It so happens I have an interest in the development of some country club homes on Deerfield Island.'

'Isn't that the island Capone tried to buy?'

Figaro grimaced through the cigar smoke.

'This is fifty years ago you're talking.'

'Maybe, but I thought that was all zoned as a nature reserve. Racoons and armadillos and such like.'

'Not any more. Besides racoons aren't nature. They're pests. You should really think it over. Go and take a look. Nine-foot ceilings, gourmet eat-in kitchens, a fitness center, intercoastal views. From as low as two-ten.'

18

'Thanks a lot Jimmy, but no.' Leaning over the arm of the sofa Dave unzipped the bag and glanced inside. 'I need this money to set me up in something. Something that feels a little more real than landfill real estate.'

'Yeah? Like what for instance?'

'I've got some ideas floating around.'

Figaro shrugged.

'Would you like to count it?'

'And leave myself with nothing to do this evening? No thanks.'

Dave decided to skip lunch with Jimmy Figaro. The sight of Jimmy's car, his two-thousand dollar suit, and the wide-eyed look on his secretary's face had been enough to remind Dave of how out of place he now appeared. The Lucifer beard and the curtain rings in his ears might have helped keep his ass out of trouble in Homestead, but things were different on the outside. In the kind of respectable, well-heeled places Dave expected to be going, maintaining the don't-fuck-with-me image would not be good for what he had planned. It was like Shakespeare said: the apparel proclaimed the man. He was going to need a complete makeover. But first he had to find a car, and well aware that he stood zero chance of driving away in something leased or rented, it made sense to keep the mean-as-shit look going for a while, at least until he had his wheels sorted. That way he figured he wouldn't get sold the kind of fucked-up automobile that might have to bring his bad ass back to the showroom.

Now that he was out of Homestead he wanted to spend as much time in the open air as possible. That meant a convertible; and in the sports section of the *Herald* he found what he was looking for. A Mazda dealer offering a selection of keenly priced sports cars. A cab took him west of Downtown, along Fortieth, to Bird Road Mazda, and thirty minutes later he was driving back east toward the beach, in a '96 Miata with CD, alloys, and only 14,000 on the clock. He had just started to enjoy the fresh air, the sunshine, the sporty stick shift, and the music on the radio – he didn't own any CDs – when, pulling up at a traffic light to turn north onto Second Avenue, he looked across at the car alongside and found himself staring into the mean eyes of Tamargo, the guard who had escorted him from his cell in Homestead not three hours before.

Tamargo was driving just $1,900 worth of old Olds and seeing Dave in a car that had cost almost ten times as much, the prison guard's sofa-sized jaw dropped like he'd had a brain hemorrhage.

'The fuck d'you get that car, Slicker?'

Dave shifted uncomfortably in his leather seat and glanced up at the still red traffic light. Serving his full sentence gave him certain advantages now that he was on the outside. Not the least of these was the absence of any nosey-fucking-parker parole officer interfering in his life. But the last thing he wanted was the city police asking awkward questions about where the money for the car had come from. The major question was whether Tamargo could be bothered reporting what he had seen. Right now all the information the cops had on his whereabouts was care of Jimmy Figaro's office. There was no sense in letting them discover the license plate on his car, and maybe a whole load of other shit as well. So keeping one eye on his rearview mirror, and tightening his grip on the leather steering wheel, Dave smiled back.

'Hey, I'm talkin' to you, motherfucker. I said, where'd you get the fuckin' car?'

'The car?'

'Yeah, the car. The one that says stolen on the fuckin' license plate.'

Still watching the traffic light.

'This is a clean car, man.'

'Oh yeah?'

'You know something, Tamargo? You're part of a detestable solution. A detestable solution, in an infernal recurrence of guilt and transgression. Those are not my words, but those of a great French philosopher. If you had a shred of fuckin' intelligence you would know that your very accusation implies the failure of the very same institution you represent. It's your kind of prejudice that's the single most important factor in recidivism. Maybe you don't know, but that's what they call it when a con commits another crime. Recidivism. The best thing you could do on behalf of the whole detestable corrections system? Drive on, and shut your fuckin' mouth.'

The light turned green. Dave revved the engine hard and slipped the clutch.

Tamargo stamped on his own gas pedal, hoping to keep sight of Dave Delano long enough to read his license plate. Instead the little sports car just disappeared, and the prison guard was more than fifty yards up the road before he realized that Dave had reversed away from the traffic light. Tamargo braked hard and twisting his bulk around in his car seat, searched the rear window for the ex-con in the convertible. But Dave was gone.

After that Dave thought he could not change his appearance a moment too soon. He was heading for Bal Harbor on Miami Beach where Figaro had told him there was an excellent shopping mall opposite a classy Sheraton, with the sea view he had stipulated. Finding a different route onto Biscayne Boulevard, and Route 41, he was soon driving across McArthur Causeway and over the intercoastal waterway with the cruise port and ship docks of Miami on his right. The sight of a couple of big passenger liners pointed toward the ocean gave him a little thrill, for he knew that if things worked out as planned, he would soon be taking a sea voyage himself. Right now he was arriving on South Beach, driving up Collins and through the so-called historic district. That just meant art deco. But that was all the history there was going in Miami, which was one of the reasons why Dave couldn't wait to leave the place. Even so, it felt good to be driving along through the gaudy pastels and flashy neon of Collins again; with all the people around, it was like rejoining the human race.

Ten minutes up Collins he pulled into the Bal Harbor shopping mall, parked the car, and still carrying the bag full of money, went in search of his new look. Straightaway he knew he was in the right place. Ralph Lauren, Giorgio Armani, Donna Karan, Brooks Brothers. Jimmy Figaro could hardly have recommended a better place for what Dave had in mind. There was even a beauty parlor offering a $200 special: a massage, a haircut, a manicure, a facial. Maybe a facial could include a shave. Dave walked inside.

The place was empty. A girl reading *People* magazine stood up from behind the counter and smiled politely.

'Can I help you?'

Dave smiled back, his best feature.

'I hope so. I just got off a ship. I've been at sea for several months and, well, you can see the problem. I must look like Robinson Crusoe.'

The girl chuckled lightly. 'You do look kind of grungy,' she said.

'Tell me, have you seen that movie *Trading Places*? You know, with Eddie Murphy.'

'Yeah. He was good in that one. But not since.'

'That's what I want. An Eddie Murphy makeover. Shave, haircut, facial, manicure, massage, the whole $200 deal.'

One of the girl's colleagues, wearing a clinical white dress and a name tag that said JANINE, had come over and was regarding Dave through narrowed eyes, the way he himself had looked at the Mazda before buying it.

'We're more *Pretty Woman* than *Trading Places* in here, honey,' said Janine. 'But we are kind of quiet right now. So I reckon we can fix you up. Make you look like a regular choirboy, if you want. Only it's been a while since I shaved a man.'

Janine turned to look at her receptionist.

'Martin. My ex, right? I used to shave him. No, really. I used to enjoy it. Naturally if I had a razor near his throat today it'd be a different story. I'd murder the son of a bitch.'

But then she smiled as if the idea of shaving Dave suddenly appealed to her.

'Well, what do you say, honey? How are you with female empowerment?'

Dave threw down his bag.

'Janine? I'm willing to take the risk if you are.'

CHAPTER FOUR

'So Jimmy. Whaddya think? Can I trust Delano to keep his fuckin' mouth shut?'

Figaro looked up from his soft-shell crab salad, and into the large blue-tinted glasses worn by the man sitting opposite. Tony Nudelli was around fifty, with a face that had as many creases as his beige linen suit. They were lunching in the Normandy Shores Country Club, just a few minutes north of Bal Harbor. Through the arched windows of the restaurant's Mizner-style layout, you could just about see Cher's $6 million mansion over the bay on La Gorce Island.

'Sure you can trust him. He spent the last five years keeping his mouth shut, didn't he? Why the hell should he rat now?'

'Because now I can't keep tabs on him, that's why. When his ass was in prison he knew that I could get to him. People I knew on the inside could fuck with him. Now that he's outside he can do what he likes without watching over his shoulder, and I don't like that. It does not sit well at ease with me.'

'C'mon Tony. The Feds could have offered him protection if he'd wanted to spill his guts. A whole change of life.'

'That's like the menopause. It just means your fuckin' life is over, in any meaningful way. You just ask my wife if that's not true. I haven't fucked her in ages. Naw Jimmy, most guys with blood in their veins would do the five years and take the money.' Nudelli selected a toothpick from a silver holder and began to search for something stuck in his upper molars. 'What about that? Did you pay him off? Was he happy?'

'I think so.'

'You think so?' Nudelli snorted, inspected the shred of

food on the end of his toothpick for a moment and then ate it. Shaking his head wearily he added: 'Jimmy, Jimmy, if I wanna know what people think, I'll read the fuckin' *Herald*, OK? From you and your six-figure retainer plus expenses, plus bonuses, I want a little more than a farmboy grin and the seat of your fuckin' pants. I want the laws of physics as described by Isaac Newton. If x then y. Do you copy?'

'I'm certain of it,' said Figaro.

'You play poker, Jimmy?'

'I'm not much of a card player, Tony.'

'That doesn't surprise me. You say you're certain of something, and yet you shrug like there were still a few doubts weighing on the padded shoulders of that expensive-looking suit of yours. Certainty looks a little more positive, Jimmy. Like you nod a couple of times? And smile some? Jesus, the fuckin' weather man looks more certain of what he's sayin' than you do.'

'Tony, if you don't mind me saying, I think you're being a little paranoid here. Believe me, Dave is very cool. While he was in Homestead he used his time to full advantage. Got himself an education, a diploma and a positive mental attitude. He just wants to get on with the rest of his life.'

'Doing what, precisely?'

'Precisely? I don't know. Nor does he. Right now he just wants to chill out, spend some of his money — '

'You paid him.'

'I already said so. In cash. With interest. I asked him what he was going to do with it and offered him some financial advice. He said, no thanks.'

Nudelli looked thoughtful as he considered what Figaro was telling him. He emptied his wine glass and then flicked the crystal rim with his fingernail.

'What were his exact words when he said that?'

'What is this, exactly? Exact? I don't know exact.'

'Jimmy, you're a fuckin' lawyer. Exact is your middle name and the birthmark on your ass.'

'He said it wasn't exactly fuck-off money. He said it wasn't the kind of money that buys you a lifestyle.'

'Well that sure doesn't seem like someone who was happy with his kiss-off.'

'I'm quoting him out of context, you understand.'

'I don't care if you're quoting him out of Bartlett's *Familiar Quotations*. What you described sounds like a man who's just had a ten-dollar Coke.'

'Tony, if you could have been there you would have seen a guy who was happy, believe me.'

The waiter appeared to refill their glasses with the California Chardonnay Tony Nudelli liked to drink. It was a little too oaky for Figaro's better-educated palate. Like drinking liquid furniture polish.

'Maybe not borne up to heaven in a whirlwind like Elijah,' added Figaro, 'but content, yeah.'

'Is everything all right here?' asked the waiter, fawning.

'Fine, thank you, yes.'

'Elijah,' oozed the waiter. 'That's a lovely name, Elijah. Why couldn't my parents have called me something like that, instead of John?'

Tony Nudelli sat back in his chair abruptly and glanced up at the waiter, his top lip drawn back with irritation from his yellowing and by now well-picked teeth.

'Because your round white face with shit on it reminded them of a fuckin' toilet bowl, you little cocksucker. And if you and your fuckin' drippy personality ever interrupt my conversation in here again, I'll fix it so that people get to callin' you Vincent. On account of how you'll only have the one fuckin' ear to stick into other people's business. Get it? Now fuck off before you *chambré* that fuckin' wine with your hot jerk-off hand.'

The waiter made a hasty withdrawal.

'I guess I'd better not order any dessert,' chuckled Figaro. Part of him quite liked it when Tony Nudelli talked tough. So long as he wasn't on the sharp end of it himself. It gave him a thrill to experience, albeit vicariously, the kind of power that Nudelli wielded.

'Are you kidding? Pecan pie here's the best.'

'I was thinking he might try and get his own back in some plausibly edible, but disgusting way.'

'People have wound up dead for a lot less.'

'He doesn't know that.'

'You're right, Jimmy.' Snapping his fingers loudly, Nudelli waved the *maître d'* over to their table. 'Goddamn little faggot might Trojan horse just about anything into a piece of pecan pie.'

'How are things here, Mister Nudelli?'

'Louis, we'd like two pieces of pecan pie. And I'd like you to serve them to us yourself. Understand?'

'Yes sir. Right away. It'd be my pleasure.'

The *maître d'* disappeared in the direction of the kitchen.

'Jimmy, let me ask you something.'

'Sure, Tony.' He chuckled as he caught sight of the cowed waiter. 'I'm all ears.'

Nudelli glanced angrily after him.

'Fuckin' dipshit. Whassa matter with waiters in this country? It's not enough you give 'em a tip. They want your goddamn assurance that you don't think any the less of them for what they're doing to make a buck.'

'Don't start me on waiters. The other day I order a steak at the Delano? And when the waiter brings it he tells me that the vegetables will be along in just a few minutes. I tell the guy, What is this? Am I supposed to eat this meal in instalments?'

Figaro laughed at his own story and laughed some more when he saw that it had amused Nudelli. Only he wished he'd thought to substitute another restaurant for the Delano. It was one of the smartest on South Beach, beloved of Madonna and Stallone, but the name didn't help to take Nudelli's mind off the one thing that was obsessing him right now, which was Dave Delano.

'What was it that you wanted to ask me, Tony? Before we got started on shitty waiters.'

'Just this. What's the statute of limitations on murder?'

'There is no statute of limitations on murder.'

'And that's precisely my point. Suppose Delano does decide to talk to the Feds?'

'Take a chill pill, Tony. Delano's no snitch.'

'Hear me out Jimmy, like a good lawyer. Just suppose he does. For whatever reason. Let's for the sake of argument assume that he holds my ass responsible for his period of incarceration. After all, jail does funny things to a man. Turns him queer. Makes him vengeful. Maybe he wants to take my quarter-mill and my liberty with it. I mean, what's to stop him? Just answer me that, will ya?'

'He probably holds me more responsible than anyone,' shrugged Figaro. 'After all, it was me representing him before that jury. But he isn't going to do it, Tony.'

'No, no, we're not talking predictive sequences here. We're addressing a hypothetical situation. You understand? Like we was two philosophers in a Roman sauna bath. What is there in the way of hard facts that enables us to say that it won't ever happen that Dave Delano won't decide to snitch? Wait, wait. I thought of something. Suppose he does something wrong. A crime. And the cops arrest him. His ass is going down for it. But he might not want to do any more time. And who could blame the guy after five years in the joint? Not me, for sure. But maybe, knowing this, the Feds figure to scare him into telling them what he shoulda told 'em in the first place. Trade his ass for mine.'

Nudelli slapped the table hard like he was killing a fly just as the *maître d'* arrived bearing two pecan pies.

'What's to stop him doing that, huh, Jimmy?'

'Here we are Mister Nudelli. Pecan pie.'

'Thanks Louis.'

'My pleasure, sir. Enjoy.'

'Well, when you put it as coldly as that Tony — '

'I do put it as coldly as that, in a frosted glass with ice in it. What's to stop him, eh?'

Figaro gouged a piece of pie onto his fork, but he left it lying on his plate for a moment.

'Nothing. Except maybe he's more afraid of you than he is of the cops.'

Nudelli raised his large hairy hands into the air and gestured in a way that reminded Figaro of the Pope benevolently greeting the faithful from the balcony of St Peter's on Christmas Day. But the lawyer could see that there was nothing particularly benevolent about the way this conversation was headed.

'You see? Maybe. We're back with uncertainty again. You put your finger right on it, Jimmy. Maybe. Now put yourself in my position. I gotta family to look after, a business to run, people whose livelihoods depend on me.' He sighed with loud exasperation and forked a piece of pie into his mouth. 'You know what the problem is here? Language. The corruption of the fuckin' language. Words don't mean what they used to because of all the fuckin' minorities we gotta tiptoe around – like we can't say this and we can't say that – and because of all the politicians who use language to say nothing at all. I give you a for instance, Jimmy. A guy says to a girl "Will you let me fuck you?" Now if she says "Maybe", you know it's a real possibility. But if you were to say to some politician, "Will you build more schools and more hospitals if we vote you into office?" and he says "Maybe", then you know for sure that he ain't gonna do it. For him, maybe means never. You see what I'm saying?'

Figaro was not sure that he did. There were times when he thought Tony Nudelli one of the sharpest clients he had, and others when he thought him as dumb as daytime TV. This extended thought had left Figaro wondering what Nudelli's original point had been. But he nodded anyway and said: 'Yeah, sure.' He decided to try and steer the conversation

to a different conclusion from the one he feared Nudelli still
had in his malicious old mind.

'You want me to have a word with Delano, Tony? Impress
upon him the absolute necessity of keeping his mouth shut?
He's coming by the offices tomorrow to talk about some
things. I can straighten him out then if you want me to.'

'Willy Barizon,' said Nudelli, shaking his head.

'What about him?'

'He's half-brother of Tommy Rizzoli. The guy you put out
of the ice business.'

Figaro smiled uncomfortably.

'Tony, I advised him to sell the business in order that he
might avoid a prison sentence, that's all.'

'Same thing. Anyway, I'm gonna get Willy to go and talk
to Delano.'

'Are you gonna whack him?'

Nudelli looked pained.

'You should eat some of this pie. It's the best.'

Figaro lifted the fork to his mouth. He had to admit it
was good.

'I hate to hear my attorney use a word like that,' Nudelli
said stiffly. 'But no, I am not going to whack him. I just want
Delano reminded, forcibly reminded, that he should still fear
me.' He licked his lips and then wiped his mouth with a
napkin. 'I think maybe I want something sweet to drink, with
my dessert. A glass of Muscat maybe. You like Muscat?'

Figaro shook his head.

'Now where's that cocksucker got to?' he grumbled, looking
around for the waiter. He stared back at Figaro. ''Sides, I'd
like to know more about these new friends of his before
I even think of whackin' him. I heard he shared a cell
with some Ivan while he was in Homestead. And that this
Ivan has some important New York connections. I'd hate to
whack Delano and find myself with those Russian bastards
comin' after me. They like killing people. I think they like
killing people more than they like making money. Well,

blood will out I guess. Killing's in their history. Making money never was.'

'The room-mate's name was Einstein Gergiev,' reported Figaro. 'People called him Einstein because he was a former physicist and computer guy before becoming involved with the Russian rackets. And then here in Florida.'

'Clever son of a bitch, huh?'

'He had some twin town scam going with the two cities.'

'Which two cities?'

'The two St Petersburgs.'

'The one on the Gulf of Mexico I heard of, but where's the other?'

'In Russia. Northern Russia.'

'I didn't know that.'

'It was quite a fraud, I hear. Cost the city of St Petersburg, the one in Florida, several million dollars.'

'Is that so?'

'Anyway, Gergiev was released six months ago and deported back to Russia. But I didn't know he was connected in New York.'

'All Russian wiseguys, the redfellas, are connected there. Brighton Beach. You should see it. Fuckin' Russkie home from home. Little Odessa they call it. Connected there in New York or in Israel. Tel Aviv. Half of them Jews that left Russia are connected. That's how they got the money to get out in the first place.' Nudelli shrugged. 'I got this cousin in Tampa. Maybe he can find out something about this Eisenstein redfella. Where's Delano staying?'

'He said he was going to check into the Bal Harbor Sheraton.'

'That's a nice beach hotel. Classy. These days you can forget the Fontainebleau.'

Nudelli straightened in his chair. The waiter was in his sights.

'Hey you, Elijah. C'mere.'

Seeing Tony Nudelli, the waiter backed toward the door

of the restaurant like a quarterback searching out one of his receivers. Seconds later he was out of the door and running through the old world Mediterranean courtyard in the direction of Biscayne Bay.

'Jesus,' laughed Nudelli. 'Whad I fuckin' say?'

CHAPTER FIVE

Dave had missed the ocean, even one as busy with people and boats as the one off Miami Beach. Sandwiched between the pale blue sky, and the pink rock dust that passed for sand, the gray snakeskin-colored sea rolled toward him in white scribbles of water. In Homestead he had often imagined having this view again. But it was not his regained sight of the ocean that served to underscore his freedom, but its accompanying salty smell and visceral, breathy sound. He had forgotten that part. Back inside the four walls of his hotel suite, luxurious though it was, it had been all too easy to conjure the nightmare of being in his cell again, in the same way that an amputee could still feel the severed limb. He had only to close his eyes and listen to the air-conditioned silence. But here on the beach, with its sounds and the smells thrusting in upon his consciousness, the feel of the wind in his neatly cut hair, and the late afternoon sun warming his smoothly shaven face like the hot plate of a giant stove, it was impossible to mistake his surroundings for anything but the outside world. Dave lay on his beach towel and breathed deep from the sky above him. He didn't even read. His other neglected senses wouldn't allow him to concentrate on anything but where he was and what that meant. A few days' relaxation in Bal Harbor would help him to begin dismantling the walls inside his head. After that he could go to work.

Willy 'Four Breakfasts' Barizon got his nickname from the time when he ate four whole cooked breakfasts – two eggs sunny side up, two strips of bacon, a sausage and hash browns each – in a Denny's on Lincoln Avenue. A little over six foot three, he weighed around 230 pounds in his shorts and 250 when he was dressed, the extra twenty being mostly referable to the two handguns he wore underneath his loose, Hawaiian style shirt. His tongue was a couple of sizes too large for his face, which meant he spoke out of the side of his wet-looking mouth as if he still had one of the breakfasts pouched in the other cheek, like a chaw. His black hair was naturally curly although the cut made it look as if he'd just had a permanent, with small dreadlocks that hung loosely over the tops of his elephantine ears, like a Hasidic Jew's. With a passing resemblance to a budget-sized giant, Willy Barizon was a hard man to miss. Besides, it was a while since he had done this kind of work, and he had forgotten how to be subtle. The ice-trucking business had been all front. Looking tough when you turned up to collect was nearly all you needed to know. It was rare that you actually had to smack someone.

Dave made Willy the minute he saw him. Or rather, he made the look the big man received from the bell-boy when Dave came out of the hotel restaurant and asked the front desk to send the fax he had written out in neat Cyrillic capitals while having his dinner. Five years of watching his ass in Homestead had given Dave eyes in the back of his head. The bell-boy might as well have shot a neon arrow into the big man's chest. 'There's your mark. Go get him.'

Dave stepped into an elevator car alongside a woman with hair as tall as a chef's hat. What was it with Miami women and big hair? With one eye on this confection of hair and the wizened doll beneath it, he pressed his floor button and stood back in the car as the woman selected her own floor. Then she moved to one side as Willy joined them. It was a second or two before he thought to press a button himself, which more or less confirmed Dave's suspicion that the big guy had been waiting to follow Dave up to his room. But the question of motive still eluded him. Not a cop, that much was certain. A cop would have pinched him in the lobby. And for

what? Suspicion Grand Theft Auto? As the doors slid shut,
Dave turned toward Willy Barizon and held out his left wrist
to display the watch he had bought in the Bal Harbor Mall
that same afternoon.

'You see this watch, man?'

'What?'

'Not what. Watch. This watch is a Breitling Chronometer.
Best watch in the world.'

Baby Doll was pretending that he didn't exist.

'Forget Rolex. I mean, that's just for the movies. And
National Geographic. This. This is a goddamn quality timepiece. Cost me $5,000.'

'So fuckin' what?' snarled Willy.

'Wait, I haven't finished. You wanna see my wallet?' Dave
took out his wallet and flipped it open. 'See that? Coach
leather. Isn't that beautiful? And there's $1,000 in cash too.'

'You're nuts.'

The elevator chimed as it reached Baby Doll's floor.

'Really,' she said, stepping smartly out on her high heels.
'Some people just don't know how to handle it, do they?'

'You're so right, lady,' agreed Willy.

Dave returned the wallet to the coat pocket of his linen suit
and took out his new fountain pen as the doors closed again.

'Then there's this fountain pen.'

'Fuck you pal, and fuck your fountain pen,' said Willy, and
instinctively patted one of the two pieces he was carrying
under his waistband.

Dave's prison-sharp eyes took in the tell-tale bulge at a
glance. 'I'm telling you all this for a reason,' he explained
coolly. 'I'm telling you this so you'll know how high I rate
your fucking chances of robbing me.'

'You've got the wrong guy, Delano. Who said anything
about robbing your dipshit ass?'

Dave took a step back in the car. The tongue almost fell
out of the guy's mouth when he talked. Dave had felt the
spittle on his face like early rain. His eyes lingered on the

tongue, momentarily fascinated by its grotesque aspect. At best it looked like the record label for the Rolling Stones that Andy Warhol had designed. *Sticky Fingers*. He still had the album in his record collection. If his sister hadn't sold it. At worst the tongue looked like some kind of hideous pink jellyfish that lived inside a ring of yellow coral. The elevator chimed again as it reached Willy's chosen floor, only he paid it no attention.

The guy had used his name. He was carrying a piece and he had followed him into the elevator. What else did Dave need to know? He unscrewed the cap of his fountain pen.

'Are you finished giving me a guided tour of your personals?'

'There's one more thing,' insisted Dave. 'There's this pen. This pen is a Mont Blanc Meisterstuck. It's called Mont Blanc because the fourteen-carat nib tells you the height of Mont Blanc, should you want to know. That's the highest mountain in France. Go ahead and take a look.' Dave held the pen up for Willy's inspection. 'Four thousand eight hundred and ten meters high. Go ahead and look because I'm gonna give you this pen as a gift.'

Willy looked.

Dave hardly hesitated, stabbing the big man in the white of his eye with the mitre-shaped point of the Cohiba-sized pen, simultaneously spattering Willy's face, neck and shirt collar with a galaxy of ink-spots.

Willy howled with pain, pressing both hands to his injured eye, leaving Dave free to hit him hard with a punch to each kidney as if was working the heavy bag in the prison gym. He finished a trio of blows with a low arcing hook to Willy's balls that had his whole shoulder behind it and felt as cruel as if he'd tugged pieces of Willy's flesh from his body with red-hot pincers. The elevator doors opened with a gasp of air that echoed the sound from Willy's misshapen mouth. Crouched down on his haunches, one hand on his balls, the other on his eye, Willy looked more dwarfish now and easily manageable. Dave could see that there was no need to hit him again. But he had questions that needed to be answered. And placing the all-leather sole of a smart new loafer in the small of Willy's back, Dave launched him into the hallway. Willy belly-flopped onto the thick-pile carpet, hit his head against a fire extinguisher attached to the wall, and then passed out.

Dave collected his pen off the floor of the elevator and stepped quickly out of the car before the doors closed. A glance both ways. No one about. He took hold of Willy's legs and dragged him down the hallway and into his suite.

Safely through the door, Dave frisked Willy carefully, relieving him of a Ruger Security-Six, worn on a belt inside his pants, that he figured was mostly for show; and, underneath a belly band, a smaller, quieter-looking .22 automatic that was probably what usually got the job done. Dave unloaded the big revolver and kept the .22 handy for when the guy came round. The name on the driver's license he found in the sweat-dampened wallet was Willy Barizon. Dave had never heard of him. There was a Mastercard, eighty dollars, a ticket from the Sheraton's valet-parking service, a slip for a dog at Hollywood, and a hooker's business card with a 305 area number: 'Foxy Blonde. Young voluptuous beauty. I visit you.' On the back was written a name. 'Tia.' Dave flicked the card into the trash.

'I don't think you'll be visiting Willy for a while,' he said, recalling the ferocity of his blow to the big man's balls. Dave ducked into the bathroom and returned with the cords from the two bathrobes with which he bound Willy's hands behind his back and then his ankles. He fixed himself a drink and gathered some matchbooks from his bar area as Willy groaned his way back to consciousness. Dave squatted down on the backs of Willy's thighs, facing his feet, and began to remove the big guy's shoes and socks. He glanced over his shoulder and said:

'How are you doin' there, Moose? Ready to have a little Socratic dialogue yet? That means I say one thing, you say another, and I get to reach a conclusion.' Dave flung away Willy's socks with distaste and sipped some of his drink. 'Ever hear of Socrates, Moose? He was a Greek philosopher, who was condemned to death for corrupting the youth of Athens. This was before television of course. Kids today, they've got cable, so they're probably already corrupted, right? This Socrates was obliged to take hemlock. That's a kind of poison. Related to the parsley family of plants, as a matter of small interest, so be careful how you garnish. Anyhow, when I read about this, in a book by Plato, I got to wondering just how the fuck do you go about obliging someone to take poison of his own volition. I mean it's not like they strapped him down on a gurney for a lethal injection like they do in the can. No, he just sat around with a few of his good friends and drank it himself. No shit. And I asked myself, why?'

'Fugg you,' groaned Willy.

'Well now, it turns out that those ancient Greeks – nasty bastards – gave you an alternative to letting you poison your own self. You know what that was? A guy would come along and torture you to death. How he did it was like this. He'd tie you down and give you some kind of drug to help your ass relax. Amyl nitrate, or its ancient equivalent most probably. Same as those S&M gays do. Those guys do all kinds of shit to each other that I can't figure. When the executioner figured you were ready, he would stick his whole fucking arm up your ass, Robert Mapplethorpe style, and just keep on going until he got a hold of your heart. When he did – and this was the most exquisite part of the torture – he would slowly crush your heart in his hand, like it was a fucking sponge or something. Can you imagine that? Talk about pains in your chest. Jesus. The real experts could make it last a while, like experienced lovers. And that – that was the alternative to poison, I kid you not. A fatal fist-fuck. No wonder old Socrates elected to off himself, right?'

'Gee-zuzz greist . . .'

'Precisely. Another writer – you're gonna hear me refer to a lot of literary figures, you spend any time with me, Moose. The last five years, I've done nothing but read. And work out. But that part you already know, I guess. Sorry I had to hit you so hard. But you're a big guy, Moose. Anyway, this other writer, name of Samuel Johnson, said that the prospect of being hanged helps concentrate a man's mind wonderfully. And my guess is that so does torture.'

'Vugg ovv . . . my eye . . . zayin' nuthin' . . . azzhole . . .'

Dave drew Willy's feet toward him.

'Moose, Moose, you wanna do something about these feet of yours. Worst case of athlete's foot I ever saw. Do you dry between your toes? You should, you know. You've got yourself a chronic case of it here, I suspect. Damn difficult to eradicate. Most of those fungal preparations? They don't work. But I've got a sure-fire way of getting rid of the tiny microbe that causes this misunderstood chiropodic condition. It's really a secret, but I don't mind sharing it with someone like you, Moose.'

Dave turned around.

'But before I do, is there some secret you'd like to share with me? Kind of a quid pro quo? Like maybe who was it sent you to see me, packing thunder, and why? Talk to me, Moose. And don't tell me you're looking for your Velma or I'll think you're being cute with me.'

'. . . the vug's Velma . . . ?'

'You're not a Chandler fan? That's too bad, Moose. I think you'd enjoy him. He's what we call hard-boiled. A bit like these feet of yours. So what do you say?'

Willy Barizon coughed painfully. 'Look Mizter, you got the wrog guy. I don't know nuthin'. Nobody vuggin zent me. My eye. There'z been zum miztake.'

'Moose, you're insulting my intelligence. And my intelligence doesn't like that. It takes offense at just about anything. But mostly it takes offense at the assumption that it isn't there. That I'm as dumb as you are.'

Dave started to thread the hotel matchbooks between Willy Barizon's malodorous and clammy toes as if he had been preparing to paint the big man's toenails.

'Ugh. Remind me to wash my hands when I'm done here.'

'What are ya doin'?'

'It's what I was telling you about, Moose. That sure-fire way of getting rid of athlete's foot? Fact is man, you've got to burn it out. Like cauterizing a wound. Extreme heat kills infection. These are matchbooks, Moose. You ever see a whole matchbook burn? It's like a Roman fucking candle, man.'

'Help,' screamed Moose and started to struggle desperately. But Dave was ready with a bar towel, stuffing it into Willy Barizon's chop-shaped mouth.

'Moose. Moose. Just shut the fuck up, will ya? You and I are going to have a Yossarian-sized problem here if we're not careful. *Catch-22*? You remember that? I mean, you can hardly answer my questions if I gotta keep a towel in that Picasso-drawn mouth of yours. But then I can hardly go ahead and let you scream the fuckin' place down either. You perceive my dilemma? So I tell you what I'm gonna do. Part of your problem here I think is your lack of imagination, your inability to visualize just how fiercely one of these little matchbooks can burn. Hence you are unable to conceptualize just how painful this will be for you. So, I'm gonna give you a little demonstration, in as nice a way as possible. And then I'm gonna take this towel out of your blowhole. At the risk of seeming otiose, that's the point at which you'd better start talkin' or I'm going to be cooking some bacon down here. So here goes with the object lesson.'

Dave placed an ashtray in front of Willy Barizon's face. Then he tugged one of the matchbooks from between Willy's toes, unfolded it, and lit it with the silver lighter he'd bought from the Porsche shop that afternoon. The cover of the book burned reluctantly for a moment and then extinguished. Dave snapped the lighter on and lit it again. This time the cover caught properly alight and a second later the matches themselves ignited spectacularly in a cloud of acrid blue smoke.

'Whooa,' chuckled Dave. 'Olympic fucking flame. Ouch. That looks painful to me. What do you say, Willy? That look painful to you?'

Willy nodded furiously.

'Ready for that dialogue now?'

Willy kept nodding.

'Good boy.' Dave hauled the towel out of Willy's mouth. 'So who sent you and why?'

'It was Tony Nudelli.'

That surprised him.

'Tony? Why? What the hell's his beef with me?'

'He wanted you to be reminded to keep your mouth shut about whatever it is that you know about.'

Dave frowned as he tried to make sense of this information.

'I've spent the last five years in the joint keeping my mouth shut.' He shook his head. 'It doesn't make sense.'

'I swear it's true.'

'Exactly how were you going to remind me? I mean were you just going to have a quiet word in my ear, or was I supposed to feel the need for silence in some non-essential part of my body?'

'I was just to smack you around some, that's all. Maybe break a few fingers. Nothing serious.'

'I've had girlfriends who might dispute that, Willy.'

'It's the God's honest truth, I swear.'

'Shut up a minute while I think.'

Dave was silent for a moment as he weighed up what Willy had told him. It was just possible that Tony Nudelli was indeed sufficiently scared of what Dave knew about him to have ordered up the goon he was now sitting on. Only Tony usually took care of things on a more permanent basis than just a few broken fingers and a busted lip. Dave knew that from personal memory. But as he thought about it some more, it occurred to him that maybe there was a way he might turn the situation to his advantage. A way of demonstrating his loyalty to Tony. A useful prelude for what was to come.

'No,' he said slowly. 'I just don't buy your story, Willy.'

'Look, you've got to believe me — '

'Why would Tony want to grease me?'

'I didn't say that. I said hurt not grease.'

'After five years, the one thing Tony knows about me is that I can be trusted not to spill my guts to anyone.'

'Look, I'm just the button. You know that. I ain't the man's psychoanalyst. I ain't privy to the workings of his mind. I owe him a favor. That's the way it works, you know that. He tells me to do somethin', I do it and I don't look for no fuckin' mission statement. I get paid to do what I'm fuckin' told.'

'You know what I think? I think the Russian sent you over here to whack me.'

'What Russian? There's no Russian involved here.'

'That's what I think. I think it was Einstein Gergiev who set this up. Isn't that right, Willy?'

'No, man.'

'Now that makes a lot more sense. The Russian. Be quite natural for you to be more afraid of him than you are of me, even with a bunch of matchbooks stuck between your toes. He's a terrifying character, that Russian. I should know. I shared a cell with him for four years. No, you've got to be lying, Moose.' Dave snapped on the cigarette lighter for extra emphasis.

Desperate now, Willy struggled underneath Dave, his neck and ears reddening with the exertion.

'Look man, I don't know about any fucking Russian. I never met anyone called Einstein whosits face. It was Tony Nudelli, I swear. Sweet mother of Jesus, I swear it's true.'

'Oooh, are you a Catholic, Moose?'

'Yeah, I'm a Catholic.'

'Tell ya what I'm gonna do, Moose.' Dave stood up and

went to the bedside drawer where he found a Gideon Bible.
'I'm gonna get you to swear an oath, on the Bible.'

'Sure, anything. Just so long as you believe me.'

Dave sat down on Willy's back and tucked the Gideon Bible
underneath his large jaw.

'Now repeat after me, Moose. As I have hope for the
resurrection of the body . . .'

'As I hope for the resurrection of the body.'

'And life everlasting in Jesus Christ . . .'

'And life everlasting in Jesus Christ.'

'What I have said here is the truth, so help me God.'

'What I've said here is the truth, so help me God.'

'Now kiss the Bible with that sucker of yours.'

Willy kissed the Bible until it was wet with saliva.

'You're not brought up by Jesuits, I hope,' said Dave. 'Only
those guys were so tricky they could swear one thing, think
another, kiss a bible and get away with it thanks to the doctrine
of equivocation.'

'No man, no — '

'OK, I believe you.' Dave stood up again and took another
sip of his drink. 'All right. I'm gonna untie you now. Just
remember though. I've got that little Phoenix Arms twenty-
two in my pocket. You try anything ungrateful Moose and I'll
take some of the pressure off that brain of yours. Give you an
extra fuckin' blowhole. You clear on that?'

'Yeah, clear.'

Dave untied Willy and stood back as slowly, painfully,
the big man sat up on the floor. Willy checked his balls
and then pressed the heel of his hand gingerly against his
injured eye. Through his one good eye Willy looked across
the suite at the man now sitting down on a large cream-
colored sofa. Laid out on the floor in front of Delano, like
the Jerry Seinfeld American Express ad, were the results of
what looked to have been a fairly major shopping expedition:
several pairs of shoes, piles of shirts, sports shirts, sweat-
ers and pants, and a brand new Apple laptop. There was

nothing cheap on view. Even the suite, with a wrap-around balcony and a sea view looked like three or four hundred a night.

'How's your eye?' Dave asked.

'Hurts.'

'Sorry 'bout that, Moose. Take a hand towel from the bathroom if you like and some ice from the refrigerator. Make yourself a cold compress. Should keep some of the swelling down.'

'Thanks, man.' Moose fetched the ice. He was regretting the passing of his ice business with cousin Tommy. But for that he wouldn't be sitting there with the risk of losing an eye. And maybe he wasn't quite cut out for the tough stuff after all. There had to be something easier.

Watching Willy fix his cold compress Dave felt sorry for the big lunk, even though he was sure that Willy would have broken his fingers like he'd said, and without any remorse.

'You can tell Tony how disappointed I am about this,' said Dave. Cruelly, he added: 'When you see him.'

'If I see him,' Willy said bitterly. 'My fuckin' eye. I think you blinded me.'

'Disappointed but not resentful. Tell him that despite this little misunderstanding, we're still friends. Tell him that. Maybe even future business associates. Yeah, tell Tony I've got a business proposition for him. Chance to make a big score. That ought to help reassure him . . . Tell him, I'll be in touch through Jimmy Figaro.'

Willy picked up the Magnum and slid it into the clip inside his pants. He glanced around for the .22 then remembered that Delano had it in his pocket. Dave guessed what he was looking for, took it out and hefted it in his hand.

'I'll just hang onto this a while,' he said. 'First rule of self-defense. Have a gun.'

'Can I leave now?' Willy sounded contrite. Contrite and concerned. 'I'd like to get to a hospital.'

'Sure, but aren't you forgetting something?' Dave nodded at

Willy's bare feet and the matchbooks between his toes. 'Your dogs, guy.'

Willy started to pick them out.

'I never figured you for no Dennis Hopper, man,' said Willy, shaking his head. 'In those clothes, you don't look so tough. More like a fuckin' college boy.'

'The apparel does oft proclaim the man,' said Dave. 'But you should have seen me at eight o'clock this morning.'

Willy pocketed one of the matchbooks.

'Souvenir,' he said. 'I collect them.'

'That should be one to remember,' suggested Dave.

'Would you really have done that? Set my toes on fire?'

Dave shrugged.

'Moose? I've been asking myself that same question.'

CHAPTER SIX

Special Agent Kate Furey stared out of the window of a third-floor conference room in FBI headquarters and stifled a deep yawn as her boss, Assistant Special Agent in Charge Kent Bowen, began to tell the story. It was one of those unpleasant, cruel stories that her male colleagues seemed to relish. Most of them were already grinning since everyone knew that the subject of the story was how Bolivar Suarez, a cousin of the Colombian Ambassador, and one of Miami's major cocaine traffickers, had met his untimely death the night before last.

'So you wanna see where this asshole lives, on Delray Beach. Jesus. Two acres of ocean-front estate. And the house is like something out of James Bond. Battleship gray, 10,000 square feet, looks like the Guggenheim Museum in New York. But inside it's a goddamn palace. Marble floors, mahogany doors and windows, art deco fixtures and lights from Paris. You get the idea. Florida living in the lap to the tune of $10 million.

'Anyway, here's the set-up. Asshole liked art, in a big fucking way. Pictures all over. He must have kept some of those New York salerooms going single-handed. Modern, but not shit, y'know? I mean I know nuthin' about art but even I could see that some of these artists had real talent. Lot of Scottish stuff, from Glasgow, which I liked of course. Asshole probably thought Glasgow was a double-glazing company. Lot of South American stuff too. I guess that he did know. Frida Kahlo. Diego Rivera. You name it. Asshole had it in a frame with a little light on. I mean, very particular. Like he couldn't just hammer a fucking nail in the wall. These pictures were positioned like he was a fucking surveyor. Story goes he once beat up his kid's nanny when she accidentally brushed against one of these canvases. And when I say beat up, I mean beat up. Apparently, he used one of those Romitron cosh things – you know, kind of a plastic ball and chain? – on her fucking hands. Damn near crippled her. No one touches those paintings except asshole himself.'

From headquarters on North-west Second Avenue it was only a couple of minutes' drive east to Kate's Williams Island apartment home. At least it was her home until the divorce came through. Howard, her husband, and a partner with one of Miami's smartest law firms, had paid almost $900,000 for the place. Her own lawyers had told her there was a chance she might get to keep the apartment as part of the settlement. But she was thinking that it hardly seemed fair he shouldn't get half. Besides, it wasn't as if she actually wanted to stay there in view of all the secretaries in his office that Howard had been balling there when, as on this occasion, Kate found herself working late.

'This information must have got out to someone in one of the other cartels,' Bowen continued, with one eye on Kate. 'Someone who wanted asshole dead. Take your pick. Hell, there's enough of them. Anyhow, whoever it was, they were real clever. Set it up while asshole was back in Bogota. The Delray place was well guarded on the highway side. Cameras, sensors, the whole protection package. But light on the ocean side. Like the stupid schmuck had never heard of boats. Anyway, CCGD Seven reports seeing some kind of high performance sports boat anchored a couple of miles up the coast, off the municipal beach, the night before asshole got hit. Sam Brockman figures they must have put a diver into the water who crawled ashore at the Suarez place under cover of darkness. There was only the one guard on the beach front. The guard says he saw nothing. Kate?'

Kent Bowen wanted her attention and approval most of all. She was one of the Miami Bureau's brightest agents, not to mention one of its great beauties and he had a thing about her. She snapped her attention back to Bowen and his interminable story.

'Here's the clever part,' he said. 'Guy gets in the house. A real pro. He selects his picture – no idea what it was – takes it off the wall and flattens out about 250 grams of C5 plastic onto the back of the canvas. Then he tapes a simple tilt detonator onto the inside of the stretcher. Just a ball bearing inside a test tube, two needles, a little battery and a blasting cap. And that's his bomb. Beautiful. A really neat job. He leaves the picture hanging slightly crooked and then skedaddles out of there. He's long gone by the time asshole returns from Colombia.' Bowen shook his head as if still amazed at the assassin's ingenuity. 'As usual the sniffer dogs go in first, but they can't get the scent of any explosives because the picture's about five feet up the wall. The asshole walks into the room and sees the picture hanging squint as Quasimodo's dick. And being the obsessive he is, right away he's over there to straighten it.'

Bowen sat back in his chair, grinning sadistically, to savor the climax of his story.

'The ball bearing rolls along the test tube, touches both points of the needles, completes the circuit, and karaboom! blows the guy's head clean off his fucking shoulders.'

Kate caught Bowen's eye and smiled thinly as he and the rest of the guys in the room laughed some more at that.

'The crime scenes investigation unit spent forty-five minutes looking for Bolivar's head. They were beginning to think one of those Colombians must have taken it for a fucking souvenir when they found it floating in the goddamn aquarium. The blast had carried it right across the room, like a basketball.' Bowen pretended to make a basket. 'Field goal, two points.'

He cackled some more, wiped a tear from his eye and thinking of another wisecrack, said:

'Now that's what I call a really mind-blowing picture.'

Bowen guffawed loudly and helped himself to a glass of water, like he'd just told a really funny story on Jay Leno. Balding and fiftyish he reminded Kate a lot of Colonel Kilgore in *Apocalypse Now*. He had the same kind of hard-ass attitude to the enemy and the same love of his staff. As soon as she started to speak she felt like the guy who wouldn't surf at Kilgore's beach party.

'Bolivar Suarez's assassination — ' she began.

'Hey, what has two asses and no head?' chuckled Bowen. 'The assassination of Bolivar Suarez.'

'Since his death would seem to leave Rocky Envigado as Miami's undisputed Citizen Cocaine,' she persisted, 'it may be that we need look no further than that particular quarter when searching for a perp.'

'One way of getting your head round modern art,' said someone else and Bowen found himself trying to keep a straight face in the presence of Kate Furey's more businesslike demeanor.

'Citizen Cocaine,' Bowen repeated. 'I like that. Did you think of it yourself?'

'No, I think I read it in a British newspaper,' she explained, aware that she could easily have got away with claiming it for herself. There were times, she knew, when she could be too honest, even by the standards of the FBI. 'When I was on vacation there last year.'

The one and only time she had been outside the States, and the last good time she had enjoyed with Howard. And yet it had been a vacation only in part. The main purpose of her trip to London and Paris had been to visit with British and French police forces who were worried about the amount of cocaine now arriving in Europe from Colombia, via Florida. But after Miami it had seemed like a vacation.

'Sorry,' she said, 'I mean when I was visiting with NCIS and Interpol.'

'Aha,' grinned Bowen. 'Now we learn the truth, Agent

Furey. You were holidaying at the expense of the American taxpayer.'

Kate smiled politely and hoped that they could get on with the meeting in progress. Its purpose was to share new intelligence about drug traffickers who used South Florida as an entrepôt for their activities. Information received from other agencies, at home and abroad. Now that Kent Bowen had told his story she could table what she had learned and then maybe go home and soak in the tub. It had been a long day.

'I had lunch with Peter van der Velden today and — '

'How is Dutch?'

Van der Velden was a detective inspector with Holland's BVD, on a two-year attachment as special liaison officer at the Netherlands Consulate in Miami.

'He's fine.'

'Go somewhere nice?'

'Don't worry, he paid.'

'I bet I know where you went. That place in Coral Gables. Le Festival. Dutch loves that place.'

'Yes, Le Festival.' She felt herself coloring a little as she made her reluctant admission.

'Is that good?' This was Special Agent Chris Ochao, a half-Cuban guy with his arm in a sling.

'Excellent,' said Bowen. 'Best soufflés in town.' He wiggled his eyebrows suggestively and added: 'Romantic too.'

'Can't say as I noticed,' said Kate.

'No?'

Someone sniggered.

Kate looked Bowen squarely in the eye. She knew it was generally suspected around the office that she was having an affair with Peter van der Velden. Every year all the liaison officers from the various consulates in Miami got together and hosted a party at the Doubletree Hotel in Coconut Grove. It was only two or three months since the last one, at which Kate had been seen leaving with the Dutch policeman after talking with him alone for almost an hour.

'Y'know, I think there's something I ought to clear up,' she said, smiling coolly. 'A little misunderstanding I know's been going around. Just for the record, I am not fucking Peter van der Velden. Nor have I ever fucked Peter van der Velden. Nor do I have any intention of fucking or being fucked by Peter van der Velden. Moreover our lunch appointment was not made for the purpose of his suggesting that he might get to fuck me, but that we might come together in a spirit of co-operation and diplomacy and get to fuck some major-league drug traffickers and bad guys. Do I make myself clear?' She looked from one end of the table to the other. Nobody said anything for a moment.

'Everyone got that?' said Bowen. 'OK Kate, you made your point. What is it that you were going to tell us about Peter van der Velden before you were interrupted?'

'Just this,' she said, pleased no one in the room had cottoned onto the occasional relationship she was actually having with the British liaison officer, Nick Hemmings. 'Peter's sources tell him that they're expecting a big shipment from Rocky Envigado. And get this. It's coming up from Mallorca, same as before.'

'Meaning?' Bowen was frowning now.

Kate took a deep breath.

'Meaning last time we must have missed it.'

'Yeah, well, if we missed it, so did the Spanish police and so did the Dutch,' said Ochao. 'We searched that boat from top to bottom. There was nothing.'

'Could be that Rocky has discovered a new way of transporting the stuff,' said Bowen. 'A way we don't yet know about.'

'Maybe he's doing it on the Internet,' suggested another agent. 'Seems like that's all that's obsessing people these days.'

'I want us to get scientific here,' said Bowen. 'Quantico. National Crime Information Center. The Smithsonian. Back issues of the *Law Enforcement Bulletin* if you have to. With all the resources at our command we ought to be able to come up with some ideas.'

Bowen stood up and tried to look inspiring to his people. It seemed easy enough until he met Kate's doubtful stare.

'Problem, Kate?'

'It might be that there really was nothing last time. That he used that first trip as a way of embarrassing us. After that little débâcle maybe he thinks now we'll leave him alone. But either way we ought to try and find the boat before we do anything, don't you think?'

'Well sure, that goes without saying, doesn't it?' He placed a carefully avuncular hand on Kate's shoulder. 'Take charge of the landing party, Mister Spock. I want some answers.'

Kate drove home in her white Sebring, fixed herself a rum punch, drank it while running her bath, and then fixed herself another before soaking in the hot water. The bathroom gave onto the wrap-around terrace and she left the blinds up so she could see across the intercoastal waterway to the winking lights of the Miami Riviera beyond. It was a big sunken tub with a Jacuzzi and just about her favorite spot in the whole apartment. A couple of times after she and Howard had taken the place they had shared a tub together. But mostly he preferred a shower and if he did take a bath he liked to have it to himself. After a while she got used to the idea that he generally took advantage of her extended sessions in the tub to lie in bed and watch the Playboy Channel on cable. He pretended he didn't of course and would switch onto Letterman or Leno the minute she came back into the bedroom. Not that she had minded him watching it very much. But what really did surprise and irritate her was that he must have believed he could take out a subscription to any new channel, let alone Playboy, and that somehow she wouldn't notice. She worked for the FBI, for Christ's sake. Noticing things was her job.

Naturally she had known that he was having affairs almost as soon as it started happening. She had hoped that he might get whatever it was out of his system. Just as long as none of it got into hers. But what finally prompted her to take action was not jealousy, nor even her love for Howard but, like the Playboy Channel subscription, the irritation she experienced at being considered too stupid to see through his lies and evasions. She was the bright one, not him. Second in her class in law at the University of Florida in Gainsville, graduating with honors, this was the same class in which her future husband had struggled to make the top fifty, and still the bastard figured he could outsmart her, like she was the dumbest short-order waitress in Oklahoma.

Kate had borrowed some surveillance equipment from the Bureau to obtain aural and pictorial evidence of Howard's infidelity and caught him banging the ladies' golf pro from the nearby Turnberry Isle Country Club. That was bad enough. Golf was such a stupid game. But it's the small things that really bother you and she had been even more appalled to discover that Howard's golfing partner was using the contraceptive gel from Kate's own bathroom cupboard for their stroke play. So with the help of a girlfriend in the Bureau's laboratory, and following extensive trial and experimentation, she had substituted the gel inside a tube of Gynogel for an identically clear and similarly scented brand of exercise balm – an alcohol and menthol-based deep heat muscle rub that was definitely not recommended for use on sensitive areas. Especially the two sensitive areas that Kate had in mind. Even now, months after the event, just the thought of the tape she had made of her husband and his lover screaming through their hottest ever session of lovemaking could still make her laugh out loud. Whoever said that revenge was a dish best served cold had obviously never listened to two generous servings of overheated genitals.

Somehow Kate had never thought of herself as the vengeful wife. With her beautiful face, her keen appreciation of art, literature and music, not to mention a strong imagination, she had always seen herself as a more romantic type. It seemed odd to think about it now, but that was the reason she had joined the Bureau in the first place, and not some sawgrass-dull firm of Downtown attorneys. She had wanted action and excitement, even the occasional danger. But of late the most hazardous thing she had done had been forgetting the safety catch on her Lady Smith & Wesson; and for all that she needed a weapon she might as well have been packing a hatpin. In the hope of getting a foreign posting, like Bogota, Caracas, Lima or Mexico City, Kate had started to learn Spanish. Meanwhile she stared out to sea and dreamed of adventure.

CHAPTER SEVEN

Everyone agreed that Al Cornaro's wife, Madonna, was an extraordinary woman. It wasn't that she was beautiful, just that everyone thought it extraordinary that Al should have married her at all. Most of the guys who worked for Tony Nudelli were married to beauty-parlor blondes with brassière-sized IQs and Condé Nast educations. Not so much trophy wives as tin cup ones, these were the kind of women who could manipulate an eyebrow pencil with more skill than they could use a pen, and for whom oral skills meant giving a good blow-job. What made Madonna different was her intelligence, her sharp tongue, her total disregard for self-image, and the size of her tits. The tits were genuine, you just had to look at the rest of Madonna to work that out. They hung around her waist like something that had been sculpted there as a dry run for Washington and Jefferson on Mount Rushmore – a monumental effect that was enhanced by Madonna's dislike of brassières – or for that matter any underwear at all – and the recent birth of her fourth son, Al junior. Al senior loved his wife, but it didn't stop him making jokes about her for Tony Nudelli's amusement. Keeping Tony amused was an important part of Al's job as Tony's business manager. Keeping him amused and taking care of business. Colonel Tom Parker with guns and jokes. Today the business included Dave Delano, but first Al wanted to make sure Tony was in a more forgiving mood than the day before when Al had had to tell him that Willy Four Breakfasts had fucked up and was now laid up in the Miami Beach Community Hospital with a serious eye injury, courtesy of his planned victim.

It was not quite ten o'clock when Al arrived at Nudelli's luxurious villa in the heart of Key Biscayne. He recognized the red Porsche convertible that was parked in the driveway and instinctively made his way to the 6,000 square foot poolhouse. He knew his boss, a keen swimmer, would be in the sixty-foot pool under the personal supervision of his coach, Sindy, a former lifeguard from Wet n'Wild in Orlando. Al liked to see Sindy, not least because she was usually naked and there was always a lot to see. He was a non-swimmer himself, but it might have been worth getting into the water just to have Sindy encourage him to learn in her own special way. From time to time she would dive gracefully off the granite deck, chase the naked Tony underwater like some fabulous dark dolphin, and then get underneath him to lick and nibble his penis. Most people thought Nudelli was called Naked Tony because of his surname, but Al knew different. Al knew that it was mostly because of what Tony and Sindy got up to in the pool. Sindy told Al that she got the idea from reading a book about the Roman Emperors, and in particular the life of Tiberius. Al wasn't much of a reader, but that was one book he just had to take a look at, and they were every bit as depraved as she had said. Sindy was tall, black and beautiful and merely looking at her gave Al a hard-on. Tony called her his Angel-fish.

Al walked into the pool-house.

'Morning Al,' smiled Sindy.

'Morning Sindy.'

Just about the first thing Al looked for after he had looked at Sindy's pubic hair and then her tits was Sindy's orange juice. Tony didn't swim a prescribed number of lengths, or even a set period, but only for as long as it took Sindy to finish him off in her mouth. If Sindy was drinking orange juice it meant that she and Tony were done.

'Party over?'

Sindy toasted Al silently with half a glass of juice and then sipped at it teasingly. Al's eyes stayed on her lips and the juice.

'Want some?' she said, offering him the glass.

'Ah no, thanks, ah, Sindy.'

There was no way Al was going to put his lips anywhere near that glass after what her mouth had been doing.

'Sure? It's um . . . freshly squeezed. Y'know what I'm sayin'?'

'Sure. I ah . . . just had breakfast.'

'Hmm. So did I.' Sindy swallowed thoughtfully. 'Rather a lot as it happens. Tony must be taking extra zinc or something.' Giggling at Al's very obvious discomfort, Sindy tapped him on the nose with one of her long, scarlet fingernails and called out to the weary looking man crawling slowly towards the poolside: 'OK, hon, I'm outta here. You OK? Want me to help you out?'

'I'm OK. And you helped me out enough already. Thanks, baby. I'll call you.'

'Later.'

Al watched Sindy's bare ass all the way back to the changing rooms and shook his head in quiet desperation.

'I should learn to fuckin' swim,' he said.

'You said it, Mary Joe.'

'Mary Joe' was what Tony always called Al whenever the subject of Al not swimming came up, after Mary Joe Kopechnie, the girl who drowned at Chappaquiddick when Ted Kennedy didn't. 'Mary Joe', or sometimes 'Pussy'.

Nudelli sank beneath the surface of the water and kicked his way toward the pool steps. Al had to admit, Tony looked good for a man of his age. His shoulders and chest were broad and he still had all his hair which was a Cary Grant shade of silver gray. Nudelli enjoyed the comparison.

'Hand me that robe, will ya Al?' Nudelli said, surfacing again and coming up the steps.

Hung too, thought Al. Like a horse. It looked like Sindy had her work cut out. For an older guy Tony sure had a whole lot going for him. Al collected a towel robe off the back of a white rattan chair and handed it over. Nudelli slipped it on. As he sat down he jerked his head toward the wet bar.

'Fix yourself some breakfast if you want,' said Nudelli, putting on his glasses and selecting a large Cohibas from the rosewood humidor on the etched glass table. 'There's fruit and coffee, all kinds of shit.'

'Thanks, I already had some.' Al started to laugh as he remembered the story he had prepared for Tony's amusement.

'No coffee?'

'Yeah, coffee, thanks. Here let me get it.' Al walked over to the wet bar, picked the Cona jug off the hot-plate and poured two mugfuls. 'Well, I say breakfast,' he said, bringing over the coffee. 'Weirdest fucking breakfast I ever ate. And that includes the ones in Holland.'

Nudelli puffed the cigar into service and flicked the match onto the surface of the pool confident that the pool man would scoop it out later on.

'How's that?'

'Ever since I was a kid I have to have a bowlful of Wheaties for breakfast.'

'I remember,' said Nudelli. 'When we were in Vegas last year you were a real pain in the ass about it.'

'The breakfast of champions.'

'Don't start on that bullshit. If there's one thing I hate in the morning it's an advertising slogan. It's like finding a turd in an unflushed toilet bowl.'

'So this morning I come down to the kitchen and Madonna's in there with the kids and it's like, y'know. Fuckin' chaos is what it is, right? And all I want to do is have my bowl of Wheaties and then get the fuck out of there before I have a cerebral hemorrhage with all the fuckin' noise there is. Anyway, I get the bowl of Wheaties and sit down at the table and look around for the cream and there isn't any left in the jug. No problem. I can see that she's got her hands full what with the new baby n'all. I'm not above fetching my own fuckin' cream from the icebox. Trouble is that there isn't any in the icebox either and so I start to cuss. What's the problem? she says. The problem, I tell her, is that there is no fuckin' cream to put on my Wheaties. I'm sorry honey, she says, I guess we must have run out. The kids drink it like they'd never heard of Coca-Cola, which is good because they need the calcium. I can see we've run out, I say, but what am I going to do? You know it screws up my whole day if I don't leave the house with a bowlful of Wheaties inside of me. You know what she did?'

'Surprise me.'

'She's walking around breast-feeding the baby, right?'

'Jesus, ya can go to the zoo if you wanna see that shit.'

'The next minute she plucks the tit from the kid's gums, leans over my fuckin' shoulder and squirts a couple of ounces of breast milk all over the Wheaties.' Al quickly mimed the action he was describing.

Tony started to laugh.

'What the fuck is this? I ask her and she says, What the fuck do you think it is, asshole? It's milk. I can see it's fuckin' milk, I tell her. I just wonder what you think you're doin' with your fuckin' tits in my breakfast. It's good enough for your kids, but not you, is that what you're saying? she says.

Tony was laughing hard now, and coughing too as his air got mixed with cigar smoke, so that he sounded like a small motorcycle engine ticking over. He took off his glasses and pinched the bridge of his nose.

'She says, How many of the other guys have wives who could do this? You should be glad. It's fresh and it doesn't cost you a fuckin' cent. The money you give me to keep this house? You're lucky you don't get this every morning, ya cheap bum.'

Tony said, 'Jesus Christ, that Madonna. I love her. She's a piece of work. She looks like Tugboat Annie, but I love that fuckin' wife of yours, Al.' He wiped his streaming eyes on the collar of his bathrobe. 'So what happened next?'

Al said, 'What happened next? I ate the fuckin' Wheaties. That's what happened.'

Both men exploded with laughter, with Al coming down first.

'I mean, it was that or no Wheaties, right?'

'Oh Jesus,' sighed Tony, finally replacing his glasses. 'How could you do that?'

Al shrugged, uncharacteristically at a loss for something to say.

'Well come on, Al. Whaddit fuckin' taste like?'

Al's face wrinkled with thought as he tried to recall.

He said, 'Warm, of course. Kind of like the skimmed you get in those little creamer cartons when you're in McDonald's. I prefer the milk that comes out of a cow, but Al junior seems to like it. Can't get enough of the stuff.'

'That Madonna. She's something.' Just the thought of the big redhead made him squirm. God only knew what she looked like when she was around the house. She looked bad enough when she was dressed to come out to dinner. Al on the other hand, Al made an effort about the way he dressed. It wasn't the effort Nudelli would have made, but still. Just now he was wearing an expensive-looking yellow Gianni Versace shirt that looked like a silk cushion cover, some black leather jeans that were made to be worn by someone a lot thinner than Al, a white snakeskin belt, and red cowboy boots – not to mention a lot of gold this n'that. Nudelli thought Al Cornaro looked like a nigger's Christmas tree, although by Miami standards he could pass for well-dressed. People in Florida knew shit from Shinola when it came to clothes and Al was no exception. They went anywhere outside the Sunshine State and Tony usually made Al wear a Brooks Brothers suit with a proper shirt and tie. A suit was business. Nudelli was an Anglophile. English shoes. English suits. He always bought English.

Al said, 'I spoke to Jimmy Figaro.'

'That putz.'

'We arranged for him to bring Dave Delano here at eleven o'clock this morning.'

There was a clock on the wall behind Tony but he didn't feel like looking around. He was a little tired after his swimming lesson. 'Time's it now?'

Al glanced up at the clock.

'Ten-thirty.'

'Whaddya think?'

'You and he are still friends. That's what Delano said, according to Willy. Wants to reassure you. Reassurance sounds good to me.'

Nudelli nodded thoughtfully.

'Sensible guy.'

'Comin' here with Jimmy, it's the smart move. It shows he doesn't bear you any malice on account of what happened. The guy's got balls, you have to give him credit for that.'

'He proved that when he became Willy's fuckin' ophthalmologist.'

'Willy must be losing his touch.'

'Either he lost it or Delano learned some when he was in jail.'

'Could be.'

Nudelli said, 'This business proposition of his.'

'A big score, Willy said.'

'He goes in the joint a numbers man, and figures to come out a major-league thief, is that it?'

'Hear him out. Maybe he learned something when he was doing time. Worked out a play. Five years is long enough for anyone to get some constructive thinking done.'

'Suppose I don't like his set-up? Is he holding a gun to my head about this, or what? Suppose I don't help set this thing up? Is he then going to go to the Feds and tell them it was me who popped Benny Cecchino? Suppose on that for a while, will ya?'

'Jesus, Tony, you got more suppose in there than Stephen fuckin' King. He kept his mouth shut all these years, didn't he?

Done his time, like he was told. If you'd wanted him popped you could have done it five years ago and saved yourself the two hundred grand. What's changed? I don't understand.'

'You wanna know?'

'I wanna know.'

'OK I'll tell you. Five years ago, I didn't know that Delano was not the guy's real name. I thought he was Italian-American, like you and me. Turns out his daddy was Russian. Well you know what my fucking low opinion is of those backward barbarians. But worse than that, he's a fucking kike to boot.'

'What, we never done business with the Jews before? This is Miami, Tony. An open city. It was the Jews who helped to develop this place for business. Meyer Lansky. People like that. Besides, as I understand it, he's only half Jewish. His mother's Irish.'

'Never underestimate a Jew, Al. Even one that's not the whole candlestick. Take my advice, and you'll stay alive a lot longer. Don't get me wrong here. I'm not anti-Semitic. Let me tell you, almost fifty years ago, when I was back in Jersey City? I met this little Jewish broad and fell in love with her. Best lay of my life, and you've seen Sindy. I'd have done anything for that little broad. Including marry her. Wanted to. Asked her often enough. Gave her a ring, the whole Tiffany deal. But it was always the same story. She couldn't do it to her parents, she said. I'm not asking you to do it to your parents, I told her, I'm askin' that you do it to me. But no, she couldn't marry out, she said. What? I said. You think my parents'll be blowing up balloons when I tell them I don't wanna marry a Catholic? You think a Christ-killer is some kind of honor for them? No way. But still she wouldn't have me. She was in love with me all right, but she wouldn't get married. To hell with Shakespeare. To hell with Romeo and Juliet and that stuff. It was like I meant nuthin' to her. Now I ask you Al: what kind of people can do that? I'll tell you what kind. The Jewish kind. There is nothing they won't put ahead of being Jewish. I know what I'm talking about. Shakespeare made Romeo and Juliet Italians because he understood what love means to an Italian. There ain't anythin' more important than how your heart feels. But it would have challenged him as a writer a lot more if Juliet had been a Jewish princess, let me tell you. Now that would have been a fuckin' play. That's a play I'd like to have seen.'

Al said, 'I dunno Tony. Delano doesn't want to fuck you. He wants to do business with you.'

'For a Jew, they're the same thing. And don't forget the Ivans. Delano shared a cell with one of them redfellas for four years. Learned to speak pretty good Russkie from what I hear. You see what I'm sayin', Al? It wasn't Italian he learned to speak, it was fucking Russkie. Which means I gotta wonder where he's comin' from. If he's in bed with these meathead slobs or what? I got enough trouble with bums like Rocky Envigado and those Colombian bastards without takin' on the Ivans as well. That's the trouble with this country. Too many damned immigrants.'

'Willy Four Breakfasts seemed to think that Delano was more inclined to believe Willy was carrying out a contract for the Ivans than he was to think you wanted him to take a beating.' Al shrugged. 'Doesn't sound like someone who's in bed with the Ivans.'

Nudelli puffed his cigar thoughtfully.

'There is that,' he allowed.

Al said, 'Hear the guy out. After all, business is business and personal shouldn't ever get in the way of that, right?'

'You're right, of course.' Nudelli leaned forward and took hold of Al by the cheek and then slapped him gently.

'Just taking care of business, Tony.'

Nudelli regarded his cigar's wet end and nodded thoughtfully.

Al said, 'I didn't know you were from Jersey City.'

'It was me or some other poor bastard.'

'What happened to the Jewish broad? The one you were in love with.'

'How the fuck should I know?'

Jimmy Figaro drove the big BMW across the Rickenbacker Causeway, just south of where his offices were located. The road soared high over Biscayne Bay and provided Figaro's uninterested passenger with an unparalleled view of the Brickell Avenue skyline. The first island was Virginia Key, once set aside for Miami's black community and a large sewage plant. The next island was Key Biscayne. Steering the car with one finger now, because everything was more laid back on Key Biscayne, Figaro came down Crandon Boulevard, heading south toward Cape Florida before turning west onto Harbor Drive.

Figaro glanced over at Dave and said, 'Tony's place is just down the road from where Richard Nixon used to live.'

'Tricky Dicky. Yeah, that figures.'

'You a Democrat?'

'What's the difference to a bad guy like me?'

'Haven't you ever voted for someone?'

'Sure. I voted for the prisoners' representative in Homestead. Choice was between a murderer and a rapist. I chose the murderer.'

'Who won?'

'The murderer.'

'What about on the outside?'

'On the outside it doesn't matter who represents you. The murderer or the rapist.'

'That's not much of a political philosophy.'

'After you've been in prison there's only one political philosophy that matters a damn and that's keeping your ass out of prison.'

The car was now gliding smoothly through an immaculately manicured community fringed with Australian pines and coconut palms and one white palace after another, like so many wedding cakes.

Figaro changed the subject and said, 'Harbor Bayfront Villas is one of Miami's most exclusive addresses. Tony's villa is right on the bay.'

'No kidding.'

Figaro slowed and turned down a private road, pulling up at a gatehouse where he gave both their names to the guard. The guard checked them on a clipboard list and then waved them on through the elevating barrier.

'Round here is the last word in European splendor,' Figaro enthused.

'Outside of Europe, you might be right.' Dave grinned. 'You really like it round here, don't you, Jimmy?'

'Wouldn't anyone?' nodded Figaro. 'I mean, wouldn't you just love to live here.'

They pulled up in front of a two-storey open bay villa with full dock and davits. Dave noted the 100-foot motor yacht that was moored there and then turned his attention to the house. With its pantiled roof, keystone columns and arches, and courtyard with fountain, the place looked as if it had been transplanted from a hill in Tuscany.

Dave said, 'I'd sure like to be able to afford to live here. If I could then I'd use the money to live somewhere nice, like London, or Paris. Miami sucks.'

'One man's meat, I guess,' said Figaro.

'And Miami is a cheeseburger.'

They got out of the car, walked up to the front door and were admitted to an atrium foyer with a marble floor and a curving stone staircase. One of Nudelli's bodyguards frisked Dave and then a butler walked them upstairs to an opulent mahogany-panelled library where Nudelli and Al Cornaro were seated inside a stockade of green leather chesterfields. The two men got up and crossed the aquamarine Bokhara rug, and Dave allowed himself to be embraced by the man who'd ordered his fingers broken.

Nudelli said, 'Hey Al, will you take a look at this guy? Five years in the joint and he looks like he spent the summer in Palm Springs. Jesus, Dave, you look great. You look like a fuckin' movie star.'

'You're not looking so bad yourself, Tony,' Dave said patiently.

Nudelli slapped his own belly hard.

'Keepin' fit, y'know? Swim every day. Watch what I eat. You want something to eat? Drink maybe? We got everything. Silver fuckin' service. We're like the frigging Admirals' Club out here.'

'No, I'm OK, thanks Tony.'

'Jimmy?'

'Just a coffee.'

'Miggy?' Nudelli was speaking to the butler. 'Couple of coffees.'

They sat down inside the stockade.

Nudelli said, 'Five years.'

Dave said, 'Five years, yeah.'

'You did good.'

'At the time, it seemed the thing to do, Tony.'

'Dave. About that little misunderstanding with Willy Barizon.'

'Hey, forget about it. These things happen.'

'It's good of you to see it that way, Dave.'

'You know after Willy's cold call I got to thinking about things from your POV, Tony. And I said to myself, I said: Dave, while you were on the inside, Tony knew where you were and what you were doing. It's a variant on what Machiavelli says about composite principalities, Tony. Being on the spot you can detect trouble at the start and deal with it pronto; but if you're absent the trouble's discerned only when it's too fuckin' late.'

Tony said, 'I heard you got yourself educated. Is that so? Machiavelli, huh? Sounds Italian.'

'From Florence.'

'That night you was with Benny Cecchino — '

'You mean in the restaurant where you shot him?'

'Yeah. What were you and he talking about?'

Dave shrugged and said, 'A business proposition. Why else would anyone talk to Benny?'

'Did you owe him money?'

'No.' Dave grinned. 'I didn't get a chance to. Your sudden arrival on the scene put paid to that.'

'You know, Benny had a mouth like a V8.'

Dave said, 'He was nothing to me. But from what I heard he had it coming.'

'Nice of you to say so.' Nudelli looked rueful. 'I had more of a temper then. Well, this was five years ago. Five years is a long time. I'm sure you of all people don't need reminding of that.'

Dave waited for Tony Nudelli to say something else and when he didn't Dave decided to segue along to the purpose of his requested meeting.

'Talking of business propositions, Tony, I've got one I think you might be interested in.' Dave unfolded his laptop computer. 'The sweetest idea you ever heard.'

'I'm always interested in sweet ideas. Isn't that so, Al?'

'Always.'

Nudelli said, 'Before you say another word, Dave.' Nudelli glanced over at Jimmy, now drinking his coffee. 'For someone like Jimmy, information is pressure. Sometimes the less he has, the more freedom and space there is for him. He likes to work in a vacuum. To know only what he needs to know. Especially if there are any inherent illegalities. So let me ask you, does Jimmy need to hear this? Or does he need to take a walk?'

'I think maybe he should take a walk,' agreed Dave.

Dave watched Figaro leave the library and when he looked back he thought that maybe Tony had false teeth and that they must have slipped off his jaw until he realized that it was some kind of little contraption made of steel and plastic and that Tony was using it to exercise the muscles in his face. Noting Dave's expression Nudelli tongued the thing onto the palm of his hand. It looked like a tiny crutch.

Nudelli said, 'My facial workout. Helps restore lost muscle tone and reshapes bags and sags. Those I got enough of already. A 250 percent increase in facial muscle strength in just eight weeks. They say all you need is two minutes a day, but I'm doin' a little more than that on account of all the fuckin' worries I've got. My wife. She wanted a facelift. Estimated cost? Ten thousand dollars. Instead I bought her one of these little gizmos for seventy-five bucks.' He chuckled meanly and popped the device back inside his cheeks. 'O ahead,' he said, opening and closing his mouth like a goldfish. 'Make your pitch.'

Dave glanced at the color screen of his laptop and found the file he was searching for.

He said, 'Chasing drug money is the new law-enforcement specialty. Banking regulations have been tightened all over the world. Banking secrecy relaxed, even in Switzerland. Used to be that you could fly into Zurich with a suitcase full of money and make a deposit, no questions asked. Not any more. It's gotten so that the Swiss have to ask questions these days. For a while back there, South America and the Caribbean were also good places to hide drug dollars.'

Al said, 'Still are.'

'If you know the right people. Not everyone does. New crime isn't connected in the same way as someone like you, Tony. Nowadays the best thing you can do is to buy a bank. And the gold medal place to buy one of those is in the former Soviet Union. Under the aegis of Gosbank, which is owned by the State, and Vnesheconombank, which is the Bank of Foreign Affairs, hundreds of banks have been formed in the last few years to take advantage of new Russian enterprise. To lend it money. To take care of other hard currency deposits. There are even tax breaks and building loans to encourage new banks.'

'It might be nice to own my own bank,' said Nudelli.

Dave said, 'Wait. There's more to this scam. OK, to do it, to capitalize your new bank, you have to get your cash into Russia. That can be difficult too, especially when the cash is the result of illegal enterprise. What's more, when it's in the quantities required to capitalize a new bank it's bulky. Let me illustrate that with a comparison. D'you like basketball, Tony?'

'Sure.'

'Then you'll know that UCF's leading scorer at seventeen points a game is Harry Kennedy. Now think of a tower of ten-dollar bills twenty-five inches wide and seventeen inches deep that's as tall as Harry Kennedy. Harry's about six-five, I believe. That's only $5 million. A tower would have to be fourteen feet high and weigh more than 2,000 pounds just to reach ten million bucks. Makes it harder to shift than any drug, with one advantage being that the dog hasn't yet been born that can sniff out money.'

'They got women for that,' chuckled Al. 'My wife can lock onto a new C-note at fifty paces.'

Tony Nudelli liked that one.

'But the Moscow gangs have fixed the transport of the cash too. Transport your money and help you set up your own bank. All for twenty-five cents on the dollar, same as if you had to launder it somewhere else. They get the cash across the Atlantic, through the Mediterranean and up into the Black Sea. Less than eight weeks after the money leaves Florida you own your own bank in the Russian city of your choice. Once there you can loan it to business, make money on it and then put it through the regular banking system.'

Al asked, 'So what's the angle? Owning a bank would be nice but we don't need no help laundering money.'

'I'm not selling any. My angle is this. I want to rip off one of these hard currency exports. The Moscow mob with some help from old KGB guys, and some new ones too, they operate an undercover dockage out of Fort Lauderdale. Just five minutes from the airport. The place is 50,000 square feet with state-of-the-art facilities, and accommodating motor yachts up to 150 feet long. They've got guys working there who really know the inside of boats. Put a new interior in your boat in no time. Except that it's not your yacht, it's theirs. One of half a dozen they own and charter. And the new interior? A new double bed in each stateroom that's literally made of money. Each one looks and feels like any other bed. Maybe a little firm but that's hardly surprising given that there's maybe two million bucks tucked away inside the base.'

Nudelli flicked the facial flex out of his mouth, wiped the saliva from his lips, and brandished the flex as if it was a cocktail stick.

'Wait a minute,' he growled. 'You look outta that window there, you can see the *Bitch*. Named after my first wife. A hundred foot long, she's got a top speed of twenty-four knots and a range of 2,000 miles. A fully equipped cruising resort, she's sleek, seaworthy and whisper fuckin' quiet, perfect for island hopping, but I wouldn't try to cross the Atlantic in her. The QE2 she ain't.'

Dave shook his head and said, 'You wouldn't have to, Tony. For around $80,000 you could book the *Bitch* a passage on a custom-built transatlantic ferry. In particular, one of the cat-tugs operated by Stranahan Yacht Transport out of Port Everglades.'

'The hell's a cat-tug when it's afloat?' asked Al.

Dave rolled the trackball on his computer, selected a picture file from the floppy disk he had made up the day before, and turned the machine to face his two-man audience. They shifted forward on the chesterfield to take a closer look at the picture on the color screen. In front of them was a shot of a 600-foot vessel that contained as many as eighteen luxury motor yachts.

Dave said, 'It has the basic hull form of a ship, combined with the wide beam and shallower draft of a barge. But it still equals the center of gravity and the buoyancy of both units.'

'Jesus,' said Al. 'That's incredible. I never seen nuthin' like that before. They really do sail this thing across the Atlantic? With all these other boats?'

Dave nodded.

Nudelli said, 'Looks kind of risky to me. I'm speaking as a yacht owner, you understand. There's the risk of lifting the boat out of the water. Then there's the risk of having your boat on an unprotected deck during the crossing.'

'Uh-uh. The cat-tug is a semi-submersible. Kind of like an oceangoing dock. You float your boat in at Port Everglades, and then float it out again when you get to sunny Mallorca, in the western Mediterranean. During the voyage each vessel is secured to the dock floor, tied down with special lines, and protected from the worst of the Atlantic by those dock walls you see. They're around twenty feet high. There are only minimal acceleration forces when the cat-tug's underway. Oh, and the er, insurance premiums for crossing the Atlantic are about a quarter less than if you went under your own steam. Always supposing that you could. SYT will carry any vessel up to one with a twenty-foot draft and there are no height restrictions.'

Nudelli said, 'I guess that's right. Looks like a schooner in amongst those other boats. Main mast should be around sixty feet high.' He leaned back on the chesterfield, the leather creaking underneath him like he was already on board a ship at sea. 'I gotta admit, it looks impressive. But this company, Stranahan Yacht Transport. They have anything to do with the Russkies?' He returned the facial flex to his mouth and began to stretch his face again.

'Nope. It's a legit company. Russkies book a passage like any other citizen. Being alongside the boats of law-abiding citizens they figure on having a certain safety in numbers. And of course the Coast Guard is looking for dope, not cash. When the cat-tug gets to Palma, Mallorca, they float out and sail on to their final destination under their own steam. It's a place on the Black Sea, where the money's finally taken out and

71

then transported by road. Another quick refit and the yacht's ready to come home again.'

'That's a lot of trust in a bunch of Russkies,' observed Nudelli. 'You say you want to rip one of these transports off. What's to stop them ripping off their clients?'

Dave said, 'Because the first time would also be the last time. And because some of these clients don't have much choice in the matter. These days there are only a few ways to launder drug money, which is what this mostly is. Being caught with dollars is almost worse than being pinched with cocaine. Some of the South American cartels are making so much money they've got nowhere to put it. Sometimes they end up just burying it in the ground and letting it rot. Guy in Homestead? He lost two million that way. Used to be that you could buy yourself a nice bank in Panama or Venezuela. But then the authorities wised up. The Group of Seven Industrial Countries set up the Financial Action Task Force back in 1989. And that's when the bad guy money started going to the former Soviet Union.

'From what I've heard, Moscow's just like Chicago was back in the twenties. If you've got the money you can buy just about anything you want. Bombs, missiles, armies, whole fuckin' towns. Country's one gigantic garage sale. All it takes is dollars. You can't buy shit with their own currency. Beats me how Uncle Sam manages to get a handle on the US economy with so much American money around. I mean what's a government for, if not to control the supply of money? It's no surprise to me our economy's a piece of shit. The dollar's carrying half the world on its green back. Anyway, coming back to your original question, Tony. These guys want to do business with Americans. With South Americans. People with dollars. Help set them up with a bank so that they can start to do business together. Contra deals, that kind of thing. Co-operation is at the heart of good business.'

Nudelli nodded and said, 'So what's your play?'

'I need a yacht to book onto the transatlantic tug. I need

another crewman to help me pull the job. Halfway across the Atlantic – that's as far away from European and American navies as you can get – we overpower the crews of the tug and the other yachts. At night, so they're not expecting trouble. We take the money from the Russian yachts and transfer it to the boat nearest the stern. Then we float out and cruise towards a prearranged rendezvous with a tanker we'll have sailing in the opposite direction, on a legitimate voyage. Something that's coming back here maybe. We put the money on the tanker and then scuttle the motor yacht, just to throw people off the scent.'

Al said, 'What's the haul?'

'The Russians have started making as many as two or three bookings per transport. Three yachts, six or seven staterooms per yacht, at two mill each.'

'Jesus,' said Al. 'That's over forty million.'

'Could be,' agreed Dave. 'But I figure a minimum twenty-five.'

'There's gonna be a lot of firepower on board to protect a piece of change like that,' said Al.

Once again, Dave shook his head, his eyes narrowing as they caught the sun. Nudelli turned around, then waved at the large expanse of window that framed their view of Biscayne Bay. South Miami and Coconut Grove lay hidden on the other side of the horizon some five miles away to the west. It was the best view Dave had ever seen of his hometown.

'Fix the blind, will ya, Al? The sun's in Dave's eyes.'

'It's OK, I like the sun.'

But Al was already unfolding louvred shutters across the window.

'Tony hates the fuckin' sun,' he explained. 'Only guy in Key Biscayne with an indoor swimming pool.'

'After five years in Homestead I could use some vitamin D.'

Nudelli tongued the flex from his mouth and grimaced. He said, 'After five years, you wanna be careful of that skin of yours. Sun ain't like it used to be. Niggers, even the fuckin' oranges go careful these days, 'cos of this hole those idiots made in the ozone layer. Even the goddamn fish are getting skin cancer. I read that somewhere. Didn't I? Al?'

Al said, 'It was me who read it to you, from the paper. And they was Australian fish. Not Americans.'

'As if it matters what nationality they are. Lots of ways Florida is like Australia. They don't call us the Sunshine State for nuthin'. Take my advice, Dave. Get yourself a hat. Everyone in our line of business used to wear a hat. Even the lousy cops wore hats. You could tell a lot about a guy from the way he wore his hat too. And with the sun we got now? Believe me, hats are makin' a comeback, and I don't mean the little peaks you see the niggers and the spics wearing. I mean a proper hat. English style.'

'Sounds like good advice.'

Al said, 'Before the sunshine interrupted us, you were about to tell us what kind of security they got to protect all this dirty money.'

'SYT allows just a couple of crew per boat. Any more than that and they'd be drawing attention to themselves. Three boats means six crew. It's reasonable to assume they'll be armed of course. But with the element of surprise I figure me and another guy could take care of them.'

'Suppose someone radios for help,' objected Al.

Nudelli grimaced irritably and said, 'Suppose he fixes all the fuckin' radios at the same time as he fixes all the crews.'

Dave said, 'That's about the size of it.'

'How'd'you find out about this?'

'You share a cell with a man for four years, a man tells you pretty much everything. Gergiev, that was his name. Clever guy. He's out of St Petersburg, right? And they're big rivals of the Moscow mob. Anyway, he knew about these transports and planned this whole thing. We were going to do the job together, only the Feds had him deported the minute he came out of the joint. One big score, that was the idea. Matter of fact

I got a letter from him the day of my release. He told me that he's trying to get back here, and that if I try this without him he'll kill me. But he's not much help back in Russia and I don't figure this job can wait. And I think he overrates his chances of ever getting another visa. Only now I've got nobody to help me set it up.'

'And you figured it was this guy who sent Willy Barizon to see you, right?'

'Gergiev was going to find the right boat, and the stake money to get it. I was going to captain it. Supply the maritime know-how. You could say that's what I bring to the deal. All my life I've been into boats. My father used to work on yachts. From time to time, I've even owned a couple of smaller ones myself. Learned to sail, learned navigation. Even got my ticket. Gergiev might figure I'm double-crossing him. But that's not true. I'll take care of him out of my end on this deal.'

'Which is?'

'If I get the right backing: someone to stake me for the boat, I figure fifty-fifty. Maybe twelve to fifteen mill each.'

Nudelli asked, 'What kind of boat do you need?'

'Not too big, not too small. Maybe sixty or seventy feet. Room enough for all that cash and with a good top speed supposing we can be nearest the stern. The main thing is it has to look the part. Like it's worth the trouble of mailing it across the ocean, y'know? I should say a value around 1.5 mill.'

Nudelli said nothing.

'Out of my final share of course,' Dave added, hoping to sweeten the deal. 'Say 60,000 bucks for the passage which I'll also cover myself — '

Al said, 'A $1.5 million boat you propose to abandon or flush down the toilet. Am I right?'

'Yes, that's right. My guess is that the authorities will spend the first few days looking for this yacht or the one we have to steal. That is if they come looking at all. Remember this is illegal cash. If anyone does come looking I figure they'll try the Azores first working on the principle that this is the nearest land to where we take down the score.'

'You seem to have thought it all out,' said Nudelli.

Dave shrugged and said, 'Had five years to think it through, Tony.'

'It's a sweet scheme, I have to admit. I got just one major problem with it.'

'What's that?'

Nudelli nodded and said, 'You. It's you, Dave. I just don't picture you for no hijacker. You ever pop anyone?'

'No, I can't say that I have.'

Nudelli said, 'There's no shame in that. But it's a fact of life that the first time is always the hardest. Ain't that so, Al?'

'The hardest. On a job like you described you wouldn't want to find yourself in a situation where you might hesitate to trigger a guy.'

Dave thought for a moment, trying to offer some guarantee for his own future ruthlessness. Pointedly, he said, 'By the way, how's Willy's eye?'

'That stupid fuck,' grunted Al. 'Maybe he'll see straight now you halved his viewing options.'

Nudelli said, 'I mean, how you handled Willy, that was impressive. Willy's no pushover. But these guys on the Russian yachts. Maybe they won't put their hands up so easy. Maybe they won't be as dumb as Willy. Maybe you'll have to take one or two of them down.'

Dave said, 'Could be.'

Al said, 'So. That's our problem. As the political analysts might say of a candidate, it's the character question.'

It was a fair question. Dave hoped that he would never have to kill anyone and felt more or less certain that he could pull off the job with the minimum of violence. But that was hardly what a character like Tony Nudelli wanted to hear. He wanted to see a convincing show of cold-bloodedness and all Dave could think of was Harry Lime. What would Harry have told this guy?

'Am I ready to take the life of another human being if I have to? I think that's a fair question,' he said with what he hoped was an amused insouciance, like Harry's. Dave stood up and walked round to the shutters and, staring out of the louvers, played a scene. He hoped that Tony and Al were not keen movie fans.

'What can I say? Except that nobody thinks in terms of human beings these days, Tony. Governments don't, so why should we? They talk of the people and the proletariat and I talk of the mugs. It's the same thing. They have their five year plans and so have I.' He turned to face them again and smiled laconically. 'The dead are happier dead. They don't miss much here, poor bastards.'

He thought he'd played it nicely. Light, amusing, ruthless, with a superficial excuse for his own behavior. If he'd started talking about how tough he was and how much of a killer he could be Nudelli just wouldn't have bought it. He was too old a hand at killing to buy anything too definite. Of course Dave was no Orson Welles. But then Tony Nudelli wasn't exactly Joseph Cotten either. Tony was right about one thing though. Dave would have done the speech better if he'd been wearing a hat. To get properly into character. A black homburg, just like Harry's.

'I'd like to cut you in, you know,' he said, for added effect. 'I've no one left in Miami I can really trust.'

CHAPTER EIGHT

It was the Florida Department of Law Enforcement – the detective branch of the State Police – that had put Kate on the trail of the boat Rocky Envigado was probably planning to use for his next transatlantic shipment of cocaine. From its offices in Pompano Beach, the FDLE had been keeping two characters, Juan Grijalva and Whittaker McLennan, under surveillance on suspicion of involvement in an insurance fraud. They tracked one of these men to a meeting with an Irishman, Gerard Robinson, who was staying at the Breakers Hotel in Fort Lauderdale. Checking through a list of Robinson's telephone calls, the FDLE found an Isle of Man number. Since the Isle of Man is a British tax haven, the FDLE thought they were onto something and so they contacted the National Criminal Intelligence Service in London for assistance. NCIS told them that the number belonged to Keran Properties, a company in which New Scotland Yard had a long-standing interest. Keran was managed by a local firm of accountants, Pater, Hall, Green, who were themselves under surveillance following a tip-off that a notorious cannabis smuggler, now doing time in a Spanish jail, was a director of Keran. NCIS also informed the FDLE that Jeremy Pater, one of the partners in PHG, owned a house in the British Virgin Islands, as well as a share in a flourishing yacht management company, Azimuth Marine Associates. The managing director of Azimuth was Alonzo Avila. A photograph of Pater, Avila, and a third unidentified man was e-mailed to the FDLE, who contacted the FBI computer records department in Miami in an attempt to put a name to the face.

Pater, Avila, and Azimuth Marine were not known to the computer records department. But the third man was. He was Chico Diaz, Rocky Envigado's most trusted *sicario* leader. As soon as Kate was up to speed with the FDLE's inquiry, she went to speak to Kent Bowen.

'Jesus Christ, Kate, you wanna run all that by me again?' yawned the ASAC.

'It is a little complicated, sir,' admitted Kate.

'Complicated? It sounds like an episode of *Soap*. Jesus Christ, Kate.'

'Well sir, Azimuth Marine is one of the leading companies in the management and marketing of luxury yachts. Management, charter marketing, crew placement, you name it, they have representation in virtually every international yachting port of call from Fort Lauderdale to Hong Kong.'

Bowen adopted a pained expression. 'Kate? Just the bottom line, if you don't mind. I've got arteries hardening here.'

Kate felt herself coloring with irritation. Never before had she worked for an ASAC with a manner as casual as Kent Bowen. 'Just the bottom line' was not the way the Bureau worked. At the FBI Academy in Quantico, the emphasis had been on building up a complete investigative picture. An investigation was not a sheet of accounts to be summarized in a simple statement of profit or loss. And now this patronizing asshole . . .

'We think we've found the boat, sir.'

'You have? Well why didn't you say so in the first place, Kate?'

'Because I assumed you'd want to know exactly what makes me believe that we've found it, sir. The intellectual and reasoning processes — '

'This is the FBI, Kate. Not MIT. Reasonable's the standard we work to here. Reasonable doubt, reasonable suspicion, reasonable this n'that. Exactly and precisely are for some schmuck in a white coat with a slide rule sticking out of his ass. In the time it takes to climb from reasonable all the way up to exactly we could lose a collar.'

'Yes sir.'

'So you reckon that this Azimuth Marine outfit have supplied Rocky Envigado with a motor yacht, is that it?'

'Yes sir.'

'Well how do you work that out?'

Biting her lip, Kate said, 'There's an offshore company called San Ferman that's registered in Grand Cayman that we've long suspected is being controlled by Rocky. About three months ago, Azimuth sold a boat to this company. We were able to trace the boat, the *Britannia*, to a dry dock right here in Miami, sir. It's on the river at Thirteenth Street. The boat is currently under surveillance. We have a stakeout at a room in the Harbor View Hospital from which we have an excellent view of the — '

'The harbor, right.'

'And the dry dock. But as yet we've been unable to ascertain if the drugs are already on board.'

Bowen nodded thoughtfully and asked, 'Kind of work they havin' done to the boat anyway?'

'Well, sir, since she's been in dock she's had new fuel tanks, an extended cockpit, re-routed plumbing, new air-conditioning, Naiad stabilizers, and quite a lot of hull work.' She smiled thinly and added, 'It would be reasonable to suppose that the modified fuel tanks might be where they plan to hide the cocaine.'

'The tanks, huh?'

'Well, yes. Except for one thing. You see, sir, I've done some calculations based on the size of the boat and the engines. The *Britannia* is 110 feet long and is equipped with twin Detroit engines each developing just over 2,000 horsepower. That would give the boat an effective cruising range of just about 2,500 miles. Which wouldn't quite get her as far as the coast of North Africa, or even the Canary

Islands, which are about 3,500 miles from the coast of Florida.'

'But with the modified fuel tanks — '

'You could stretch her cruising range to about that distance. Maybe even 4,000 miles. But that would leave you with another dilemma. Where to put the coke. Assuming that the purpose of extending her fuel tanks is to — '

'Yes,' snapped Bowen. 'I take your point. She can't make the distance and carry the dope in her tanks.' Bowen picked up a paperweight from his desk top and began to toss it in his hands like a baseball. 'You know, I've been giving this matter some considerable thought, Kate, and I've come up with an idea of my own.'

'You have?' Kate sounded a little more surprised than she could have wished.

'Yeah. Wanna hear it?'

Kate shrugged. She hadn't explained the rest of her theory to do with the *Britannia*'s fuel tanks. But at the same time she was aware of how little Kent Bowen knew about boats and reflected that she really couldn't afford to antagonize him. She said, 'Sure. Go ahead.'

'Well, I was thinking.'

Good start.

'We know they can compress cocaine, color it, mix it with cellulose, even combine it with glass fiber to create a hard material that can be molded into any shape you like.'

'Ye-e-es.'

'Well, d'you remember a few years ago? The dog kennels?'

Kate nodded patiently. Bowen was referring to a narcotics seizure made by federal agents back in 1992. A Colombian drug cartel had manufactured fifty dog kennels made from cocaine. Ground down and treated with chemicals, the dog kennels had had a street value of almost half a million dollars.

'Suppose Rocky Envigado brain-celled a way to do the

81

same with a boat hull. Polyurethane? Glass fiber?' Bowen shrugged as he waited for Kate to step in with an exclamation at her ASAC boss's genius. Instead she looked puzzled, as if she hadn't quite grasped the ingenuity of what he was suggesting. 'Well, you said yourself they were working on the hull in this dry dock of yours down on Thirteenth.'

Kate said, 'You know something? I would never have thought of that. Not ever. That is an incredible idea.'

Impervious to Kate's sarcasm, Bowen said, 'It is kind of sneaky, isn't it? I mean think about that.' He uttered a little chuckle of appreciation. 'Goddamn it Kate, when you think about it some more, it really begins to make sense.'

'It does?'

'For instance. Most yachts are white, aren't they? It's the perfect disguise for a ton or so of cocaine. Jesus Christ, a motor yacht made of pure cocaine. Now that's what I call a goddamn sports boat.'

Kate smiled thinly and wondered how many more weak jokes he might yet wring out of his hare-brained theory.

'Now if that isn't the last word in custom-built motor yachts.'

She let him ramble on for a minute or two before deciding to bring him down to reality again.

She said, 'Yes, it's certainly an interesting possibility. Albeit a remote one. However. Suppose there was a way to make the transatlantic shipment without using any fuel at all. Of course you'd need enough diesel to cover the secret compartments for the cocaine. But taking into account the dimensions of the yacht and the position of the engine room, which is aft — '

'Aft? Where's aft?'

'Nautical term. It means in or near the stern of the boat.' She paused for a second and then added, 'The back of the boat.'

'Oh aft, yeah, I know.'

'Taking that and the construction of the interior bulkheads into account – it's just light aluminium plate coupled with honeycomb composites – well, I estimate you could store up to 1,000 keys of coke and still have as much diesel as the boat was originally designed to hold.'

Bowen grinned uncomfortably, certain now that he was out of his depth. He replaced the paperweight on his desk and said, 'So what are you saying?'

'Just this. Maybe this time, instead of trying to sail the boat across on its own, via Bermuda and the Azores, they're planning to book the yacht on a transatlantic yacht transport. They are kind of oceangoing ferry boats. For expensive plastic. If you want to get your twenty-four-inch beam Broward over to the South of France for the Cannes Film Festival for instance, you'd probably have it ferried across the Atlantic. It would be perfect cover for someone like Rocky Envigado. His boat rubbing fenders with what passes for high society here in Florida.'

Bowen said, 'I had no idea — '

That much was true at any rate.

'That you were so knowledgeable about boats, Kate.'

'Before Howard, my husband – before he and I separated, we used to spend a lot of time together on his sport-fisher.'

Kate smiled as she recalled the fishing they had done together – marlin, tuna, even the odd shark – and the 78-foot Knight & Carver boat they had owned. Correction, he had owned. The *Dice Man*. With bait well, fish-freezer and professional tackle center, not to mention three large staterooms finished in rare Hawaiian koa wood, the *Dice Man* had been a really luxurious but true tournament fishing platform. She missed the boat more than she had realized. Certainly she missed it more than she missed Howard.

She said, 'That's where he's been living since we split. On the boat.'

'Well I'm from Kansas,' said Bowen. 'Reckon that's as far away from one or t'other ocean as it is possible to be.'

She said, 'I've never been in Kansas.'

'It's kind of a square-looking state when you see it on the map. A lot like a picture frame. You'd be hard pressed to recognize its outline if it came up as a question on *Let's Make a Deal*. Now Florida – you're from Florida, right?'

'Titusville.'

'Florida is the most recognizable state outline in the whole Union.'

'Yes it is,' said Kate. At least they could agree on something.

'You know what I'm reminded of when I look at that outline, Kate?'

Kate shook her head.

'A handgun. Short barrel, large grip. Kind of like that Ladysmith you carry. Every time I see that state outline on a road sign I'm reminded of why I'm here.'

'And why is that, sir?'

'To combat crime. This is the crime capital of the United States. Didn't you know that?'

But Bowen wasn't waiting for an answer.

'Mostly on account of all the scum who've come to settle here from places like Cuba, Haiti and the Dominican Republic.'

'I think that's all a little — '

He said, 'Titusville. That's up the coast, isn't it?'

'Yes.'

'Were you always into boats?'

'Ever since *Gemini 8*.'

'*Gemini 8*? What's that got to do with anything?'

'When I was a kid we used to go out on the ocean aboard my daddy's boat and watch the launches from the Kennedy Space Center. It was best view around for miles. Yes, I've been around boats nearly all my life.'

Bowen said, 'Well, you know boats. But I know law enforcement. You probably heard I was deputy sheriff of Dodge City before I joined the Bureau.'

Kate nodded wearily.

'Of course this was quite a few years ago. And Dodge was cleaned up before I ever got there.' He uttered the familiar little chuckle that Kate had learned to detest. 'Old Wyatt Earp saw to that. One of the reasons I joined the Bureau in the first place was to escape from there. But not before I learned the job the hard way. On the street. Only place you get to develop a nose for it. And right now my nose is telling me that we ought to at least check out this theory of mine. About the boat hull bein' made of cocaine n'all. You say you know boats?'

'Yes sir.'

'Then I want you to speak to some boat-builders and see if it can be done. I hear what you say about fuel tanks, Kate. But I think you're down a gator hole. Those boys have got a lot more ingenuity than you give 'em credit for, Kate. Never underestimate your opponent.'

Kate smiled back at him as he tapped his temple with a forefinger. Underestimating her boss was beginning to look almost impossible.

He said, 'Think big. That's what they do. That's what I do. These bastards don't conform to the common order. Neither do we, Kate. Neither do we. And when you've seen if it can be done – and frankly I'd be very surprised if it couldn't – well then maybe you can organize some kind of covert team to go into that dry dock and take a closer look at that hull. I'm willing to bet you'll find some kind of an anomaly.'

'Anomaly, yeah.' Kate restrained herself on the edge of a remark she knew she would later regret. She wanted to tell him, yeah, there's been some kind of an anomaly, all right. I normally get an ASAC for a boss with a brain in his fucking head.

Driving home that night, through the banyan-lined streets of North Miami, she was tuned to Magic 102.7, an oldies station, and there was an early Rolling Stones song she had always loved. And although she had heard the song a thousand times before and knew the words by heart she still found herself thinking of Kent Bowen and how she was going to prove him wrong as she sang along.

Time was on her side.

CHAPTER NINE

In Dave's suite, the telephone rang. It was Jimmy Figaro.

'Got a passport?'

'You've got it,' said Dave.

'I have?'

'I had to surrender it before the trial. Remember?'

'If you say so. Still valid you think?'

'Should be, yes.'

'OK, let me get Carol to find it and then I'll come back to you.'

'You know, I'm glad you reminded me. I was going to have to call you about it anyway. Does this mean the job is on?'

'I don't know anything about a job.'

'Oh yeah, I remember. You're on a need to know basis.'

'All I know is what Al Cornaro told me.'

'And that is?'

'That you and he are flying down to Costa Rica.'

'Costa Rica? What's in Costa Rica?'

'Some pretty good coffee, last time they looked. Maybe you could bring me back some beans.'

'What am I, Jimmy? Starbucks or something?'

'That and a boat. Al said to say that he's found you a boat.'

'Great. He say what kind of boat?'

'The love boat. How the hell should I know? I'm a lawyer not Herman Melville.'

'Yeah, well, call me back, Ishmael. About that passport, OK?'

*   *   *

San José, the capital of Costa Rica, was a thousand miles south of Miami and a two and a half hour flight aboard an American Airlines jet that was full of tourists in search of difficult surf and easy sex.

Dave returned to his first-class seat from the toilet and said, 'This flight. It's like *Big Wednesday* back there.'

'Big what?'

'Surfing movie. John Milius. All about the perfect wave.'

Al grunted and settled back with his third vodka martini. He said, 'You know what that means to me? The perfect wave? It's Madonna saying goodbye as she takes the kids on a six-week vacation with her mother.'

'Madonna's your wife, right?'

'Right.'

'Do you mind me asking you a personal question?'

'Not if you don't mind a slap in the mouth if I think you're out of line.'

'Why do you stay married to her? I mean, you make jokes about her all the time.'

Al said, 'It's a husband thing. You wouldn't understand. We get along pretty good, she and I. She asks no questions, which means I tell her no lies. Like going down to Costa Rica. What I do when I'm down there? Maybe find a couple of nice little *ticas* and get myself laid? She won't ever ask. Won't even sniff my fingers when I get home. There's an understanding there. A *modus vivendi*, know what I'm sayin'? Sides, even if I wanted to get rid of her, I wouldn't. I'm a Catholic. Marriage is for keeps. Like herpes.' Al laughed obscenely and finished his drink.

Dave said, 'Nice to know that true romance is not dead.'

'*True Romance*. Now that's what I call a fucking movie.' Al waved his empty glass at the stewardess and laughed some more. 'That's what a lot of the beach bums back there are really after. True romance. Surprising as it might seem. Local classifieds in CR are full of ads from soft-headed Americans looking for a cute little *tica* to settle down with.'

'Then you've been before?'

'CR? Yeah. Lots of times.'

'And what are you looking for, Al?'

'Me, I'll settle for getting my cock sucked.'

Dave looked out of the window.

'Sa matter?' Al demanded. 'Somethin' wrong with that?'

'No, nothing at all.'

'Y'know prostitution's legal in CR. Country's a regular pussy K-Mart.'

Dave took the *New Yorker* he had bought at the airport out of the seat pocket and started to turn the pages.

Al frowned and said, 'Y'know, most guys out of Homestead be quite interested in gettin' theirselves laid. You turn fag or somethin' while your ass was in there?'

Dave said, 'No. I did not turn fag while I was in there. But people who've got something against fags are generally trying to cover up their own fears that they might be gay themselves. Well how about it, Al?'

Al shrugged and said, 'You're right. I am gay.' Another obscene laugh. 'I'm a lesbian trapped inside a man's body. Means I'm interested in seeing two girls partying with each other before they party with me. I think that about covers my sexuality.'

Dave laughed and said, 'Me, I'm more like one of those soft-headed guys you were talking about. In the local classifieds. The ones looking for true romance? I guess that covers it for me.'

'Your fuckin' loss.'

Al opened the copy of *Penthouse* he had bought at the airport and began to pick his nose. Absently he inspected his forefinger and frowned as he caught sight of the blood on it. The next second there was more blood dripping in large bullet-hole-sized gouts onto the magazine and his cream polo shirt and pants.

'Fuckin' nosebleed,' groaned Al.

He made a futile attempt to stanch the flow using first his

own paper napkin coaster and then Dave's, stuffing one up each nostril, but it was not until the stewardess, arriving with another drink and a napkin, had tipped Al's seat back in the reclining position that the bleeding finally stopped.

Dave looked at the man stretched out beside him and sighed wistfully.

'Shit,' he said. 'My first time out of the States and I've got to travel with Jake La Motta.'

It was in the taxi, on the way into town from Juan Santamaria Airport, that Dave began to experience his first misgivings about the trip.

'Shit,' he complained. 'Something bit me on the leg.'

'Probably just a mosquito,' said Al.

'A mosquito?'

The idea of taking any medication for the trip hadn't occurred to him until now, and Al certainly hadn't suggested anything. But Dave turned to the *Fodor's Guide to Costa Rica* he had bought at Miami Airport, just to make sure. The health precautions there did nothing to reassure him.

'You dumb bastard,' he said, snapping the book shut.

'What's the problem?'

'Malaria,' he complained angrily to Al. 'This fucking place is full of it. Not to mention a whole load of other diseases.'

'So?' Al slapped a mosquito flat against his own blood-stained cheek.

'So I haven't had any shots, Al. And I don't want to get anemia, kidney failure, coma, and death.'

'Listen, who needs shots? Most of those drugs don't work anyway. I read about it in the paper. They just have what they call a placebo effect. That means that for all the good they do you might as well swallow green M&Ms. They just make you feel better in your mind about bein' around diseased spics and bugs and tropical shit. Whereas, on the other hand, the drugs that do work, do it at the expense of your system. Just look at what happened to those army motherfuckers after Desert

Storm. They took all kinds of drugs and now a lot of them have got some serious fucking medical problems. So try and be cool. 'Sides, we ain't gonna be down here long enough to make any of that south of the border medication worthwhile.'

'Fuck that. As soon as I get to the hotel I'm going to find a drugstore. Jesus Christ, I can't believe you're so blasé about this shit. I mean just one bite from an anopheles'll do it man.'

'There ain't no fleas in the hotel we're checking into. You can take it from me. Place is class.'

'Not fleas. Anopheles. It's a mosquito, Al. According to the book the whole country's lousy with them.'

'You read too many books.' Al delved into his flight bag. 'Relax, will ya? Naturally I brought something to keep the bugs off, just to be on the safe side.' He handed Dave a sweet-smelling tube of cream. 'There you go. Slap some of that on your chicken-shit ass.'

Dave read the label with incredulity.

'Avon Skin-so-Soft Moisturiser? This is it?'

'That'll do the job. I bring some every time I come down here, and I've never been bitten yet.'

'Al, I want to repel insects, not give them a nice smooth landing on my so fucking soft skin.'

'And you better believe that stuff'll do it. Bugs can't stand the stuff.'

'What is it they don't like? The advertising? The brand image?'

'Don't ask me why, but it works, right? Marines comin' down to these parts for jungle warfare training have been using the stuff for years. Better than DEET or any of those other insect repellents, they reckon. And I didn't read that in any fuckin' book.'

L'Ambiance was American-owned and comfortable. Formerly a colonial mansion, it was located in the Barrio Otaya district of San José. Dave's room, furnished with antiques, was much bigger and better than he had anticipated. His only criticism was that when he opened the french windows onto his balcony, he could hear and smell the animals in the Simon Bolivar Zoo a block to the north. To that extent it was like a home away from Homestead.

As soon as he was unpacked Dave went out and bought some mefloquine in a local pharmacy. It made him feel a little more relaxed. And later on, after a good dinner and an excellent bottle of wine, he felt sufficiently well disposed toward both the country and his travelling companion to accompany him to what Al insisted was the best bar in San José.

Key Largo, with its Western-style saloon, big oval bar and live music, was housed in yet another handsome colonial mansion. The place was full of gregarious gringos and a seemingly endless supply of dollar-hungry *ticas*, many of whom were in their teens. Al found a table, ordered a couple of bottles of *guaro* and left Dave to soak up the atmosphere while he went in search of some female company. He returned a couple of minutes later with not one but four of the best-looking hookers Dave had ever seen. One of them, a blonde with a tight pink cotton sweater and very large breasts, sat down next to Dave and, smiling sweetly, told him her name was Victoria. He felt his eyes climbing up to the half-timbered ceiling as a languorous-looking brunette took hold of his other arm and asked him for a cigarette. When Dave's eyes came down from the ceiling again they were met by Al's, already filled with delight.

'Whad I tell ya? Isn't this place somethin'? Every time I come here it's like I died and went to pussy heaven.'

Finding the brunette a Marlboro, Dave glanced sideways at the pink sweater and then back at Al. Grinning he said, 'Pink. I always did like pink.'

He lit the girl, whose name was Maria, and then smoked one himself. The other three girls were already helping themselves to glasses of *guaro*. Despite Dave's best intentions, he was beginning to enjoy himself.

Al toasted Dave with the local firewater and said, 'They all speak pretty good American, so I hope you can decipher what I'm sayin' to you now. They're fit for human consumption, if you know what I mean. Forget about the Andromeda Strain, OK? What they do is legal down here so they have to get themselves periodically checked out by the local Surgeon-General. Anyway, s'all fixed. Stock is bought and paid for, whether you take up your share option or not, my friend. That's for their benefit as much as yours. After all, they have to make a living. So it's your choice, sport. They don't mind one way or the other.' Al downed the glass of *guaro* in one as he saw Dave's grin persist. He added, 'You can read 'em a poem or you can show 'em your cock, it's up to you. Just be friendly, that's all.'

Dave toasted Al and then the two girls sandwiching him. 'Me? I'm Jay Leno, man. I'll sit and be friendly to any of the guests who come on tonight's show.'

Al chuckled obscenely and said, 'If I don't come on tonight's show, it won't be for want of the right encouragement.'

It was well after one when Al announced that he was taking his two *tican* friends back to the hotel before he was too drunk to party. Dave had enjoyed the company of Victoria and Maria. The evening had been relaxed and light-hearted and he had no desire to offend Al by an obvious display of priggishness. But in life you were either a john or you were not and a long time ago Dave had decided he was not. So he decided to go with the flow and cut the two girls loose as soon as Al had retired to the hotel's presidential suite with his two friends.

Which is what he did.

There were no recriminations, no petulant displays of rejection. The girls accepted it with as much pleasant good grace as they had accepted Al's original invitations. After they'd left in a cab, Dave took a long cold shower and tried to persuade himself that he had done the right thing. Five years of Homestead seemed like degradation enough for one lifetime. Now he wanted to feel good about himself, like he was in control of where he was going and what he was doing. And to do that you had to be strong. To command power over yourself and your desires. Being a john was way short of that.

He threw on a bathrobe and went out onto the balcony. Above the buzz of distant traffic he could hear the roar of a large cat, a lion or a tiger caged in the nearby zoo. He imagined the poor beast as it paced up and down its small cage, and for a moment he was reminded of being back in his cell in Homestead. Hearing the dreadful sound of that immobilized spirit as it gave itself up to its despairing ritual dance, to and fro, to and fro, forever pacing the cell, he realized that for the first time since being released he understood what it meant to be free.

'Have a good time last night?'

It was a cruel question because Al looked like yesterday's shit. His normally dark, swarthy face was pale and sweaty and his eyes were as mean and puffy as a couple of hot snakes. If his head had been left on a pole somewhere in the jungle, he could not have looked any worse.

'Jesus, Al, you look like a fuckin' movie star,' mocked Dave, echoing Tony Nudelli. 'You look like Ernest Borgnine on his free day.'

Al whispered hoarsely, 'Where the fuck's Chico with the four-wheel-drive?'

Ahead of them was a three-hour drive to Quepos on the Central Pacific coast. Parked out front, next to the hotel's Spanish-style courtyard, their driver was waiting in a Range Rover. Al climbed slowly into the back seat, let out a profound sigh that was half a groan, and closed his bloodshot eyes.

Half an hour into the journey and Dave, sitting up front alongside Chico, wished that he had sat in the back with Al. Almost gleefully Chico informed him that Costa Rica had the world's highest auto fatality rate.

'But hey, don't worry,' he added. 'Range Rover is very good car for Costa Rican roads. Is English car, but very tough. I think maybe roads in England are as bad as here. English drivers too. But is no problem in Range Rover. This is car that say get the fuck out of my way, *hombre*.'

Highway Three from the central highlands of San José down to the coast, was a two-lane blacktop with steep drops and sharp bends. It was in reasonable condition only as far as Carara. From there on Chico halved his speed to take account of the many potholes, some of which would have broken the axle of a lesser vehicle. One volcano-sized crater bounced everyone off the roof, awakening Al from his crapulous sleep-off.

After a moment or two, he said weakly, 'Gotta get out.'

Chico glanced back across his shoulder, saw the color of his passenger's face, and steered hard to the right off the road, pulling up close to a steaming stew of swampland.

Al opened the door and forgetting the height of the car, half stepped, half fell onto the ground.

Chico watched as he staggered toward the edge of the swamp and then, laughing, lowered the window to call out after him, 'Watch out for crocodiles and boas.' He looked at Dave and let his eyes roll for a moment. 'Aiee. The boas, they are worse than the crocs. Very aggressive.'

'But they're not poisonous.'

'Maybe so, Señor Dave, but they still have teeth. Such teeth they have. You give me a choice between being bitten by a boa and a viper, every time I will choose the viper.'

Lurching to a halt, Al leaned forward, his hands on his knees, and began to throw up. Dave got out of the car to take a leak, and then meandered over to Al's one-man huddle.

'You all right?'

Al was still retching and Dave felt his nostrils prickle with disgust as a strong smell of nail polish wafted his way. It was the stink of *guaro*. The stuff was coming back up from Al's gut as neat as if he was pouring it straight from the bottle.

'All right?' Al groaned a bitter laugh. 'I'm about thirty fucking clicks west of there,' he said breathlessly and then retched some more.

Dave said, 'Someone ought to record that sound. A sound effects guy for a movie. Last night, on the hotel room cable channel, there was this movie with Mel Gibson? At the end they tear his guts out and burn them in front of his face. They could sure have used you in the recording studio, Al. That is one medieval sound. Could be the start of a whole new career for you.'

'Thing about throwing up . . . is not to give up on it . . . before you're done . . . otherwise it don't achieve what it's supposed to . . .' Even more retching. 'Matter of fuckin' stamina.' He belched, retched again and then spat several times. 'Don't quit on it . . . before you're through . . . less you have to . . .' A last heaving, coronary of a gag. '. . . Or you just have to repeat the process . . .'

Panting, as if he'd sprinted the hundred, Al straightened up, took a deep unsteady breath, and grinned horribly.

Dave swallowed uncertainly and said, 'Jesus Christ, Al, you should puke for America.'

Dave knew very little about the boat they had come down to fetch back to Miami. And every time he asked, Al told him to wait and see. But nearing Quepos, on a road so thick with dust Chico had the headlamps on, Dave said, 'This is a long way to come for a fucking boat.'

'Ain't you heard? Broke don't get to pick.'

'Yeah, but look at this place.'

They were driving past a warren of houses built on stilts and connected with a virtual freeway system of planks and corrugated iron sheets.

'Kind of a boat are we going to find down here anyway? Fucking banana boat. Sampan maybe. Jesus.'

The dirt road led past the fishing village and through extensive mangrove swamp.

'Fucking airboat is what you need down here,' complained Dave and irritably slapped something crawling on his neck.

'Told you to use that Avon shit. Me, I ain't been bitten once.'

'The bug that bit you would probably die of alcohol poisoning.'

Al shrugged and said, 'Feelin' better, as a matter of fact. A nice cold beer would slip down a treat.'

Dave caught a glimpse of a crocodile as, disturbed by the Range Rover, it slipped into some brackish water.

'The horror,' he muttered darkly. 'The horror.'

'The fuck you talkin' about? Relax will ya? We're nearly there.'

The road led south along a beach-front drag.

'Is Quepos,' grinned Chico. 'The town. It is nothing to write home about, no?' He turned into a large harbor north of a bridge. 'But here is better. Here has been a lot of development. Lots of gringo tourist fishermen. December through August. Snapper, amberjack.'

Suddenly Dave saw why they had come, for the bay was bristling with the marlin towers and flybridges of dozens of long-range luxury sport-fishing boats, some of them worth a million dollars or more.

He said, 'All right. That's more like it.'

'Wahoo, tuna. But mainly they come for the marlin and the sailfish.'

'Whad I tell ya?' said Al.

'Is more protected from winds down here than Guanacaste Coast, I think. But don't even think of swimming. Is contaminated. Not to mention currents and the fucking sharks.'

Al laughed and said, 'Swimming? Fuck that.'

'So why you come to Quepos?'

Dave said, 'To pick up a boat.'

'For the fishing,' Al added quickly.

Dave looked at Al and frowned. Al shook his head as if he didn't want Dave to contradict him.

'Most gringos, they come here, and bring plenty of rods and equipment. But you guys — '

'Ours got stolen at the airport,' explained Al.

'Is no problem. I can recommend somewhere. They will supply all equipment if you want. Good price too.'

'Thanks, but no. We made a booking with an outfit back in San José. Charter company called Vera Cruz. Somewhere north of the bridge is all I know.'

Chico asked the way at a gift shop and they were directed to a small *ranchita* on stilts over the water in front of the bridge leading into Quepos town. While Al paid off Chico, Dave strolled up the marina, relieved to be out of the car and getting some fresh air. Backed up against a thickly forested hill, with a muddy beach in front, Quepos looked a strange place to find a bay full of luxury yachts. A couple of kids were doing wheelies on ancient mountain bikes up and down the harbor in front of a row of shops and restaurants. When Al glanced in the door of the Vera Cruz office one of the bicycling kids came and told Dave that the Vera Cruz gringo had gone somewhere for lunch. Dave gave the kid a five-colon note and then went to tell Al.

Al nodded at the restaurant and said, 'OK, let's eat. My stomach feels like a basketball net. 'Sides, there are one or two facts of fuckin' life that I want to get straight between us. Like some do's and fuckin' don'ts till I say when, motherfucker. Savvy?'

'Since you put the invitation so graciously, I don't see how I can very well refuse you, Al.'

'You just stick with that attitude and you and I are going to get along just fine.'

They went inside the restaurant and straightaway ordered a couple of *cervezas* apiece, while they looked at the menu. After a few minutes Dave decided on the rice and the beans, while Al elected to have turtle, laughing unpleasantly as he made his selection.

He said, 'Jesus, I wish my kid Petey was here to see me eat

this. Those fuckin' Ninja turtles he's always playing with, they drive me nuts. I hate the little green bastards. I hate the song, I hate the show, and I hate the characters. Leonardo. Donatello. What kind of a world are we buildin' for 'em, I ask ya? When a kid grows up and thinks that Michelangelo is a fuckin' turtle instead of a famous historical painter.'

'I had no idea you were so interested in art,' said Dave.

'All Italians are interested in great painters. It's part of our heritage. Soon as I get home I'm gonna tell him, I ate a fuckin' turtle.'

'But won't that upset him?'

'Damn right it'll upset him. Listen, you ain't a parent, you wouldn't understand. Thanks to Hollywood, there's hardly an animal that hasn't been turned into some cute little cartoon character. Whales, deer, rabbits, baby elephants, crabs, n' turtles.'

'A turtle isn't an animal. It's a reptile.'

'Whatever. Daddy, you can't eat Bambi. Hey son, just watch me.'

'But what's the point of that?'

'It's a tool for learning, that's what's the point. When you eat the animal you teach the kid about the real world. Half the problems kids have today are to do with their fuckin' fantasy worlds. Bite on reality, that's what I say. Food for thought. Helps 'em grow up. When I was a kid I saw my father kill chickens and turkeys all the time. My kids have never seen any kind of food killed. Not even a fish. Somethin' wrong there. I may not be able to kill the animal like my old man. But I can sure make a point of eating it when the opportunity arises.'

'You're a regular Doctor Spock, y'know that?'

'All these animal welfare whackos. Most of them have been reared on bullshit about little animals with cute personalities. Two things I want for my sons. I want them to know who the real Michelangelo was. And I don't want them growing up vegetarian. Vegetarian is for faggots.'

Dave said, 'Michelangelo was a faggot.'

'Says who?'

'Everyone. Look at the *David*.'

'Bullshit. OK, if Michelangelo was a fag, would the Pope have had him redecorate the ceiling of the Sistine Chapel? I don't think so.'

Dave could see that Al wasn't about to be persuaded, so he just grinned and said, 'Lesbian trapped inside a woman's body, huh? Now that I can understand.'

Pleased to change the subject himself, Al laughed and said, 'Yeah. You should have seen the two of them party. They licked each other from end to end. I love to see that. That is such a beautiful sight. Man I bet Michelangelo would have painted that if he could have gotten away with it. What about you? Kind of a time did you have yourself?'

'Good,' said Dave. 'They were good.'

Al waited for details, but when none came he frowned and said, 'OK, here's the deal, wiseguy. We're down here on a repo. Fucker who owns the boat I've chartered? Guy by the name of Lou Malta. Malta owes Tony a shitload of money. What with the vig n'all it totals over a million bucks. Six months ago Malta was in Fort Lauderdale, paying his bills and everything was cool is the rule. Then next thing? He floats his ass down here without so much as a fuckin' postcard to Tony. Like he disappeared without a trace. But how's this for a co-fucking-incidence? Day after you pitch your outline to Naked Tony? The private dick he hired to find Malta's dumb ass e-mails Tony with the full longitude and latitude of his exact whereabouts. Like it was ordained that you should have this boat for your caper. Now Malta doesn't know me from John Doe but it would be best if we didn't tell him we just flew in from Miami and other eyebrow-raising shit like that. You keep your mouth shut and help me out here and the boat's yours for the long hot summer ahead.'

'Malta. You going to kill him, Al?'

'Not unless he makes it necessary.'

'Only I won't help you kill him.'

'Believe me, blood is not on today's menu.'

'Not even as a tool for learning?'

Al shrugged. 'Like I say, not unless he obliges me to do it.'

'What if I don't help you out?'

'Then I got a boat with no one to sail it back home. And you got no boat to pull your caper. Not to mention no ticket home.'

Dave nursed the cold *cerveza* in his hand for a moment wondering if he really had a choice.

'What kind of boat is it?'

Al took out his wallet, unfolded a black and white photocopy, and handed it over. 'A real beauty. Eighty feet, twenty beam, six draft. Powered by two 1,500-horsepower engines, she's got a top speed of about thirty-five knots.'

Dave noted the name painted on the stern in the picture. 'The *Juarista*,' he said. 'Vera Cruz. It figures.'

'That's all I know. That and the color. She's white.'

Dave said, 'White is good.' He chugged some beer down his throat. 'Shows the dirt, but still, it's good camouflage. It'll help us to blend in with all the other boats.' He smiled and folded up the picture. 'Can I keep this?'

'Be my guest.'

'So how d'you wanna play this, Al? You know, Malta might not be willing to give up his boat without a struggle. Then there's the paperwork. We'll need proper paperwork to get this boat onto SYT's next transatlantic voyage.'

'Paperwork was all taken care of when the boat was still parked in Lauderdale. Collateral for Malta's loan from Tony. Tony lent Malta the money when none of the banks would touch him. However I take your point. We're a long way from home and Malta might figure that gives him some liberties. I tell you what we're gonna do. We're gonna get out to sea, just like we was a couple of tourists. We'll get away from shore, somewhere secluded I hope, put down some bait, like we really are going fishing. And then I'm gonna give him the Forbes

101

Fact and Comment on how much his ass will be worth if he thinks he can fuck with Tony's portfolio.'

'Kind of like an investment analyst. I get it.' Dave finished the first beer and started the second. 'OK, I'll help you out with this on one condition.'

'I thought we already had that. No killing.'

'This is as well. I want you to let me do the talking.'

'What the fuck for? You don't think I can handle the dialogue on a simple repo?'

'I think you can handle it just fine. I just worry about all that fact and comment bullshit.' Dave shrugged and lit a cigarette. 'You're much too confrontational.'

'This is a repo we're talking about, not an AA group. Give me one of those cigarettes.' Al lit up angrily.

'Yeah, but you gotta understand human psychology, Al. You lip the guy and he'll react badly, just the same as if you were to put a gun to his head.'

'He's lucky I'm not gonna blow his fucking brains all over the deck.'

'But don't you see? You talk hard to him maybe you provoke him to do something dumb. He does something dumb, it almost guarantees a violent outcome to the situation.'

'What are you, a shrink all of a sudden?'

'I saw it a lot in prison. The way the guys got mad and the way some of the guards could talk them down. We want to do this thing peacefully, which is the way I want it. Then we've got to be subtle.'

'Oh yeah, yeah.' Al was laughing. 'This is the guy who blinded Willy Barizon in one eye with a fucking fountain pen. That was very subtle.'

'Haven't you heard the expression the pen is mightier than the sword? Well Willy wasn't armed with a sword, but with two guns. I'd say I was just about as subtle as I could be.'

'Tell that to Willy, next time he almost sees you.'

'Those are my conditions.'

'OK, OK, you do the talking. What do I know? Maybe you're Warren fucking Christopher or somethin'.'

They ate lunch and then went outside.. On the short walk along to the Vera Cruz offices, Al spotted something he wanted to buy for his son, Petey, in the gift shop. It was a baby hammerhead shark specimen, about a foot long, preserved in a jar of formaldehyde.

Dave watched Al hand over twenty colons for the curio and asked, 'What's that? A tool for learning?'

'He'll love it. Petey loves sharks.'

'Does that mean you're planning to give it to him, or eat it on his birthday?'

Al smiled thinly. 'That smart mouth of yours. It's a wonder you lasted out the five.'

CHAPTER TEN

The *Juarista* was indeed a beauty. Lou Malta explained her construction history inside the enclosed flybridge while they were getting underway.

'Sh-she was built in San Diego,' he explained in his stuttering drawl. 'The way the hull's constructed means she has a low center of gravity and a deep V-entry in the water. Producing a very comfortable ride for you people, whatever the sea's like. I never knew anyone to get sick on this boat. Not even from Pepe's cooking. Of course we've got the thrusters and stabilizers to simplify handling, but it's the hull that makes the difference. And a reverse sheer below the transom there makes backing down as smooth and d-dry as if you were standing on the sh-shore. Where'd you say you boys were from?'

Dave said, 'LA.'

'LA, huh? Which part?'

'All over.'

'Mmmm. All over. My favorite place.' He giggled. 'Just ask Pepe. Well, you picked a pretty good time of year to come after marlin and sailfish. January's usually our best month.' He gave them a searching north to south look. 'How much sport-fishing experience have you boys had anyway?'

'Enough,' said Al.

Malta shrugged. 'W-well whatever. Pepe and I? We get all levels of experience on this boat. Just a few weeks ago, we were fishing for wahoo with these three types from New York. And I swear I found one of them trying to kill the fish with his cellular telephone.' He giggled again. 'I swear, it was the funniest thing I ever saw. Wasn't it, Pepe?'

Pepe grinned and said, 'Yes, Lou.'

Pepe was a beautiful black boy of about thirteen, wearing a navy blue T-shirt with a white Nike swoosh logo and a pair of baggy Guess jeans. He was down on the cockpit, tying off ropes and smiling broadly at Malta whenever their eyes met. CR had a big gay scene and Al and Dave could see that Pepe was Malta's *cachero*. Malta himself, wearing a pair of sky blue Lycra cycling shorts and a white T-shirt with Garfield the cat on it, was a curious-looking man. Fortyish, Rod Stewart haircut, pink Pilsbury Doughboy face, rimless eyeglasses with blue frames, and a large gold earring with a cartouche to match the one hanging around his pudgy neck, he looked more hairdresser than fishing skipper.

'Pepe will fix you up with some tackle. We've got more or less everything you'll need, although you two are the lightest travellers I've ever seen down here. Talk about the accidental tourist. Don't you think so, Pepe?'

'Yes, Lou.'

'Like I said,' Al growled. 'We got a lot of our gear stolen in San José.'

'CR is a very pretty country,' said Malta. 'But the thing about the country is that it's just so impossibly p-pretty that it seduces you into a false sense of security. There are thieves all over.'

Dave said, 'That's true of everywhere.'

'Well yes. But really.' Malta tutted and sighed loudly and shook his head in apparent despair. 'A man's fishing equipment is something sacrosanct. Isn't it, Pepe?'

'Yes, Lou.'

'You boys were insured though?'

'Yeah, we got insurance,' said Al. 'You got insurance?'

Malta picked up the slight note of threat that was carried in Al's remark.

'Oh you boys'll be safe enough on this boat, won't they Pepe? We've got every creature comfort. TV and VCR in every cabin. Air-conditioning. We've even got a misting system to keep those rippling muscles of yours cool when you're in the fighting chair. It gets pretty hot out there when you've got a big one. I even put a little patchouli oil in the mist reservoir just to make the air smell nice. I don't know about you, but fish isn't my scent of choice. And Pepe's a pretty good little cook, despite what I said. And I don't just mean he knows how to use the microwave. He can cook up pretty much anything you want. Pepe knows what men like to eat. We have plenty of s-supplies. You just tell him if there's anything in particular takes your fancy. Just as long as it's fish.' He giggled again. 'Just joking. We've got lots of steaks in the freezer. And plenty of beer. You boys want a beer?'

'Beer'd be good,' admitted Dave.

'But what am I thinking of? You'll want to see your cabins. Naturally you each have your own head and bath. Go on, take a look around while I get the beers. Only pay particular attention to the salon. I'm kinda prouda that. Designed it myself. It's ornamented with custom-made glass by Lal-Lalique.'

Al and Dave went below. The boat was as luxurious as Lou Malta had promised. And with the headroom reaching seven feet in the salon and in the staterooms, it had an impressive amount of interior volume. Dave didn't much care for the taste – it was too fussy – but it was plain to see that no cost had been spared in fitting her out with every conceivable extra.

Dave said, 'Hey, Al. This boat's worth a lot more than a mill. Say not much change out of three and you'd have been more accurate.'

'So?' Al was more interested in investigating Lou Malta's sleeping arrangements than his own. Inspecting the cedar-lined drawers and closets he sneered and said, 'It's like I thought.'

'What is?'

Al glanced up at the mirrored ceiling and then spat onto the black silk sheets that covered Malta's double bed.

'He's fucking that kid. My Petey's not much younger than that Pepe kid.'

'What of it? Those two girls you were with in Key Largo last night weren't much older than Pepe. They were maybe fifteen or sixteen at most.'

'Bullshit. But even if they were it's different for girls. Number one, girls mature quicker. And number two, that was straight sex.'

'I thought you said you had them going down on each other?'

'That was for my benefit, not theirs. That kind of sex don't count. That was just like a couple of actresses playing a gay part for a movie. With me being the camera. It don't make them queer. But this — ' He bent down to pick up a magazine from the cabin floor and Dave caught a glimpse of older men having sex with younger boys before Al flung it aside in disgust. 'This is something else.' He looked angrily at Dave. 'What?'

Dave shrugged. 'I still think this is a lot of boat to repo for the loan of a million.'

'Yeah, well that's the nature of collateral. Ain't you heard? We're in a recession. Money's tight.' He laughed cruelly. 'And I bet that's a lot more than I can say for that faggot's ass.'

'I'd better go and give him the bad news before we get too far offshore,' said Dave.

'You do that. Sooner those two fags are off this boat, the better I'll feel. There's magazines and videos in that creep's fuckin' drawer that would give Hannibal Lecter a nightmare.'

Lou Malta wrung his hands and wept, 'What am I going to do?'

Dave and Malta were sitting at opposite ends of an L-shaped sofa in the now stationary boat's salon. Malta was on his second pink gin, although it looked large enough to have been a third and a fourth as well.

'Get some things together,' Dave told him. 'And the thousand bucks we paid you up front for the charter? Keep it. We'll turn the boat around and head back towards Quepos.

When we get in sight of the CR coastline, you and Pepe can take the inflatable and row ashore.'

'But this boat. It's my whole life.'

Dave said, 'Not any more. What you've got to hang onto here is the fact that you still have your whole life. You may not have the boat, but you're going to live. If it was up to the gorilla on deck, you'd be lip-gaffed, hoisted for a fuckin' picture and then dropped over the side for the sharks.'

Malta trembled visibly and emptied his glass.

'Jesus Christ, really?'

'Really. He's a violent man. And he works for a violent man. Tony Nudelli? I've seen what he can do to people.'

'I had no idea that, um . . . that Tony was so mad with me.'

'Sure you did, Lou. Sure you did.'

'I guess I did at that,' said Malta. 'It was a stupid thing to do, wasn't it?'

'Yes it was, Lou.'

Malta got up from the sofa a little unsteadily and walked toward the stairs down to the cabins.

'I'll get that bag.'

'Lou? You won't do anything else that's stupid, will you? Like come out of that stateroom with a gun in your hand. That's just what the gorilla wants. An excuse to kill you and Pepe. You understand me?'

'Yes sir.'

'Good boy.'

Dave stood up and followed Malta to the top of the stairs. He had no idea if Al was carrying a gun. Just because he couldn't have brought one aboard the plane didn't mean he wasn't carrying now. San José looked like the kind of place you could buy one easily, no questions asked. And someone like Al wasn't the type to leave anything to chance. No more did he know if Lou Malta had a gun. But if Dave had run out on a man like Nudelli, a man who lent the loan sharks their money, then he'd make sure he always had a gun around.

Probably two or three. So he followed Malta downstairs and looked through the door of his stateroom to make sure. Lou was staring into an empty sports bag, as if wondering what to take.

Dave said, 'C'mon, we haven't got all day.'

'All right, all right, I'm doing my best for you, you inhuman bastard.'

'Doing your best for me?' Dave shook his head and yawned. That was the thanks he got for keeping the guy alive.

Malta started to stuff things into the bag: wallet, passport, jewelry, a bottle of Obsession for Men, Walkman, toilet bag, cellular phone.

'I think you'd better leave the phone,' said Dave.

'Oh yeah. Sh-ure. OK. Well, couldn't I just take the operating chip out of it and leave that behind? It's useless without — '

Growing impatient now, Dave said, 'Lou. Will ya leave the fuckin' phone?'

Malta shrugged and stared at the contents of his bag almost incredulously for a moment, then zippered it up. 'I'm done,' he said tearfully and came through the door.

Dave grunted, needing to take a leak. He said, 'Go up on deck and tell Pepe you're both leaving. I'll be there in a minute.'

Emerging onto the lanai deck a couple of minutes later, Dave blinked furiously in the bright Pacific sunshine and took a deep breath of the fresh sea air. Below there was a decadent smell of Obsession and something else that he didn't much care to try and put a finger on. Al was leaning over the rail looking down onto the cockpit from where the serious fishing was done. Hearing Dave he turned around and Dave saw that for the second time in thirty-six hours the other man's white polo shirt was covered in blood.

Dave shook his head and said, 'What? Another fuckin' nosebleed?'

The very next second he heard a loud splash, like the sound

of someone jumping into the water, and turned toward the bow of the boat. Instinctively, he said, 'Where's Malta?'

'He hit me,' shrugged Al, and threw a jagged piece of broken glass over the side. It was part of the jar containing the baby hammerhead he had bought for Petey. The dead fish now lay on the teak deck at Dave's feet. It was surrounded by a lot of blood spots like so many shiny red coins. Al rubbed the back of his sparsely haired head and looked vaguely sheepish.

Dave was frowning now, suspecting something was wrong. 'Al? Where the fuck is that faggot?'

'Man's got a speech impediment,' said Al and jabbed a thumb at the cockpit behind him. 'He's dead.'

Lou Malta lay in a spreading pool of blood like something they had just hauled up from the depths of the ocean, his legs twitching spasmodically as if with one good jerk he might propel himself back into the life-preserving water. The broken jar had crossed through the midline of Malta's throat with such force that his neck had been severed from shaving line to spine.

'Jesus fucking Christ,' exclaimed Dave. 'What happened?'

'What could I do? He tried to brain me, the lousy faggot.'

A monkey wrench lay on the lanai deck a short distance from the baby hammerhead as if confirming Al's story. Malta's bag stood inside the doorway of the salon, as if he had put it down there before stepping outside with intent. But Dave was suspicious. It was possible that Al had left the wrench there himself before stabbing Malta with the souvenir. And yet that wasn't the most obvious murder weapon Dave had ever heard of. Surely if Al had meant to kill Malta he would have chosen something a little more wieldy. Something he hadn't been planning to present to his son.

Lou Malta stopped twitching before Dave could get to him. It was obvious there was nothing to be done.

Dave said, 'So who jumped off?'

'The kid, I guess. Pepe must have seen me kill his boyfriend and figured he was next.'

'Not an unreasonable conclusion.'

Dave climbed up to the flybridge to get a better view of the water surrounding the *Juarista* and, about fifty yards away, saw a small figure swimming strongly in the direction of the mainland. Sitting down in the cream leather pilot's chair, Dave started the engines and took hold of the helm.

Al yelled up to him, 'What are you doing?'

'Going after Pepe. It's five miles back to shore, against a riptide. He'll never make it.'

Down on the cockpit deck Al said nothing. Instead he started to maneuver Lou Malta's body over the edge of the transom, all the time cursing him for a lousy faggot.

Dave drew the boat close to Pepe, slowed the engines and then threw the boy a lifebelt on the end of a line. But Pepe, terrified of what he had witnessed back on the boat, was too scared to grab it.

'C'mon, Pepe,' Dave called down to him. 'Take the line. Nobody's going to kill you, kid, I promise.'

Treading water for a moment, Pepe shook his head. He said, 'No way, man,' and began to swim away from the boat again.

Dave returned to the pilot's chair, gave the engines a short burst of gas, and then revved back the same way as before. Coming outside again he spoke to Pepe in Spanish, gently telling him that the other guy hadn't meant to kill Lou; that it had been an accident; and that anyway it was Lou who had attacked Al in the first place. Giving Al the benefit of the doubt. Ten minutes passed in this way and still Pepe was too scared to take the line.

'Throw him the inflatable and let's get the fuck out of here,' urged Al.

Dave's eyes caught something else surfacing briefly in the water near Pepe. It looked like a harmless tarpon, he thought. Around eighty to a hundred pounds in size, it was a good one too. Good silver color, big dorsal. By the time he realized what it was there were others, all of them summoned by the blood from Malta's body.

Dave's heart missed a beat and he yelled down to the boy, 'Look out. Pepe, get out of the water. For Christ's sake, grab the fucking line.'

Seemingly unaware of the sharks, Pepe shook his head as if Dave's angry outburst had merely confirmed what he'd suspected all along. By the time he understood what Dave had been yelling about, it was already too late.

As if sensing that Malta would wait, the sharks concentrated their attack on the swimming boy. Dave could only stand and watch, horrified, as the sharks hit Pepe like a gang of playground bullies – first one, then another and then all at once, with an audible snapping of jaws that Dave felt in every nervous fiber of his being. Pepe screamed, slapped the water in front of him and, gulping air and water, disappeared briefly under the foaming confusion of reddening water. It was then Dave saw what species of shark these were. Hammerheads. Bigger deadlier versions of the baby that still lay on the deck. Dave felt himself shiver at the ferocity of their apparent revenge. Pepe reappeared only once, water and blood bursting from his screaming mouth, a hand already missing from his arm. He kept shaking his head as if he couldn't quite believe what was happening to him and Dave was almost relieved when the boy finally disappeared under the surface of the water.

Al yelled, 'Did you see that?' Did you see that?' He laughed as if callously enjoying the horror of what he was witnessing and with no more sympathy for Pepe's savage fate than if the boy had been part of some B-movie's lengthy body count. 'Fuckin' *Jaws*, man. Jesus, I never thought I'd see something like that. That was totally awesome.' He shook his head. 'I knew I was right. I knew it. Don't ever get in the fuckin' water.' And then, like a man who had witnessed the birth of a child instead of the death of one, Al lit a large Macanudo.

Dave watched the frothing boil of shark, water and young blood until he was certain that Pepe wouldn't surface again, and then cut loose the lifebelt, once pure white, now bright red. Slowly he climbed down from the bridge, sickened. Seeing the baby hammerhead, he stamped on its T-bone head and then flung it angrily into the ocean.

Al was still standing on the lower deck occupying the bloody space where Lou Malta's body had been, the cigar chomped between his teeth jutting out over the shark-infested water like a warship's gun barrel. Springing down the steps into the cockpit Dave snatched the big cigar from Al's mouth and flung it into the sea after the baby hammerhead.

'What the fuck — ?'

'You dumb ox,' snarled Dave. 'Don't you know anything? Pushing Malta's body into the water when you did was like sending the sharks an e-mail. Jesus Christ they must have thought it was Thanksgiving.'

Al looked around evasively.

'OK, I'm sorry,' he yelled back at Dave. 'It never occurred to me.'

'And while we're on the subject, did you have to kill Malta? What happened to the deal we made?'

'He came at me with the wrench. I grabbed the jar, smashed it against the side of the boat, and let him have it. I didn't mean to kill him. Just to mark him up a bit.'

'Mark him? You damn near sawed his head off.'

'Yeah, well I ain't sorry I killed him. Goddamn pedophile. My son Petey's not much younger than that kid Pepe.'

'Not any more he isn't. Thanks to you, Pepe is dead. Thanks to you Al, Pepe just got eaten by the fucking sharks. Thanks to you this boat and Lou Malta were probably the best it ever got for Pepe. Think about that when you smoke your next premium cigar.'

With slow defiance Al pulled another Macanudo from the pocket of his bloodstained pants, sucked its length as if it was his own forefinger, and then lit up. He puffed the cigar in Dave's face and said, 'OK, I'm thinking. What the fuck happens now?'

Dave met Al's eye, hating him, finding the hate returned

in spades. He shook his head and turned away, disgusted at Al's display of cold-bloodedness.

He said, 'Let's get out of here. We've got a lot of sailing to do.'

The bridge of the *Juarista* was fully computerized and it took Dave less than an hour to familiarize himself with the electronic chart plotter, the radar system, and the auto pilot. But once he had keyed in their course for Panama and the Canal there was very little else to do except periodically look at the monitor screens. With a fuel tank containing nearly 4,000 gallons, a 600 gallon per day fresh-water maker, and a freezer full of food, they were completely self-sufficient for their voyage back to Miami.

It was a twenty-four-hour cruise down to Panama City and the entrance to the Canal and, keen to be away from the scene of Lou Malta's murder, Dave decided to avoid any ports of call and sail through the night. Happy to keep out of Al's murderous way, he stayed up on the flybridge, snatching the occasional hour or two of sleep on the sofa. Al himself remained in his stateroom, drinking beers, watching movies on his VCR, and eating several microwave meals before falling asleep around midnight and sleeping until well after lunchtime the next day, when they arrived off the coast of Panama. The journey through the Canal itself took a full day and a half, and, Dave decided, was probably the most interesting thirty-six hours he'd had in five years. Three sets of locks – Gatun, Pedro Miguel and Miraflores – raised ships entering from the Pacific side on a kind of liquid stairway to the Caribbean side. There were no pumps. Gravity performed all the necessary water transfer.

Summoned by Dave's calls to come and take a look at one of the modern wonders of the world Al finally emerged from his cabin, reeking of sweat and beer and wearing a Dolphins shirt and a pair of cutoff jeans. He nodded without much enthusiasm as Dave explained what a feat of engineering the Canal was and seemed quite unimpressed by the close proximity of so many larger vessels.

Al said, 'So what's in it for them?'

'Who?'

'The fucking Panams, that's who.'

'The Canal's controlled by some kind of international body.'

'Yeah? And what's their angle?'

'They charge a toll to get through the canal, of course.'

'You mean like on the Florida Turnpike?'

Dave smiled slowly and said, 'Kind of. Except it costs a little more than a quarter.'

'What?'

'Tolls are based on a ship's tonnage.'

'What?'

'OK, they once charged a guy who tried to swim the canal thirty six cents. And that was back in 1928. So guess how much it is for a boat like this today?'

'What is this? *Family Challenge*? How the fuck should I know. Five, ten bucks? What?'

Dave was enjoying his anticipation of Al's reaction. Finally he said, 'It was $1,000.' He smiled as Al's jaw hit the deck.

'Get the fuck out of here. It was not.'

'I swear.'

'A thousand bucks? You're putting me on.'

Dave handed Al the receipt. 'Average toll for a big cargo ship is around $30,000.'

'Get the fuck out of here. And they pay it?'

'They've no choice but to pay it. Unless they want to go round Cape Horn.'

'Shit man, that's what I call a shakedown.' Al looked up uncomfortably at the oil tanker that was moored alongside them in the Pedro Miguel. 'Most expensive fucking drain I've ever been in,' he said and, without another word, returned to his stateroom to watch the US Military's Channel Eight on TV.

Dave suspected that Al's reaction was mostly based on fear. Being at the bottom of a forty-foot screw lock as it filled up with millions of gallons of water felt very claustrophobic. He had set a north by north-west course for Cancún on Mexico's Yucatan Peninsula, a distance of some 900 miles. From there he intended to sail north by north-east across the northern coast of Cuba. It was a course he hoped would keep them close to land in the event that they encountered anything worse than the roughish sea that, according to the weather station on the radio, now lay ahead of them. The boat was fitted with Gyrogale Quadrafin stabilizers but, in an effort to make time, and because he also wanted to punish Al for what had happened to Pepe, Dave avoided using them altogether. He himself was an excellent sailor. Al, he had already surmised, was not; and by the time the coast of Honduras was behind them, Al was looking as green as a wet dollar bill.

Watching him throw up over the side for the third time in eighteen hours, Dave grinned sadistically. 'Seems like you've thrown up just about everywhere in Central America. You're one hell of a tourist, I'll say that much for you, Al. Kind of like a tiger, the way it marks out its territory with piss. Only you seem to prefer to use vomit.' He glanced back at some seagulls now making a meal of what Al had just thrown up. 'The gulls seem to like you anyway. At least they like what you had for breakfast.'

'That smart mouth of yours again.' Al collapsed on the flybridge sofa and closed his eyes biliously.

'Smart?' Dave smacked his lips experimentally. 'You mean, as in not covered with flecks of vomit? Yeah, I guess it is at that.' He glanced down at one of the screens in front of him as the auto pilot made a small course correction and simultaneously stored the information in the computer's dead-reckoning log. Then, taking a deep, ostentatiously euphoric breath, Dave stood up, stretched and said, 'Hey, Al. Doesn't this sea air give you an appetite? Reckon I'll go below and fix myself a big lunch. Right now I could really murder a big plate of rock oysters.'

Al swallowed loudly and said, 'I'm gonna murder you if you don't shut the fuck up.'

'Not hungry, huh?'

'How long,' groaned Al, 'before we get to Florida?'

Dave checked the bottom of the screen where real time displays of position, course, track and ETA were updated every second.

'Well, according to Hal here, be another forty hours or so before you see the historic city of Miami again. That is if we don't hit any really bad weather. Which could slow us up some. But I can't see it changing very much from what it is now. It looks like you and your internal affairs had better get used to this kind of sea.'

Al smiled grimly. 'And you, motherfucker, had better get used to having me around. Maybe I haven't yet told you. But I'm your chaperon for the Atlantic caper.'

Dave laughed scornfully. 'You? I've seen poisoned camels that would make better sailors than you.'

Al shook his head as if too ill to think of some insult to hurl back in the younger man's tanned and healthy-looking face. Exasperated he said, 'The fuck d'you want all that money for, anyway?'

'That's an odd question for you to ask. Like one hooker accusing another of promiscuity.'

Al stood up abruptly and, with one hand clamped over his ballooning mouth, went outside the bridge and leaned over the side. During the minutes he was gone Dave did a little philosophical thinking. He thought about the heist and he thought about the money, but mostly he just thought about where he was: on the high seas, with nothing in front of him except the prow of the boat, and not a bad boat at that – it was just about worth the effort of going all the way down to Costa Rica to fetch it back home. Maybe it wasn't worth the lives of two people, but he could hardly have anticipated anything like what had happened in San José. He was enjoying the voyage, an enjoyment made all the sweeter by the knowledge of how much Al was hating it.

Al stepped uncertainly through the flybridge doorway, wiping his mouth on the sleeve of his football shirt. He sat down at the chart table and drank some whiskey in an attempt to settle his stomach.

Dave said, 'Been thinking about your question, Al.'

'What fuckin' question?'

'Why I want all that money.'

'You were right. It was a dumb fucking question.'

'You ever read books, Al?'

'Books?' Al finished the whiskey in his glass and poured another. He was considering the possibility that being drunk he might not notice being seasick. 'I only ever read three books in my whole life. Three that I remember, anyway. One was Hoyle on Gambling. The second was the *Jaguar Owner's Handbook*. I gotta Jaguar. Supercharged XJR. Beautiful fuckin' car. And the third book I read was about the Roman Caesars. On the whole if I want to read a book I generally wait for the movie.'

'You should read more, Al. Most of the travel I've done in the last five years has been in the pages of books. So, in answer to your earlier question, I want to buy myself a yacht and see some of those places for myself, y'know?'

'Madonna wants to go to Europe. But I like Vegas.'

'One book I read was *Seven Pillars of Wisdom*, by Lawrence of Arabia.'

'Good movie.'

'It was all about how he fell in love with the empty space of the desert, right? That's what I want to do. Fall in love with some empty spaces.'

'I could introduce you to a cousin of mine. Best lookin' empty space I ever saw. The lights are on, 'cept nobody's home. But built like a fuckin' palace.'

'The desert. Or maybe the wilderness. The Australian

outback. The Yukon. And of course the sea. The sea, I love.'

Al shook his head and grimaced. He said, 'I hate the fuckin' sea.'

'The kind of yacht I want to buy, it's nothing like this, man. I want a proper boat, with sails. Can't be too big, or else I have to have a large crew. Two people, including myself'd be about right. Gotta picture of the kinda boat I'm gonna buy right here. Want to see it?' Dave took a piece of paper out of his pocket, unfolded a picture he had torn from an old copy of *Showboats International* and showed it to Al. He said, 'Now that's what I call a boat. Seventy-five foot ketch, clipper bow, wineglass stern, transom windows, Scheel layout. Boat like that costs a lot more than two hundred grand anyway. Kind of boat to see the world in.'

Al looked at the picture and then floated it back to Dave. 'All those sails? Looks like hard work.'

'That's the point, Al. It's you and the sea.'

'The sea's a bitch. And a bitch who's really out of your league. The kind of bitch who, even when you take her on, you know she's gonna fuck ya around, and that you're gonna live to regret it. But still you go ahead anyway and persuade yourself that maybe it won't turn out that way. But it does turn out that way. If anything she behaves worse than you ever imagined was possible. She's cold, she's hard, she's cruel and she doesn't give a flying fuck what happens to you. A real ball breaker. That's the fuckin' sea, man.'

Dave looked at Al appreciatively. He smiled and said, 'Well what do you know? Hey, Al, you're a romantic too.'

CHAPTER ELEVEN

Kent Bowen parked his Jimmy and walked up a long slope toward the hotel entrance. The Hyatt Regency occupied a prime site in Fort Lauderdale, on the west side of the Seventeenth Street Causeway Bridge. From its revolving Pier Top cocktail bar you could see for miles around and Bowen had good reason to remember the place with special affection. It was in the Pier Top, last St Valentine's Day, while drinking delicious Margaritas, that he had asked Zola to marry him. On her accepting his proposal they had adjourned to a beach motel on Bayside Drive where they had taken a room for the night to consummate their love. A Scot by descent, and thus, by his own estimation a thrifty, hard-headed man, Bowen had never been the kind to throw money around. But that ranked as one of the most perfect evenings of his life.

He walked in the door of the hotel and made for the elevator, pausing only to buy a copy of *Luxury Florida Homes* in the gift shop. There was nothing like seeing how the other half lived on Florida's premier real estate to encourage the dreams he had when he bought his weekly lottery ticket. Not that he would ever throw his wealth around if he did win. Bowen liked to think of himself using his as yet unfound wealth with discretion. Enjoyment with anonymity. Dressed from head to toe in Tilley Endurables, he felt as anonymous as the situation now required, mixing unnoticed with the guests who were staying in the hotel.

Bowen rode the elevator up to the floor below the Pier Top, and walked round the hall to the east-facing suite where the stakeout was located. Standing in front of the door, he glanced one way and then the other before knocking carefully. A few seconds passed and then the door opened on the chain.

Kate Furey almost laughed. Most of all it was the hat that got to her.

'Hi, it's me,' he said, as if he had been wearing a Santa Claus outfit.

'Of course it is,' she said and let him in.

Bowen advanced through the door and glanced around the suite before she ushered him into the bedroom.

'Hi there.'

At the window, behind an arsenal of high-powered lenses mounted on tripods, two bored-looking men grunted back. A third, wearing headphones and facing a whole sound stage of eavesdropping equipment, remained silent, unaware that someone had come into the room. Kate left all three unidentified. She knew that Bowen wasn't looking for introductions. More than likely he had driven up from Miami in search of a free lunch.

'Nice room,' he remarked. 'Very nice indeed.'

Kate shrugged as if she herself didn't much care for it and said, 'Actually, this is supposed to be a suite.'

'A suite? Jesus, Kate, how much is that costing?'

'Same as a room. I got a rate.'

'How come?'

'My can't-happen-soon-enough-ex-husband acted for the hotel in a personal injury suit. I seem to remember it was some dim-witted dork who injured himself in the revolving bar upstairs. It's really tacky, but a great view. I guess that's why they go there. The airheads.' Kate laughed with undisguised contempt. 'Give them something to talk about when they think they're being romantic. You want to take a look at it before you go.'

Bowen said stiffly, 'Thanks, I already did.'

Kate giggled. 'I guess they think it's pretty *soigné*, but I thought it was like being inside a really cheap sports watch.'

'Hardly that cheap, I'd have thought,' bristled Bowen.

'Damn right,' said one of the men on the cameras. 'Last night I paid ten bucks for the worst goddamn Margarita I ever tasted.'

Kate looked at Bowen. 'There's not much you can see up here when it gets dark,' she offered by way of an excuse.

'I guess not.'

Kate said, 'I could show you some pictures, but right now you can see the live action.'

Bowen clapped his hands together purposefully. 'Then let's take a lookee-see what we can I-spy, shall we?'

The big lenses were focused on the opposite side of the Stranahan River and the Portside Yacht Club where some of the biggest and most expensive boats in Fort Lauderdale were moored. The cameraman who reckoned he knew a good Margarita when he tasted one, took Bowen through the cameras like a salesman in a Sharper Image store.

'This one, the 500-mill, gives you a pretty good view of the whole boat and what's happening on the mooring.'

Bowen swept off his Tilley hat and pressed his eye close to the viewfinder. At 110 feet long the *Britannia* was hardly the biggest vessel in the harbor. Not with Trump about. And she was dwarfed by the 150-foot triple storey moored alongside. But with her large flying bridge and elegant lines she was a graceful-looking boat. Fun too, if the small speedboat, Wet Bikes, Jetskis, and Hobiecat she had on board were anything to go by. Not to mention the naked female occupant of the Jacuzzi on the bridge.

Bowen grinned and said, 'I'll have me some of that. Who's the little lady with the bubbles?'

Kate sighed wearily and said, 'So far as we can tell her name is Gay Gilmore.'

'Gary's sister, huh?' sniggered Bowen. The girl in the Jacuzzi rubbed some bubbles over her breasts. 'Hey, let's do it, babe.'

'Actually, she's from New Zealand. Until a few weeks ago she was working illegally as a table dancer at a joint on

Collins. Right now, she seems to be the *Britannia* captain's main squeeze.'

The Margarita man said, 'You can see him on the 800-mill here. Name of Nicky Vallbona. He's the ugly bastard on the aft deck.'

Reluctantly, Bowen changed cameras and found himself looking at a dark man with a pencil-thin mustache. He said, 'You're right, he is an ugly bastard.'

'He's clean as far as we're concerned,' said Kate.

'What does a babe like her see in a hog like him?' mused Bowen.

The second cameraman stirred on his chair to put out his cigarette. He snorted and said, 'The boat, I shouldn't wonder. Chick seems to like it as much as she likes him. Comes and goes pretty much as she pleases. Always in that Jacuzzi. I believe she's quite popular with the folks looking through the telescope up on the Pier Top. She's becoming a regular tourist attraction.'

Bowen moved back to the first camera to take another look at Gay Gilmore.

'Me I prefer the boat next to the *Britannia*,' said the Margarita man. 'That one belongs to Sean Connery.'

'OO7's got a boat here in Lauderdale?' Bowen's voice betrayed excitement. 'Any pictures of the big guy himself?'

The two cameramen exchanged a guilty look and then shook their heads simultaneously.

'No,' lied one.

Bowen said, 'You're right though. It is a nice boat. Sean Connery, eh? Matter of fact my own ancestors were Scottish. From Edinburgh. Just like him.'

'I guess there are lots of other similarities,' said Kate.

But Bowen was too interested in Connery's boat and the naked girl on the *Britannia* to be aware of Kate's sarcasm.

Kate said, 'I checked out your theory, sir. With Palmer Johnson Yachts right here in Fort Lauderdale. They're one of the biggest makers of boat hulls in Florida. The guy I spoke to, Luis Madrid, said it was possible that you might get a hull made of compressed cocaine that might look like the real thing when covered with a linear polyurethane coating. But that it would hardly perform to the same standard.'

Bowen had moved back to the 800-mill lens to get a closer view of Gay Gilmore's naked body. She was touching herself all over now, almost as if she knew that people were watching. The thought occurred to him that maybe she was acting as some kind of distraction to keep people watching what was happening in the Jacuzzi and not somewhere else. But swinging the camera lens all around it didn't seem that there was much else to see. Just Vallbona talking on the cellular.

'I wonder who Nicky's talking to on his Nokia,' he murmured.

'Right now, it's his bookmaker,' said Kate.

Bowen looked up for a moment, surprised.

'You can really tell that from up here?'

'Sure. We've got a Cellmate System,' said Kate. 'We have intercepted one call I think you'll find is of particular interest.'

She went over to the man wearing the headphones and tapped him gently on the shoulder. The man, bearded and stale looking, as if in need of air and sunlight, lifted the headphones from his appropriately large ears.

'Colin. This is Kent Bowen, the ASAC in charge of this operation. Could you play him the SYT tape we made?'

'Sure thing, Kate.'

Colin drew his laptop toward him, pulled down a menu and chose a file from the list of recordings he had made. The Cellmate was connected to the laptop via an SCSI cable and to a digital tape recorder by means of a parallel interface. The Cellmate itself looked like a larger cellular telephone with some additional controls.

'SYT file coming up,' said Colin and hit the return on his laptop.

Kate said, 'The first voice you'll hear, the guy with the

Spanish accent, is the shipping agent, Juan Sedeno. Nicky Vallbona is the second voice.'

Bowen nodded and pulled up a chair and listened as the tape began to play:

'*Stranahan Yacht Transport.*'

'*I'd like to book my vessel aboard your ship for the March voyage to Palma, Mallorca. From Port Everglades.*'

'*All right sir. Your own name, the name of your vessel, and the name of her owner?*'

'*I'm Nicky Vallbona and I'm the captain of the* Britannia. *She's owned by Azimuth Marine Associates in the British Virgin Islands.*'

'*Virgin Islands . . . Can you tell me please, what are the dimensions of your own boat?*'

'*Length is thirty-four meters, beam is 7.3, and the draft 1.8.*'

'*One point eight . . . Any bow pulpit?*'

'*No.*'

'*Swimming platform?*'

'*Yes, it's three feet long.*'

'*Three feet. What about tender storage?*'

'*On-board.*'

'*Hmmm. March, you say . . .*'

'*Yes.*'

'*Yes, we can accommodate you, Captain Vallbona. The cost will be approximately 93,500 American dollars. That figure includes stevedoring on both sides of the Atlantic, diver's assistance, all lashing and securing, keel blocks and chine supports, passage for two crew members, and all insurances.*'

'*Sounds good.*'

'*Do you have our booking form, Captain?*'

'*Yes.*'

'*Could you please complete it and fax it back to us as soon as possible?*'

'*No problem. I'll do it right away.*'

'*Thank you for calling. Goodbye, Captain.*'

'*Goodbye.*'

The conversation ended and the tape turned itself off automatically.

'Wanna hear it again?' asked Colin.

Bowen said, 'Hell no. Speaks for itself, doesn't it? Obviously the boat isn't seaworthy on account of how the hull's probably made of pure cocaine. So they're doing what I always suspected they would do. Getting someone else to ferry it across the Atlantic for them. Perfect cover too. When you think about it. Rocky Envigado's boat rubbing fenders with what passes for high society in these parts.'

Listening to Bowen claim her theory – or at least half of it anyway – as his own, Kate felt her jaw muscles tighten. She wanted to remind him, to tell him that he was so full of shit he made her sick. Only he kept talking, on and on, like some asshole politician on TV. In a perfect world she could have reached for the remote and hit the mute button. Or maybe just forced the remote into his big stupid mouth and battered it down his throat with the heel of her shoe. But all she did instead was turn her back on him in an attempt to hide her anger.

'The only question is what we do about it,' continued Bowen. 'Whether we choose to pass the matter on to the Spanish police or mount some kind of undercover operation of our own.' He paused and glanced around. 'What do you think, Kate?'

Kate cleared her throat and tried to struggle out of the sea of resentment in which she had suddenly found herself. But when she answered him it still came out bitter and sarcastic.

'Me? What do I think?' A hollow laugh tumbled out of her mouth. 'What? I tell you, so you can tell me later? Is that the kind of what-do-I-think you mean, sir?'

Bowen frowned and said, 'Something bothering you, Kate?'

Even when she was being offensive he didn't pick up on it. Kate shook her head, pitying him as she would have pitied a dog left in a car on a hot day.

Only Bowen managed to misinterpret that too. He said,

'Good. Because, you know, March is just around the corner. There's no time to lose here.'

Kate wondered exactly how Kent Bowen had got to be an ASAC in the first place and considering the possibility that there existed within the Bureau some kind of affirmative action policy on behalf of dumb deputy sheriffs from Kansas. Quietly, she said, 'I've got some ideas.'

'Well, I want to hear them.'

She led him through to the sitting room next door, waved him toward a big horseshoe-shaped sofa and went over to the mini-bar.

'Want something to drink?'

'Just a Diet Coke.'

Kate came back with two regulars on ice and put them down on a table that was a sheet of round glass atop a Corinthian capital. It wasn't just the Pier Top that looked tacky; it was the furniture as well. But this was true of nearly everywhere in Florida. You just had to look in the copy of *Luxury Florida Homes* Kent Bowen had with him to know that.

'Mind if I smoke?' she said. She picked up a pack of Doral and lit one without waiting for an answer.

'Go right ahead,' said Bowen and winced in response to her first inhalation.

Still holding her cigarette she pushed her dark hair clear of her face and marshalled her thoughts. She said, 'OK, this is *my* idea.'

Bowen nodded and said, 'You made your point, Agent Furey.'

'I did?'

'It slipped my mind that you were the one who predicted Rocky would use the yacht transport. I apologize.'

Kate shrugged. Maybe he wasn't so bad after all. 'Forget it,' she said. 'It's not important. What's important is that we nail the perps. Here, and in Europe, right?'

Bowen looked doubtful. He said, 'Can't say I give much

of a shit what happens in Europe. But please don't tell any of those liaison officer friends of yours I said so. It would be bad for diplomatic relations.'

'I wouldn't dream of telling any of them anything I wasn't supposed to,' she said, aware of how earnest she sounded, but wondering if Bowen still harbored any suspicions about a relationship with the Dutchman. She took another life-threatening drag on her Doral and added, 'Nevertheless, the Assistant Director has recently gone on record to say that he believes helping the Europeans win their war on drugs may be one way of helping us to win ours.'

This was news to Bowen. 'He did, huh?'

'It was in the FBI Foreign Intelligence Coverage folder last month.'

Bowen smiled, dismissively. 'Oh, that.'

'And in response, there was a Miami SAC memo. Presley Willard wrote to the Director just a couple of weeks ago, assuring him that Miami General Investigations would do everything it could to support this initiative.'

Bowen, who had no knowledge of this memo, closed his eyes briefly and said, 'I remember that.' He swallowed some of his Coke and began to crunch on a piece of ice as if it were peanut brittle. It was her turn to wince now.

'I take your point, Kate.'

'Then as I see it, we need to keep the narcotics under surveillance for the duration of the voyage. It's no good just waving goodbye to the yacht transport when they exit Port Everglades.' Kate pointed out the window. 'That boat should never leave our sight. Which means we have to book a boat of our own aboard the same transport. Crewed by two FBI agents, in radio contact with a US Navy submarine and, when we cross the Atlantic, the British and the French navies too. While we're aboard the transport it will give us a chance to get a closer look at Rocky's boat, which, so far, we've been unable to do. Moreover, we can keep a close eye on things just in case they try to unload the dope while they're still at sea.

Maybe even transfer it to another boat on the same transport, just to put us off the scent.'

Bowen, who hadn't thought of that, swallowed the icy shards and pulled a face.

'This idea of yours. It sounds expensive. Number one, where are you going to get a suitable boat? And number two, who's going to pay the costs of transportation? You heard how much it costs. Ninety thousand dollars. I can't see the SAC authorizing that level of expenditure.'

Kate smiled and said, 'As a matter of fact, I've found a boat. Or rather Sam Brockman's found me one. Seems like the Coast Guard boarded an abandoned boat off Key West the other day and found it full of dope. Eventually, of course, it will go into government auction, but right now it's moored in Miami and available for a covert operation. The Coast Guard were planning something themselves, only it fell through and now they're offering it to us. It's ideal for our purposes, sir. Eighty-four feet long, twenty-two knot cruising, and all state-of-the-art facilities. I'm talking about a really luxurious yacht, here. As for the money, well I've an idea where we can get that too.'

Bowen said, 'You're going to suggest that latest tranche of Gulf Stream money, aren't you?'

Operation Gulf Stream had been another undercover Miami Bureau op in the early 1990s, mounted against one of the biggest money-laundering machines in Florida. A Miami gold and jewelry business run by one of the larger Colombian cartels had laundered millions of dollars through the Bank of Credit and Commerce International, shut down by the Bank of England in 1991. Weeks before BCCI's collapse, the jewelry business had withdrawn large sums of cash and placed them in safety deposit boxes throughout the state. Even now, several years afterward, boxes full of cash were being discovered by Bowen's own department – the latest, just a few days ago in a Liberty City bank, containing 200,000 British pounds sterling.

Kate shrugged and said, 'Why not? It's not as if it's even been entered in the report yet.'

'It'll have to be accounted for.'

Kate said, 'Sure. Eventually.'

'What's a British pound worth these days?'

'About a dollar fifty.' Kate pursed her lips and looked thoughtful. '$100,000 worth of that versus the European street value of a 1,000 keys of coke? I'd say that was money well spent.'

'And I suppose you're going to tell me that you're the best person to handle this little operation?'

'Sure. Why not?'

'Well for one thing, you've never worked undercover before.'

'I was a pretty good actress in high school.'

'I don't doubt it.'

Kate said, 'Undercover's just about being a good liar. How difficult can that be? Men do it all the time.'

'And for another, you're a woman.'

'Is that an objection, or merely an informed guess, sir?'

'Now don't go bristling like a hairbrush, Kate. It's just my impression that it's mostly men who crew and captain these motor yachts.'

Kate took a long drag of her cigarette with eyes narrowed against the smoke and the sexual prejudice. Since when did the captain of a boat have to be a man? Women had sailed solo around the world. There had been female pirates. These days there were even a couple of female admirals in the US Navy. Kent Bowen, on the other hand, didn't look like he could have captained a chair around his own desk.

'As a matter of fact,' she said acidly. 'It so happens that one of the other vessels booked onto the SYT transport this March is captained and crewed entirely by women.'

Bowen grinned. 'What are they, Amazons, or something?'

'Boat's owned by Jade Films.'

'Jade Films? The porno people?'

Kate made a performance out of looking surprised. She said, 'You've heard of them?'

Bowen shook his head casually. 'There was something in *Newsweek* about them, I think. To do with the guys who work in the sex industry.'

'I read that article,' she said. 'It was a good piece. But I don't think I remember anything about Jade Films in there.'

'Oh come on, Kate,' said Bowen, uncomfortably. 'I'm not that kind of guy.'

She thought, none of them were. Not until you got a look at the cable company account, and then it was just a bit of harmless fun.

Bowen said, 'What takes them across the Atlantic, anyway?'

'The Cannes Film Festival.'

'Cannes?'

'It's in Spain,' she said, knowing full well that Cannes was actually in the South of France.

'I know where it is. Cannes. That's kind of like the Oscars, isn't it?'

'Only classier.'

Bowen sniggered. 'With Jade Films in attendance? I hardly think so.'

'In attendance, but not in competition for the Palme d'Or. Cannes is a marketplace for just about anyone who's involved in the movie industry. And that includes people like Jade Films. Anyway, the point I'm making here is that this is a 160-foot twin screw diesel yacht captained and crewed entirely by women.'

'Twin screw, huh?' smirked Bowen.

Kate smiled patiently, waiting for the ribald punch line she felt certain was coming.

He said, 'Would they be identical twins, or just sisters?'

Kate kept on smiling as Bowen laughed his Beavis and Butthead laugh, trying her damnedest to look amused. Crushing out her cigarette like she was pinching him hard, Kate let her eyes drift sideways as if they were slipping off Bowen's oleaginous personality. But only *he* could OK putting her plan in front of Presley Willard, the Miami Bureau's Special Agent in Charge. Be nice, she told herself. Don't piss him off. Maybe he is an asshole but you don't have to stick the toe of your shoe in there. Be accommodating. This is the dork who could green-light a free trip across to Europe. To some real adventure.

'How'd you find out about that anyway?' he asked. 'Jade Films going on the transport.'

'Same way we found out about Rocky's boat. We've been intercepting all SYT's calls. I thought we ought to know about some of the other people who are going. Look, sir, you yourself said we have to move fast. March is just around the corner and there's only so much space left aboard the transport. If we leave this too long it will be nothing other than a great idea that might or might not have worked out for us.'

Bowen stood up and went over to the sitting-room window. To the south of the bridge was Port Everglades, the deepest port in Florida. Formerly known as Mabel Lakes it had been a shallow marsh in the wide section of the Florida East Coast Canal until President Calvin Coolidge threw a switch that was supposed to detonate an explosion to open the inlet. Except that the long-distance switch from Washington didn't work and someone had to set off the explosion locally. Another great idea that didn't work. Ordinarily Bowen was suspicious of good ideas. But he had to admit, Kate's idea about getting their own boat aboard the SYT transport was a good one.

Out in the harbor, Bowen could see as many kinds of boat as there were varieties of fish. Military ships, Coast Guard and police boats, island freighters from the Caribbean, tugs and tankers, cruise ships full of holidaymakers wondering if they were going to get mugged in Miami, sailboats, schooners, barges and motor yachts. Everything but a guy floating in a barrel.

The scent of perfume made him turn around. Kate was

standing a foot or so behind his shoulder and handing him a pair of binoculars. He lifted them to his eyes and let her describe the port facilities.

'Going anticlockwise, you've got passenger and cargo terminals. That's where our SYT ship departs from. Then the US Customs building. Gasoline storage tanks. This is the biggest gas station in the south. Did you know that?'

Kate was letting him know that she knew the port. It was her way of reminding him that she knew boats and that she was ideally qualified for the operation she had outlined. 'Those four red and white chimneys? You can see them for miles out to sea. Yachtsmen use them as navigation aids. They belong to the Florida Power and Light Company. Coming left of there you've got Port Administration, the World Trade Center, and more cargo terminals. Coming further back round to us again, and that's the Naval Surface Warfare Center.'

Bowen was thinking: she smells as good as she looks. It might be fun to go undercover with Kate. Best-looking girl in the Miami Bureau. The two of them aboard a luxury yacht together? He might even get lucky with her. Hadn't he always suspected that she had a soft spot for him? That was why she gave him such a hard time. Because she was trying to disguise the fact that, in reality, she was powerfully attracted to him. Why else would anyone speak to their boss the way she spoke to him? And it wouldn't be like they'd actually have to do very much on the boat. As she herself had said, it was just a question of keeping a close eye on Rocky's boat and maintaining radio contact with a navy submarine. There was even a sub in port. What could go wrong?

Kate said, 'I'm not exactly sure what the sub is called, but the aircraft carrier is the USS *Theodore Roosevelt*. Oh yes, and up on the point there? That's a restaurant owned by Burt Reynolds.'

'Burt Reynolds? Really?'

Kate grimaced as Bowen eagerly tried to get a better focus on the mission-style building that housed the restaurant. He was such a putz, such a tourist that it might have been only yesterday he'd left Kansas.

'Burt Reynolds,' he repeated dumbly.

'Actually,' she admitted, 'I'm not sure if it's still owned by him. Not since he filed for bankruptcy anyway.'

'You know, back in the seventies, he was just about my favorite movie actor.'

Kate's grimace became even more pronounced. Jesus, that clinched it. She was with the one guy in the whole world who enjoyed *Smokey and the Bandit*.

Bowen said, 'You know, I think I can probably persuade Presley that this is a good idea.' He handed back the binoculars.

'Great.'

'You said two crew?'

'Just two.'

'Any undercover mission is not without its dangers,' he said pompously. 'But it's just possible that we might also have some fun along the way.'

Kate swallowed. 'We?'

Bowen glanced at his cheap sports watch.

'Why don't we go to Burt's place and discuss it over lunch?' he said.

'Burt's place?' She wondered if Bowen hadn't heard what she had said about the bankruptcy.

'It's still open, isn't it?'

'Yeah. OK. If you really want to,' said Kate, wondering if there was some kind of opposite for the saying 'Every cloud has a silver lining.'

In Bowen's Jimmy, driving toward 'A' dock and the restaurant, she managed to buoy herself up with the thought that she might be able to deflect him – put him off the whole idea of coming along. Perhaps she could paint a picture of a transatlantic crossing that was a wave or two higher than Géricault's great masterpiece *The Raft of the Medusa*. A few well-chosen images over lunch that might scare the landlubbing shit out of him. By the time they reached Burt & Jack's, Kate was on an even keel again and paid little or no attention to a news report on the radio about an air traffic controllers' strike. Even if she had listened more carefully she would have had no reason to think the strike would last more than a couple of days; nor to suppose that it would have implications for the March voyage of SYT's semi-submersible vessel, the *Grand Duke*. There was only one thing on her mind now and it was that she somehow had to put Kent Bowen off a transatlantic voyage without jeopardizing his backing for the whole operation. Entering the restaurant she got ready to tell her boss a story that would make the storm in *The Caine Mutiny* look like another Pleasant Valley Sunday.

CHAPTER TWELVE

Inspired by Jimmy Figaro's purchase of a sculpture for his office, Tony Nudelli bought a bronze for his pool-house. A life-size Marilyn Monroe as she had appeared in *The Seven Year Itch*, her white skirts frozen voluminously as she stood over the subway vent.

'Nice,' said Al. 'Real classy.'

'Glad you like it,' said Nudelli. 'Cost me a fuckin' fortune. And then some. The refinements I had done were almost as much as the original bronze.'

Al frowned and then looked a little more closely at Marilyn. The halterneck dress, the big breasts, the same look of ecstatic delight on her dippy blonde face. She looked exactly the way he remembered her from the movie. Right down to the red polish on her toenails. Finally, admitting defeat, he said, 'OK, I give up. I can't see no difference. Exactly what were these refinements you had done?'

Nudelli grinned. 'Take a look under her dress,' he suggested.

'You're kidding.' But Al bent down, peeked between Marilyn's legs, and let out a loud guffaw. The white panties she had been wearing in the movie were gone. And what was there instead looked as realistic as if she'd been a table dancer flashing her pussy in your face in return for a bill underneath her garter. Right down to the gash in the pubic hair.

Still laughing Al said, 'Now that's what I call a conversation piece.'

'I thought so.'

'She's beautiful, Tony, just beautiful.'

'I'm thinkin' of having her up on some kind of table. It can't be this one, she's too heavy for glass. But I want to be able to look at that trim now and then, whenever the fancy takes me.' He lit a cigar and puffed it, happily watching Al as he squatted down to take another, closer look.

'Can I touch her pussy?'

'Be my guest.'

Al reached up and pressed the palm of his hand over Marilyn's private parts, laughing like a kid. He said, 'I never thought I'd get to give Marilyn Monroe some index finger.'

'You and Bobby Kennedy.'

'Not forgetting Jack.' He sang, ' "Happy birthday, Mister President." '

'She looks like she's enjoying it, Al.'

'I've always known how to please a woman, y'know? It's all in the wrist action. Man, this feels good.'

'Who says modern art don't mean nuthin'?'

'Not me. You won't hear me complaining.'

For Tony's benefit, Al sniffed his forefinger experimentally, each nostril vacuuming along its hairy knuckled length as if it had been the choicest cigar from Tony's rosewood humidor. He said, 'Too bad you couldn't get it made scratch 'n' sniff.'

'I'm workin' on it.' Nudelli waved his Cohiba at the seat in front of him. 'Sit down, Al. We've got some business to discuss.'

'I figured.'

'This longitude and latitude that Delano gave you. I had the guys on my boat look it up on their charts. Seems like it's a spot north-west of the Azores along the Mid-Atlantic Shelf. Anyway I fixed everything. Just like Delano wanted. A freighter out of Naples is gonna meet you at this nautical position. She's the *Ercolano*. Carrying break bulk cargo. Loose items like spools of wire, lumber, steel beams, shit that's too large to be containerized. But mostly Italian marble for the luxury bathrooms and gourmet kitchens of America. I'll come back to that in a minute. The *Ercolano*'s agent in Naples is a company called Agrigento. I've done business with them before and they're 100 percent reliable for our purposes. The captain's been told to expect to find a vessel in distress at that position and to pick up a passenger and cargo. He's going to hide the money in a marble sarcophagus that's on its way to some rich dead guy in Savannah.'

Al nodded. 'Got it.'

'Also, you'll note I said "passenger". Not plural, but singular. Meaning your individual ass, Al.' Tony puffed the cigar and looked momentarily uncertain of something. 'It's up to you how you do it pal, but I don't want Delano comin' back here to Miami with the money. The long and the short and the in-between of it is that I want him dead. I figure you'll need him alive only as long as it takes for you to make the rendezvous with the *Ercolano*. If I was you I'd let him have it before you get on the *Ercolano* and then sink the yacht, like he planned. Only with his dead son-of-a-bitch body still on board.'

Tony paused and studied Al's big open face for a moment, aware that Al had got to know Delano reasonably well on the voyage from Costa Rica. He studied the red-hot gray end of the cigar for a moment, feeling the heat on his cheek, and said, 'You gotta problem with any of that?'

Al shook his head. 'No problem at all. Delano's got a smart mouth. On the way back from CR he was breakin' my balls about this n'that. There were a couple of times when I felt like popping him right then and there. You know what I told him? I told him I was surprised someone didn't grease him while he was still in Homestead.' Al shook his head bitterly. 'S'gonna get worse too, I'm sure of it.'

'What do you mean?'

'Him fuckin' with me. Like for instance, this air traffic controllers' strike?'

Tony said, 'Don't remind me. I got to take the train to New York because of those fuckers. Country's going to shit.'

'Unfortunately there's no train to Europe. It seems as if a lot

of boat owners who want to get over the Atlantic this spring
have decided to beat the strike and travel with their boats.'

'So?'

'So Delano made the booking with SYT describing himself
as the owner and me as the crew. He's gonna be giving me
orders all the time. Breakin' my balls, like I'm the hired
help.'

Tony tried not to laugh. He said, 'Just remember something,
Al. With the smart mouth comes an even smarter brain. Don't
forget, he's a Jew, and Jews are clever. Don't make the same
mistake as Willy One Eye. Don't underestimate that kike.'

Al nodded impatiently. 'Yeah, yeah.'

'And don't let yourself get needled. There may be a reason
behind it. So be cool and turn the other cheek. Two things
you gotta bear in mind if he starts riding you, Al. One, when
this is all over you get to waste his smart ass; and two, you
get to keep his share of the money. That should make your
cross easier to bear. Huh? What do you say to that?'

Al said, 'Yeah, you're right. Thanks, Tony.'

'One more thing. Watch out that it's not you who gets
double-crossed. The Atlantic is a big place, Al. And recent
history teaches us that a lot can go wrong in an ocean.'

'You're telling me,' said Al. 'That kid I told you — '

'If it does . . .' Nudelli puffed out a cloud of smoke and
watched it hang in the air between them, as if considering
the size of the threat he wished to convey to the other man.
The smoke slowly drifted up Marilyn's white bronze skirt
adding an infernal touch to her famous pose. He'd actually
met Marilyn once, not long before she died, when she was
hanging around with Sam Giancana. A nice girl. A shame
what had happened to her. Only it hadn't been Sam who'd
helped hasten her death.

He said, 'If it does go wrong, you can depend on this.
That I can be as cruel as any of them fuckin' Kennedys. Joe
included.'

*　　*　　*

They were never a close family. The way Dave looked at it, they were never a family at all.

It was the usual stuff. A father who drank. That was the Russian in him. A mother who lit out. That was the Irish in her. And his sister, with an unwanted pregnancy and a boyfriend who didn't marry her. Well, that was hardly Nick's fault. Nick Rosen would probably have married Lisa if someone hadn't cut his throat first.

By the time Dave was twenty he'd more or less given up on them all. With the occasional exception of Lisa. Not that he'd really been much help there either. Just making it through life on his own had seemed challenge enough without having to shoulder the badly packed luggage of their problems as well. But at least he'd tried to help her. Once. Maybe now, after five years, it was time to try again. Maybe. That was how he found himself driving over to her dismally suburban two-bedroom bungalow off Hallandale Beach Boulevard a couple of weeks after he got back from CR.

Dave got out of the Miata carrying his Nike sports bag and walked up the path. He knocked on the warped wooden door and a big dog started to bark inside the house. He waited. It wasn't yet midday. A stupid time to go visiting. She might have been out working except that the drapes were pulled and there was an old and battered red Mustang parked on the drive. A car that had once been his. How could she have let it get that badly rusted?

He knocked again. This time when the dog barked he heard someone curse the animal. And after a minute or two the door creaked open and there, gathering a thin, kimono-style robe around her overweight, naked body, stood Lisa. Older than he remembered. Well of course, she was. But harder too. As if life hadn't been especially kind to her. Maybe if Nick hadn't died it would have been different. But the hell with that, he told himself. He was the one who'd spent the last five years behind bars. And had she thought to come and visit him? To do more than write a couple of badly spelt letters? She had not.

'Dave, my God,' she said, obviously flustered. 'My, my. You're out.'

'Hello, Lisa.'

An impossibly large dog came to the door, nudging her behind with a muzzle the size of a shoebox and growling quietly. It looked like a Dobermann that snacked on chocolate chip steroids.

She pushed the dog back indoors, and said, 'It's just my kid brother.'

Dave wasn't sure if she was talking to the dog or to someone else in the house. He had a glimpse of a dingy interior behind her and his keen eyes took in an ancient-looking TV, a grimy moth-eaten sofa, a table with a half-empty bottle of bourbon and, next to the bottle, looking like recent and incongruous arrivals, two new $100 bills.

He said, 'I wasn't sure if I'd find you in.'

She shrugged back at him, still trying to find a smile. When it came it looked uncomfortable. 'Well, here I am.' Glancing back over her shoulder, she added, 'You should have called.'

'I was in the general area,' he lied. 'Passing through. So I thought I'd stop, say hello, see how you were.'

'Only it's a little inconvenient, right now.'

Dave thought he guessed what he had disturbed.

'New boyfriend?'

Lisa smiled thinly and nodded with little more conviction. 'Yeah.'

'That's good.'

'We were — ' A sheepish look filled in the blanks. 'I'd be embarrassed to let you in. My underwear is all over the floor.'

Dave grinned and said, 'Same old Lisa.'

She was looking past him now, around the neighborhood. 'Hey, less of the old Lisa, will ya? I'm only five years older than you.'

That was right. He remembered now. She had been just his

age now when he went inside Homestead. Dave was about to pick up on that but then let it go. He wasn't here to reproach her, but to help.

He said, 'I brought you a present.' He handed over the bag. Inside were two parcels, each containing 50,000 of the 250 grand plus interest Jimmy Figaro had given him. 'Actually, there's one for Mom as well.'

'Why thank you, Dave,' she said and, hesitantly, brushed his hair with her hand.

As she touched him his nostrils detected a sweet cloying smell that for some reason made him start thinking of babies. It was on her hands. A kind of sheen.

'Just promise me that you'll only open it when you're alone,' he said.

'Sure, OK.' She frowned and laughed at the same time. 'Whaddya do? Rob a bank or something?'

'Not yet.'

'Look, why don't you come back, in about an hour, and we can talk. I'm not much of a cook, but hey. What the hell? You never complained when you were a kid and big sis fixed your dinner.'

Now he remembered the smell. It was baby oil. Johnson's Baby Oil. Only Lisa had never had her baby. It had been stillborn. And what with the two C-notes and the anonymous boyfriend back in the bedroom an unpleasant thought began to strut its way along the sidewalk of Dave's imagination.

'Whaddya say, little brother? Be like the old days.'

It was Dave's turn to be evasive now.

'I'd like to, Lisa, really I would. But I'm on a pretty tight schedule.'

There was no need for him to say anything. He told himself it wasn't his right to do so. Whatever family obligation he'd had, he'd fulfilled, hadn't he? Fifty thousand dollars a head was a lot of payback for not much of an upbringing. Now he just wanted to get the hell away from there. Forcing a smile that was the equal of the pinched nerve that was Lisa's own, Dave backed toward his car.

He said, 'Another time, huh?'

'Sure honey, but call first, OK?' she told him. Like he was some john.

'I'll do that.' He jumped into the open car and started the engine.

'Nice car,' she said. 'Are you sure you didn't rob a bank?'

'Not yet,' he repeated and waving stiffly, drove off, trying not to floor the gas pedal and look like he was suddenly desperate to be away from her. And at the same time ashamed. Ashamed for what he felt he was. Just another john in his sister's life, giving her money and then going away again. His own sister. His own sister.

Kate Furey was giving Kent Bowen a tour of the boat. The *Carrera* was moored alongside dozens of other yachts on Fort Lauderdale's intercoastal waterway, and a stone's throw from R.J.'s Landing, one of the dockside area's better restaurants. Bowen had already suggested lunching there, but Kate had told him they had too much to do getting him up to speed with the lexicon of yachts and their equipment. She had already figured out a way around his lack of boating knowledge, but she wanted to punish him a little for not being scared off with all her best stories about squalls and seasickness. A water taxi slipped by with a couple dressed up to get married. They waved, and from the sunny skylounge aft deck where he and Kate were standing, Bowen waved back.

'You haven't been listening to a word I've said.'

'Sure I have,' said Bowen.

Unconvinced, Kate pointed toward the davits above their heads. She said, 'OK, what are those?'

'You mean those things holding up the boat?'

Kate made an inhuman noise that sounded like the wrong answer button on a TV game show.

'Incorrect. That isn't a boat. It's a tender. As in *Tender is the Night*. But don't get any ideas. And the tender is attached to? What?'

'A crane, I guess.'

Kate made the noise again. She said, 'Davits. Those are davits, dammit. Look sir. Kent. This isn't going to work unless you become a little more familiar with the right names for things. You won't, thank God, have to try and sail this boat. But the chances are you'll have to talk about her with people from other boats. You know? Like you're proud of her? And by the way, those shoes you're wearing? They'll have to go.'

Bowen glanced down at his Air Nikes.

'What's wrong with them?'

Kate shook her head firmly and said, 'They're not proper boat shoes, that's what's wrong with them. A real boatman wouldn't be seen dead in those things. But we can fix that. We can stop off somewhere along Las Olas on our way down to the port. There's bound to be a man's shop, or a chandler's somewhere on the boulevard. Docksiders are best. Leather uppers, flat rubber soles. At least you can look the part even if you screw up on the glossary.'

Kate walked through a glass doorway and into the salon where a large and extremely comfortable leather couch, arranged aft to port, faced an enormous TV. A smaller sofa and narrow built-in counter with maple wood cabinets lined the starboard side of the salon. The arrangement of furnishings prompted Kate to ask Bowen yet another question. She pointed at a circular, six-place dining table that was located forward of where they were now standing.

'Am I pointing to port or to starboard?'

Bowen thought for a moment. Impatiently Kate started to click her fingers at him.

He said, 'Port.'

'C'mon, it's got to come faster than that. Like the difference between your right and your left.'

He followed her through the salon casting a look of regret in the direction of the 27-inch TV. He wished he could fetch himself an ice-cold Corona from the refrigerator and go and watch the play-off game on the TV in his stateroom. Dragging his fingers across the satin-finished wood he said, with just a hint of sarcasm, 'So what's this part of the boat called in that *McHale's Navy* glossary of yours?'

'The dining room.'

'Ask a dumb question.'

They climbed a few thickly carpeted steps.

'Hey, swell kitchen,' remarked Bowen. 'Look at this.'

Kate made the wrong-answer noise again.

'It's the galley,' she said.

Bowen sighed, 'As in slaves, right? Jesus, I'm never going to remember all this shit.'

'Well it probably won't matter that much. I already thought of a way to explain your ignorance.'

'You did, huh?' Bowen contained his momentary irritation.

She went on: 'For the purposes of SYT's insurance cover, I was obliged to describe you as the boat owner and me as the captain. A lot of owners have decided to travel with their boats because of the air traffic controllers' strike. It looks as if it's going to drag on for a while. So, under the circumstances, it won't seem that unusual, you coming along on the voyage.'

'I can't see how that helps,' said Bowen. 'Why should the owner know any less than the crew?'

Kate smiled. 'For a lot of yacht owners, a luxury yacht is just a floating den. Another expensive toy. Believe me, it's not uncommon for these guys to know jack shit about their own boats.' She was enjoying this. 'So, it's possible your complete and total ignorance won't be noticed.'

'OK.' Bowen looked around with a proprietorial air. 'You know, I always did kind of fancy owning one of these things.'

'I also took the liberty of inviting Sam Brockman to join our crew and make up the numbers.'

'Sam Brockman?' Bowen couldn't help but look disappointed. 'From the US Coast Guard?'

Kate noted the look on his face and smiled. Coast Guard. That was a laugh. More like bodyguard, just in case Bowen was thinking of trying anything when they were at sea.

'Well, think about it. It would have looked odd with just me crewing,' said Kate. 'And after all, it is his department's boat, at least until it goes up for auction. We're going to pick him up at the Lake Mabel station on our way down to SYT's cargo terminal.'

Bowen tried to feel positive about Sam Brockman's imminent arrival on board. 'I'm sure it's a good idea. Especially with all his, um, nautical knowledge.'

But Kate hadn't finished. 'That does of course mean that when we're in company we ought not to be too familiar with each other. I'll call you sir, as usual. Everyone'll assume you're just another Miami plutocrat with more money than sense. Sir.'

'I've no problem with any of that, Kate.' Bowen was already thinking of a way to exploit his new status as a rich boat owner. 'You know what? I'm going to find a bathroom.'

'Head, sir.'

For a moment Bowen couldn't believe his luck.

'I beg your pardon?'

'On board ship, sir, we call the bathroom the head.'

'Oh. The head. Whatever. Well, that's where I'm headed, anyway.' He laughed. Now he had thought of a way. 'Then I'm going to find me a cold beer and, like any convincing plutocrat with more money than sense, I'm going to put my feet up for a while and I'm going to watch the big game on TV.'

'We really ought to finish our tour of the boat, sir,' advised Kate. 'There's still a lot you should know about. The engines. The communications system. The ship's computers.'

Bowen shook his head. 'Kate? The only thing I want to see right now is the Chiefs taking the Dolphins apart.' Noting Kate's expression, he added, 'I'm from Kansas, remember?' He walked back down the steps. 'Let me know when we're underway, Captain. I'll be in my quarters.'

Kate watched him go, mouthing a silent 'asshole' at Bowen's back. A second or two later she had the satisfaction of hearing him fall down the circular stair connecting the midship accommodations deck with the formal salon and dining room.

'Asshole,' she said and climbed the portside companionway to the wheelhouse skylounge, where she began to get to grips with the *Carrera*'s computer-based dynamic reporting system. She was almost disappointed to discover how easy it would be to sail the boat. With its exhaustive on-line diagnostic testing and troubleshooting, the *Carrera* was so well equipped that even Bowen could have piloted it. And she wished that the part of her mission in which she was actually obliged to sail the boat could have lasted longer than the few minutes it would take to cruise down to Port Everglades.

Kate started the engines and then went out on deck to pull up fenders. She might have asked Bowen for help except for the inevitable joke that it would have produced:

Now Kate, you don't have to worry about fending me off . . .

Kate's lip wrinkled with distaste. 'Not any more,' she said, and began to pull on a rope she wished had been knotted around Bowen's stupid neck.

CHAPTER THIRTEEN

Jack Jellicoe, master of the *Grand Duke*, stood on the bridge wing and surveyed the scene below him with mounting distaste. It was bad enough that he was obliged to transport these expensive toys across the Atlantic – if they'd bought proper yachts with sails in the first place they might have made the crossing unaided. It was bad enough that he had to have contact with their overpaid and underqualified captains – most of them didn't know a fart from a fo'c'sle. It was bad enough to learn that some of the obscenely rich bastards who owned the floating Tupperware now being sailed onto his ship would be coming along on the voyage. But to be told by his own shipping agent that their owners, captains and crews were to be allowed free access to their vessels during the voyage was more than the tall Englishman could stomach.

'Let me get this straight, Mister Sedeno,' he said crisply, addressing the smaller, bespectacled man standing beside him. 'You expect me to sail across the Atlantic, one of the most hazardous oceans in the world, to safely deliver $50 million worth of waterproof caravans and motor homes, not to mention their Forbes Five Hundred owners, while at the same time permitting these same flat-footed cretins to clamber about my ship in all weathers without any of them falling overboard and drowning themselves?'

'Come on, Jack,' Sedeno said wearily. 'That's all bullshit. We both know that it won't be particularly hazardous. Going via the Canary Islands is not a route in which you'll encounter all weathers, as you say.'

Jellicoe stared off to starboard as if searching the dockside for a better argument. 'Well, what about the ship's insurers? What do they have to say about it?'

'We are only responsible for each vessel. Not for the supernumeraries who come aboard them. They have made their own personal insurance arrangements.'

Jellicoe thought for a moment, his long bony jaw quivering as he racked his brain for yet one more objection.

'Batteries,' he said triumphantly. 'Ships' batteries.'

'What about them?'

'Only this: that if they go on board their yachts, where will they get their power? Eh?' A small grin of satisfaction appeared on his lean bearded face. 'Tell me that, if you can? Without running engines their batteries will be flat in no time. And I'd like to see the multi-millionaire who can do without his microwave lobster dinner and the TV to watch while he's stuffing it down his neck.'

Sedeno shrugged.

'Many of them have solar power panels, while others need only run their engines in neutral to charge up their batteries. This can be organized in rotation, so as to minimize any fire risk. No, this is not a problem.'

Jellicoe twitched visibly. 'Next thing you'll be asking me to organize a game of quoits on deck. I'm the master of a cargo ship, not a cruise captain. What am I supposed to do with them? I've enough to do with the running of this ship without the effort of being nice.'

'Jack, Jack, surely that's not much of an effort,' argued Sedeno.

One of the other two officers who were on the bridge laughed out loud and Jellicoe looked around angrily. Like himself they were dressed in the tropical uniform of the British Merchant Navy – white shoes, white socks, white shorts, white shirts with epaulettes, and white cap.

'Something amusing you, Two-O?' he asked his second officer.

'No sir.'

'Then get on with your work. I shall of course expect visual bearings for position before we leave port. Not the radar range and bearings. There'll be none of that kind of slackness on this ship, d'you hear?'

'Yes sir.'

'And Three-O? I shall want you to execute a full stowaway search before we sail. On every one of those picnic trays called yachts.'

'There are seventeen of them, sir,' protested the ship's third officer.

'I'm sure I don't have to remind you, Three, that a stowaway search is normal shipping practice on leaving port. I shall want a signature to that effect from every supernumo yacht captain.'

'Someone looking for me?'

The voice belonged to a tall, blonde Amazon of a woman dressed in a pink Ralph Lauren shirt and shorts. Jellicoe wheeled around fiercely. Like cats and alcohol, women were never allowed on Jellicoe's bridge.

She said, 'I'm Rachel Dana, captain of the *Jade*.'

'Are you indeed?'

Jellicoe caught Sedeno's eye and stretched his face into a smile.

Rachel pointed to the largest yacht, nearest the bridge.

Jellicoe followed the line of her well-muscled, tanned forearm and a long pink fingernail.

'Very handsome,' he allowed.

'Isn't she just? She was built in 1992 to ABS A1 and AMS Classification.'

Jellicoe tried to look impressed although he hadn't the faintest idea of what any of this meant.

She said, 'Normally we run with a crew of about ten, but for the purposes of this voyage, we're down to just three.'

'Really? And how do the, um, how do the men find having a woman as ship's captain?'

'You noticed that, huh?' Rachel shook her head. 'There are

no male crew on the *Jade*. Just us girls. We're an entirely female crew. You might call it the owner's little conceit. Like *Charlie's Angels*.'

'Outside the pages of Homer, I never heard of such a thing,' Jellicoe said brusquely. 'Well, well.'

'Anyway, I thought I'd better come and introduce myself. And I couldn't help but overhear what you were saying just now. Is there a problem?'

'Jack?' said Sedeno. 'Is there a problem?'

Jellicoe said nothing.

'If you still object to all these supernumeraries, I can always sign the way bills myself,' Sedeno added.

'Did I say I had a problem with them? I was merely doing what any responsible captain would do under the circumstances. I was voicing all the potential safety concerns.'

'Supernumeraries, eh?' said Rachel. 'That's what you call us passengers, right?'

Jellicoe found himself both attracted to and irritated by the woman in pink. Women aboard a merchant ship were always a distraction. Especially when they were good-looking women like this one. He saw that his officers had already noticed the outline of Rachel Dana's nipples on her cotton polo shirt. Not to mention the large and thrusting breasts.

'That's right,' said Sedeno. 'You see, we can't call you passengers because that would mean we'd have to conform to a different set of shipping regulations. We'd have to do things like have a doctor aboard, instead of making do with the ship's carpenter.' He laughed at his own little joke. 'So we call you supernumeraries. Or supernumos, for short.' His grin widened as he smoothly added a compliment. 'It looks like we got the super part right, if you're anything to go by, Captain Dana.'

'Will you be joining us on the voyage?' she asked coolly.

'I'm afraid not. Business here in Fort Lauderdale prevents me.' Sedeno extended a hairy hand and said, 'Felipe Sedeno, ma'am, at your service. I'm the shipping agent. And this is the ship's master, Captain Jellicoe.'

'Pleased to meet you. This is such a fascinating ship you have here, Captain.'

'Is it?' Jellicoe advanced to the window of the bridge, towing Rachel Dana in his wake, and stared gloomily down at the sculpted, almost sensuous flowing shape of the *Jade*. 'It's not much more than a glorified car ferry. No different from all the other ro-ro freighters that come and go in this port.'

'Ro-ro?'

'Merchant shipping term. Cargo that can be rolled on and rolled off. I suppose we're rather more flo-flo, if you follow me. Anyway, beauty's not our strong suit. We leave that kind of thing to our customers.'

Mistaking Jellicoe's baleful gaze as admiration of her ship, Rachel Dana asked him if he would like to see round the *Jade*. 'Thank you, but some other time,' he said. 'I have business on deck.' Jellicoe turned to the second officer. 'Where's the chief?'

The second officer pointed outside.

'Supervising the cargo loading,' he said in a where-else-would-he-be? tone.

Jellicoe replaced his cap.

'You have the bridge, Mister Niven. I'll be on deck.'

'Yes sir.'

'I'm afraid you'll find us much less formal on the *Jade*,' she said.

'Oh, we're not so very formal, you know.' Jellicoe glanced warily in the direction of his two officers as if defying their contradiction.

'Well, I'd better be getting along myself,' announced Captain Dana, and she followed Jellicoe out of the bridge and onto the narrow walkway that led along the twenty-foot-high dock wall that was the *Grand Duke*'s starboard side.

Under the watchful eye of a short, balding officer wearing the same tropical gear as Jellicoe, an assortment of steve-dores and yachts' crewmen were drawing an 80-foot luxury sport-fisher toward the stern of the *Jade* by means of two pairs of headlines that were attached to the sport-fisher's bows.

'Watch that bleedin' bow pulpit,' roared the chief in a broad cockney accent. 'You'll have it through her arse. D'you hear?' He averted his eyes as the pulpit stopped a couple of inches short of the *Jade*'s stern. 'Dozy bugger,' he muttered and then sighed wearily as he saw Jellicoe advancing on him with Captain Dana following on behind.

The chief said, 'It's all right. Everything's under control. No damage done.'

'I'm very glad to hear it,' said Dana. 'I'd hate to get this voyage started with a lawsuit against your company for negligent cargo handling.'

Jellicoe looked around and shook his head. Already she was confirming his worst fears for the crossing.

The chief laughed wryly and jerked a grimy thumb at one of the port stevedores. 'Might help if some of these dozy buggers could speak English. This bloody city gets more like Havana every time we dock.'

'Don't tell us,' said Rachel, climbing onto the *Jade*'s coachroof where a sunpad big enough for half a dozen sunbathers was located. 'Tell that bastard Castro.'

When she had gone, the chief frowned and said, 'What's up with her?'

Jellicoe sighed loudly. 'Just get on with it, Bert,' he said. 'I'll be in my cabin.'

'All right for some,' grumbled the chief, then scowled at the stevedore standing on the sport-fisher's deck, an orange fender the size of an armchair lying uselessly at his feet.

'Hoi you,' yelled Bert. 'Are you going to sit on that bloody fender or put it over the side like you're supposed to?'

The man looked up at Bert, and said in Spanish, '*No comprendo. Màs despacio, por favor.*'

'You what?'

A bare-chested Dave Delano came quickly out of the wheelhouse, slid down the roof onto the deck, and, while the stevedore was still debating the purpose of the fender and the meaning of the chief's words, picked it off the deck and lowered it over the starboard side.

Bert waved and said, 'Bit more. OK that's enough. Tie it off.'

Dave wiped his forehead, and said, 'Thanks a lot.'

'No bother,' said Bert. 'Bloody hell.'

'What's up?'

'Your bloody stomach, that's what's up.'

Dave glanced at his own stomach and said, 'What about it?'

'Just look at it,' grinned Bert. 'It's like a bloody washboard. Look at mine.' He jerked his chin down at the large belly straining at the waistband of his white shorts. 'It's like having an extra limb wrapped around you in case of an emergency.' He laughed and slapped his belly hard with the flat of his hand. 'A lot of beer went into that. Here, I 'spose you've got one of them abdomenizers, have you? What a country this is for people worrying about their bellies. What goes in them, and what they look like. Every time I turn on the TV there's some bastard trying to sell you a flat stomach. Well, I don't 'spose I'll ever have one of those again. Certainly not like yours, mate, abdomenizer or not.'

Dave grinned. 'I don't have an abdomenizer,' he said.

'Well, how d'you do it, then? I mean, get the old six-pack stomach?'

'You have to be able to isolate the muscles when you exercise them,' said Dave. He might have added that the best way to do that was to isolate the man at the same time. Like maybe keep him in prison for five years. Homestead was full of guys with torsos that looked like they'd been drawn in an anatomy class.

Both men looked around as one of the pink ladies from the *Jade* came up on deck and walked off toward the bow of the ship. Generously hipped, she looked even more Amazonian than her captain. Bert grinned wolfishly and said, 'It's

154

not bellies with women, is it? It's their bottoms they worry about. Not that there's anything wrong with her butt. But for all I know, the buttockizer already exists. To give women smaller butts.'

As the Amazon finally disappeared, Dave shook his head and said, 'Now why would anyone want to do a thing like that?'

Bert laughed. 'Yeah,' he said, 'who'd want to do that, eh?'

Dave and Al watched as a diver came up from under the *Juarista*, having made sure that she was safely secured to the special support welded to the floating dock floor. Lashed tightly to the dock wall and carefully fendered against the boats to starboard and to stern, it was a snug fit and the boat looked as immovable as if she'd been mounted on a trailer and parked on a hard deck.

'Naturally you brought scuba gear,' Al said sceptically.

'Naturally.'

Al frowned, surprised at the apparent extent of Dave's efficiency. He said, 'Just don't expect me to go down. Takin' a bath's the only time I go in the water.'

Dave sniffed the air loudly. He said, 'Not so as you'd notice.'

'Wiseguy. I suppose you noticed how boxed in we are here. I thought you said we were going to try and be at the back of the boat so as we could make a clean getaway?'

'You go where that man and his clipboard tell you. A computer figures out all the positions according to the length and breadth of your hull. It would have looked kind of odd, us going up against the computer. Don't you think?'

Al said nothing.

Dave said coolly, 'It's like I told you already. When we're ready to rumble we'll just steal the boat that's nearest to the stern of the ship. That's what we call the back of the boat. You know, if you're going to pretend to be a boat captain it would help if you get a handle on the way we talk about this shit.'

'The only thing that's going to get a handle on it is your fuckin' head, wiseguy.'

'Relax will you, Al? The only thing's not under control round here is your temper. Take my word for it. We're cool.'

'I sure hope so. Tony don't appreciate hearing about the unexpected. I gotta tell him anything that happens out of the ordinary.'

Dave shook his head. 'Forget it, Al. It's radio silence from now on. Like we're in a submarine with Clark Gable, and some Japs are trying to get a sonar fix to drop a depth charge on our ass. You give Tony the broadcast news on our progress and I guarantee there are sixteen other boats in this man's navy who will pick it up on their radios. The same goes for your cellular phone.' Dave tossed him a quarter. 'You want to tell Tony something? Then I suggest you go ashore now before we set sail and use a pay phone. Because on this ship, it's silent running. Understand?'

Al glared at him.

Dave said, 'Look, I've got this all figured out. All the angles are in our control. About the only thing that can go wrong here is that you'll fuck it up with this "Tony don't appreciate" routine. What's got to happen here is that you and I have to get along and trust each other so that when the time comes to make the score, we're working as a team.' Dave shrugged. 'And if the unexpected does happen, we'll improvise. Flexibility is the key to our success here. Steady can go to random at any time. From our side, you and me Al, we're covered. Outside of that we've got the sea, we've got the weather, and we've got other people, all of which adds up to quite a lot that's random. We have to appreciate that and be ready for it. OK?'

'OK.'

'Now why don't you and I do something constructive? Like maybe take a little stroll around and acquaint ourselves with the layout of this oceangoing marina?'

'Good idea.'

'And try to look a little more user friendly and less like an argument for genetic engineering. Got our story straight?'

'I think so. You're some financial hotshot, right?'

'Right.'

'And a big motor-racing enthusiast. So we're on our way to Monte Carlo, for the Grand Prix they got down there. After which we're heading to Cap d'Antibes, in the South of France, where you've rented a house for the summer. Got some business associates from London coming down to join you there. Maybe take in another couple of races while you're in Europe, depending on how the business goes.'

'OK, what kind of financial hot shot?' asked Dave.

'Commodities. But I'm supposed to be a little vague about this, right?'

'Right. If anyone asks you just say it's some kind of metal, maybe copper, and leave it at that. They won't expect you to know any more.'

Dave moved toward the gangway and then turned back. He said, 'One more thing. The Coast Guard and Customs people will board us when we're ready to sail. So just so as I know, where'd you stash the Alamo?'

'They got enough to worry about what's comin' into Miami without giving much of a fuck what's going out.'

'True. But I'd still like to know.'

'It's in the fish-box. Under a shitload of ice. And you can take it from me. Improvisation won't ever come into it. Gunwise, we are covered against every eventuality. Steady. Random. Whatever the world may throw at us.'

Dave had never told Tony or Al the names of the boats that would be carrying the money. It was understood that this was Dave's best guarantee of trust between himself and Tony. And even now, as Dave and Al picked their way along the starboard side of the ship toward the smokestacks in the stern, Al saw him give no sign which of the boats now loaded and lashed within the high walls of the *Grand Duke*'s extraordinary hull were carrying cash bound for Russia and the purchase of a whole bank.

'Ya see 'em?' asked Al. 'The boats? Our boats?'

'All three. Just like I said.'

'Yeah? Which ones? Where are they?'

'When we're at sea, I'll tell you. But not before.'

Al laughed bitterly. ' "Get along and trust each other," he said. Like fuck.'

'You wouldn't want me to make those guys feel self-conscious, now would you? Pointing them out like some kind of tourist attraction? "Hey look, there are the boats that we're going to rip off." ' Dave tut-tutted and shook his head. 'I bet they're nervous enough as it is. Besides, these are heavy guys, Al. They've probably got a fish-box just like ours. Let 'em relax, think they're on a summer cruise. Better for us, better for them.'

They turned as a white boat with an angled red racing stripe came alongside the *Duke*. It was flying the Stars and Stripes in contrast to the ship's British Red Ensign.

'Customs?'

'Uh-uh,' said Dave. 'Coast Guard. We must be getting ready to leave port.' Dave glanced at his watch. It was five o'clock in the afternoon and it had taken the best part of a day to float the *Duke*'s peculiar cargo on board. A couple of seconds later they heard an announcement over the ship's tannoy in the unmistakable voice of the chief officer.

'Crew to close all hatches and stow all gear.'

Al smacked his lips.

'I'm goin' back to the boat to make myself a sandwich. Want one?'

'No thanks. I'll be along in a few minutes. I'm going to the stern. To take a look at our getaway boat. See what we've drawn in the lottery.'

But Dave had another mission in mind. Of necessity he had lied to Al, to reassure him. Al was enough of a pain in the ass already without alarming him any further. But now he wanted to reassure himself that the last information he had received from Einstein Gergiev had been correct and that the boats were indeed on board the *Duke*. He already knew that none of them was on the starboard side. So he waited until Al was out of sight before walking round to the port side of the ship, all the time turning over in his mind the names of the three boats he was looking for like a mantra. His heart gave a leap as he spotted the first boat; then the second; and then the third. Just like he'd been told. He could hardly believe it, but the three boats carrying the money were in a line along the *Duke*'s port wall. And, like the *Duke*, they were all flying the Red Ensign which meant that they were registered in the British Commonwealth – somewhere like Bermuda, Antigua, Gibraltar or the British Virgin Islands. There was a 100-foot raised pilothouse, cockpit motor yacht called the *Beagle*; a 70-foot Burger Cruiser called the *Claudia Cardinale*; and a 112-foot triple-decker custom Hatteras called *Baby Doc*.

Everything was just as he'd been told.

Dave still couldn't get over the last boat. Even back in Miami, when he'd been given the three names, he had thought *Baby Doc* was hardly a name to have on a boat you were likely to sail anywhere near Haiti. After years of dictatorship by the Duvalier family – Papa Doc and then his son, Baby – the locals would probably have torched it on the quayside.

None of the crewmen of the three boats looked particularly Russian. Not that Dave had expected them to. They did look very tough, of that there was no doubt. One guy sunbathing on the roof of the *Beagle* was built like a wrestler, while a black guy tying off a length of rope aboard the *Claudia Cardinale* had arms that were the size of Dave's legs. More than ever, Dave realized that the success of his plan depended on the element of surprise and not much else. Halfway across the Atlantic, he hoped the opposition would be less on its guard than they looked now. Even with the Customs and Coast Guard around he was pretty sure that one of the guys on the *Baby Doc* was carrying a gun underneath his shirt. Dave didn't much care for the idea of a firefight with these characters. Guns had never been his thing. He preferred to shoot with his mouth.

'Go to stations,' the voice on the tannoy ordered.

Dave thought that was probably a good idea, before any of them noticed him watching.

Back at the *Juarista* Dave could just about see Al through the smoked glass of the galley window. He stepped onto the flybridge and found himself almost face to face with a girl on the bridge of the ship to port of him. She looked around thirty, with shoulder-length brown hair that belonged in an expensive shampoo commercial, and eyes that made the sky look as gray as the aircraft carrier moored outside the port's main turning basin. Stretched out on a big white leather sofa on the back of the bridge, she was the kind of woman Dave had met many times lying on the bunk in his cell in Homestead, but had only ever seen in the glossy magazines.

'Hi there,' he said affably, expecting she'd be too snooty to reply.

'Hi.'

She didn't say any more than that, but her eyes stayed on him, as if they didn't mind what they saw.

Dave looked quickly up and down her boat and then nodded appreciatively. She was probably married to some company chief executive old enough to be her father.

He said, 'Nice-looking boat. Fast too, I'd say.'

'She rides as flat as a railroad car,' said Kate.

'The *Carrera*, huh?' he said, reading the name on the side of the bridge. 'I'll bet you've got the car to match.'

Kate smiled.

'I've never liked Porsche very much,' she said. 'I think they're too clinical. If it was up to me I'd have something British. Like a Jaguar XJS. I prefer something a little more luxurious for my money.'

'I never could tell.'

'You seem pretty comfortable there yourself,' said Kate. 'And I'll bet your boat's faster than mine. Looks like it has plenty of range for long-distance fishing expeditions too. Why don't you come aboard and have a beer and tell me about her?'

She knew cars. She knew boats. And she was friendly. Already Dave was impressed. 'I sure can't think of a reason not to,' he said.

As he climbed onto the *Carrera* he caught a brief glimpse of two men sitting inside the salon watching TV, then he stepped up onto the bridge. The woman got up from the leather sofa and smiled pleasantly.

She said, 'Kate Parmenter,' using her married name for what she hoped would be the very last time.

Dave shook her hand while noting that there was no ring on the other one. That was good. The kind of women who married older, rich guys usually made sure they got a good rock out of it. So maybe she wasn't married after all. He said, 'David Dulanotov.'

'Like in *The X Files*?'

'No, that's David Duchovny.'

'Well, pleased to meet you anyway, David.' Kate wondered if he was crew. Mostly the guys who owned boats like the *Juarista* were pink, fat and balding, like her soon-to-be ex-husband Howard. The sportiest thing about Howard had been his Rolex submariner. But this guy, David, with his hard body and easy smile looked too fit to be spending much time behind the kind of desk that made enough money to buy a two, maybe three million dollar sport-fisher.

'And to meet you, Kate.'

'Your boat?'

'Yeah.'

'She said, 'The *Juarista*. An unusual name. What does it mean?'

'The Juaristas were Mexican revolutionaries,' explained

Dave. 'They tried to free their country from the French-supported Emperor Maximilian.'

Kate looked sheepish. 'I didn't even know the French had been involved in Mexico.'

'Mexico, Algeria, Vietnam. Every lousy cause.'

She went forward to fetch a couple of cold Coronas from the flybridge refrigerator. 'I must say, you don't look like someone who'd be interested in revolution.'

'Me?' Dave shrugged. 'Well, I've got a lot of Russian blood. But actually I'm more interested in movies than commies. Most of what I know about the Juaristas comes from a movie called *Vera Cruz*. Gary Cooper and Burt Lancaster. 1954.'

'That's a little before my time.'

'Mine too. But it's still a good movie.' Dave took the bottle she offered and drank some cold beer. 'Is that your crew watching TV?'

'I'm the captain, not the owner. He's one of the guys watching the football game on TV. You're not a sports fan?'

'Oh sure, but I can watch a game any time. It's not every day you set sail on a voyage across the Atlantic Ocean.' For a moment Dave stared off the port side and then added, 'I feel I'm about to suffer a sea change, into something rich and strange.'

Kate smiled. 'Is that poetry?'

Dave, who reckoned becoming something rich was at least a strong possibility, supplied the complete quotation and said, 'It's Shakespeare. *The Tempest*.'

Kate raised her bottle, 'Here's to one not finding us.'

'Is that at all likely?'

'Not really. Not at this time of year. But sailing in the tropics, you never can tell.'

They fell silent for a minute or two as if immediately comfortable with each other, enough just to sit there and watch the *Grand Duke*'s crew make ready to leave the mooring. Occasionally, Kate would glance to the stern of the ship where Rocky Envigado's boat, the *Britannia*, was now loaded and lashed. She was feeling a little more relaxed. The *Britannia* had been the very last boat to float into the *Duke* and, for an hour or so, it had seemed that she and her two colleagues might have found themselves setting sail without the target of their surveillance.

A tugboat tooted to port, lines were thrown off the quayside, a klaxon sounded, and Kate and Dave felt a low rumble on the starboard side as bow and stern thrusters began to turn over. There were now only two lines connecting them to land and seeing these slacken, men on the wharf lifted the eye of each rope clear of the bit and then dropped it into the rainbow streaked water.

'All gone and all clear,' someone shouted.

Having checked the whereabouts of Rocky's boat, Kate watched David out of the corner of her eye as he watched the thrusters push the ship gently away. Maximum points for quoting Shakespeare. And he was right, there was something rich and strange about a voyage like this one. Maximum points too, for not being interested in football. What did a game matter when there was the leaving of America by ship to contemplate? She had begun to believe that men like David Dulanotov simply didn't exist. Romantic men, who were content to sit in silence instead of trying to talk their way into your pants. Looking at his big brown eyes fixed on the distant horizon, she wondered what other surprises the voyage might have in store for her and how many of them might include this handsome man.

CHAPTER FOURTEEN

Some of the crew and yacht-owners stayed aboard their own vessels for dinner. But mostly they went to the accommodations block in the forehouse, curious to see more of the ship and to meet the captain, his officers and their crew. Officers and crewmen on the *Duke* ate separately and in different messrooms. In the British Merchant Navy, it had always been done this way. Now Jellicoe gave orders that owners and their captains would be permitted to dine in the officers' saloon. Crewmen, however, would have to eat with the crew of the *Duke* in the crewmen's mess. So it was that Dave found himself sitting down to dinner with Jellicoe, those of his officers who were not on watch, and a couple of dozen assorted owners and captains, including Al Carnaro, Kate Parmenter and the captain of the *Jade*, the handsome Rachel Dana.

Rachel said, 'Captain Jellicoe, I was wondering, what's the purpose of those two brass cannon on your fo'c'sle?'

'What the hell's a fo'c'sle?' grumbled Kent Bowen.

'It's the deck above the forecastle in the bows of the ship,' explained Jellicoe, and marked Bowen down as a complete idiot in all matters relating to the sea and seafaring. Turning toward Rachel, he smiled bleakly.

'As a matter of fact,' he said, 'there's a bit of a story attached to those cannon. You see, on our way back from the Balearics . . .' He nodded toward Bowen. 'That's the small group of islands including Mallorca, that is, of course, our destination. Well, we had to stop for repairs, pretty close to Lanzarote . . .' Another nod to Bowen. 'Which is of course in the Canary Islands. Anyway, we were lying at anchor close to some cliffs for the best part of a day while the chief engineer sorted out the engines and the boys started to get rather bored. Now at the top of these cliffs were two ceremonial cannon. And I thought that it would be a pretty good way of keeping them out of mischief, if we climbed to the top of the cliffs, along the lines of a film I once saw and, instead of blowing up these particular guns, stole them instead.' Jellicoe was chuckling as he relived this exploit. 'So that's exactly what we did. It took most of the day, since, as you can no doubt imagine, they were rather heavy. Anyway, they're in full working order. We fire them once a year, to commemorate Admiral Lord Nelson's victory over the French at the Battle of Trafalgar . . .' He nodded toward Bowen again. 'Famous sea battle during the Napoleonic wars – 21 October 1805, in case you should be wondering. Fought not so very far north of the Canaries, as a matter of fact. You see, the cannon were originally British. Came off a ship in Nelson's squadron that was wrecked in Madeira. For a while the cannon stayed there, until the governor lost them in a card game with the governor of Lanzarote. Something like that, anyway. So you see we were merely reclaiming naval property. England expects, eh Chief?'

Bert Ross smiled a wintry smile and helped himself to some more of the execrable white wine that was served aboard the *Duke*.

'How heroic,' said Rachel. 'Perhaps you should be in a film yourself, Captain.'

Kate wondered what kind of film Rachel Dana could have in mind. She said, 'Captain Jellicoe, if that's how you keep your men out of mischief, I'd love to see what might happen when you were planning on causing trouble.'

'Come, come, Captain Parmenter. It was just high spirits, that's all.' Jellicoe looked at Dave and said. 'Wouldn't you say so, sir?'

'It sounds a blast.' Dave grinned back at him, wondering

how Jellicoe would react when he and Al enacted their own high-spirited caper. Badly, he thought. Jellicoe was the kind of guy who'd have called what Dave was planning 'Piracy'. Well, that was OK by him. He'd always kind of liked Errol Flynn and Tyrone Power. When he was holed up somewhere, several million dollars better off, he might even grow himself a small mustache. Maybe even wear an earring again. When you were worth several million dollars you could wear more or less what you wanted and no one ever complained.

'A blast?' Jellicoe said. 'Yes, I suppose it was.'

Kate smiled at Dave. 'A few too many beers is as wild as it gets on the *Carrera*.'

Dave smiled back. 'Same here,' he said, although he was thinking that what had happened to Lou Malta and his boy Pepe would count as pretty wild.

Al, who had wisely stayed silent throughout dinner, leaned toward Dave's shoulder and murmured, 'That her? That the babe you were talking to earlier?'

'Yes it is.'

'Cute. Very cute. The question is, does she have a good-looking friend?'

Dave looked at Al and shook his head. 'No, Al, the question is, do I?'

After dinner, Dave asked the chief officer, Bert Ross, which of his officers was the radio officer.

'Radio officer?' Ross sounded surprised.

'Yeah, only I've got a fist-mike that's cutting out on me.' Although this was true, Dave knew pretty much how to fix it. His real purpose was to find out where the ship's radio was. The first part of his plan, when eventually it kicked in, would involve immobilizing the *Duke*'s VHF.

'We've got an electrical officer,' said Ross. 'Radio officers went out with flared trousers. We're all satellite and microchip these days. Fax, telex, digital selective calling, you name it. Most of the lads on this ship think Morse Code is the capital of

Russia.' He laughed and glanced at his watch. 'As it happens, Jock – our electrical officer – he'll be on the blower now. Gettin' the soccer results from England. Come on, I'll take you there myself.'

'Thanks. That'd be great.'

'No problem. What you want to do anyway? Have a chat with your personal trainer or something?' Ross led the way out of the officers' saloon. 'After that dinner you'll probably need a couple of hours in the gym.'

'It was kind of heavy,' admitted Dave, thinking how much the food had reminded him of the chow back in Homestead.

'What we don't eat, we use as ballast.'

They went along to a cabin close to the bridge where a thin, undernourished-looking man with the reddest hair Dave had ever seen that wasn't on a dog, was seated in front of a series of teak-mounted transceivers and loudspeakers. In his hand was a digital telephone handset and on the table next to him was a sheet of paper covered with team names and scores.

'This is Jock.'

The red-haired man looked up and nodded.

'He's Scottish, so don't expect to understand a bleedin' word he says.'

Jock replaced the handset on the cradle and sat back on his plastic office chair.

'How'd the Arsenal do, Jock?'

'Lost, three-nil.'

'Bastards.' Ross sighed and looked away in disgust. 'Jock, this is Mister Dulanotov. One of our supernumos. He's got a problem with his VHF.'

Dave answered a few rudimentary questions about the VHF system aboard the *Juarista* while at the same time he considered what would be the best way of taking out the ship's radio. The sailor in him recoiled from the idea of simply putting a bullet in the radio and leaving a hundred people stranded on the ocean with no means of communication. But he could see no obvious alternative. At least that was how it seemed until, backing out of Ross's way, he caught and tore the pocket of his chinos on the heavy steel door.

'Sorry about that,' said Ross.

But Dave was more interested in the discovery that there was a key in the door than in any apology. All he would have to do was steal the key and then hide it somewhere.

Jock leaned forward in his chair, frowning with puzzlement as through the loudspeaker came a sound like a fax machine in transmission. He said, 'Odd. There it is again.'

'What is?' asked Ross.

'That sound. One of the supernumos must be broadcasting a signal using a digital scrambler.'

'So?'

'So, it's a little unusual, that's all.'

'What channel?' asked Dave, curious.

Jock hit the squelch button on the transceiver to try and filter out the background atmospheric noise. He shook his head and said, 'It seems to be between frequencies.'

Ross shrugged and said, 'Whoever it is is probably trying to have a private business conversation, that's all. There are a lot of nosey bastards around these days. You never know who's listening to your blower. I was reading about it in the paper. Industrial espionage is on the increase.'

'That's true,' said Jock in an accent as thick as porridge. 'But digital's sophisticated.' He looked accusingly at Dave. 'Even for some mega-rich supernumo. Normally it's only the military and the intelligence community who get to play with these kinds of toys.'

'Are you sure it's coming from the *Duke*?' asked Dave.

'Positive. Look at that signal strength. We're right on top of it. And what's more, VHF has a very short range. Fifty miles max. If someone's broadcasting then it's to someone else who's quite close.'

'Can you get a fix on it?' asked Dave.

'Not with this kit.' Jock picked up a half-smoked cigarette and puffed it back into life. 'There is another possibility, if the signal's not actually coming from the ship.' He took a drag, stubbed out the cigarette in a saucer, and started to roll another.

Ross said, 'Well, don't make us change our underwear for it.'

Jock licked his cigarette paper and said, 'It's possible. Just possible, mind, that we're over a submarine.' He put the cigarette in his mouth and scraped a match alight. 'Those bastards play all sorts of stupid games. If it is a sub, he's probably using us as the subject of an exercise. Right now he could be going through the motions of firing a torpedo at us.'

Dave said, 'That's a comforting thought as we prepare to go to bed.'

Ross said, 'Yeah. And to think that it's to help us all sleep soundly in our beds that they do these bloody stupid things.'

Aboard the *Carrera*, Kate finished her conversation with the first officer of the USS *Galveston*, the 688-Class attack submarine that was, she had just been informed, 200 feet below the twin hulls of the *Duke*. She felt a lot better knowing they had company, even though it would only last as far as the Sargasso Sea. After that there would be several hundred miles across the Cape Verde Basin before they picked up their French nuclear sub escort at another underwater landmark, Great Meteor Tablemount.

She and Sam Brockman were seated behind the drawn shades and closed doors of the wheelhouse skylounge. Brockman was keeping one eye on the electronic chart, more out of habit than of necessity. A tall man – too tall to be really comfortable on the yacht: at six feet five his steel-gray hair was forever brushing along the *Carrera*'s suede-covered ceilings – Brockman had the air of someone who'd seen it all before. Kate liked him, finding confidence in his steady demeanor, admiring his attention to duty, but most of all enjoying the fact that he shared her own low opinion of Kent Bowen.

Kate said, 'Where is His Excellency?'

'Asleep. In his stateroom. He and the beer got well acquainted during the game on TV. And then there was the wine he had at dinner. I guess he's drunk as much as he's breathed today. Looks like he intends to play the part of lazy fat cat to the whiskers, Kate. Not so much under cover as under the influence. It amazes me that he's managed to keep such a tight rein on his mouth. So far.'

'I should never have suggested it,' Kate said. 'You're right, Sam. He's acting like he's Donald Trump. This owner thing really has gone to his head.'

'It's not just his head. Did you see the way he was coming onto the captain of the *Jade*?'

Sam grinned. 'I wonder why?'

'Oh come on, Sam. Not you too. Those are tits in her polo shirt. Not golden apples.'

'Can't say as I noticed her tits. But I love that woman's ass.'

'*Sam.*'

'Sea air does strange things to people,' he explained. 'There'll be all kinds of shit before this voyage is out. You just see if I'm wrong.'

'I hope so. I could use some action. Miami Bureau's been a little dull of late. Bowen sees to that. Dullest ASAC I ever worked for.'

'Don't you worry about a thing. You did right. Believe me, he's playing the dumb schmuck owner to perfection. I should know, I worked for plenty. During college vacations I used to crew yachts. One particular asshole I worked for, heir to a sanitary napkin fortune, he owned this classic three-masted schooner. Two hundred feet long, built in 1927, a real beauty. His private plane flew him down to meet the yacht at Tierra del Fuego, in Argentina. This was after us radioing him to say that the weather was real quiet. We picked him up and he spent forty-eight hours on board going round Cape Horn just so that he could boast to his yacht club pals back in

Manhattan that he'd actually done it. Two days later, we dropped him off the coast of Chile and he flew home. Asshole. As soon as he got back to Wall Street he put the yacht up for sale.' Sam shook his head with disgust. 'Yes, I think he and Kent Bowen would have gotten along real well.'

'It's kind of you to say so, Sam.'

He stretched his long arms and yawned. 'Bowen's right about one thing, though. That early night. I'm bushed. Mind if I turn in?'

'You go ahead. I'm going to stay up a while and enjoy the night air. It's not every day you set sail on a voyage across the Atlantic Ocean.'

Sam smiled politely and rose to his feet. He had no great love for the ocean. Fort Lauderdale was one of the busiest stations in the service. They'd performed over a thousand boardings the previous year and Sam never worked less than a seventy-hour week. The Coast Guard motto was *Semper Paratus* – Always Ready – and boy, did they mean it. Sam had never married. He'd never found the time, let alone the right girl. The kind of girl who would put up with a rival like the sea. Kate, he liked. But already he knew her for what she was. Someone like himself. Someone prepared to put her job ahead of any relationship. And there was no future in that for either of them. So he said goodnight and went down to his stateroom.

Kate went to the back of the bridge and stared out to sea. The ship was making good speed at almost seventeen knots, although she would hardly have noticed but for the low noise and dull vibration of the engines. The sea itself looked as calm as if they'd been sailing in one of Lauderdale's intercoastal waterways. The moon was full, as big as a soccer ball, and there was only a light warm breeze as they cruised through the night.

Kate lit a Doral and meandered barefoot around the deck.

In the moonlight you might have believed all of the boats on the ship were made of cocaine, they were so white. A poet at least might have appreciated Kent Bowen's half-baked theory. And it was easy to think of all their passengers as supernatural voyagers from some Greek myth, or maybe flying Dutchmen set to sail the seas forever.

Someone cleared his throat, and, turning towards the *Carrera*'s starboard side, she found herself facing the moonlit captain of the *Juarista*. He said, 'Lovely evening.'

'Isn't it?' Kate put out the cigarette. She never felt she looked her best when she was smoking.

'You could ask me aboard again, if you wanted to.'

'You want a beer?'

He seemed to take this as a yes, for the next moment he was leaping athletically from his bridge to hers.

'Oh,' she said, a little nervous of him. 'Here you are. Well, well.'

'Well, it's a marvellous night for a moondance.'

To Kate's surprise Dave put his arm around her waist, picked up her slightly reluctant right hand in his left, and began to dance with her, all the while quietly singing his favorite Van Morrison song, smiling when their eyes met and without a trace of shyness, as if he serenaded a girl like this every night.

At the end of the song, when she thought he would surely kiss her, he released her hand and stepped back.

Kate let out her breath and said, 'That was nice.' She was a little shocked to hear herself add, 'I could listen to that all night.' She turned away so that he couldn't see her grimace with embarrassment. 'I'll get you that beer.'

'No,' he said. 'Really I'm OK. I don't need a beer.' He smiled. 'I was thinking. How about you go to the movies with me tonight? *The Third Man*'s playing at the *Juarista*. It's a little movie theater somewhere off the Bahamas.'

'I know it,' she said. 'It's right by the *Carrera*.'

'Afterwards, we could check out a cocktail bar I know

nearby. The barman there makes these really excellent Margaritas.'

Kate frowned, wondering why she should suddenly be reminded of the Pier Top at the Hyatt in Fort Lauderdale.

Dave went on: 'Then, if you've still got the energy, we could go dancing.'

'I'm not much of a dancer,' admitted Kate. Didn't Howard always say so? I've seen a book of random numbers with more rhythm than you have, Kate, he had told her.

'Sure you are,' he said. 'You know all the moves.'

'I think that's you you're describing.'

'Oh, you mean moves like in chess.'

She nodded.

'As in a gambit?'

'Mister Gary Kasparov,' she said.

'Could be,' he allowed. 'Only a gambit involves some kind of sacrifice.'

'So what have you got to lose?'

Dave said, 'I had the naive idea of simply expressing my feelings as they occurred. Will that do?'

'Sure. But maybe we'd better skip the movie. We might disturb the other patrons.'

'OK, but how about that Margarita?'

'If you think it'll help with that naive idea of yours. Just the one though, and remember this. One: I'm driving home. And two: I like to lick the salt off my own lips.'

Dave helped her to cross to his boat and, while Kate cast her eye over the salon, he stepped downstairs to make sure that Al was fast asleep. The first decent girl he'd met in five years, the last thing he needed was Al sticking his nose in. Behind the polished cedarwood door, the TV was still on, but Al was snoring loudly. Dave went back up to the salon to fix the drinks.

'Al's asleep,' said Dave. 'He won't disturb us.'

'Tell me about Al.'

Dave said, 'I guess you could say that Al's pretty much the

guy next door. That is if you happen to live next to a zoo, or a pig farm. But he's useful to have around, y'know?'

Kate laughed. She was looking at the mock-glass aquarium by Lalique that surrounded the sofa and thinking that the boat's interior was a lot less obviously masculine than she had imagined. Quite apart from the glass there were the scatter-cushions on the sofa. She had never known a man to possess cushions aboard a sport-fisher.

'Nice interior,' she pronounced politely.

'It's OK,' he allowed. 'A little fussy. I'm not sure that the glass works. So I'm thinking of a refit in the winter.' He handed Kate her Margarita. 'Something more practical, perhaps.'

She sipped her drink. 'Mmmm. Just right.'

'That's the way I like them.'

'A perfectionist.'

'That would certainly explain why I'm attracted to you.'

'Flattery's my favorite compliment.'

'I'd have thought you were used to it by now.'

'Not really. My ex-husband was a little stingy with his good opinions. He made up for it with his bad ones, though.'

'The ex part sounds good.'

'He's well out of my life,' she lied. 'Short on compliments, but he'd always take his hat off to a pretty woman. Only trouble was, it never stopped at just his hat.'

'Philanderer, huh?'

'Like his name was Phil, and er . . . he came from er . . . Philadelphia.'

Dave grinned. 'Who writes your dialogue?' he said. 'I love the way you talk.'

'Little guy, with a battered Remington, upstairs in my head, looks a bit like William Holden.'

'William Holden. He used to be big.'

'He is still big,' declared Kate, with mock solemnity. 'It's his arteries that got small.' She was pleased that he liked the way she talked. Howard had never cared for Kate's wit. She was always too quick for him and he had hated that. Sometimes she was too quick even for herself, saying things, funny things she would later regret. If her mouth had been a gun she'd have been the Sundance Kid. But in her own opinion it wasn't that Howard had lacked wit or intelligence, merely that he took himself too seriously.

'It's good that you and I share a sense of humor,' she had once told him. 'The only trouble is that I've got 95 per cent of it.'

There was certainly nothing wrong with David's sense of humor. Kate was pretty keen on the way he talked too. She said, 'You're not so badly off yourself. After all, you've got Van Morrison on your case. I always liked Van the Man. Where are you from, Van?'

Dave smiled and looked away for a moment. 'It doesn't matter,' he said. 'What matters most is where you're going and how you get there.'

'Uh-huh. So you're from Miami,' Kate said.

Dave laughed.

'People are always coy about being from Miami,' she explained.

'You're right,' he said. 'It's like saying you were born in a K-Mart.'

'You've lost most of your accent,' she observed.

Ever since he'd started learning Russian Dave had been trying to improve the way he spoke English too. To use conjunctions and prepositions. Except when he spoke to Al. It hardly seemed to matter the way he spoke to Al. Dave said, 'I didn't lose it. I wiped it off my shoe.'

'Self-improver, huh?'

'Isn't everyone? What about you? Where are you from? Or are you coy too?'

Kate said, 'Me and coy never got along that well. Him and his sister meek? I never liked them.'

'So you don't believe that the meek shall inherit the earth?'

'If they do it'll be because they had a good lawyer. Actually, I'm from the Space Coast. It sounds better than saying I'm from Titusville, doesn't it? If Miami's a K-Mart then I don't know what that makes T'ville.' She considered the matter for a moment and then said, 'A local church thrift shop, probably. No, the only good thing about T'ville was the view of the rocket assembly building twenty miles away. I kind of grew up with the space program. When I was a kid I wanted to be an astronaut. To be the first American woman on the moon.' She shrugged, smiling brightly. 'And now I crew luxury yachts.' She finished her drink and licked her lips. 'A logical career move.'

Dave said, 'Do you want some more? I made a whole pitcher, in case you changed your mind about having just the one.'

'A man who knows female psychology.' She handed him her glass. 'Shall we add that to your list of accomplishments?'

Dave took the glasses, salted the rims and then refilled them to the brim.

'Who's counting?' he said.

She waited until Dave sat down again, looked him straight in his big brown eyes and answered him with a frankness she found almost exhilarating. 'I am.' Then she raised her glass before he could get too close, wanting to control this for as long as possible. 'Well, that's how I come to be the captain of a yacht. How do you come to be an owner? I mean this is a pretty expensive boat.'

'I guess I know what I like,' said Dave, with what he hoped sounded like evasive modesty. 'And then, if I can, I go and get it.'

'Do you go after everything you like?'

'No. Not everything. But it's the way I'd pick out a woman.'

'You make it sound like choosing a necktie.'

'Choosing a necktie is a serious business,' said Dave. 'It can be hanging around your neck for up to twelve hours a day.'

'Twelve hours a day? Sounds like you're in something that's high pressure. Exactly what do you do for a living?'

'Exactly?' Dave grinned. 'A bit of this, a bit of that.'

'That sounds like a really nice job. Which of them pays better?'

'Generally, that.'

'That's what I thought.'

'I work in the South East Financial Center, on Biscayne Boulevard.'

'Sure. The tallest building in Florida.'

'It has to be, for all the stories I have to tell my clients.'

'So you're a practiced liar, is that what you're telling me?'

'Not practiced. Perfect.'

Kate smiled. 'You must be doing all right.'

Dave looked noncommittal.

Kate said, 'I mean, we've already established that this isn't exactly the Sloop John B. A boat like this must cost the best part of three million. That's a lot of tall stories. Even for someone in the Financial Center.'

He put down his glass and said, 'What would you do if you had three million dollars?'

'Is this *Indecent Proposal*?'

'I said, three million.'

'Well, naturally there'd be some change.'

Dave slid along the sofa and put his arm around her shoulders. He said, 'Where are we on the King's Gambit?'

And then he kissed her.

You could tell a lot about a man by the way he kissed you, thought Kate. Sometimes you could tell what he'd had for dinner. But mostly you could tell right away if you wanted to go to bed with him. Kate knew pretty much as soon as he pressed his mouth to hers that she wanted to have it pressed to other parts of her body as well. When eventually he drew back to look for her reaction, she said, 'I think it has probably been accepted. Only the White Queen is badly placed here. She ought to move if she's to avoid mate.'

Kate put her Margarita down on the coffee table, slid a hand around the back of his neck and pulled his mouth back to hers, as if she was already addicted to its narcotic effect. Dreamily she closed her eyes and gave herself up to the acute intoxication of his lips, which were still flecked with crystalline salt from his glass. The last man who had kissed her had been Nick Hemmings, the British liaison officer. A nice guy but not much of a kisser. And before that Howard, of course, who kissed like a clam. But this – this was a real Schedule II buzz: high abuse potential. The kind of $200 an ounce kiss that felt like she was vacuuming it up through her dilating nostrils and finding it, seconds later, tingling in her toes.

'Mmmm,' she said, deliciously, and brushed his warm cheek and hot ear with her glowing lips. 'You could cut that feeling with a credit card.'

'Have you ever felt really wide awake and all you wanted to do was go straight to bed?'

'I've never done anything straight,' said Kate, revelling in the new role she was creating for herself. Barbara Stanwyck. Lauren Bacall. Bette Davis. She pushed Dave gently away. 'If I had, I'd have become an astronaut. Still, as rocket rides go this has been quite fast enough. Just look at me. Breathless.' She sat up and collected her near-empty glass off the table. 'Running low on fuel and oxygen. I think I'd better get back to the mother ship.'

Dave picked up a cushion and placed it on his lap. He said, 'That's probably a good idea.' He finished his Margarita, waiting for Kate to show some more obvious signs of wanting to leave. Like standing up.

When she stayed put on the sofa he helped himself to one of her cigarettes while he thought of appropriate lines of poetry. There was some Andrew Marvell that fitted the situation very well, only he'd relied on other people's words too much already. It was time to be himself. Or as much of himself as he could ever reveal to her, given what he was planning. So he said simply, 'You know, for a ship's captain, you're a pretty nice girl.'

'It's not a condition of the job that you have to look

like Charles Laughton and walk around the deck carrying a rope's end.'

'Al makes Charles Laughton look like Cary Grant.'

'It's probably just as well he does,' suggested Kate. 'Think how embarrassed you'd both be if this was him sitting here now.'

The obscenity of that picture made Dave laugh out loud. He said, 'It would make it easier to say goodnight.'

'You know, David, for a millionaire, you give up real easy.'

'And I thought I was demonstrating an admirable restraint.'

'Your admirable restraint is nice, don't get me wrong. It makes a very welcome change. But how shall I put it? OK, as butlers go, there's too much English and not enough of Rhett. Quite obviously I'm in two minds about what to do here now. Maybe I just need a little financial center salesmanship.'

'Frankly, my dear, I don't feel up to bullshitting you. What it boils down to is that I like your stock too much to sell it short. I'd rather force the price up than down. When I buy into something it's not because I'm after a quick killing, but because I believe in the company. You should only sell when you're sure of that yourself. A deal's only a good deal if both parties think so.'

'I love it when you talk that way,' said Kate. 'It makes me feel like Bell Atlantic.' She kissed him and stood up. 'I'll be waiting for your offer, Rhett. You'll know where to find me. You just look out to sea in the morning and then turn around.'

'Want me to walk you home?'

'That's OK, I brought my sea-legs with me.'

'So I noticed. As a matter of fact I've been noticing them all evening. They look good on you. Like one's called Cyd and the other's called Charisse. They make a pretty good duo.'

'And contrary to whatever impression I may have given you, Dave, they're seldom seen apart.'

'I didn't doubt it,' said Dave, escorting her toward the stern of the yacht. 'You know Kate, this wasn't, isn't, just a casual flirtation. I meant a lot of what I said. That's not something that happens to me very often, believe me.'

'And if I told you I already had the same feeling?' She stopped his mouth with another kiss, and then added, 'We've got ten days to find out if this means anything more important than just human biology.'

Dave frowned, momentarily at a loss. He said, 'Ten days?'

Kate said, 'That's how long we've got on this floating tin of sardines until we get to Mallorca, isn't it?'

'Oh sure,' said Dave, whose mental clock was only set for a five-day voyage.

Kate said, 'You'll let me know if you plan to get off early, won't you, David? Only I'd hate to wake up in the morning and find you'd checked out.'

Dave forced a smile. 'Where can I go? There's only the moon and stars.'

'You know the night's magic, Van the Man. You said so yourself. Remember?'

CHAPTER FIFTEEN

'Kinda late when you came back on board last night, wasn't it Kate?'

'Kent,' she protested. 'You sound just like my father. Besides, I'm surprised you noticed after the amount of alcohol you put away yesterday.'

They were in the galley, Bowen seated behind the L-shaped dinette, Kate standing behind the inlaid faux-granite counter pouring boiling water on top of some Folger's Crystals. Down the portside companionway, nearby, they could hear the sound of Sam Brockman singing in his shower.

Bowen said, 'Well, here's the thing: what with the play-off on TV and the luxury of this boat, and setting out on this voyage, and because I was in your attractive company, Kate, and because there really wasn't much else to do yesterday except relax, I guess I did drink a little more than I should have done. But you certainly wouldn't have noticed it affecting my ability to do the job.'

'I wouldn't have seen that, no,' she admitted. Adding, under her breath, 'Mostly I try not to notice you and your abilities at all.'

'What's that?'

Kate shook her head. 'So what's your problem with my time-keeping, sir?'

'I was just wondering what it was that kept you up so late?'

Kate saw no point in denying where she had been. Very little had actually happened. Unless you counted a small trip before maybe falling head over heels in love. Certainly nothing had happened in the bed department. She shrugged and said, 'The guy on the next boat invited me over for a drink, that's all. He makes a pretty good Margarita.'

'I'm interested to hear it. Margarita's my favorite cocktail. And would this be the same guy who came over here for a drink yesterday afternoon?'

'The same guy.'

Bowen looked thoughtful.

'Something wrong with that?' asked Kate.

'He's certainly a good-looking fellow,' he remarked.

Bowen started grinning at Kate in a way she found offensive. Like he was some jealous sugar-daddy or something.

'Meaning?'

He said with apparent innocence, 'Meaning, he's a good-looking guy.'

Kate placed a cup of coffee on the table in front of him and then retired behind the galley counter, just in case she felt tempted to tip the hot coffee into his lap. She watched him take a sip and almost wished that the coffee was poisoned, like Bowen's mind. At the very least she wanted to take the brim of his stupid Tilley hat and tug it down hard, over his eyes and ears, just to see if it would make any difference to the way he conducted himself.

Bowen said, 'Since he and I are to be neighbors, I guess you'd better tell me his name.'

Kate sipped her coffee and stared out of the full-width windshield, her mind wandering. Although the time was not quite ten o'clock, it was already a hot day. The Tropic of Cancer was only a hundred miles to the south. Confident of her figure, she wanted to wear a bikini for Dave's benefit; but the idea of wearing anything more revealing than a nun's habit around Bowen filled her with disgust. She was hoping to go up on the coachroof sunpad and catch some rays while listening in to the bug that had been planted aboard the *Britannia* during loading by one of the Port Everglade stevedores. The trouble was, a single device had not proven to be enough and Kate was going to have to place another on Rocky's boat herself. She was still undecided about her costume for the day.

Bowen kept on grinning through Kate's obdurate silence. 'He does have a name, doesn't he? The captain of the *Juarista*?'

'His name is David Dulanotov and he's not the captain, he's the owner,' Kate said quickly. Almost immediately she regretted her alacrity. Telling Bowen anything was as good as telling him too much, for it was plain he was jealous.

'The owner, eh? Same as me.' Bowen allowed the grin to become his irritating chuckle. 'I should have known. As soon as I saw him, I felt he and I had something in common.' He drank some more coffee. 'Peer recognizing peer. You know the kind of thing. And you know boats. So tell me, Kate, how much do you think a boat like the *Juarista* would cost?'

Kate was uncertain if she should leave him in impotent ignorance or tell him and make him feel small. Finally she couldn't resist rubbing his nose up against Dave's obvious wealth. She said, 'I don't know. Maybe three million dollars?'

'Three million bucks. Jesus, he must be worth a bundle.'

'It's hardly the biggest boat on the ship, Kent. Rocky's boat has twenty or thirty feet on David's.'

'David?' Bowen smiled. 'You know how long it would take me to get that kind of money together? Maybe fifty years.'

'Don't tell me, tell your Congressman.'

'And if that's what he spends on a goddamn boat, can you imagine what kind of house he lives in?'

Kate found she could imagine all kinds of things about David Dulanotov and most of them involved her being naked.

'What are you? A real estate agent?'

'I mean, you don't spend more on the boat than you do on the house. It stands to reason the guy's house has got to be three or four times as much as his boat. It's got to be a seven or eight million dollar place, he's got. Imagine that. Jesus.'

Kate sighed and looked into her coffee cup.

'What's he do for a living? Young fellow like that. Rob banks? Smuggle cocaine?'

'I see there's nothing wrong with your imagination. As far as I know he works in the Financial Center on Biscayne Boulevard. Commodities or something.'

'That's as good as robbing a bank. Better. Those guys are harder to catch when they get up to something. Fraud, insider dealing, shit like that.'

'What are you? The Securities and Exchange Commission? Kent, you haven't the first idea what you're talking about. You don't even know the guy.'

'I know the type,' insisted Bowen. 'Maybe better than you think. Maybe better than you.'

Exasperated, Kate tossed the rest of her coffee into the sink.

'It's not every day we rub shoulders with multi-millionaires, Kate. It's natural we should feel curious about these people. That we should be dazzled by them and their wealth.'

'Is that a personal observation? What is this?'

'I just want you to be careful, that's all. We've got a job to do here. Don't get distracted by anything. Don't get your head turned by anyone. By this guy, for instance.'

'You know what this is? This is connected to something else,' said Kate. 'Which is that you feel uncomfortable on a personal level with me talking to other men. I think you're jealous.'

'Me, jealous? That's ridiculous.'

'I don't think so.'

'I just don't want you to get hurt. I don't want you to screw things up for yourself, or for this whole operation.'

Kate smiled bitterly. 'And I suppose the way you were conducting yourself with the captain of the *Jade* last night somehow evades the category of foolish, does it?'

'Look Kate, I'm a little older . . .'

'That's something we can agree on anyway. Better not push your luck and try wiser, OK?'

'I know where to draw the line.'

'Don't you mean spin a line? You were coming onto Rachel Dana like you owned Kansas.'

'Now wait a minute — '

'No, you wait a goddamn minute. You're trying to make me feel guilty. To wrong-foot me about this. Well you can save your shoes. I don't feel guilty for anybody. And don't lecture me about keeping my mind on the job, *sir*. Keeping my mind on the job cost me a husband. Did you ever lose a marriage because of your work? It has its depressing moments. One of the things that gets you through to the other side is the idea that your job means something. That it's important. That doing it makes a difference. So don't lecture me about my job. You can leave that job to my husband's divorce lawyer. Sir.'

Kate walked swiftly out of the galley. A minute or so later Bowen saw her going along the high side of the ship and stopping to speak to the owner of the *Juarista*. Bowen finished his coffee and then went up to the flybridge. He sat down in one of the pilot's chairs, switched on the digital scrambler, and picked up the radio handset.

'This is turkey in the hay calling turkey in the straw. This is turkey in the hay calling turkey in the straw. Are you receiving me? Over.'

There followed a short pause filled with the noise of static and then Bowen heard the voice of the USS *Galveston*'s duty radio man.

'Turkey in the hay, this is turkey in the straw, receiving you. Are you secure? Over.'

'Turkey in the hay, all secure. I want you to relay a message back to FBI headquarters in Washington. Have the Records Division run a check on a David Dulanotov. That's D-U-L-A-N-O-T-O-V. Also other permutations of that name. Spelling was never my forte. In addition, I'd like to have them check on a boat called the *Juarista*. That's J-U-A-R-I-S-T-A. Originally registered in San Diego, California. Everything and anything. Oh yeah, one more thing. All of this information is to be

given up by you only on my specific request. Me. ASAC
Kent Bowen. It is to be withheld unless specifically asked for.
Got that? Over.'

'Turkey in the hay, this is turkey in the straw. We copy.
Over.'

'This is turkey in the hay, over and out.'

Bowen turned off the radio and leaned back in the fine
leather chair. He was quite impressed that Kate could make
sense of all these computer screens. Several times he'd watched
her run various troubleshooting sequences – that's what she'd
called them anyway – and still he had no idea what she'd
been doing. Maybe she did know a lot about boats, but
he knew about investigation and all things forensic. Being
inquisitive, finding out about people, knowing exactly who
you were dealing with – all of that helped keep you ahead
in the game. Bowen believed that most rich people usually
had something to hide. Along the lines of the old saying that
behind every great fortune was a great crime. It would be
interesting to see what David Dulanotov's secret was, and
what Kate's reaction would be when eventually he got to tell
her all about it.

'The boat at the stern of the ship, the one we're going to
steal and use as our getaway, it's called the *Britannia*,' Dave
told Al.

They were sitting on the double bed in Al's stateroom. With
no windows or portholes, it was the most secure place on the
Juarista. And since Al had never bothered to change his sheets
since Costa Rica, it was also the most malodorous.

'It's not as fast as this boat, but looking at her I'd say she
can do twenty-five knots, no problem. She's got twin bow
thrusters, so there won't be any difficulty maneuvering her
out to sea. Power's not going to be a problem either. I've
been watching them. She's got more solar panels than a
fuckin' space station, and the captain – who, incidentally,
looks just like Gilbert Roland – he keeps the engines turned

over. The only outstanding question I have about her is how much fuel she has on board.'

Al frowned. 'Who the fuck is Gilbert Roland?'

'Played a lot of Mexicans in movies.' Dave shook his head as Al's face remained a blank. 'It doesn't matter.'

'And what about the money?'

'What about it?'

'What I mean, motherfucker, is that you don't know how much fuel there is on this other boat, so maybe you don't really have a fuckin' clue about how much money there is either.'

'That's a complete *non sequitur*,' said Dave. 'Your pain-in-the-ass conclusion does not follow from the premises you stated. Believe me. It's there.'

'If you were Jesus Christ and you swore on the holes in your hands and the wound in your side the money was there, I'd still say, what makes you so fuckin' sure?'

'Ye of little faith. Will you forget about the money? The money's where it's supposed to be. Which is more than I can say of your attitude. Why can't you be more like one of those other disciples, Al? Not having seen and yet believed. Just be cool about the fuckin' money.' Dave shook his head, weary of Al's doubt. Changing the subject, he said, 'Did you find somewhere to lock everyone up?'

Al said, sullenly, 'I think so. I went right over the accommodation block and the best area seems to be on the lower deck. There's an engineer's workshop and end storeroom alongside the engine room. Apart from some tools and shit, place is more or less empty. Door's good too. Solid steel, outside bolt. If we left the tools, they could probably hammer their way out in a few hours. By that time we'll be long gone, right?'

'With the wind.'

Al bent down and drew a baseball kit bag toward him, still wet-looking and smelling bad after several days in the fish-box. He said, 'Me and you, Scarlett, it's about time we got to meet our partners in crime. All of them combat veterans. And the first to do the boogie is the nine-mill Heckler & Koch, M5 submachine gun. Weighs no more than a newborn baby, and it's just as fuckin' loud. Fires thirty rounds. Effective range around 100 meters.' He handed over the weapon and showed Dave how to eject the magazine.

'It's slung on a length of rubber tube, SEAL style, in case we have to take a bath with it. Fitted with waterproof laser sights, takes a nine-volt battery for up to thirty hours of continuous play. You'd have to be Stevie Wonder not to hit the target with this mother. Guaranteed accuracy or your money back.'

Al reached into the bag and came up with a pistol.

'Next to do the boogie is the Heckler & Koch forty-five ACP Special operations handgun. Brand loyalty's a big thing with me, in case you hadn't noticed. I always eat the same fuckin' breakfast cereal and I always use the same gun. Two most important things in your day are a good start – that means a good breakfast – and a good gun. There's enough uncertainty in the world already without trusting new shit that you haven't used before.'

'Pretty good *Weltanschauung*,' said Dave.

Ignoring him, Al said, 'And with this pistol, believe me, you got the whole world in your hands. This is the Big John Cannon of handguns. Detachable sound suppresser 'cos we're gonna' be working at night and we don't want to wake folks up before we're ready. Laser aiming module, like before. Matter of fact, same as they used on the F-14 fighters in Desert Storm. You could hit Baghdad with this artillery. Fires eight shots. Guaranteed take down. But there's a heavy recoil. So we'll wear these weightlifters' gloves. Not because we wanna look like a couple of S&M faggots but because they let you keep a tight grip.'

The last weapon out of the bag was a shotgun.

'Last, but by no means least to boogie on down is your pump action twelve-gauge shotgun. Mossberg Model 835. Cut back to eighteen inches, same as my dick. I've taken off the magazine plug and replaced the front bead. Looks pretty mean, doesn't it?' Al chuckled. 'Well, this'll sweep the fuckin' hall for ya, and no mistake. You'll only have to fire this mother once and your problems are solved. When we're outside and on the boats I recommend you stick to the submachine gun and your pistol. Dealing with the ship's crew, the shotgun will be the most effective friendly persuasion.' Al worked the slide, and pulled the trigger on the empty chamber. 'Not for nothing is this called a riot gun. And with these three weapons, we are loaded with fuckin' opportunities.

'But in case we have to play anyone with a similar hand to our own, we'll be wearing Kevlar. Tested at the Aberdeen Proving Grounds by the US Government Edgewood Arsenal, this body armor will stop the ACP and the nine-mill, but maybe not the twelve at close range. This is what you want to be wearing when you attend your next local meeting of the Branch Davidians. The truth hurts, but not if you're wearing Kevin Costner.'

Next to the folded white torso of the body armor, Al laid a walkie-talkie. He said, 'And of course, our communications devices, in case love tries to tear us apart.' Al waved his hand at the guns and equipment that were now spread on the bed like Christmas presents. 'At the risk of sounding like Gunny Sergeant Highway, get to know this shit. Become familiar with it. Could be it'll save your life. More importantly, you might save mine. Oh yeah. One more thing. What I call the *Alias Smith and Jones* factor.'

Dave nodded and said, 'Starring Pete Duel and Ben Murphy.'

'All the trains and banks they robbed, they never shot anyone? Bullshit. Nobody gives up a fuckin' payroll without someone gettin' shot. Remember that. Someone gets in your way and you gotta grease the fucker, then you'd better fuckin' do it or it could be your ass that's down. You wanna be very popular with everyone but the railroads and the banks? Then you'd better try stand-up comedy instead of robbery. You wanna take down a score like this one, then you'd better be ready to drop some fuckin' brass. And lots of it. You understand? It's survival of the fittest. *Capisce?*'

Dave grinned back at him. He said, 'All that testosterone, Al. You wanna hear yourself. Like a goddamn pit-bull terrier. Survival of the fittest? That was Charles Darwin's theory. It was an explanation of natural selection and evolution and shit like that. When he said survival of the fittest he didn't mean those who were prepared to be the baddest motherfuckers would survive. Fittest doesn't mean bad, Al. It doesn't mean anything except what it says: most likely to survive. Fact is that old Darwin thought that being predisposed toward co-operation might well be adaptive and would thus be selected for.

'The way I look at it, Al, that's what we're after. A little co-operation. We wave our guns and make some noise, sure. But let's do this cleverly. In a social way. A certain amount of aggression may well be called for, sure. It may confer some benefits. But it also has its costs. Most animals have got built-in codes for conflict that set limits to the violence they do to each other. A lot of it is just bluff. Threat displays n'shit like that. To hear you Al, you sound like you actually want to kill somebody. And what you've got to understand is that if we use our brains we probably won't have to use our guns. Your *Alias Smith and Jones* example is all wrong, man. The point was not that they were too yellow or too dumb to shoot anyone, but that they planned their robberies with sufficient thought and style, and then kept their cool so as they didn't need to shoot people.'

Al laughed scornfully. 'And you believe that?'

'Al, it's your example, not mine. The question's kind of academic, on account of how it wasn't meant to be true in the first place.'

'Sure it was true,' insisted Al. 'It was history. Said so right at the beginning of the show. "Hannibal Hayes and Kid Curry, the two most wanted outlaws in the history of the west." Sure it was true. The only part that wasn't true was the part how they never shot anyone. They just did that to make sure they picked up the family audience.'

'Al, it was a fictional scenario, based only very loosely on two historical characters.' Dave checked himself from saying more. What did he know? What did he care? What the fuck did it matter? He was debating a point with someone whose idea of an effective argument was a bigger handgun than the next guy.

Al said, 'You know your trouble? You read way too much. Every time you open your mouth some other guy's thoughts come out. Like you were a vent's dummy or something.' He lifted the empty .45 automatic, pointed it at Dave's reflection in the large mirror behind his bed, and pulled the trigger harmlessly. He said, 'I've said it before and I'll say it again, it beats me how you did all that time.'

Dave said, 'Whatever I did, Al, I did for you and for your boss. Try and remember that sometime.'

Al winked unpleasantly.

'Hey, it's always on my mind.'

Dave carried his gear back to his own stateroom, put it in the drawer underneath his bed and then stretched out.

The five years he'd done in Homestead were of little consequence to Al, but Dave knew the experience would be on his own mind for the rest of his natural. He thought about the time and then he thought about the man Tony Nudelli had shot, and the ramifications that had ensued. For Dave and Dave's fucked-up family. There was no way Naked Tony was going to get away with what had happened. He had some payback coming.

But mostly he thought about Kate and what had happened the night before. Already she was on his mind in a way he'd hardly have thought possible on the strength of one day's acquaintance. First thing that morning his thoughts had been about her. It's the girls who resist that you most want to kiss. He could not recall feeling this way about a girl in years and it seemed unthinkable that in four or five days' time he might sail off into the sunrise and simply never see her again. What made it even more awkward was the certainty that she felt the same way about him. With the only difference being that she wasn't expecting him to turn thief and take off with millions of dollars of drug money. There could be no question of not going through with the caper. Even if he'd had second thoughts there was still Al to consider. But maybe there was a third possibility. How much did the captain of a small yacht make anyway? Thirty, forty thousand dollars a year? What was that next to some real money? She talked like she'd be willing at least to entertain the proposition. If there was one thing Dave liked it was a good-looking girl with lip. Of course, the timing would be critical. He could hardly tell her what he was going to do before he had done it. Suppose she objected and then gave the game away? No, he wasn't quite sure how, but he would have to check her out and make sure of her in some other way, up front. He would have to devise a fictional scenario or pose, in order to test her.

After a while Dave went up on deck, and looked toward the *Carrera*. There were signs that someone had been sunbathing on the roof but Kate was nowhere in sight. Al was up on the side of the *Duke*, talking to the *Jade*'s captain and grinning wolfishly. Seeing Dave, he shouted down.

'Hey boss, we just got ourselves invited to a cocktail party.'

'That's nice,' said Dave, climbing up onto the wall alongside them. 'Thanks a lot, Captain Dana.'

She said, 'Eight o'clock. Everyone's invited. And please, it's Rachel. With so many captains around this ship is starting to look a little top heavy.'

Dave saw Al glance surreptitiously at Rachel's tits. Al's thoughts were an open book to Dave; certainly where they concerned the top-heavy Rachel Dana.

Dave said, 'Dana. That's a good name for the captain of an American boat. Any relation?'

'As a matter of fact he was a distant ancestor of mine,' confirmed Rachel.

Al bit his lip and said, 'Who?'

'A famous writer,' Dave said, teasing him. 'R.H. Dana.'

Al rolled his eyes and was about to make another disparaging comment about books when it suddenly dawned on him that Dave was supposed to be his boss, and this Dana guy was a writer who was related to Rachel.

'He wrote one of the best books ever about the sea,' said Dave. '*Two Years before the Mast*. But you wouldn't be interested, Al. Not being much of a reader n'all.'

'Says who?'

'I have a copy in my cabin, if you'd like to borrow it,' said Rachel.

'I'd love to read it,' insisted Al.

'Maybe when you've finished reading it, you can tell Rachel what you think,' said Dave. 'Give her your literary critique.'

'Yeah, sure. Why not?'

Rachel smiled pleasantly and ushering Al onto the *Jade*, said, 'Well then let's go and get it, shall we?'

Later that same day, Dave walked round to the port side of the ship to check on his three target vessels.

Up on the roof of *Baby Doc*, one of the crewmen, with more tattoos than a Maori Hell's Angel, had the bell cover off the Tracvision antenna and was attaching a wire to the satellite dish.

'Afternoon,' said Dave.

'So I was led to believe,' said the guy, not even looking round.

'You got a problem there? Maybe I can help.'

The guy looked around slowly with a who-the-fuck-are-you-to-be-offering-me-advice expression on his smug, tough face. After a moment or two, he finished chewing the inside of his lip and said, 'We're not getting a TV signal.'

Dave smiled to himself, marking the guy down as someone with little experience of boats. He said, 'Too far away.'

'From the satellite?' The guy sounded incredulous.

'Hell no,' said Dave. 'From the coast. That thing only works up to the 200-mile limit. After that it's just white noise and space, the final frontier.'

'No kidding?'

'No kidding. Leastways until you get to Europe. But their TV's shit so don't hold your breath.'

'Shit,' said the guy. 'What are we gonna do?'

'Gotta VCR?'

'Yeah, but no tapes.'

'Not a problem.' Dave pointed toward the bow of the *Duke*. 'See that big boat up front? The 160-footer. That's the *Jade*. She's owned by Jade Films. They've got plenty of videos for loan. That is, if you like porno.'

'Does Sinatra like spaghetti?'

'Well then you're in luck. They've got a video library like a Triple X on Times Square.'

Dave was only reporting what Al had said after collecting Rachel's copy of *Two Years before the Mast*. His eyes had been out on stalks.

'As a matter of fact they're having a cocktail party tonight, at eight. Open invitation. Surprised you haven't heard about it.'

'Oh, we haven't been very sociable so far. Some chick came around earlier but we were all still in bed. Had a few drinks ourselves last night.' He grinned ruefully. 'More than a few.' The guy turned a little friendlier. 'Hey, you wanna drink?'

'Sure. Why not?'

'Then step aboard, my friend. Step aboard the *Baby Doc*.'

This was better than Dave could have hoped for. He leaped

onto the rooftop alongside the tattooed guy and followed him down to the deck. He said, '*Baby Doc*. What was this, the Duvalier family yacht or something?'

'Nope. Guy who owns her runs some kind of fertility clinic in Geneva. Makes a shitload of money out of women who can't have any babies. And other gynecological odds and ends. I don't think he'd ever heard of the Duvalier family or the Tonton Macoutes. Fact is I don't think he even knew that Haiti existed. Not until he started to sail it around the Caribbean.' The guy laughed and handed Dave a cold Bud. 'Found out soon enough then, of course. He's planning to refurbish her in Europe. Gonna rename her at the same time, I think. If he's got any sense. Dumb fucker.'

Dave grinned and looked around the shabby interior, wondering how much money might be concealed inside the worn leather furniture. Two big sofas and two matching easy chairs. The rest of the lounge looked suitably clinical. Like a rest room for the guys on *E.R.* They'd worked the story well enough and certainly picked the right boat. The guy, who told Dave his name was Keach, hadn't exaggerated. A complete refurbishment was what the *Baby Doc* needed. And ripping out the interior furnishings would cause no great expense.

Dave took his beer and dropped onto the sofa, hoping he might witness some discomfort under his ass or on Keach's face. The sofa felt firm enough. Maybe too firm at that. More like an office chair than a comfortable sofa. The stitching on the old leather looked a little too pristine. Like it was new. As if someone had stitched something up inside the leather. Money. Meanwhile Keach's face, with its puffy eyes – like he'd maybe taken a few punches in his time – and lugubrious mouth stayed cool.

Dave recognized the look. It was the same long-range, armor-piercing, full-metal-jacket stare you developed when you were in the joint. The don't-mess-with-my-shit-or-I'll-fucking-kill-you kind of look. So Keach was an ex-con, just like himself. Dave wondered if the guy maybe got the same smell off him.

'C'mon,' Keach said coolly. 'Let's go outside. You can point out your own boat.'

Dave stayed on the *Baby Doc* for another fifteen minutes meeting one of the other crewmen, a heavy-set black guy wearing a buzz haircut in a Keith Haring design and the kind of granite face that looked like he'd had it custom-made on Easter Island. Catching sight of his own reflection in the two watchtower gun-barrels of the black's sunglasses, Dave thought that he himself looked like a fairly regular guy. Hardly the kind of guy who had a gun for all seasons underneath his bed. He looked like just the kind of guy that Kate might take on.

Taking on these guys aboard the *Baby Doc* looked like a rather more difficult proposition.

On his way back to the *Juarista*, Dave found his progress along the narrow gangway impeded by a solitary figure staring out to sea. As Dave excused himself, squeezing past the guy, he realized that he knew the face.

'Hey,' he said. 'Aren't you Calgary Stanford? The movie actor?'

'Yes, I am.' Stanford's tone was sad, almost as if being Calgary Stanford was a little too much to bear. Or maybe it was the role he was reported to be planning. Calgary Stanford was the same movie actor who had attended the execution of Benford Halls on the day that Dave had been released from Homestead. Dave was familiar with stories in *Première* about the methodical prep work some movie actors did to get into character. On the whole he thought it was right that they should have to do some work, maybe even endure some hardship in return for the money they got paid. But he drew the line at attending a guy's execution and wondered if, before the voyage was out, there might not be some way of getting even with the actor on the executed man's behalf.

Dave said, '*The Cruel Sea*, huh?' When Stanford looked blank, Dave explained it was a book.

'I think I saw the movie. British movie, right?'

Dave nodded, wondering if guys in prison were the only people who read books any more. 'As a matter of fact, I thought you must be watching out for the hurricane.'

'What hurricane?'

'You haven't heard? There's one coming up from the west.'

This was true. It had been on the radio just after midday. It was a long way behind them, but Dave wanted to spook the actor some.

'Jesus Christ.'

'Actually no,' said Dave. 'It's called Louisa. But Jesus'd be a pretty good name for a hurricane when you think about it. Hurricane Jesus, or Hurricane Holy Shit, or Hurricane Holy Mother of God. I've known some mean bitches in my time, good for spending your money and giving out grief, but none of them could trash a place up the way a real storm can. The way a rock group can. Hurricane Led Zeppelin. That's a better name for a hurricane. Or Hurricane Keith Moon. Boy, I'll bet that's a hurricane that could do some real damage. Not just the TV or the Rolls-Royce that ends up in the swimming pool, but the whole damn hotel.'

'They say what category this Louisa is?' asked Stanford.

'A three, I think.' Dave sniffed the air. There was a definite smell of marijuana coming off the actor's breath. The guy was a little stoned. Probably came up on deck to clear his head.

'That's not the top category,' said the actor in his laid-back LA drawl. 'But it's still dangerous. Did you know that in one day a hurricane can release as much energy as 500,000 atomic bombs?'

'What size of A-bomb do you mean?' asked Dave. 'Hiroshima, or something bigger?'

Calgary Stanford thought for a moment, blinked hard and

then said, 'I don't know. But either way it's a lot of dead people.' He started to laugh.

'You seem to know a lot about them,' observed Dave. 'Hurricanes, I mean.'

'Did a movie about a hurricane once. Piece of shit. You wouldn't have seen it. But that's the kind of trivia you tend to collect when you're getting into a role.' He paused and looked out to sea again. 'I've never been in a real hurricane. Sounds like a blast.' He laughed again.

'I have,' said Dave. 'It was pretty scary.'

'Where was that?'

It had been when he was in Homestead. Even behind several feet of reinforced concrete, Dave had thought that the place would blow down. Unfortunately it hadn't. But for days afterward the inmates were clearing up the damage. 'Just Miami,' he said.

'Where's this one, right now?'

'Over Cuba. And heading north-west. Maybe it'll blow itself out by the time it reaches us. Or maybe the ship will outrun it.'

Stanford snorted and said, 'Now if it was my boat, that might be a possibility.' He pointed to the sharp-looking flybridge motor yacht that occupied the space immediately in front of the *Britannia*. 'That's her there. The *Comanche*. British built Predator. Three 846 K engines. That's forty knots. But she still sleeps eight.'

'Nice-looking boat,' Dave admitted.

'But this ship. This ship couldn't outrun Orson Welles.'

'He was kind of quick on his toes in *The Third Man*,' Dave argued. 'Running through all those sewers in Vienna.'

Stanford blinked blearily and snorted again. 'Not quick enough, as I recall. Besides, from what I've read about that movie, Welles didn't like being down in those sewers and most of those shots were covered by a body double.' Noting the look of disappointment that momentarily clouded Dave's face, Stanford added, 'It's a very mendacious business, the movies. Nothing is ever what it seems. And nobody is ever who they're supposed to be.'

Dave dismissed his small shattered illusion and said, 'Then to that extent, I guess the movie business is just like life.'

CHAPTER SIXTEEN

Dave met Jock, the *Duke*'s electrical officer, and Niven, the second officer, on their way out of the bridge wing.

'I was going to come and check the handset on your radio, wasn't I?' admitted Jock.

'Hey, no problem,' said Dave. 'Fixed it myself. But what about this hurricane? Is it going to catch us up, do you think?'

'We're on our way down to the radio room to get the latest weather report,' said Niven. 'You're welcome to join us, sir, if you're interested.'

'Thanks, I'd like to.'

Dave followed the two men along the corridor to the radio room.

As Jock waited for a detailed weather map to be printed out on the fax machine, Niven said, 'I wouldn't worry about the storm, if I were you sir. It's my job to lay off courses and to take account of any hazards to navigation. That includes storms. If Hurricane Louisa looks like it's getting too close, we'll simply alter course and try to get out of her way.'

Niven's comment sent up a small distress signal in Dave's head about the rendezvous. 'By how much do you think we would have to alter course?' he asked.

'That all depends, sir,' said Niven.

'Storm Force Nine,' said Jock, reading the map. He tore the fax off the machine and handed it to Niven. 'Heading north-west toward the North Atlantic Plateau. Straight for us.'

'I'd better give this to the captain,' said Niven. On his way out of the radio room, he called back, 'Provided Louisa stays on course we should be able to sidestep her without much of a problem.'

Dave nodded, although he was not much reassured by this latest news.

'The second officer's right, sir,' said Jock. 'We'll probably just go a bit further south, that's all. Might put us slightly behind schedule, only you wouldn't want to be on this ship in a storm, sir. Because of the high profile, see? The *Duke*'s like a floating multi-storey car park. What's more, there's not much in the way of freeboard.'

'Freeboard?'

'In the tropical zone you expect the best weather, so you load more cargo with a consequent reduction in freeboard,' explained Jock. 'Increased freeboard increases the safety of the ship in bad weather. And vice versa. Plus, we're working on the summer loadline. That also decreases our freeboard.' Jock grinned and began to roll a cigarette. 'Ach, don't worry yourself. If we do have a problem we can always radio that submarine.'

'You really think it's there?'

Jock lit his cigarette, flicked a switch on the radio to change channels, and Dave heard the sound that he had heard before. Jock said, 'There it is. Broadcasting right now.'

Dave remembered Keach screwing around with his Tracvision antenna and wondered if the signal could have anything to do with the *Baby Doc*.

'Wait a minute,' he said. 'Before, you said you thought a sub was only a possibility. That it might be one of the boats on this ship that was broadcasting.'

'Aye sir, that was the first possibility. The sub was the second. And now that I think about it, there's a third as well.'

'What's that?'

'One of the boats on this ship is broadcasting to the submarine.' Jock sucked on the cigarette with slow precision and half swallowed his inhalation of smoke.

'You really do think it's there, don't you?' Dave repeated dumbly.

'I'm no sonar man,' said Jock. 'But there was something there on the echo sounder, last time I looked. It's not very accurate, mind. All it does is give you the depth of clear water underneath the hull. But anyone could see there should have been more water than there was on the sounder. Of course, for all I know it could have been a reef, or even a friendly whale.'

'But you don't really think that, do you, Jock?'

'No sir, I think it's a sub.'

'What about the captain? What does he think?'

'Granny?' Jock laughed. 'All he cares about is his garden and that woman on the *Jade*. Fancies his chance, by all accounts. He doesn't give a shit about any submarine.' Jock flicked ash across the radio table. 'Quite exciting when you think about it. A spy aboard the *Duke*.'

'But why?' said Dave. 'Why would anyone want to spy on this ship?'

'Ah well, that's the question, isn't it, sir? Why indeed?'

Jack Jellicoe was sunbathing in his garden. This consisted of several terracotta pots filled with lobelia and scented geraniums, which were arranged around one of the bow engine towers on top of the bridge. Lying on his sun-lounger, with a cool-box of ready-mixed pink gins by his side, and a novel by P.D. James, the captain was in his element. But he knew, as soon as he saw his second officer approaching, that something must be amiss. Niven was a competent officer and would never have disturbed him unless it was something important.

'What's up?' he barked.

Niven handed over the fax. 'Weather map, sir. I thought you ought to see it straight away.'

'Thank you Two-O.' Jellicoe scrutinized the map carefully. Niven said, 'Hurricane Louisa, sir. Following us. Thought

I'd better lay in a new course. I've marked it up on the fax, sir.'

'I see,' Jellicoe said sourly. 'The only problem with this new course is that it takes us straight along the Tropic of Cancer.'

'Yes sir. I thought if we stayed south the storm would pass by well north of us, heading toward the Azores.'

'And where do you propose that we should sail north to ourselves, when we want to head toward Gib and the Med? Which is, after all, where we are ultimately bound.'

'Well sir, just north of the Canary Islands.'

'Just north of the Canaries, eh?' Jellicoe smiled bitterly and then pointed to the two brass cannon that were pointed out to sea. 'What about those?'

'How do you mean, sir?'

'In case you'd forgotten, we stole those from the island of Lanzarote. Which, if memory serves, is one of the smaller Canary Islands. Thus placing me and my ship in rather bad odor with the local government's chief budgerigar. You see my point?'

'Yes sir.'

Jellicoe took another look at the map.

'We can't possibly go anywhere near there.'

'No sir.'

'Here's what we'll do, Two. I've seen this kind of thing before. The storm will have largely blown itself out by the time it gets to us, take my word for it. No, we'll stick to our original course. However, just to be on the safe side, tell the chief engineer to give us maximum revs. We'll try to put some distance between ourselves and Louisa. It'll probably get a bit rough, but nothing we can't handle. You know, Two, contrary to popular opinion, the best place you can be during a storm is at sea. When Hurricane Bertha struck the American coast, US Navy officers ordered their ships to sea, to save them from being thrown against the harbor walls. That should tell you something.'

'What about the ladies on the *Jade*, sir?'

'What about them?'

'Tonight's their cocktail party, sir.'

'Oh, that.' Jellicoe took another look at the weather map and shook his head. 'Should be all over by the time the sea starts to get up.'

'You know they might not be used to this kind of thing, sir. I mean it's going to get pretty rough.'

'Oh, I don't think you need worry about Captain Dana and her crew. I'm sure they've encountered a bit of squally weather in their time.'

'Yes sir, but a boat like that. They'll be fitted with stabilizers, won't they? They're not much good to them while they're aboard the *Duke*, sir. The only stabilizer on this ship is the cook's coffee.'

'That'll be all, Mister Niven. Better tell the boys to go to blues. It's going to get cooler. And tell the helmsman it's steady as she goes.'

'Aye sir.' Niven started to walk away, shaking his head. 'Steady as she goes? Fat bloody chance of that.'

'Something to add, Mister Niven?'

'No sir.'

'Then get on with it.'

Jellicoe watched his second officer retreat. Calmly he folded away his sun-lounger, then collected up his cool-box, his novel and the weather map. Heading back to his own cabin he was chuckling happily. It looked very like the supernumos were going to get a real taste of the Atlantic after all.

Kate had walked down to the stern of the ship to take a closer look at the *Britannia* and her crew, and to see if she could plant another listening device on the hull.

The captain, Nicky Vallbona, the other crewman, a guy named Webb Garwood, and Vallbona's girlfriend, Gay Gilmore, were nowhere to be seen. Kate strolled up and down the dock wall alongside the *Britannia* a couple of times, affecting a greater interest in the *Duke*'s engine towers and open stern but there was nothing to see except a lot of seagulls picking over the garbage floating in the *Duke*'s wake. The *Britannia* looked as shipshape as any other boat on the transport, and that included the *Carrera*.

Kate looked both ways and then knelt down to tie the lace of her boat shoe. The listening device was no bigger than an earplug and it was a simple matter to lean across and stick the bug to the boat's coachroof. She was already walking away, when a man's voice behind her brought her to a halt.

'Talk to me,' said the man. 'Don't just stand there. I mean, have you given any thought to having kids, for instance?'

Half expecting to see Howard standing on the dock wall behind her, Kate glanced around. There was no one in sight.

'Your biological clock,' said the voice. 'Well, it's hardly slowing down, is it honey? I mean you leave it until you're in your thirties and it becomes a lot harder to conceive, doesn't it?'

Kate realized that the voice was coming from an open window near the bow of the *Britannia*. Who needed bugs when you had open windows? Not that there was anything about this conversation that was of particular interest to the FBI. It could easily have been Howard. How often had Kate heard him utter these same remarks?

'What's it to you?' answered a woman's voice. The accent was New Zealand. This was Gay Gilmore and Nicky Vallbona talking.

'What's it to me? Honey, I kind of thought that was one of the reasons why we were going to get married. To have kids.'

'Is that right? Well you can think again, mate. The only biological clock I've got is the one that tells me when it's time to have another fuck. And it's got nothing to do with having kids. It's just that I like fucking a lot more than I do the idea of having kids.'

'What about maternal instinct?'

'What about it?'

'Every woman's got some.'

'Like hell they have.'

Kate stayed where she was, fascinated. It was like hearing actors reading dialogue she might have written for them. *Scenes from a Marriage*, or something of the kind. So far, she liked the actress playing herself.

'Listen, Nick, I've got other plans, OK? If I've got a maternal instinct then it's fulfilled by you licking my nipples and me remembering my mum's birthday.'

Kate almost applauded: she would have to remember that line.

'Motherhood is definitely not for me. I've got enough problems just looking after myself.'

Nicky moaned, 'I just don't understand a woman who doesn't want to have children.'

There was a short silence during which Kate thought about what she had in common with Gay. At least, their choice to remain childless. She wondered how much Gay knew about the drugs that were hidden in the boat's fuel tanks. She hoped nothing at all – Kate was already feeling sympathetic toward her. Enough to want to help her out when the time came to make the bust. It would be a shame if Gay had to go to prison. Nicky Vallbona's reaction, on the other hand, had been just like Howard's: unreasonable and selfish.

Gay said, 'Nicky, you haven't really thought about this. You and I. We're not the kind of people to be bringing up children. It wouldn't be right. When we get to Europe, when this is all over? We'll have lots of money. Why don't we just do what we do best? Enjoy ourselves. Have a good time. Just the two of us. No worries.'

'Yeah, OK. I guess you're right at that, honey. Shit, I'm not even sure why I mentioned it. But I'm chilled. You won't hear another word about this. I promise.'

Kate walked sadly away. Sad that her own husband couldn't

have been as accommodating on the issue of children as a drug smuggler; and sad to hear that Gay probably did know what she was involved in. Not having children would be a lot easier for Gay when she was in prison.

Sometimes the job was difficult, in ways you could never foresee. Like discovering that dope smugglers could have the same conversations about ordinary human things as any law-abiding person.

Kent Bowen had just come off the radio and received the information he had requested – some of it anyway – when the man himself came knocking at the sliding glass door of the *Carrera*'s skylounge.

Dave said, 'Hi there. Hope I'm not disturbing you?'

'Hell, no,' said Bowen, keen to meet Dave and get another look at the guy now that he knew a little more about who and what he was. 'Come on in.'

Maybe he did work at the Financial Center in Miami, they were still checking that out. But of greater interest was the revelation that before coming into the ownership of an offshore company in Grand Cayman Island, David Dulanotov's boat had been owned by a wiseguy by the name of Lou Malta, a small-time racketeer and former associate of Naked Tony Nudelli, one of the biggest hoods in Miami. It didn't prove that Dave himself was a mobster, but it was enough to be going on with. Bowen promised himself that before the voyage was out he would know everything there was to know about David Dulanotov. He was going to be right about this guy. Dulanotov was a crook.

'You have a beautiful boat,' said Dave. 'What's her displacement?'

'Come again?'

'The tonnage.'

'Forty. Forty tons.'

'Really? I'd have said she looks nearer sixty, myself.'

'You're probably right,' grinned Bowen. 'I'm just the owner.

If you want full specifications, you'd have to ask Kate. She knows everything there is to know about this boat. Me, I just enjoy having her.' Saying that gave him an idea. Maybe he could put this guy off in his own way. By just dropping a broad hint that she was already spoken for, in the form of a joke – the kind a real owner would have made. He winked at Dave. 'And the boat.'

Dave smiled thinly while Bowen got off on his own joke. Somehow he couldn't see Kate fucking this guy. 'Is Kate around?'

'Let me go and fetch her,' he said, happy to leave the skylounge before Dulanotov asked him any more questions about the boat that he couldn't answer. Even Bowen thought you could play the dumb owner too far. 'I think she's down in her room. Help yourself to a drink, if you want one.'

Dave sat down in one of the black leather wheelhouse pilot chairs, smoothing his hand over the black lacquer tops on the maple units. Right away he noticed that the touch control handset for the radio was still warm, as was the transceiver's slimline, diecast aluminium casing. It was only a few minutes since he had been in the radio room with Jock, since they had both heard the sound of another digitally scrambled broadcast from one of the boats on board the ship. Dave had no way of telling if the *Carrera*'s radio was fitted with a scrambler. All radios looked a little unusual after you'd been out of circulation for five years. But there could be no doubt, someone had been broadcasting from the radio on this boat. And if not to a submarine, then to what?

All of which begged the question. Who was Kent Bowen? And, more importantly for Dave, who was Kate Parmenter?

'Hi there.'

Dave turned around and frowned. Kate looked like she'd been crying.

'Are you OK?' he asked.

'I had something in my eye,' she explained. 'I'm fine. But I must look like I just sat through *Gone with the Wind*.'

'Kind of.' Dave grinned. 'Is your boss coming back up?'

'I don't know. He comes and goes, y'know?' Realizing Dave probably wanted to be private with her, she said, 'Tell you what. I've a mind to go and see those ceremonial cannon. The ones that Captain Jellicoe stole from whoever it was. Shall we go and take a look?'

They crossed over onto the *Juarista* and then climbed up onto the *Duke's* dock wall. Coming along the starboard side of the *Jade,* Dave said, 'The reason I stopped by was to find out if you were going to the party tonight.'

'Only if you are,' she said. 'Not that Kent would let us miss it. Ever since he found out what kind of films they make, his tongue's been hanging out. The man has a libido that's as big as his boat. Except he probably thinks a libido is something the French wash their feet in.'

Dave laughed and led the way up the gangway to the accommodations block.

'Are you and he — ?'

'Jesus, no. Whatever gave you that idea?'

'As a matter of fact, he did.'

'What? You're kidding.'

'Just a remark he made. Nothing specific. But he seemed to imply there was something going on between you.'

'That bastard. The only thing that's ever been going on between us is me putting up with all his bullshit.'

'What does he do anyway?'

'You mean when he's not being an asshole?'

Kate had given some thought to Kent Bowen's cover story. Bowen had wanted to claim he was something glamorous like a film executive, or even a writer. But Kate had managed to persuade him that it should only be something he actually knew about. Maybe she could also persuade him to throw himself overboard and save her the trouble of doing it.

'He owns a string of shops selling security and counter-surveillance merchandise. You know the kind of thing. Bugs that look like electrical plugs, and little safes that are inside a dummy can of Coke. Paranoid shit for paranoid times.'

Kate paused to light a cigarette and then followed Dave all the way forward to the bow of the boat. The sun-lounger was still there, but the cool-box and Jellicoe were gone.

'He wants to open a chain of spy stores across Europe,' she lied smoothly. 'Tech Direct. That's what the shops in the States are called. Anyway, there's this big trade fair for all kinds of electronic gadgetry in Barcelona in two or three weeks' time. Kind of every man his own James Bond. That's where we're headed, after we get to Mallorca.'

Dave nodded, asking himself if any of this might help explain why Kent Bowen had been using a digital scrambler on his radio. Meanwhile Kate thought it was time she changed the subject.

'What about you?' she asked. 'What takes you to Europe?'

'The Monaco Grand Prix,' Dave lied with equal facility. 'I like to watch motor racing. After that we're sailing to Cap D'Antibes. I've rented a house there for the summer.'

'By yourself?'

'Some friends'll probably drop by. From England.'

A gentle breeze stirred Kate's hair and Dave found himself reaching to touch it. Her hair felt like silk against his hand. There was her perfume to think about too. After Homestead, all women smelt good to Dave. But Kate smelt especially good. Like something rich and luxurious.

He said, 'You should come by, yourself. That is if you can get away from Q, Miss Moneypenny.'

'I wonder, how many other girls you've invited down there.'

'You're the first,' said Dave. 'In love's affairs, I'm a sweet beginner.'

'That I don't believe.'

'I feed on hope's uncertain dinner.'

Kate checked herself, realizing he was reciting something again.

'For me the object on life's chart is mysterious and enticing, something to think hard about, suspecting that wonders will accumulate. And so I'm sure, a kindred spirit will be joined to me by fate.'

She could hardly help but feel impressed.

'Who's that? she asked. 'Van Morrison again?'

Dave shook his head. 'It sounds better in Russian. No, it's Pushkin. Freely rendered.'

Kate smiled and said, 'I wasn't offering to pay. But it's nice. Did Pushkin find his kindred spirit?'

'Yes, but it wasn't a happy ending.'

'What happened?'

'Someone shot him. Guy called D'Anthes.'

'No gun law can stop a madman,' she shrugged. 'If, as you said, I can get away from Q, I'd love to come visit. Cap D'Antibes, huh? I guess it's very chic down there.'

'Like Valentino.'

'That's the part that worries me. Alone, in a foreign country, without even a native guide. Anything could happen.'

'Last night it almost did.'

Kate smiled and said, 'Last night? Oh, that wasn't anything at all. That was just sex. Today it feels more like a subject on *Oprah*. A whole show. How the two of us met. Or some stuff like that.'

'Don't worry,' said Dave. 'I feel the same way.'

'D'Antibes. D'Anthes. Don't worry. You're a regular red light, you know that, Van? Anyone would think you're trying to send me some kind of signal.'

'Hailing on all frequencies, Lieutenant Uhura.'

'Go ahead, Captain.'

'It sounds kind of stupid, but I'm falling in love with you. Maybe it wasn't exactly love at first sight. If that's what it was I'd have said so yesterday. But it runs a pretty close second.'

'Photo-finish, I'd say.' Kate stroked Dave's cheek with the

back of her hand. 'Besides, it's having second sight that counts. Ask any fortune teller. You know something, Van. You remind me of my lawyer.'

Dave laughed. 'Your lawyer? How's that?'

'You remind me to call him and find out what's holding up my divorce.'

'Do you think you and I would make a good team?'

'Could be.'

He paused for a second, as he deliberated the best way of checking her out. It was one thing for her to say she loved him. After all, she thought he was a regular guy, or as regular as you could be when you also happened to be a millionaire. It would be quite another thing for her to say that she was willing to hook up with a thief. And not just any thief. A very uncommon thief.

'Together, you and I, we could make some real money.'

'Yeah?'

'Wouldn't you like to make some real money?'

'That all depends on what I'd have to do to get it. I don't see the two of us winning a mixed doubles at Forest Hills.'

'What if I told you I was about to play a game of cards with four aces in my hand?'

'I'd ask if this hand was on the table or up your sleeve?'

Dave was silent.

'Uh-oh,' said Kate. 'Sounds like there's a racket involved after all. I don't know, Van. I'd say Monte Carlo's a pretty neat place to go with four aces.'

'What if I said it was five aces?'

'They've got names for people like that, Van. Numbers too. And you have to watch your ass when you're taking a shower.' She grinned uncertainly. 'This is a joke, isn't it? You're not a gambler, are you?'

'I was speaking metaphorically,' said Dave.

'Oh I see. A metaphor. I'm glad. Here was me thinking maybe I'd met a cheat.'

'But there are risks involved. And high stakes. For big rewards.'

Kate kept on smiling. She felt if she stopped she might find it hard to start it up again. The conversation had gone in a completely unexpected direction. For a moment there she'd thought they were going to declare undying love and talk about getting married. But now she didn't know what to think. She said, 'Next thing you'll be telling me you're really some kind of high-class jewel thief now living quietly in a hilltop villa on the Côte d'Azur. Like Cary Grant in *To Catch a Thief*. Come on, Dave. What is this?'

Dave considered the suggestion carefully for a second or two. Why not? Being a high-class jewel thief would do very nicely for the kind of litmus test he had in mind. After all, if she was prepared to take on a cat burglar then she ought to be prepared to take on a pirate, or whatever you wanted to call a guy who took down a score on board a ship.

'I'm perfectly serious, Kate.'

Still trying to keep her good humor, Kate's smile became a little strained. She said, 'To be quite frank with you? I've never seen myself in any of Grace Kelly's roles. For one thing, I'm a much better driver. For another? Well for another, does that film have a happy ending or not? I can't remember. And wasn't Cary Grant a reformed jewel thief trying to clear his name?' She stopped, exasperated, good humor disappearing now. 'Jesus, David, you don't do this kind of thing to a girl you've just fallen in love with. You know, when people get married and they say for richer, for poorer, for better, for worse? There's nothing about for right and for wrong.' Now she was feeling anxious. Like she'd won the lottery and couldn't find her ticket. 'It's not supposed to happen like this. Look, maybe you got the wrong idea about me. That Rita Hayworth, Gilda thing last night? It was just an act. I'm just a small-town girl. From T'ville, remember?'

'What happened to the girl from the Space Coast?'

'Houston, we've got a problem. I think the rocket just blew up on the launch pad.'

Dave kissed her again, as if to reassure her. Then he said, 'Are you sure about that?'

'No,' she said weakly, and kissed him back. 'But I've got a feeling I'm not going to land on the moon. My guidance systems have gone haywire.'

'You just need some time to get them realigned, that's all. You can still complete your mission.'

'If you say so.' Kate smiled wryly. 'Listen to me, Dave. Can we talk sensibly for a moment? This isn't a movie. This is real.'

'What's real? Someone once said that we wouldn't know how to fall in love if we hadn't read about it first. Well, it's kind of the same with movies. Maybe even more so. Sometimes, when I look back on my life all that I can remember are the good movies and favorite TV shows. Most of the best times I've had have been in movie theaters. I think that's true of people everywhere, Kate. Some of our most extraordinary experiences are in the movies. Not watching them, you understand, because if it's a good movie, it's like you're part of it. Now that's what I call virtual reality, not some motorcycle helmet you have to stick on your head to see the hand in front of your face.' Dave shrugged. 'So, what's real? I don't know. What I am sure about is that things are only as ordinary as you want them to be. If you want your life to feel as exciting as a movie, then that's the way you've got to live it.'

Kate laughed and kissed him quickly.

'OK,' she said. 'What have been your most extraordinary experiences?'

Dave thought for a second. Then he said, 'Walking into town with the Wild Bunch. Easy riding a motorcycle alongside Captain America. Running north by north-west from that crop-dusting airplane. Being seduced by Mrs Robinson. Escaping through Vienna's sewer system. Showing a clean pair of heels to a ten-ton rollerball in an Inca temple. Riding a chariot against Messala in the Circus at Antioch. Destroying the Death Star with my last missile. Playing chess with Death. Kissing Hedy Lamarr. Kissing Grace Kelly. Kissing you.'

'You're right. You have had an interesting life.'

'It's like I told you, Kate. Everyone has movie moments they remember. And this can be one of them. If you want it to be.'

'You could be right,' said Kate. 'But like you also said, I need some more time to think about how I'm going to play this particular scene.'

'Don't take too long about it,' urged Dave. 'In a few days we start shooting.'

CHAPTER SEVENTEEN

Guests arriving on board the *Jade* entered an atrium incorporating a life-size sculpture featuring a naked girl being penetrated from each end by two well-endowed men. The sculpture, which was also the logo of Jade Films, was executed in considerable anatomical detail; this, and the 'organic' staircase surrounding it, provided the yacht's focal point. Greeted by Rachel Dana and her crew in the spectacular reception area in front of this atrium, the guests were each handed a glass of Cristal and told that movies were on continuous show in the special theater that was to be found at the top of the curving mahogany staircase.

As soon as Al saw the sculpture he felt sure this was a party he was going to enjoy. A wolfish grin spreading on his blunt features, he said to Dave, 'Will you take a look at that fuckin' artwork? Boy, I sure wish Tony was here to see this. He's a real art lover. Buys quite a bit of sculpture himself. He'd love to have that in his collection.'

'Sounds as if Tony's a regular Solomon Guggenheim,' said Dave. 'I bet he's got Norman Rockwells, Dali prints, Tretchikopfs, everything.'

'He knows what he likes, y'know?'

'When it comes to buying art, nearly everyone has the same problem,' said Dave.

Others arriving at the party looked at the sculpture and seemed less certain of enjoying themselves, among them Kate and Captain Jellicoe.

'It's by Evelyn Bywater,' explained Rachel. 'An English artist.'

'Don't you mean proctologist?' said Kate.

'Her work is very well known throughout Europe and the Far East. She's is something of an institution in Japan.'

'Is that institution as in mental institution?' said Kate and left Jellicoe's side to go and talk to Sam Brockman.

'Jesus. What's wrong with her?' said Rachel. 'You'd think she'd never seen a naked human body before. What about you, Captain? Do you like our work of art?'

'Well,' he swallowed. 'I know nothing about art. We see very little of that kind of thing in the Merchant Navy. But I do have some rather nice prints in my cabin. Old schooners, tea clippers and British warships. But nothing like that. No indeed.' Jellicoe frowned. 'What sort of films does your company make anyway?'

'There's one showing upstairs, if you're interested.'

'Seems hardly sociable to clear off upstairs,' Jellicoe said stiffly. 'Television killing the art of good conversation and all that sort of thing. I've only just got here.'

Rachel took his arm in hers, and said, 'Come with me. I think you'll find it interesting. Most people seem to think our films are actually an aid to conversation. Kind of a therapeutic thing, y'know? It's not like television at all. And you wouldn't have seen any of our films on TV. I can guarantee it. We're much more video-oriented.'

She led Jellicoe up to the viewing theater under the envious eyes of Kent Bowen.

'It's OK,' Kate told him. 'She's taking him up to the viewing theater, not her bedroom.'

'They're screening movies up there? Jade movies?'

'I thought that would interest you.'

Sam Brockman raised his eyebrows and said, 'What are they showing?'

Bowen laughed coarsely. 'It's not re-runs of *The Brady Bunch*, you can be sure of that.'

'Jade Films are in the hard-core porno market,' said Kate.

'Is that so?' Brockman sounded genuinely surprised. 'You

know, I've never seen a real porno movie.'

Bowen glanced at Kate, teetering on the edge of ridiculing the Coast Guard lieutenant before suddenly realizing that this could work as a strategy to circumvent Kate's contempt. He said, 'You know something, Sam? Neither have I. What do you say we go and take a look for ourselves?'

Kate fixed Bowen with a gimlet eye. While she could easily believe Sam, she found Bowen's show of innocence harder to swallow.

'Yeah, come on, Kate,' said Brockman. 'Chill out. It might be a blast.'

'Maybe she's already seen one,' offered Bowen.

'I have not.' Kate was sufficiently well informed about what went on in real hard-core porno to know that Howard's subscription to the Playboy Channel hardly qualified as the real thing. 'What do you take me for?'

'It'll be an experience,' urged Brockman.

Kate thought poor Sam was looking more and more like some horny high-school kid. His glasses were a tad foggy, and by now it was obvious that he really hadn't ever seen a porno movie and badly wanted to remedy this omission.

'An experience?' Kate snorted. 'An experience is generally what you learn to call an error in judgment.'

Brockman raised his glass of champagne.

'Then here's to errors in judgment,' he said. 'Things would be Dullsville, Arizona without a few of them. Which, so far, has been my own life's story. Sam Brockman, they'll say. Exemplary career. No mistakes. But the CEO of Bromide Incorporated.'

Kate smiled sympathetically. She had much the same opinion of her own life, with Howard Parmenter being her only major aberration. Filing for divorce had been the most interesting thing that had happened to her in ages. That, and setting up her undercover operation aboard the *Duke*. Seeing Dave coming toward her she suddenly perceived an extra dimension to what Sam was talking about. Life was about taking risks. And not always calculated risks either. Maybe even a risk like Dave. Sure, making a mistake was always unfortunate. But not to have the opportunity of making a mistake was a catastrophe.

'OK,' she said. 'Why not?

'Attagirl,' said Brockman. 'You only live once.'

'That's been the prevailing theory,' said Kate and indicated the staircase. 'You guys go on ahead. I'll catch you up.' She watched them go up the stairs and then turned to face Dave.

'Hi.'

'Hi.'

For a moment neither of them spoke. Then Kate said, 'I've been thinking, about what you said.'

'Come to any decisions?'

'I haven't ruled anything out.'

'The sea's a pretty good place to float an idea,' he said. 'It's all to do with the freshwater allowance.'

To Kate's keen perception, Dave looked and sounded just a little distracted.

'Don't tell me you have to pay duty on water as well?'

'Fresh water has a lower density than sea water,' he explained. 'Things float deeper in fresh water. There's an F-mark on the ship's Plimsoll line. Difference between S and F is known as the freshwater allowance. You and I are nearer S than F. I'm surprised you didn't know that, you being a boat captain.'

Kate lit a cigarette.

'What's this? The Master Mariner's Certificate? Maybe you'd like to put me through my paces? See if I can fit new impellers in the dark, that kind of thing.'

When Dave made no reply, she smiled and said, 'Don't tell me you've never heard of impellers?'

Dave looked ready to admit defeat.

'It's like a propeller,' she said mischievously.

'Oh yeah, I think I know —'

'Only spelt different. More 'im' than 'pro'. Matter of fact that's really only as far as the similarity goes.' She smiled triumphantly. 'If the impeller packs up, so does your fuel pump and so does your diesel, so it's important to be able to get it out and fit a new one. Even at sea, in the dark, in a storm. Can be kind of tricky if you don't know how.' She blew some smoke across his shoulder and watched the grin spread on his face.

Dave jerked his head toward the top of the stairs.

'What were you guys talking about?'

'They'd just finished persuading me to go and take a look at the hard-core action.'

'That's where Al is,' said Dave. 'He's a real movie fan. Sees everything.'

'That's what's on show,' said Kate. 'Everything. You want to take a look?'

'Sure.'

Kate was a little disappointed. She had hoped he'd be the type to shake his head at the very idea of watching porno. Instead here he was, taking her by the elbow and steering her toward the movie theater upstairs. He could at least have pretended to disapprove, for a minute or two anyway. She was swiftly coming to the conclusion that all men were probably interested in this kind of shit.

She said, 'Beats me why more guys just don't become gynecologists.'

'Relaxation becomes harder to find when a man's hobby becomes his work,' said Dave.

'Is that an observation based on personal experience?'

'That and a lot of wishful thinking.'

'You're no gay bachelor, I'll say that much for you, Van.'

She felt his hand in the small of her back as they mounted the stairs. Near the top he stopped and took a step down again.

'Suddenly I need to visit the head,' he admitted.

'I thought that was after you'd seen the movie.'

'You go on in. I'll be there in one minute,' he said.

'One minute? In a movie like this? You could miss the whole story.'

'As long as it's got a happy end, I don't mind.'

Kate started upstairs again. 'Happy endings are what this crap's all about. Lots of them. In slippery close-up.'

Dave thought he had about ten minutes before Kate started to get suspicious. He left the *Jade* from her stern, climbing straight onto the *Juarista* and then onto the *Carrera*. A minute after leaving Kate at the party he was down the circular stair that connected the *Carrera*'s salon and dining room with the midship accommodations deck.

The master suite was the full width of the boat and featured a sitting area, a large walk-in closet, and a generous bathroom with a Jacuzzi. Dave guessed this was the cabin occupied by Kent Bowen. Lying on the floor of the closet were some garishly colored sports shirts he thought he had seen Bowen wearing. And there was no mistaking the sweet antiseptic smell of Brut aftershave that always signalled Bowen's presence. Quickly, Dave opened some of the drawers and almost immediately found what he was looking for: a medium-frame .357 Magnum in a ProPak undercover shoulder holster, and a wallet containing business cards. Dave thumbed one out and read it quickly. The embossed gold roundel in the top left-hand corner of the card was easily recognizable. It identified the Department of Justice just as surely as the printed information alongside. Kent Bowen was an Assistant Special Agent in Charge at Miami's FBI HQ on Second Avenue.

'Jesus Christ,' he exclaimed.

Dave replaced the card, closed the drawer carefully and then went next door to search Kate's stateroom. This was tidier than Bowen's. The bed was made, with cushions scattered across the silk brocade spread. Clothes were neatly hung in the closet, but there was nothing in the built-in drawers to interest Dave. Apart from some very sexy underwear.

'Just the facts, ma'am,' he muttered and, closing the drawer, he backed out of the closet.

His heel struck something hard underneath the spread. Guessing that there was probably a linen drawer under the bed just like the one in his own stateroom, Dave dropped to his knees, threw back the spread, and grabbed hold of the drawer handle. Hauling it open he found everything he would have expected to find in a linen drawer. He had to reach right to the back to put his hand on the familiar shape he'd been half expecting. The next second he was looking at a Smith & Wesson Airweight .38, holstered in a nice leather Vega, although the gun's shrouded hammer made it about perfect for a handbag. Attached to the holster's strap was an ID wallet containing an FBI badge and card identifying Kate, not as Kate Parmenter, but as Kate Furey, Special Agent. She looked younger in the photograph and her hair was different. But there was no mistaking that launch-a–thousand-ships face.

Dave nodded with bitter satisfaction. He didn't know whether to whoop or to wail.

'A Fed,' he mumbled. 'She's a goddamn lousy Fed.'

The only question was what she and Bowen and the other guy, who was probably a Fed too, were doing on the *Duke*. There was no way they could know about Dave's score. Unless it was the money they were onto.

'Fucking Feds.'

He dived back into the drawer in search of something that might tell him what this was all about, but found nothing. He shut the drawer and went into the head. His eyes noted the brand of her perfume for future reference, a small bottle of Murine eyedrops, some suntan lotion, and an impressive array of mouthwash, dental floss, toothpicks and plaque-disclosing tablets that helped explain Kate's Ford model smile. The drawers were empty, but in a closet under the basin he found a TEAC reel-to-reel tape machine. The kind of tape that wasn't meant to play Handel's *Water Music* when you were lying in the tub. Dave knew it was set up to record from some kind of listening device. But planted where? On whose boat?

Twisting a knob he rewound the tape for a couple of seconds. The least he could do in the time available was verify that the Feds weren't interested in him, or in the Russkie money.

The tape began to play.

He was listening to the voices of a man and a woman. The man was American but the woman sounded as if she was from Australia. The accent would help to narrow it down. Not that it really mattered. None of the Russian boats had any female supernumos. And these two weren't saying anything interesting. Just some shit about this and that. Dave switched the tape off and started to grin. The Feds were watching someone else's boat. Someone Dave didn't even know about. Everything was fine. His five year plan could go ahead more or less as scheduled. Submarine permitting. And seeing those FBI shields and ID cards had given him an idea.

For about ten minutes Kate was too shocked to notice Dave's prolonged absence. Her imagination was abruptly ordered somewhere else, as not the smallest aspect of human anatomy escaped the attention of the camera: every mucous tract, subcutaneous fold and sebaceous follicle. But what was most surprising to her was not the explicit intimacy of what was depicted, but that there should be any women who were still willing to have unprotected anal intercourse. Just where had these women been for the last ten virally preoccupied years? Did they imagine that just because they were doing it in a movie they would be protected by the special effects department?

Almost as fascinating to Kate as what was happening on the screen were the faces of the audience. Bowen grinning like an ape. Sam Brockman cleaning his glasses every few minutes and making a silent whistling noise from time to time. Rachel Dana watching Jellicoe and enjoying his thunderstruck demeanor. Two of the targets from the *Britannia*, Nicky Vallbona and Webb Garwood, laughing loudly and cracking the most tasteless jokes. Kate wondered if Bowen had even registered that they were there.

She'd heard men – Howard was one such – claim that porno was boring, but somehow she'd never quite believed it. Bowen looked anything but bored. Even in the half-darkness of the *Jade*'s viewing theater, she could see a light sheen of sweat glistening on his upper lip which he wiped periodically with the back of his hand. But after a while she realized she really was bored. It wasn't so much the lack of story she found tedious as the monotonous serial continuity, as if what was being enacted was a precise ritual. The girl always sucked the man before he licked her; then, always, he penetrated her vagina as a prelude to sodomy, before finally he came all over her face as if by this final act of degradation the reality of what was happening was there revealed. To Kate this last act in the ritual pointed up the lie of porno: no man had ever come in her face, and if it ever did happen – woe betide the guy who thought he could get away with that shit – she would hardly have been disposed to treat his load as if it had been the choicest Beluga.

Dave sat down beside her and said, 'Aren't you grossed out yet?'

'Where have you been?' she demanded.

'I got detained. Did you know Calgary Stanford is on this ship?'

'The movie actor?'

'I've just been talking to him.'

'What's he like?'

'Kind of ordinary, really.'

Dave glanced around the little theater and caught sight of Al, and then one of the guys from the *Baby Doc*. Al's face was something by Goya; grotesque. Kate was shaking her head.

She said, 'People just do not behave like this. Even in

movies. They don't go around fucking each other like rabbits. It's just not feasible.'

Dave looked sideways at her and said, 'Feasible? You sound like you've got the latest Nielsen figures on this one, Kate.' He looked back up at the screen and then grimaced. 'Anyway, these aren't movies. Not the ones I go to.'

'Hey, I'm the one who's supposed to say that. C'mon,' she said. 'Let's get out of here before the next money shot. While I've still got an appetite.'

Going downstairs, Dave said, 'Why don't you come back to my boat and let me make you a sandwich?'

'Sounds good. Besides, I need a little air. The breathing's getting kind of noticeable in there. Like a locker room in winter. Now I know what it's like to sit in a car with a hosepipe attached to the exhaust. I guess that's why it's called a blue movie.'

Kate watched Dave make the sandwiches. He did it carefully, and with a touch of panache, as if he enjoyed cooking and preparing food. In some ways he was quite the new man. In others he was reassuringly like all the old ones. She liked the way he wasn't always speaking, as if he was used to his own company and didn't mind it. Self-contained, she thought.

'You can be quiet if you want, Van,' she said. 'I don't mind. I like a bit of Dolby in my men. The thing that cuts down on noise, y'know? Like an electronic blue pencil. I bet you're the kind to let a girl talk herself into bed.'

'Could be.' Dave returned to the sofa with a plate of neatly cut sandwiches.

Kate waited until he had picked one up and was teeing up his first mouthful. She said, 'Take me to bed, Van. Right now. No more hard-boiled. From now on, I'm zip-lipped.'

Dave looked at her and then back at his sandwich which stayed about an inch away from his mouth. He said, 'You mean right now?'

'Before I think about it some more and change my mind.'

Kate had no intention of changing her mind. Maybe she did have one or two reservations about what he had told her: her best guess was that he had fed her this story in order to find out if it was him or his money she was really interested in. She would probably have done the same thing herself. She understood about money, even if she was not much interested in it herself. For Howard, money had been the major motivation of nearly everything he did. He was driven by money, as if it turned up at the start of every day with a peaked cap and a mobile phone. For Kate it was merely the means to an end, and right now it had little or no relevance to what she wanted most, which was to go to bed with Dave. But she enjoyed making him choose between having a sandwich and having her. She leaned toward him and nuzzled his ear with the tip of her nose.

'Where I'm taking you now,' she said, 'the cooking's wonderful, painstakingly prepared, and the service is excellent. So don't even think about eating anything else. Not if you ever want to be welcome back to this restaurant.'

Dave put down his sandwich. He was hungry but there were some things better done on an empty stomach.

'Did you sleep OK?'

Dave stretched on his king-sized bed and rolled toward her.

'Weird,' he said. 'I dreamed I had Alzheimer's disease. Only trouble is I've forgotten what happened.'

Kate glanced at her watch.

'Still joking at six o'clock in the morning, I see.'

Dave grinned and rolled on top of her.

'Can you think of anything else to do?'

'I could make you breakfast,' she offered. 'I feel kind of guilty about making you sacrifice that sandwich.'

'I've forgotten about that too. Breakfast sounds good, though. I could eat a horse.'

As he slipped out of bed, Kate said, 'I already did.'

Dave grinned again. 'You haven't forgotten about my proposition, have you?' he asked.

'What proposition is that, lover?'

'You know? Living with the famous Phantom, in the South of France?'

'Oh yeah, that. The *Pink Panther* thing. No, I hadn't forgotten about it. I'm like an elephant. I never forget a name or a face.'

Dave nodded. A good memory for names and faces was probably a job requirement for a Fed.

'And?'

'This is some kind of test, right? Like the three caskets in *The Merchant of Venice*. Gold, silver and lead.' Kate searched Dave's face for some sign that he recognized she knew what he was up to. 'All that glisters is not gold?'

'So which is it to be?'

She rolled across the crumpled sheets toward him and sat up. 'With you? I don't know. If I said I chose lead, you'd probably shoot me.' Kate wagged her finger at him. 'Come on, Dave. I'm not interested in the money.'

Dave flinched. 'What money?'

'Your money. The Dulanotov family fortune.'

'Oh, that.' He lit a cigarette. 'Maybe I didn't make myself clear. But it's like I told you. The money's based on crime. There's no family fortune. I'm a thief, Kate. I steal for a living. Like old Cary Grant.'

She shrugged. 'OK. If you say so. Well then I haven't ruled out becoming Grace. Not yet.'

Like hell she hasn't, thought Dave, and went to take a shower.

Kate frowned. He really was serious about this test of his. Couldn't he see she wasn't remotely interested in his money? As soon as she heard the water running Kate started to search the room. It wasn't that she shared Kent Bowen's suspicions of him. That was just stupid jealousy. But Dave volunteered so little about himself and she wanted to know more than the crumbs she had gleaned from the few questions he had honored with straight answers. She didn't think for a moment he was a thief. How many thieves knew Shakespeare and Pushkin? But there was something he wasn't telling her, of that she was sure. Something that she needed to find out. At the FBI training academy she had learned to recognize when someone was hiding something. For a brief period in her early career she had entertained notions of joining the Behavioral Science Unit. But after *The Silence of the Lambs* came along it seemed that everyone wanted to be Jack Crawford or Clarice Starling, and she had ended up in General Investigations and Narcotics. Now, looking over the room, she had no idea what she was searching for. The large number of books only seemed to underline what she already knew – that Dave was widely read. Most of the clothes in his closet were predictably new and came from expensive shops, as she had expected. There was no cash lying around. Nor any travellers' cheques, credit cards; not even a driver's license. Most infuriating of all, she could not find Dave's passport. The explanation was inside Dave's walk-in closet. A combination wall safe. Just what any self-respecting millionaire would have had. You didn't stay rich by leaving money lying around.

Kate came out of the closet and sat on the edge of the bed. If only she had taken the safe-cracking course instead of psychology. Absently she stared at Dave's bookshelf. It was like a reading list for a summer school. Many of the titles were classics. Tolstoy, Turgenev, Dostoevsky, Nabokov. Even a few published movie scripts. A nod to post modernism. Some philosophy too: Wittgenstein, Kierkegaard, Gilbert Ryle and George Steiner. But the more she stared at the books the more it started to seem that for all its apparent inclusiveness, there was something missing, like a piece from a cutlery set. Yes, that was it. And not just one piece. Maybe one whole item. Like a set of fish knives. Gradually she perceived what it was. There were no books on business. Not one. And this struck her as curious. Millionaires were interested in money, weren't they? Especially if they worked in Miami's Financial Center. Howard had been forever reading books about making money. *Beating the Dow. One Up on Wall Street. The Midas Touch. The Three Minute Manager.* He must have bought that one just around the time he was reading *The Two Minute Lover.*

Kate picked out Dave's well-thumbed paperback edition of *Crime and Punishment.* She hadn't read the novel since she'd been in Law School, when it really had seemed like one of those books that might change your life. Or, at the very least, the way you thought about criminals. Idly she was turning back the cover when something caught her eye. Something was printed there, on the inside cover, in bright blue ink.

Something was stamped on it.

She stared at it incredulously, as if she had been admiring some clever bookplate, reading the words printed inside the simple roundel with more care than if they had been a visa on the passport for which she had been searching.

But this was something much more revealing.

She whispered the words out loud, as if she needed to hear them spoken in order to absorb what was implied.

'Property of the Miami Correctional Center at Homestead?'

Could it be that Dave really was a thief? And not just a thief, but an ex-con?

Hearing his shower end, she closed the book and returned it quickly to the shelf. Then, slipping into the spare dressing gown, she left the stateroom and went up to the galley. Maybe she could rustle up a relaxed, loving and laid-back sort of face along with some breakfast.

In the galley Kate put on the kettle to boil, and started to fry some ham and eggs, all the while considering the evidence that was before her: the new clothes; the bookshelf more typical of some jailhouse auto-didact than a millionaire; and the five aces Cary Grant-style proposition he had made her. There seemed to be no other conclusion that she could form. Dave really was a thief, and a convicted one too. She realized that he had been perfectly serious, as indeed he had said he was.

Al, summoned upstairs to the galley by the smell of fresh coffee and frying sausage and ham, brought home to her this wasn't a Cary Grant movie. Al was Luca Brazzi, Tony Montana and Jimmy Conway all squeezed into the one short-barrelled pump-action shotgun. Right down to the rifle sight, the hardwood stock attitude, and the blue metal jaw.

'Time is it?' he growled.

'Just after six,' she said, perky as an airline stewardess responding to a first-class passenger. You got all sorts going first class these days.

'Six o'clock? Jesus, what are we doing, abandoning ship or something? Six o'clock.'

'You want some breakfast?'

Al sighed uncomfortably and stooped to look out of the galley window, checking on the weather. He sniffed loudly, like he was hunched over a couple of lines of coke, and said, 'I can't make up my mind if it's better to eat so that I got something to throw up or if it's better not to eat so that I don't throw up at all.'

Kate smiled sweetly, trying to overcome her nerves. Who were these guys? And what were they doing on the ship? Was it possible they had anything to do with Rocky Envigado?

'Al?' she said. 'Have you heard the expression, the cook could use a hug? This particular cook only requires a "yes please" or a "no thankyou". The ultimate destination of this food I'm cooking, be it toilet bowl or ocean, is of absolutely no account to me.'

Al grunted biliously. Uncertainly he eyed the breakfast Kate was cooking. Rubbing his bare belly, for he was only wearing shorts, he said, 'Maybe I'll just have some Wheaties.'

'Have you got a hangover or something?'

'Naw. I'm feeling sick in anticipation of feeling sick, on account of the weather.' Al poured out a bowlful of cereal, then some milk, and began to shovel the stuff into his mouth.

'The weather? What about it?'

'You don't notice it, huh?' he remarked with milk dribbling down his unshaven chin. 'Must be another good sailor. Like the boss.'

Kate glanced out the window. What with making love and her shock discovery about Dave, she had hardly noticed the swell underneath the ship. Outside the sky was gray and threatening and a stiff breeze was whipping the flag on the stern of the *Jade* in front of them. It looked as if the storm was catching up to them after all.

'Me, I ain't much of a sailor,' confessed Al. 'I get sick looking at a glass of salt water.'

'It does look kind of rough,' Kate admitted.

Coming into the galley, Dave said, 'Are you talking about Al, or the weather?'

Al sneered, dumped his empty bowl in the sink, and reached for the coffee jug. Kate stepped fastidiously out of his way as from a large and smelly dog.

Noticing her flinch from Al's bare torso, Dave said, 'Couldn't you put a shirt or something on, Al? It's like having a giant coconut rolling around in here.'

Al slurped some coffee and said, 'Some women like hairy men.'

Dave said, 'Dian Fossey and Fay Wray don't happen to be sailing with us.'

'Let me tell you about this gorilla thing,' said Al. 'Hairy guys have got more intelligence than smooth as shit ones like yourself, boss. Now that's a fact. It was in the *Herald*. Scientists have done a survey and proved it. Smart guys have hairy chests. Lotta doctors. Lotta college professors. Not many lawyers. No cops. Lotta writers. And the really smart guys have hairy backs to match.'

'Say anything about hairy brains in that survey, Al?' laughed Dave. He looked at Kate, who smiled back at him faintly. 'Well that's a new one on me. It certainly puts a different spin on the story of Samson, I suppose. It's not the guy's relationship with God she screws when she cuts his hair, but his IQ.'

'You can laugh all you like,' said Al, marching out of the galley. 'But that's a fact.'

Kate cleared her throat nervously and kept on trying to get her smile right, even when Dave smiled apologetically. Now that she saw him again, he did look like he might be a high-class jewel thief. He probably relied on Al to drive his getaway car, or to provide muscle when it was required.

When Al had gone, Dave shook his head. 'Al,' he said simply. 'Some guy, huh? I told you he was an animal.'

'I think that's the first time I've seen the two of you together,' she said.

'That's easy to explain.' Folding her up in his arms, Dave inspected the breakfast that Al had declined. 'We're like Jekyll and Hyde. Mmmm, that looks good.'

'And which one of you is Mister Hyde?'

'Well he is, of course. Didn't you notice the hair on the backs of his hands? The guy's like a goddamn doormat.'

Kate pulled away and started to serve Dave his breakfast.

'Something the matter?' he asked. 'You still cool about last night?'

'Everything's fine,' she said, and anxious to reassure him, she added, 'You know what?' she said. 'If you were Mister Hyde? I'd be Missus Seek.'

'That sounds promising.'

He wondered if there was anything at all in her show of prevarication. Was she just trying to amuse herself during an otherwise uneventful undercover surveillance? Or was there genuinely something more there? It seemed impossible to find out until the heist itself was out of the way. He sat down at the dinette table and began to eat what was put in front of him. He said, 'I'm sure I'd rather share a divided consciousness with you than with Al. Think about it. A fifty-fifty partnership. Straight down the middle.'

Kate said, 'Straight? You've hardly been that.'

His mouth full of food, Dave stretched his eyebrows back at her.

'What I mean to say,' she explained hurriedly, 'is that you've not exactly told me very much about what you do. I can't just leave Kent's employment without knowing a little more about you. About what you do. About where you live.'

'I told you,' said Dave. 'I steal rocks. Same as old John Robie in *To Catch a Thief*. The Cat. Actually, I don't bother with a handle. Or a white monogrammed glove. There's no point in making it easy for the police to nail me for a lot of other scores in the unlikely eventuality that I get caught. Naturally I only steal from those who can afford it. Matter of fact I thought there might be some nice stones on this ship. Until I discovered the owners seldom travel with their boats. That was before the air traffic controllers heard about my predicament and decided to try and help out.'

'It's over,' said Kate. 'The strike. It was on the radio yesterday afternoon.'

'Is that so? Well this trip has been very disappointing, at least from a professional POV. No jewels, no cash, not even a small Picasso. Makes you wonder what people are spending their money on these days. Security and porno, I guess. There's not much of a margin in that for someone like me, Kate.' He sighed. 'I hope things are better on the Côte d'Azure.'

'You're really serious about this?'

'I'm always serious about partnership, Kate. After last night you should know that. But for another reason too. I already have a partner. There's Al to consider.'

Kate felt herself recovering some of her poise.

'Replacing Al, well it's very flattering,' she said. 'But you know, business could sound more promising. You could try selling me the terms of our agreement. What's in it for me? What can I do? That kind of thing.'

'I've told you, that's not my style. Besides, you know the terms. Yesterday I heard you say them yourself. For richer for poorer, for better for worse. Fifty-fifty, Kate. With all my worldly goods I thee endow. What do you say?'

'You're really asking me to marry you?'

Dave forked some ham into his mouth and nodded.

Kate smiled. 'But I don't even know you.'

'People who don't know each other get married every day. I know. I read it in the paper.'

She sat down opposite him, flabbergasted. Would he be half as keen to marry her if he knew she was a Fed?

'When does your divorce come through?' he asked.

'Couple of months.'

'Get married then.'

He was enjoying her predicament. He sensed that she loved him as much as he loved her. Perhaps she even wanted to marry him and but for her being a special agent working undercover, she might have agreed. At the same time he was thinking how good it had been last night. And how comfortable he felt with her now. How reluctant he would be to leave her. Time was running out, fast. In eighteen hours he and Al were going to do the job. After that he might never see her again. The truth was that he meant what he said. If keeping her had been merely a matter of marrying her, he would have done it right away. About the only card he had left to play was that he knew what she was. A Fed. But he would only play that one when the time came to leave, when she knew more or less everything, but not before.

'You like going fast, don't you, Van?'

'I'm going to the Monaco Grand Prix, remember?'

'I thought it was the financial guy who was going, not John Robie.'

'Grand Prix is good for cat burglars. Makes a lot of noise. People don't hear much during and after a Formula One motor race. And Monte Carlo is always Monte Carlo. There're always a lot of stones around. It's like Tiffany's with a roulette wheel and a nice beach.' Dave straightened his knife and fork and reached across the table to curl a length of Kate's hair around in his fingers. She hadn't had a shower yet and she still smelt great. 'Shouldn't be too much of a problem for a girl from the Space Coast. The kind of girl who wears Allure.'

'How did you know I wore that?'

'I recognize it. It's my favorite perfume. At least it is now.'

Kate cupped his hand to her cheek and sighed wistfully. Howard didn't know one brand of perfume from cigar smoke. It was just her luck to find a guy who had fallen in love with her at first sight when she was pretending to be someone else. A guy who knew poetry. A guy who was not a selfish lover. A guy who knew perfume. A guy who was a thief and an ex-con. It was just another of the curved balls life was wont to pitch at you. She stood up.

'I still need some more time,' she said, glancing automatically at her watch. 'And I'd better be getting back. Kent gets a little funny about this kind of thing.'

Dave was hardly surprised by this information. In his experience the Feds could get funny about all kinds of things.

CHAPTER EIGHTEEN

Dave was reading a book when he heard a footfall on the cockpit deck.

It was the ship's electrical officer, Jock. No longer wearing white, he was wrapped in a thick woollen navy blue sweater and navy blue pants.

'Come tae look at your boat. Check your ropes are all holding up.'

'And are they?'

'For now. But if the storm catches up wi' us, we could all have some problems. Right now we're just ahead of it. Making good time. We're going like a racing dog's cock.'

'But we're still on course?'

'Oh aye. On course right enough. But if this keeps up we'll be arriving well ahead of schedule.'

Dave frowned. Being early for the rendezvous might be every bit as disastrous for the heist as being late.

'How much ahead?'

'Can't say for sure. Soon as the weather improves we'll get a better idea. By the way, how's your handset?'

Dave said nothing, distracted by the latest information. It looked like they were going to spend more time aboard the getaway boat than he had figured. From now on he would need to keep a close eye on their position with the aid of the boat's GPS receiver. About the same size as a cellular telephone, the GPS could accurately tell you where you were, in what direction you were heading, and how fast you were going: every time you turned on the receiver it worked out its location by tracking the signals broadcast by satellites in the GPS constellation until it had enough information to determine its own relative position.

Jock repeated his question.

'Oh, still working OK, thanks. You want a beer?'

'Why not? Might as well be wet inside as well as out.'

Dave glanced out of the window. Rain lashed the roof of the *Juarista* and even behind the walls of the *Duke*, the boat's deck felt more like a surfboard. He handed Jock a Corona. 'Right,' he said. 'It's like *Moby Dick* out there.'

'A wee bit tricky walking along the ship's walls,' Jock admitted. 'But not half as bad as we thought. The skipper was right. It should blow itself out soon enough.'

Jock drained half the beer from the bottle. Hearing a loud retching noise from the bowels of Dave's boat, he glanced at the stairwell. He grinned slightly and said, 'Someone's Uncle Dick, are they?'

Dave frowned momentarily as his ears and understanding tried to penetrate the Scotsman's speech. Finally it dawned on him.

'Yeah. It's Al. He's not a good sailor.' He seemed unconcerned, although he was growing worried by the thought that he might end up tackling the score on his own. The only possible benefit of the bad weather was that the crews of the Russkie boats might be feeling as sick as Al.

'But you're all right?' said Jock.

'I'm fine.' Dave said. 'You wouldn't happen to have something I could give him, would you? I've tried Kwells and other shit like that, but they don't seem to help.'

Jock finished his beer and pulled a face.

'That stuff's for kids,' he said. 'What other shit have you tried?'

'Antihistamine. Didn't work either. Just made him sleep for a bit.'

'When was his last dose of that?'

'Hours ago.'

'Well, if it's me, I take hyoscine. Blocks the para-sympathetic

237

autonomic nervous system. Stuff's commonly used as a pre-anesthetic to prevent reflex vagal stimulation of the heart.'

'There's nothing sympathetic about Al's nervous system,' said Dave. 'I'm not even sure he's got a heart.' He lit a cigarette. 'What are you, some kind of doctor as well?'

'On this ship, aye. My father was a veterinary surgeon. I learned a lot from him.' He shrugged. 'Bastards on this ship are all animals anyway, so it makes no bloody difference.' He took one of the cigarettes Dave had offered him, and lit it quickly. 'Does your pal suffer from glaucoma, at all?'

Dave had no idea, but he shook his head anyway, sensing that Jock was about to prescribe something useful. The hyoscine perhaps.

'Aye, well I've got some Scopoderm. It's good stuff. Not available over the counter.' He pinched the cigarette from the corner of his mouth and inhaled through clenched teeth. 'Expensive, though. If you know what I mean.'

Dave thought he did and grinned back at him. 'I think so.'

Jock looked apologetic. 'You're the one with the flash boat, not me. I'm just trying to make ends meet.'

'How much?'

'Fifty bucks. Enough to see you through the bad weather.'

'Done.'

Jock took a small packet from his pocket.

'You had it with you?'

'Quite a few people are feeling like shit today,' laughed Jock. 'Business is good.'

'That's a nice little racket,' said Dave, handing over the five Hamiltons.

'You make it any way you can.'

'Sure do,' agreed Dave.

'These are tablets and plasters,' Jock explained, giving Dave the packet. 'Give him one tablet now and stick a plaster to his arm. He'll have difficulty in passing water. Maybe blur his vision a bit. And it'll stop him sweating altogether.'

'I can't wait,' said Dave. 'How soon does this shit kick in?'

'Right away. An hour should see him on his feet again. Then one of the plasters and one of the pills every six hours. Just don't mix the stuff with any alcohol.'

'Right.'

'Thanks for the beer.'

'Pleasure doing business with you, Doc.'

Jock walked precipitously toward the stern.

'Oh yeah. I meant to tell you. That sub. I reckon it's gone. No one's been broadcasting in a while and there's nothing on the echo-sounder. Must have got bored, and pissed off.'

'Must have done,' agreed Dave.

'It's that kind of voyage,' said Jock. 'I can't think why I ever imagined going to sea would be more interesting than becoming a vet. Nothing ever bloody well happens on this boat.'

'No, I guess not.'

Al was lying on the floor, one arm wrapped around the toilet bowl as if it was his best friend. Dave knelt down, wrapped one of Al's anaconda-sized arms around his own neck, and dragged him into the stateroom.

'One thing I like about you, Al. You know your proper station in life. It's been a pleasure sailing with you, you know? A guy out of the can, like me? It's been a great comfort to have been around someone lower than myself.'

'Fuck you,' groaned Al.

Dave dropped him onto the bed and finding a towel he began to dry Al's arms carefully.

'The doc was just by to give you something,' said Dave. 'To be completely honest with you, he's really a vet. But I knew you wouldn't hold that against him, you being a fuckin' gorilla n'all.'

Dave unwrapped the supply of Scopoderm and taped a plaster to the inside of each chunky forearm.

'Normally the guy only treats domestic animals but I per-suaded him to make an exception in your case. I told him to pretend you were a domestic ass and y'know something? He didn't seem to have any problem with that.'

Dave placed one of Jock's tablets on Al's lolling, beige sock of a tongue, and then closed his jaw before reaching for the glass of water on the bedside table. The glass was in his hand and then almost on the floor as he realized with disgust that the water covered a set of dental plates.

'Jesus, what the fuck is this?' Dave laughed and then lifted Al's slack lip on the edge of his finger. Grinning, his own teeth shining perfectly, Dave peered into Al's pukey mouth. He said, 'Man, there's not one tooth in the whole fucking bowling ball.' Dave kept on looking, fascinated and feeling like the bitch in *King Lear* come to gloat over some old guy's empty eye sockets. Until Al's big hairy paw swept Dave's hand away.

'Fuck you.'

'OK, you gotta sit up now and swallow this bitter little pill, Al. Make you feel better. It's a seasickness pill, so be a good fellow and just swallow the goddamn thing. Stuff cost me fifty bucks.'

Al sat up, swallowed the pill and, taking the glass out of Dave's hand, drained it of the water covering his dentures.

'You bastard,' he whispered and collapsed back onto the bed.

'Yeah, I know. All my patients say the same thing. My manner's more dockside than bedside.' Dave wiped Al's forehead with the towel. 'Takes a little while for the Scopoderm to kick in. The dope's attached to your arms as well, just in case your stomach's paying less attention than your brain. Just one note of precaution. No booze while you're tripping on this stuff. That means no booze until we're off this ship, right? You and I have got a job to do.' Dave glanced at his watch. 'In less than twelve hours. You want some character motivation? Then think about that for a while. This time tomorrow you and I are going to be multi-millionaires.'

*   *   *

'So,' said Sam Brockman. 'We're on our own now. Excepting when there's a NATO exercise, the Navy generally stays this side of the Atlantic. It makes things less complicated for the ASW people.'

'ASW?'

'Anti-submarine warfare,' he told Kate. 'French'll pick us up in a few hours, just west of the Azores.' He sighed. 'Shit.'

'What?'

'Just that I almost wish something would happen. Seems kind of a shame to hand the collar over to Interpol.'

Kate agreed without much enthusiasm. For her there was more than enough happening already. More than she had bargained for, anyway. Since breakfast she had stayed on the *Carrera*, grateful that the bad weather gave her the excuse not to go up on deck and see Dave. Perhaps it was as well the sub had gone. It meant that there was no temptation to get a message relayed back to FBI HQ and check on Dave's criminal record. Assuming Dulanotov was his real name.

A very green-looking Kent Bowen came up to the galley and stood breathing heavily over the sink for a moment before fetching a glass and taking some water from the faucet.

'How are you feeling, Kent?' Sam asked the ASAC.

'Like dog shit.'

Kate gave Bowen a look as if to say dog shit was what he was. She hadn't yet worked out a way of paying him back for implying to Dave that he was fucking her. But she was working on it.

'The Dramamine not effective?' said Sam.

'That's the top of the news,' said Bowen. 'I take any more of that stuff and I'll fall asleep. I'm nearly out on my feet as it is.'

'You know, nothing much is happening right now,' said Kate. 'Turkey in the straw has signed off. There doesn't seem much point in staying awake if you're feeling lousy. Why not go to bed?'

Bowen smiled weakly. 'Why not go to bed? Is that your personal motto or something?'

Kate bit her lip. 'What's that supposed to mean?' she said evenly.

'I think you know what I'm talking about, Agent Furey.'

'God, you sound just like my mother.'

'I doubt that. I doubt that very much. Clearly your mother can never have offered you anything in the way of moral guidance.'

Kate felt her cheeks color. Then she laughed scornfully. 'Listen to Bob Guccione. What would you know about moral guidance?'

Persisting, Bowen said, 'If she had — '

'I'm assuming it's the Dramamine that's making you sound like an asshole, Kent.'

'If she had, you'd have returned to this boat last night.'

'Did you come up here especially to insult me?'

'You don't deny it then?'

'Deny what?'

'That you slept with that guy?'

'Actually we didn't really sleep at all. We were too busy fucking.'

'I was right, then.'

'But what I did or did not do last night is really none of your goddamn business.'

'If it affects the integrity of this operation, it is.'

'And you'd know all about that, watching porno all evening.'

Bowen leaned forward and retched into the sink.

'You make a lot more sense with your head in a toilet bowl,' she sneered.

Bowen straightened and wiped his mouth with a paper towel. 'It was not all evening.'

'It was a couple of hours, Kate,' said Sam. 'Maybe three.'

'So don't lecture me on integrity,' said Kate.

Sam said, 'Never seen that kind of thing before. Probably won't ever see it again. Last night, I reckon I saw everything it was possible to see. There was one particular female – ' He glanced awkwardly at Kate. 'Well, I'll just say this. That now I know what it really means to have your head screwed on.' He laughed. 'Anyway, I don't see that any of us have affected the integrity of this operation. Nothing happened last night that's anyone's business but his or her own. Now why don't we just leave it at that, huh, Kent?'

'That kind of adolescent behavior may be OK in the Coast Guard,' hiccuped Bowen. 'But Agent Furey's illicit sexual activities are not in the best traditions of the FBI.'

'Who do you think you are?' demanded Kate. 'J. Edgar Hoover? Illicit sexual activities, my ass.'

Bowen grinned through a wave of nausea that drained the last shade of color from his face. He said, 'Well, I know who I am. Yeah. That's right. I know who I am.'

'The secret files of Kent Bowen.'

'But can you say the same about your sexual partner? Answer me that, if you can. Exactly what do you know about Mister David Dulanotov?'

'This is bullshit,' said Kate. But the truth was that she had spent the whole morning asking herself the same question.

Bowen took a deep breath and said, 'I am a pillar of strength in a city of weak men and women. And I will maintain the law. But Mister David Dulanotov is something else. He is not a righteous man. The rancorous eye and the finger of scorn are pointed against him.' He exhaled unsteadily.

'Pillar of shit more like. What are you talking about?'

'I'll tell you. I've done a little checking on Mister David Dulanotov. And it turns out that the boat he owns is registered in Grand Cayman.'

'There's no law against that.'

'The previous owner was a guy by the name of Lou Malta, formerly an associate of Tony Nudelli. Even you must have heard of Tony Nudelli.'

Kate stayed silent.

'Naked Tony Nudelli. I say formerly an associate, because Lou Malta is listed with the Miami Police Department as a missing person. No one has seen him in months.'

PHILIP KERR

Kate shrugged and said, 'I don't see what that proves.'

'Nothing. Except maybe that this Lou Malta guy has been murdered.'

'All we ask of someone when they sell us something is that they possess a proper title to the goods. Not that they are a proper person.'

'S'right, Kent,' agreed Sam Brockman. 'Guy who sold me my first car was one of the biggest crooks in Florida.'

'Keep out of this,' said Bowen.

'Be careful, Sam,' said Kate. 'Or the crazy son of a bitch'll open a file on you too.'

Bowen said, 'I haven't been able to find out about the other guy. The knuckles he has for company. But I wouldn't be at all surprised if he was some kind of mobster too.'

'You sound like you've already established a *prima facie* case against David,' said Kate. 'What I've heard so far is about as circumstantial as the time on your cheap watch. Boy, when you throw up it's not just last night's dinner, is it? It's a lot of other bile and rat shit as well. In case you've forgotten, Kent, it's dogs that are interested in puke, not the DA. He'd laugh you out of his office with what you've told me so far.'

'I never said I had anything other than — ' Bowen stopped, gulped biliously before covering his mouth and then waiting for another wave of nausea to subside. After a moment or two, he added, 'Other than a strong suspicion, that he was not, a proper person for an agent to become, associated with.' Then he belched.

'Most intelligent sound you've made all morning, Kent,' said Kate, standing up. 'I'm going outside. The air in here is getting kind of sour.'

'Agent Furey? I haven't finished yet,' said Bowen, and threw up into the sink.

'It sure doesn't look like it,' said Kate, squeezing out from behind the table.

Almost as soon as Bowen had straightened again, a large fly landed on his puke, buzzing loudly.

244

'Well, what do you know, Kent?' said Kate, on her way out of the galley door. 'Looks like one of your friends just dropped by.'

Kate spent the rest of the afternoon alone in her stateroom, avoiding everyone, Dave included. She heard him come aboard just after six, but when Sam came down to tell her, she told him to say she was sick and that she'd catch him tomorrow.

She was hardly to know that the next time she saw Dave he'd have a gun in his hand.

By dinnertime, with the squall still blowing hard and the sea as rough as ever, Dave returned to Al's cabin with an omelette he had cooked for him, a piece of lemon pie, and a cup of strong black coffee.

'Your in-flight meal,' he said, coming in the door. 'How are you feeling?'

Al sat up on the bed and yawned cheesily. He returned the dental plates to his mouth and said, 'Better. Thanks. That stuff really works.'

'I think you'd better eat something.' Dave laid the tray on the bed. 'It's you who needs to be ready to rumble, not your stomach. With all that we've got to do, you're going to need some energy.'

Al nodded, then wolfed down the omelette hungrily.

'How about a beer?' he asked.

'Uh-uh,' said Dave. 'See those two Bandaids on your arms? Health warnings. They say the Surgeon-General has determined you remain dry until we're aboard the *Ercolano*. Because of the medication. After that it's champagne for the rest of your life.'

'I don't like champagne,' said Al, attacking the pie. 'It gives me gas.'

'That's the whole idea.'

'Yeah?'

'Sure. It's the gas that lets you get loaded quickly.'

Al looked as if he hadn't ever considered this possibility and spooned the rest of the pie into his mouth. Dave wondered if Al had ever heard of indigestion.

'Thanks for the meal. 'Preciate it.'

'No problem.'

'My stomach was as empty as a fuckin' campaign promise.' Al burped happily and then drained his coffee cup. 'Fuckin' weather, huh? Reckon it's going to slow us up any?'

Dave said, 'If it keeps up like this, it's certainly not going to make things any easier.'

'How come you don't ever get seasick?'

'Mind over matter, I guess. I don't mind. And it don't matter.' Dave lit a cigarette and grinned. 'Besides, I figure thirty, forty million bucks'll cure just about anything that ails me. Shit, man, I may never get sick again.'

Al grinned back. There were times when he quite liked the younger man. Times like this one. He promised himself that when the time came to kill Dave he'd make it quick. A bullet in the back of the head. The guy wouldn't know a thing. It seemed the least that he could do.

CHAPTER NINETEEN

Jimmy Figaro believed in history. But what was the use of it if you didn't learn from it? You didn't know about it, you were doomed to repeat its mistakes, and one thing Figaro could not afford was a mistake. Not with his client list. With some of these guys you fucked up just once and that was it. Then it was you that was history.

One of history's lessons was to do with being the bearer of bad news. A cop he once knew in Orlando got woken in the middle of the night by another cop on his doorstep telling the guy he had some bad news for him. As it happened the bad news was just that the guy had been ordered to take charge of an accident investigation in which a lot of kids had drowned, and the cop was going to have to look at the kids' bodies. But the guy was so annoyed with the other cop when he found out it wasn't really bad news for him at all, and that none of his own family were dead or anything, that he pulled a gun and shot the cop on the doorstep dead.

There were a lot of permutations on the don't-shoot-the-messenger theme. Nobody liked the guy who brought bad news. And that nobody could turn nasty when he was someone like Tony Nudelli. It was ironic how Figaro's own bad tidings were tied up with the very same thing that had taught him to be extra careful of Nudelli and his quick temper in the first place. Which was Benny Cecchino.

Benny Cecchino had been a made man, a loan shark who had borrowed $250,000 from Tony, at half a percent per week, to put out on the street at whatever vig he liked. One percent, or a hundred percent, Tony didn't care who got

charged or how much just as long as he got his 1,250 a week
from Cecchino. Cecchino had lent $4,000 to an individual
called Nicky Rosen, who promptly disappeared. Three weeks
later Cecchino had been driving up Collins and thought he
saw Rosen in another car. By the time Cecchino realized that
the guy was someone else he had smashed his Mercedes into
the lookalike and put him in hospital. An honest mistake,
except that the lookalike turned out to be Tony Nudelli's
own brother-in-law. It was just bad luck and Nudelli might
have excused this, but for the fact that Cecchino had gone
around the Beach talking about it like it was the funniest
thing that had ever happened. Like he didn't give a shit
whose brother-in-law it was. And the minute Nudelli heard
about that he took a gun, drove down to the restaurant where
Cecchino was usually to be found, which was a mob-owned
place, and took care of the insult himself. And not just any gun
either, but an awesome little Derringer-sized twelve-gauge
pistol, firing one single capiscum round that was capable of
crippling a grizzly bear. It was like having a shotgun in the
palm of your hand. A make-sure killer's gun that left most of
Cecchino's head in his lap.

After that happened it wasn't just Jimmy Figaro who gave
Naked Tony extra respect. It was everyone. David Delano
included.

As Figaro parked his BMW on Nudelli's drive, he reflected
that it was curious the way history was always rewriting itself.
How years after you thought the chapter was closed, new facts
came along to alter your perception of something you thought
you knew very well already.

It was Figaro's client, Tommy Rizzoli – Tommy of the ice
trucks and the mango trees – now cleared of all racketeering
charges, who had supplied the original crumb of information
that caused Figaro to go and check out a few things himself.
What he discovered was that on the night Dave Delano saw
Naked Tony walk into that restaurant and shoot Benny
Cecchino, Dave had been there to make a deal with Cecchino

on behalf of Nicky Rosen, the guy who had disappeared with Cecchino's four grand. Rosen, it turned out, had been engaged to be married to Dave's sister, Lisa, and Dave was trying to make sure that the same thing didn't happen to his future brother-in-law as had happened to Naked Tony's. The lookalike guy. Except that the twelve-gauge capiscum had put an end to the negotiations.

No one ever found Benny Cecchino's corpse. But it wasn't long before the word got out that Nudelli was involved and that Dave Delano had been the last man to talk to Cecchino before he got himself killed. The State tried and failed to put together a case against Naked Tony, which was when the Feds, already trying to make a Rico case against Nudelli, subpoenaed Dave to give evidence before a Grand Jury. Just a few weeks after Dave's five-year sentence for contempt, Naked Tony had taken over Benny Cecchino's vig list. Three months later, Nicky Rosen was found dead in a boatyard at Dinner Key. Someone had sawed his head half off with a broken bottle.

It wasn't that Jimmy Figaro thought that Dave was planning to double-cross Nudelli or anything. He had no idea what business he and Dave were involved in, merely that Dave and Al Cornaro were somewhere out of town and doing it. Actually he didn't think the news was so bad. But with the paranoid way Nudelli had greeted the news of Dave's release from prison, Figaro couldn't see his client treating this latest revelation with equanimity. So he had made sure to bring some really good news as well.

With a face like a rock, Nudelli listened to Figaro explain the whole story, and then stretched the cheeks across the bones with his fingers while he gave the matter some thought. Finally he said, 'And what's the silver lining you want to sew into this fucking cloud of shit you brought me, Jimmy?'

'Just this,' smiled Figaro, shifting excitedly on the leather sofa. This was the moment he had been looking forward to.

'The Court of Appeal affirmed the lower court's decision throwing out the challenge to the public portion of our new hotel's financing. It means the city properly created a redevelopment district to finance its share of the project.'

'That's good news, Jimmy.'

'Isn't it great?' Figaro smiled. He had worked it well, he thought.

'So the builders can start when?' Nudelli asked him.

'Just as soon as you give them the down payment, Tony.' Nudelli remained silent.

'There's no problem about the money, is there? Twenty-five million in cash. That's a lot of green. But without it — '

'The money's on its way. Be here any day now. Soon as Al gets back to Miami. So don't worry about a thing. Now when do you think we can open the hotel?'

'By early '98.'

'Then I think this calls for a bottle of champagne.' Nudelli pushed a button on his library desk to summon Miggy, his butler. 'I can't tell you how happy this makes me, Jimmy.'

'I'm glad. And I'm relieved. To be honest I was a little worried how you'd take the other thing. About Dave Delano.'

'I appreciate your concern, Jimmy. Maybe now you'll understand me a little better, huh? I had a nose about that kid, remember?' He pointed a finger at Figaro. 'You thought I was being paranoid.'

Jimmy Figaro started to disagree but Nudelli wasn't about to be contradicted on this point.

'Don't fuckin' argue, it's true.' But Nudelli was laughing as he said it, still wagging the finger at Figaro. 'I seen it in your eyes. You were thinkin' it, even if you weren't saying it. Well, I got an instinct for these things. Maybe this is why I am where I am. Not by havin' no college education, or no rich daddy, or by marrying some classy broad. Some hope. I got to be where I am by trusting to my fuckin' instincts, y'know? Just like I knew we could get past this redevelopment district bullshit.'

Nudelli's finger tapped the side of his nose and then the side of his temples. He chuckled as he said, 'It's a basic instinct. Like Sharon Stone's pussy. You see it only once, for a second, but it's always there. Waiting to go into action.'

Figaro grinned back at him and shook his head in apparent wonder. 'I have to admit, Tony, you were right, all along.'

This was all Nudelli wanted from Jimmy Figaro. The acknowledgment.

'So what happens now?' asked Figaro. 'About Delano?'

'How do you mean?'

'I had the impression that some sort of business relationship had been concluded.'

Nudelli looked up at the grandfather clock against the wall of his study. Twenty thousand dollars' worth of time-keeping. It was English. A George II walnut eight-day long case, the height of a basketball player. The same height as the pile of cash he expected Al to bring back from the Atlantic score.

'Concluded? Yeah.' Tony Nudelli laughed. 'In just a few hours that's what it's gonna be. Concluded.'

CHAPTER TWENTY

Dave was out of breath. A walk to the accommodations block along the narrow side of the ship at night and in a high sea could do that for you. Several times he and Al had to stand still and hang on to the guide-rail until the swell passed and they could move again. Usually the journey took five minutes. This time it took more than twenty. And when finally they reached their objective they were both soaked to the skin. For a moment there passed through his head the thought, 'What the fuck am I doing here?' Then he got it together again, and left the question unanswered in case Al should take offense. Both of them realizing the size of the task they had taken on, they parted silently for fear of giving expression to the doubts that each man now felt. Dave headed toward the radio room, and Al made his way down below to secure the engine room.

Outside the radio room Dave pressed his ear to the door, listening long and carefully, making sure there was no one about. Like Raskolnikov, ready to bash the old woman's head in. Not that he was planning to kill anyone. Least of all Jock. But although it was after twelve, someone was in there. He could hear the sound of a machine in use. If Jock was inside, Dave hoped the Scotsman wouldn't be foolish enough to try to resist. Then, glancing at his Breitling, he realized that he could wait no longer. They were working to a pretty tight synchronization. The storm had made sure of that. There would be no time for mistakes. Dave had only a minute or two to lock up the radio room and then capture the bridge before Al went into action down below.

He opened the door to darkness and a small green light,

like the single eye of some nocturnal animal. The radio room was empty and he saw that the noise was coming from the fax machine spewing a long roll of paper onto the floor. Turning on his flashlight to check on what info was being sent through, in case it affected the rendezvous, Dave saw that it was only the midweek soccer results from England. And Arsenal, whoever they were, had lost again. Dave locked the door from the outside, slipped the key into the pocket of the hunter's vest he wore over his bulletproof vest, and went along to the bridge.

The watch had changed just around midnight when the third officer was relieved by the second officer, Niven. Normally this was the quietest of all the watches, lasting until 4 a.m., when Niven would be relieved by the chief. But the weather had given the watch crew plenty to do, keeping an eye on the ship's collision and avoidance program. This involved taking the radar range and bearings with the ship's ARPA, to get the vector of ships that might be in the area. The Duke was doing 105 revs. Niven had just heard the helmsman say 'Port One', and acknowledged the computer's one degree of helm adjustment to their course, when he found himself staring into the silenced barrel of Dave's submachine gun. The red light emanating from the laser aiming module underneath the gun barrel confirmed that the bearer meant business.

Dave hoped that the men standing on the unsteady floor of the bridge would hear what he had to say above the beating of his heart.

'Be dead, or order dead slow ahead.'

Niven did not hesitate, realizing that it was only in films that anyone ever thought to question a man holding a gun on you. Straightaway he picked up the engine room telephone and gave Dave's order, and waited until it had been confirmed by the second engineer. Still holding the phone, he said, 'Dead slow ahead it is.'

'Set the gyro for automatic steering,' ordered Dave.

'It's already set. You can check it yourself if you like.'

Dave grinned. 'Why would you lie?'

Niven swallowed hard. Dave jerked his gun toward the bridge window.

'Any crew astern?'

'Not in this weather.'

Dave took the phone from Niven's trembling hand and waved him back. He said, 'Let me speak to the man with the gun.'

There was a short pause and then he heard Al's voice:

'Engine room secure.'

'Bridge secure,' said Dave. 'We're on our way down.' He tossed the receiver back to Niven who in his fear, fumbled and then dropped it onto the bridge floor.

'Sorry,' said Niven, retrieving the receiver slowly and replacing it on the wall cradle.

'Just be cool and you'll be OK,' Dave advised. 'From here on it's an attitude thing. Having one could be unhealthy. Follow me?'

'Like Moses.'

'Good boy,' said Dave. 'OK, let's go below.'

'Excuse me, but what about the helm?' asked Niven.

'We're on automatic,' said Dave. 'The computer will watch the ARPA.'

'Yeah, but all the same. In this weather, it's as well to keep an eye on things.'

Dave didn't have time to argue. Silently, he waved the gun toward the bridge wing and the stairwell that led below deck. The two men gave the gun and then Dave a wary, attentive look and went through the door. A few minutes later they and the man who had been down in the engine room were meekly stepping into the workshop. Dave watched Al shove the engineer roughly inside with the barrel of his shotgun and then bolt the door behind him.

'He give you any trouble?' Dave asked him.

'He's alive, isn't he?' Al said ominously.

'Don't be such a fuckin' hard ass. Smith and Jones, OK?'

Al shrugged and it was then Dave noticed that he was

wearing a crucifix on one of the gold chains around his neck. Al wore a lot of gold, but this was the first time Dave had seen him wearing a crucifix. Grabbing it in his half-gloved hand, he said, 'What's this?'

'What's it fucking look like, asshole?'

Al tugged the little crucifix out of Dave's fingers and tucked it behind the hard sternum of his bulletproof vest.

'You really believe God is going to look out for you with a shotgun in your hand?' laughed Dave.

'Who are you? Billy fucking Graham? What the fuck do you care what I believe?'

'I think a man ought to be self-reliant, that's all. I don't like the idea that there are any second chances in life. Makes people careless. The only one who's watching your ass round here is me, Al. Not God. Try and remember that.'

'You just watch out for your own shit and leave me to mine. I can handle the discordant notes in my set-up. I'm cool to the contraries inherent in my situation. Know what I'm sayin'? So why don't you get your nose out of my fuckin' conscience and let's go and kick some ass.'

With three men locked up that left fourteen others to be accounted for. All the officer and crew quarters were on the same deck. Most of the men were asleep. A few were drunk. Either way they offered Dave and Al no resistance. With the exception of Jellicoe. He was the last to be hauled roughly from his bed at gunpoint. Seeing the rest of his men standing meekly in the corridor under Dave's armed guard seemed to bring out in him something of his country's proud tradition of resistance.

'You know what this is, don't you?' he said stiffly.

'Shut the fuck up.'

'It's bloody piracy, that's what it is,' Jellicoe persisted. 'It's an offense against the law of nations, that's what it is. Well, mark my words, outside the normal jurisdiction of a state, I'm the law round here. And I can tell you bastards, you won't get away with this. Regardless of your nationality or domicile you can be sure that I will pursue you, arrest you, try you, and punish you as I am so empowered to do under international — '

Al jabbed the shortened barrel of his shotgun under Jellicoe's nose and racked the slide, silencing him with immediate effect. Then, wearing an expression of intense irritation, Al looked at Dave as if he held him personally responsible and said, 'OK, I'm cool to this Smith and Jones shit. But if he gives me any more of the Admiral Halsey I'm gonna pump one up each fucking nostril.'

'Do as the bastard says, sir,' said one of Jellicoe's crew. 'For Christ's sake. Or you'll get us all killed.'

Al turned his malevolent gaze back to Jellicoe and said, 'You hear that, you fuckin' fag? It's good advice. One more crack out of you and you're gonna be huntin' Red October, so help me God. Understand?'

Before he locked the workshop door, Dave took Jock aside.

'Sorry about this, Jock. Look, there are some tools and things on the floor that'll help you escape. Only I wouldn't start until around six. It's likely to make Al nervous if he hears you guys banging away and when he's nervous he gets trigger happy. Know what I mean? The ship's going dead ahead slow on auto-pilot, so you've nothing to worry about there. One more thing. You'll find some people handcuffed on the *Carrera*. The keys to their handcuffs as well as the key to the radio room are in the safe on my boat. It's a four-digit combination. The first number is keyed in already for you guys. You just have to work your way through the other 999 possibilities. Shouldn't take you more than a couple of hours. I know, I've already tried it myself. Understand?'

'Aye, I think so,' Jock frowned. 'What's this all about anyway?'

'It's like you said yourself, Jock. You make it any way you can.'

*   *   *

Clearing the accommodations block and locking up the crew was the easiest part of the plan. But scrambling from one yacht to another, and moving owners and crews off their vessels and along the dock wall in darkness had always looked more problematic. Now, in a high sea, it looked impossible. As Dave and Al had discovered on their own trip to the block, it would have been only too easy for someone to have fallen from the ship's dock wall and into the sea, where they would certainly have drowned. But Dave was nothing if not flexible in the way he approached his plan, and stumbling across those FBI shields and IDs had given him an idea how a lot of crucial time and effort might now be saved. And as soon as the ship's officers and crew were safely out of the way, Dave told Al about the change in plan.

'Al,' he said quietly. 'I've got a present for you. Now, I don't want you getting alarmed when you see what it is, OK? Because normally you would be, right? Under normal circumstances you would look at what I'm about to give you and feel very uncomfortable. And I wouldn't blame you one bit. But with anything creative, if it's any fuckin' good, there's usually a certain amount of improvisation involved. Like good jazz, y'know? Or Jimi Hendrix?'

'Improvisation?' Al's frown deepened. 'What the fuck is this? What are you talking about, improvisation? Do I look like Lee fucking Strasberg or something? We're taking down a score here, not some fucking director's notes.'

They were standing on the empty bridge staring down at a vague outline of the captive flotilla of yachts. Apart from the two lights on the ship's stern, everything was dark. Dave nodded and said, 'That's good, Al. Lee Strasberg is good. A much better example than Jimi Hendrix because there is going to be some acting involved. Did you ever see yourself as an actor, Al?'

'I hate fucking actors.'

'That's good too. See if you can hang onto that. Because

the best way of manifesting your contempt for actors would be to demonstrate just how easy acting is.'

'Get to the point, motherfucker.'

'OK, here's your part.' Dave unfolded Kent Bowen's FBI identification wallet and handed it over. He hoped that in the half-light of the bridge Al wouldn't recognize Bowen from his photograph. 'Your name is Kent Bowen and you're an Assistant Special Agent in Charge with the FBI.'

Al scrutinized the card. 'Where the fuck did you get this shit?'

'Never mind that now. That and the other one in my pocket are going to save you and me a lot of legwork.' He glanced at his watch. The change in plan was now looking essential. 'Dangerous and time-consuming legwork,' he added. 'Just look down at those boats and think about this. That it's a lot of fuckin' boats to be gettin' on and off of in the pitch dark, and in this fucking weather. Right? This FBI thing is just a way of streamlining this particular phase of the operation. You dig?'

Less effort for the same return was OK with Al. 'I guess so.'

Dave took back Bowen's FBI wallet and tucked one half inside the strap of Al's vest, so that the badge was hanging out in the front.

'There you go,' he said. 'You look just like Al Pacino. Right, now here's the set-up. You and I are going to board these boats posing as a couple of Feds. We'll tell them that we've been keeping one particular boat on this ship under surveillance because it's smuggling drugs. Only now we've got to move in and make the arrest before they transfer the stuff onto another ship. So we're asking everyone to stay in their cabins in case there's any shooting and to be real quiet. Think you can handle that?'

Al glanced at the badge he was wearing. He shook his head, and said, 'Jesus, this feels weird. I can handle this shit, yeah. Acting. Nothing to it. If Arnie Schwarzenegger can do it, then anyone can. I'm Jack Webb, no fucking problem. When I was a kid I watched *Dragnet* all the time.'

'Now you're talking,' said Dave.

'Who am I supposed to be again?' asked Al and before Dave could distract him, he had the wallet out of his vest and was scrutinizing Bowen's ID. 'I'd better get into character here.'

'Your name's Bowen,' said Dave, hoping to distract Al, worried about how he might react to the presence of three real Feds on board the *Duke*. 'And you're what the Feds call an ASAC.'

'Sack of shit more like,' muttered Al. 'Y'know, this is pretty good ID. With these fuckin' creds I could — '

'Yeah, yeah, c'mon Al, let's get moving.'

'Wait a minute,' Al frowned. 'Wait just a fuckin' minute. I recognize this joker. This is the guy on that broad's boat. That broad you've been — '

'Al, there's really no time to explain.'

'It is, isn't it? That's where I've seen this character. And this ID. This is Coca-Cola. This is the real thing.'

'None of this is relevant.'

'The hell it isn't. Show me your ID.'

'These really are going to make things easier for us, Al, if only you'll let them.'

'Hand it over, asshole.'

Dave could see there was no point in arguing. He handed Al Kate's ID and watched the big man's ugly face wince with horror.

'Jesus, she's a Fed too. You fucked a Fed, didn't ya? I don't believe it. You fucked a Fed. What the hell were you thinking of? Didn't it make you feel nervous or nothing?'

'I didn't know she was a Fed when I fucked her,' lied Dave. 'I was snooping around her pantie drawer and that's when I found her wallet.'

'What about the other guy? The tall guy with the glasses? Is he a Fed as well?'

'No, he's with the Coast Guard.'

'Did you fuck him too? Or is it just Feds you've got a thing for?' Al shook his head in wonder. 'Jesus Christ. I can't believe this. Doesn't it make you feel nervous? It makes me feel like running for Mommy's tit.'

'Relax will you? Everything's cool. They're no threat to us, believe me. For one thing they're working under cover – keeping Jellicoe under surveillance. They suspect him of smuggling drugs or guns or some shit like that. It's nothing to do with us. Nothing. You understand? And for another thing, I took their guns at the same time as I took their IDs and threw them over the side, just in case.'

Dave thought the story about Jellicoe was better for Al's peace of mind than saying he really had no idea who was under surveillance, or why, except that it certainly wasn't the two of them.

'They had guns?'

'Well of course they had guns. They're FBI, not fucking *Baywatch*.'

'I still don't like it.'

'You don't have to like it, Al. All you gotta do is act, for Chrissakes.'

'And what about them. The Feds. What are you going to do about them?' Al threw Kate's ID back at him.

'Chill out. I'll handle them.'

'Romantic goodbyes, is that it?'

'Something like that.'

'I gotta hand it to you, pal. Fucking a Fed. That's quite a pelt for any guy to have on his bedpost. But for someone like you. An ex-con, straight out of the federal joint. Wait till I tell Tony. He ain't gonna believe it. You. Dave Delano. Mister Sang Freud. That's French,' explained Al. 'Means you got composure. Like there was ice running in your veins.'

Kate lay on the gently rocking bed in her stateroom, drifting in and out of sleep. The prints and photo fits of vague thoughts piled up in her head; but she couldn't concentrate on any one of them. What was she going to do? She could hardly ignore Dave for the remainder of the voyage. Suppose he *was* involved with the mob? Was that better or worse than being a jewel thief? Was there anything he had said that she thought she could actually believe? Yes. He loved her. Even wanted to marry her. That much she did believe. And not because she wanted to, but because she just knew that it was the truth. In which case, since she felt the same way about him, did anything else really matter? What was being in the Bureau and staying on in Florida really worth compared with what she felt for him? And hadn't she wanted something like this? Something out of the ordinary? What did it really matter that she didn't know him? As Dave had said, people who didn't know each other fell in love and got married every day. Were their marriages any less successful than anyone else's? She and Howard, for instance. They'd known each other for three years before getting married. And look how that had turned out . . .

It was not so much sleep that she awoke from. More like returning from oblivion. As if something had disturbed her: something other than the storm still lashing at the porthole window. As if someone had come into her cabin. Kate rolled across the bed toward the lamp and found a hand pressed over her mouth before she could reach for the switch.

'It's me, Dave. Don't scream.' The next second he took his hand away and replaced it with his mouth.

For a minute or two she gave herself up to his kiss, pushing all her doubts to the back of her mind. He was here with her now and that was all that counted. Putting her arms around him she tried to draw him down on top of her, wanting him to make love to her, regardless of what she now knew about him. She whispered, 'Jesus, Dave, you're all wet. Is there something the matter with the ship?'

'No.'

'Well, I'm still glad you came.'

'Kate, I have to talk to you.'

'I've been avoiding you, I'm sorry. I guess you've swept me off my feet. I didn't know how to respond . . . What are you wearing? Here, let me turn the light on.'

But Dave held her still, and sensing that he didn't want the light, she began to think that something might be wrong.

He said, 'I want you to know I meant everything I said. About loving you. About wanting to marry you.'

'I know you did, I know.'

'And?'

'Can't we talk about this after we've made love?'

He sighed and moved away from her in the darkness.

'I'd like to, really I would. But you see, I'm getting off the boat. Tonight.'

'Getting off? Dave, what are you talking about? What's happening?'

'Listen carefully. Two things.'

Kate reached across and turned on the light. At a glance her eyes took in the bulletproof vest, the .45 automatic, the submachine gun, the night sights, and the walkie-talkie. He looked like some kind of navy commando. Or maybe something worse.

'Jesus.'

Dave shrugged apologetically and said, 'Well, that's the first thing.'

'What the hell's going on here?'

Dave started to answer, but she silenced him as quickly. Her mouth narrowing with disapproval, she said, 'No, don't tell me. I think I can guess. This is a hijack, isn't it?'

Dave said, 'Sure you don't want to change your mind and come along with me?'

Kate laughed with contempt. Only the contempt wasn't for him. It was for herself. To have been proved wrong about this man, the man she loved, and by Kent Bowen of all people. He would never let her forget it, the bastard. She heard herself say, 'Me, on the lam with a drug hijacker? I don't think so.'

'That's too bad,' said Dave. So he had been right about there being drugs somewhere on board the ship. That's what she thought he was planning to steal. 'Because I meant every word.'

'Yeah, you said that.' She smiled bitterly. 'You said a lot of things that don't mean a thing now. And me? I really fell for that millionaire routine, didn't I? Then the gentlemen jewel-thief bullshit. You had me dangling on a string, and how.'

'So, I'm a liar,' admitted Dave. 'Everyone in this world is pretending to be something they're not.' He paused, hoping she might volunteer something about her own deception.

She said, 'No worse? Don't fool yourself, Dave. If that's your real name. You're just another cheap recidivist from Homestead.' Kate smiled at the look of surprise on Dave's face. 'Yes, I know all about that.'

Dave tried to figure how she made him an ex-con. She was still uncertain of his real name, but could somehow connect him with Homestead.

'You want to be more careful whose books you steal.'

So that was it. There must have been something in one of his books. A bookplate or something. He should have been more careful. Dave realized he had underestimated her.

'I guess you think you've figured out all the angles.' Kate slipped slowly off the bed and onto the floor. 'Well, I'm not going to wish you luck. Your kind isn't interested in leaving things to luck. You want a sure thing. But there is something I'd like to give you, in the way of a keepsake. Something to remember me by. When you're doing time again.'

Dave watched her coolly lift the bedspread, admiring the way she was handling herself. Him armed to the teeth and her, dressed only in pyjamas, still going for it, undeterred, thinking she still had a chance to nail him. Reluctant to admit defeat. There was no doubt about it, he had picked a really special one. Kate Furey was one hell of a woman.

Slowly she pulled out the bed drawer and said, 'A little souvenir, of our love. So you'll always know exactly what you missed when you lost my good opinion of you, Dave.'

Smiling, Kate reached into the drawer, all the way to the back where she kept her identity card and the Ladysmith .38. The way he was sitting there, legs akimbo, arms folded, smiling slightly, like the score was already in the bag. The last thing he was expecting was a weapons-trained federal agent coming out of that drawer with a gun pointed at his balls.

Dave watched her search become more urgent and the sly little smile she had been wearing quickly disappear. 'Looks like you've missed something yourself,' he said. And taking her ID out of the pocket of his huntsman's vest, he flipped it open over his forefinger. 'Is this what you're looking for, Agent Furey?'

Kate lunged for her wallet.

'Uh-uh-uh,' he said, and returned it to his pocket. 'This and the gun that was with it. What would you have done if you had found it? Would you really have shot me?'

Kate sat back and folded her arms calmly. 'We'll never know, will we?'

'Agent Furey. I prefer that name. It suits you a lot better than Parmenter. Agent Furey sounds like something the Army might have used in Vietnam. A defoliant, maybe. You certainly shook the leaves off my tree, I don't mind telling you. They're all over the grass.'

'Parmenter is my married name.'

'That part true? About you and he getting divorced?'

'Yes.'

'Is he FBI too?'

'No, he's an attorney.'

Dave nodded.

'When did you find out?' she asked.

'Oh, I could ask you the same question. But I'm afraid we're out of time.' Dave reached into his vest then tossed a pair of a handcuffs onto the floor. 'Just on the one wrist please, if you don't mind.'

'And if I refuse to comply? Do you think you can shoot me?'

'Nope. I couldn't even point a gun at the contents of your closet. But I wouldn't mind betting I could give that boss of yours, Kent Bowen, a good crack on the ear.'

'That makes two of us.'

'And Al – well, Al is capable of just about anything where a Fed is concerned.'

'I figured.' Kate snapped the cuff on one wrist. Much as she disliked Kent Bowen she really hadn't the stomach to see any harm come to him.

'Just in case you were wondering, Bowen and the other fellow are safely handcuffed in the luxury of their own staterooms.'

Kate held up the wrist wearing the cuff. 'Can you get me the earrings to match?'

Dave pointed inside the head. 'In there, please.'

She got up and went through. He told her to sit down on the floor and to open the closet underneath the sink where the reel-to-reel tape machine was hidden.

'Nice stereo,' said Dave. 'By the way, who was it that you guys were really after?'

'What? You expect me to finger the dope for you, is that it?' Kate assumed he was being flippant. That this was just another way of taunting her. 'You. We were after you and your friend, Al.'

He said, 'No, you weren't. I already listened to your tape.'

'Then why are you asking me?'

'You're right. It doesn't matter. Now reach around the waste pipe and manacle the other wrist.'

When she had done it, he dangled the keys and said, 'I'll put these in my safe. I assume you know where that is. My guess is you already tried to open it when you searched my room. The key to the radio room's there as well. It's a four-digit combination. The first number's keyed in. It takes about two hours to work your way through the 999 remaining possibilities. The ship's crew are all locked up in the workshop, but it shouldn't take them more than a few hours to break out. I've told them you're here, so you shouldn't have long to wait. Of course, we'll be gone by then.'

He took out a roll of surgical tape. Just in case she started hollering and putting the crews on the Russkie boats on alert.

'I'm sorry about this,' he said. 'Really I am. You have the most attractive mouth — '

'Save it for the judge, asshole.'

'Anything I can get you first? A glass of water, perhaps?'

'How about a glass of water and a goodbye kiss?'

'Easy.' Still apologizing, Dave fetched her some water from the faucet and helped her to drink. She swallowed most of it but as he moved closer to kiss her, she squirted a jet of water right back in his face.

Laughing she said, 'There you go. There's your kiss. A big wet one you'll always remember me by.'

Dave picked up a towel and wiped his face. Trying to smile he said, 'In the next life you'd better come back as a fountain.'

'You should thank me. You may never feel this clean again.'

When he had finished taping her mouth he asked her if she could breathe all right. She nodded sullenly.

'Sure you won't change your mind? Come with me? We could be good together.'

She shook her head.

'OK, if you should ever change your mind . . .'

Kate looked the other way.

'Then keep an eye on the Tuesday editions of the *Miami Herald*. Classified section. Lost and Found. Look out for, Lost at Sea. Siberian Husky. Answers to the name of Rodya. It'll say No Reward, just to stop any cowboys from telephoning. There'll be an answering service. You can leave a message.

If you want.' Dave paused and let out a long sigh. 'I hope
you do.'

Kate kept her head averted. A second or two later she heard
the door close behind him.

CHAPTER TWENTY-ONE

'What took you?' growled Al. 'Or did you feel impelled to fuck that Fed bitch again? For old times' sake.'

'You wouldn't understand,' Dave told him. 'The way it turned out was something rather more poetic than just a straight fuck.'

Al laughed. 'Nothing's more poetic than a straight fuck, shit for brains. Except maybe one that deviates up her ass or something. All those books in prison must have turned your dick to Jell-O.' Al wiped his sweating forehead and bare arms with a bar towel he had taken from the last boat he'd been on. 'You were right about one thing though.'

'I'm glad to hear it.'

'This FBI shit works better than a gun. You just tell people what to do, snap your fingers like Mary fuckin' Poppins, and they do it. It's better than a gun. And no questions asked.'

Dave said, 'It's like I was telling you. Alias Smith and Jones. There's no need to shoot anyone if you're wearing that badge on your chest.'

'Tell that to David Koresh. One thing though. You do uncover a lot of bad shit when you just walk in on people uninvited. That bitch on the *Jade* for instance. Rachel Dana?'

'What about her?'

'Bitch was in bed with one of the girls in her crew. Pair of them as naked as the day they hatched. I didn't know whether to flash my dick or my badge. Lesbians, the pair of them. I swear they were both attached to the same fuckin' dildo. Like they was on a life-support system.'

They were on the *Duke*'s port stern stack, looking back

up toward the bow of the ship. Al threw the towel into the pitching sea with disgust and lit a cigar.

'I'd forgotten about your homophobia,' said Dave. He shrugged, 'Hey, whatever floats your boat.'

'I'm not homophobic,' Al insisted. 'But I just can't figure that dildo shit. I mean if you're a dyke, it means pussy's your thing. If you want eight inches of length inside you, you might as well choose the real thing, right? 'Stead of some plastic dick looks like it belongs in a toy store. I mean, how do you figure it?'

'Doctor Ruth, I'm not,' said Dave. 'What did they say, after you interrupted them?'

'They were kind of pissed at me. But I told them I didn't care what they got up to. Or what got up them. They could fuck a cat with a broken back for all I cared just as long as they stayed on their boat. Less they wanted to get their heads blown off.'

'That was cute,' said Dave. 'OK, how many boats have we got left to visit?'

'Apart from our three Russians? Just the one.' Al pointed at the *Britannia*. 'That one. The getaway from it all boat.'

'Good work. You've been busy.'

'Like I said. This FBI thing works like beetlejuice.'

'Take a breather. I'll handle the *Britannia*.'

'Be my guest. Hey did you know Calgary Stanford is on this ship? The movie actor? He was hitting a pipe when I caught up with him. Lousy doper.'

'Takes all sorts to make a world, Al. Least that's what it says in the Bible, doesn't it?' Dave started to walk down the stairs toward the stern of the *Britannia*.

'How the fuck should I know?'

'Well, you're the Catholic, aren't you?'

'Ain't you heard? Catholic Church don't like people reading the Bible. They used to grease you for it.'

In the moonlight the sea looked like something animate, like the scaly skin of some enormous reptile. Perhaps even the one he was feeling like. He thought he'd given Kate a choice – to come with him or to stay on the boat. But really he'd given her no choice at all. And she wouldn't have been the girl he loved if she'd agreed to come with him. He knew that and it didn't make him feel any better about himself.

Dave stepped onto the deck of the *Britannia* still unaware of the special cargo that was concealed inside the yacht's enlarged fuel tanks. He was set to impress those on board with his impeccable credentials. With all that he and Al still had left to do, he'd forgotten that Kate Furey and her Fed friends had been keeping someone else under surveillance. There was no way he could know that the *Britannia's* crew might feel a little less sanguine than most about being boarded by the FBI. His heart was still in bed with Kate. His mind was already boarding the first Russian boat where he expected to encounter the real resistance. Not to mention the money.

The *Britannia* looked quiet enough, although the owner's taste left something to be desired. Flashing his Maglite around the lounge, Dave liked the furniture well enough, but the art on the oak-panelled walls was the worst kind of kitsch – the kind of bland stuff you bought with both eyes on the room's color scheme. He went downstairs. When he had real money he was going to buy some real art. Paintings. Not interior decoration.

Below deck, in the three en-suite staterooms, all was quiet. Dave opened the first door to find a twin-bedded cabin. There were clothes all over the place but the beds were empty. He opened the second door to find a sophisticated art deco room more to his taste, and a double bed with a naked man and woman staring at him blearily through the hard flashlight he'd aimed at them. There was no window or porthole in the cabin, so Dave closed the door quietly behind him and turned on the light.

'Who the fuck are you? What the hell's going on?' the guy was demanding.

'US Federal Bureau of Investigation, sir,' said Dave, waving Kate's badge. 'I'm sorry to break in on you people in the middle of the night like this. But if you could just keep your voices down, I'll explain what this is all about.'

The woman slapped the sheet around her with both hands and shook her head bitterly.

'I don't believe it. I just don't believe it. Oh Jesus. Well, that's just fucking great,' she said. 'Shit. Shit. Shit.'

Dave said, 'Take it easy, will you? Look we're about to make an arrest on another boat. Some drug smugglers. But before we do, we're trying to warn all the passengers to stay put in their cabins. If you do hear shooting, then you should lie down on the floor, until you hear from us that it's all clear. Just in case. It's only a precaution. I don't think there's any need to worry.'

'Oh Christ,' said Nicky Vallbona.

'You stupid bastard,' said Gay Gilmore, punching him hard on the shoulder.

'Me? What the fuck did I do?'

'I told you they were onto us, didn't I? Back in Lauderdale. I said they were watching us. But no, you wouldn't listen. Not you. You knew better. Mister Pro-Fessional Arsehole.'

'Did you hear what I said?' asked Dave.

'You couldn't believe that I would have spotted something you didn't. Well, if you think I'm going to prison for a prick like you, Nicky, you can forget it. I'm not. I'll tell them everything. I've got the rest of my life to live and I'm not doing it inside jail.'

'Will you please keep your voices down?'

'Fuck off,' snarled Gay. 'What difference does it make? If you're going to arrest us, then arrest us, but don't expect us to be happy about it, mate. Or is being arrested normally some kind of party? Tell me, Mister G-Man. I'd like to know how I'm supposed to react to this shit.'

'Arrested?' Dave frowned. Suddenly it dawned on him. Hers was one of the voices on Kate's tape. This was the boat with the drugs. No wonder they were so unnerved by his presence. Now if he could only get her to shut up for a second then he might be able to explain.

'We did some coke earlier on,' explained Vallbona. 'She's still a little high.'

'Not any more, lover. I'm on a fucking downer now, thanks to you.'

'Will you shut up?' snapped Dave. 'Shut up. Just for a minute. Look, this is not a bust. You're not being arrested.'

'You said to lie down on the floor,' Gay insisted.

'Then do it, for Christ's sake.' Dave jerked his silenced .45 at the floor. He was going to have to get rough with them anyway, when the time came to steal their boat. Maybe now was as good a time as any. 'I don't have time for all this bullshit.'

Suddenly the door behind him opened, banging against Dave's head. He heard someone in the corridor outside say, 'What the fuck's going on?'

It was all the opportunity the two in bed needed. Each reached for a handgun.

The big automatic in Dave's hand seemed to take charge of what happened next and with the laser-sight it was as easy as taking a photograph with some idiot's idiot-proof camera. In a split second his entire world was reduced to a red circle with a central dot floating inside it, and Dave had fired several times more before the door behind him banged hard open again, knocking him onto the blood-spattered bed.

Dave slipped to the floor, pursued by this new assailant, whose hand gripped the fist holding Dave's gun as tightly as the other held his windpipe. Dave punched the man hard underneath the chin, but with no result and the two struggled to their feet only to crash through the door of the en-suite head. For a second, the grip on his windpipe released, and Dave could smell the cordite in the air from when he had fired the shots. He might have shot his attacker too if the barrel of his gun had been shorter. They collapsed over the edge of the empty bath, Dave's wrist caught on the shower door and the gun clattered into the bath underneath him. Dave lunged at the man with the top of his head, butting him hard in the mouth, then fell back against the tiled wall. He reached down below him for the gun but by the time he had the grip in his hand, the man had hauled the nylon clothes line out of the wall-mounted spindle and had wound a good length of it around Dave's neck. This time the grip was tighter and Dave kicked out in front of him, his boot smashing the glass in the shower door. The guy was strangling him. Twisting one way and then the other, like a dog on a short lead, Dave tried to elbow the guy in the stomach, but his own vest and the machine gun got in the way. Another minute and it would all be over. Another sixty seconds and he would be dead. Already he could feel the edges of his world becoming dark and hazy, as if the void was closing in upon him.

The head door slammed open and something spat twice into the air, jolting the man behind him like a bolt of electricity. The pressure on the line around his neck slackened and hot steamy liquid trickled down the back of Dave's neck. It was another second or two before he realized that it was blood from the dying man who groaned as Al lifted Dave clear of his attacker. Then Al stood back, levelled the silencer and fired another shot into the guy's throat, just to make sure.

Al looked anxiously at his coughing partner and asked, 'You OK?'

Trembling, Dave took a deep and unrestricted breath. Holding his nylon-burned neck, he stuck his throbbing head under the cold shower, hardly paying attention to the blood still running out of the dead man's bullet wounds and washing down the plug. When Dave finally answered Al, his own voice sounded as if he'd smoked a couple of cartons of cigarettes.

'I think so. Thanks. He'd have strangled me for sure.'

'Don't mention it. Kind of fuckin' actor are you anyway? I mean, there are no Oscars for what happened down here. Not even a lousy Emmy. Goddamned bedroom. It looks like *The*

Wild Bunch through there.' Al lit a cigarette for Dave. 'Here. This'll help you get your breath. What did happen in there, as a matter of small academic interest?'

Dave pulled a towel over his head and sighed.

'Damned if I know.'

'It's like I said, then. The Alias Smith and Jones factor? It's bullshit. People carry guns, people get shot. Stands to reason.'

'They gave me no choice. I had to shoot them. It was them or me.'

'No doubt about it. I guess there was something about your manner they objected to. Me, I can relate to that. Your small talk can be like fleas sometimes. It itches like fuck. The sight of that badge drove 'em to it, perhaps. Who the fuck knows? But it's lucky for you I came down here or you'd be John Brown, man.'

'They thought we were pinching them. They thought it was a real bust. That's why they went for their guns.'

But Al hardly cared to listen. He was already heading back through the stateroom where the two bodies lay grotesquely twisted on the bloodstained bed, on his way upstairs. He said, 'The fuck difference does it make now? They're dead, ain't they? For them it was a real bust. Dead's the biggest bust there is.'

Coming upstairs into the moonlight, Dave took a deep breath of the cool night air. The *Britannia* looked so pure and white that it was hard to connect it with the bloody scene in the master stateroom below. It was a couple of minutes before he realized what else had happened.

'The storm's died away,' he said.

'That's what I came down to tell you,' said Al. 'Happened just like that.'

'I guess that's something.'

'Still want to do this the hard way?' asked Al.

'Meaning?'

'No killing.'

'More than ever.'

'You're being a mite particular, aren't you? These guys ain't gonna be any more co-operative than the three we just greased.'

'Al it's my understanding that you're a professional killer. But me? I'm a rank amateur. Like I said before, I didn't want to be a killer. And now that I've killed two people – the first two people I ever killed – I want to be a killer even less. What I did back there makes me feel sick to my stomach.'

'Hey, don't let it spoil your evening. That was self-defense. Them or you, just like you said. It's intention that counts. Even the law knows that much. A real Fed would have blown them away just the same as you did. So being dead is their fault, not yours. They were fuckin' stupid. Had to be stupid to think they could pull a gun on a man carrying your kind of heat.'

'One of them was a girl, Al.'

'That much I noticed. Nice-looking broad too. Good tits. But a nice-lookin' broad with good tits and a handgun. Makes all the fuckin' difference in the world. And the next one, too, if it comes to that.' Al shrugged. 'I still reckon we should grease these fuckers. That's why we've got the silencers on the ends of our dicks.'

'Tell you what, Al. I'll make you a deal. If we can avoid any more bloodshed, you can have half my share.'

Al thought about this for a moment. Since he was planning to murder Dave the minute he saw the *Ercolano* sailing toward the rendezvous point, and since Naked Tony had already promised Al Dave's share anyway, the deal didn't sound so good. But he had little choice but to agree, or else risk Dave's suspicion. He was a nice guy for a dead man.

'OK, you gotta deal. Half your share and no more human tragedies.'

'We stick to shooting only in self-defense.'

'Right,' sighed Al. 'But don't go soft on me, Dave. Remember, I'm supposed to be the one with the conscience. Not you.

I'm the Catholic round here. You. You're an atheist. You don't believe in shit.'

Al tripped and fell upon the explanation for the lack of any resistance they met on the *Baby Doc* almost as soon as they had set foot inside the smelly lounge. The boat's shabby interior was littered with empty vodka bottles and on top of the dining table was what looked to have been a serious game of Monopoly – not least because it had been played with real money. There were loose piles of dollars all over the place and in Dave's eyes it was easy to see what must have happened.

First a hell of a lot of drinking; although few, if any, of the three crews were actually Russian, it was as if the idea of Russianness had exercised such a powerful effect on the crewmen that they had felt an obligation to live up to the hard-drinking reputation enjoyed by their employers; second, the idea of playing the ultimate game of Monopoly, with some of the real cash that was being smuggled to Russia; and third, a lot more hard drinking. One of the crewmen lay insensible on the lounge sofa, and another had passed out on the floor of one of the heads. A third they found dead drunk in the wheelhouse, curled up like a baby in the cockpit chair. The rest of the three crews were sleeping it off in the *Baby Doc*'s staterooms. Most of them so drunk that even after Dave and Al had tied them up with plastic ties, they stayed asleep, or unconscious.

'Will you look at these drunken bastards?' laughed Al, when he had tied up the last man in his stateroom. 'Be a while before they even know we've been and gone. Jesus, that's some fuckin' Monopoly game they got upstairs. Must be a couple of hundred thousand dollars on that game board.' He stood up, checked the knot, then kicked the man in the small of the back. The man grunted and rolled quietly away. 'How many's that?'

Dave was checking the three crews off against the ship's

own list of supernumeraries. He nodded and said, 'That's all of them.'

'Bet you wish you hadn't made that deal now,' Al said harshly. 'This was a piece of sponge cake.' He picked up a half-empty bottle of vodka, unscrewed the top and took a short pull from the neck. 'Wasn't it?'

Dave said nothing, and it was then Al noticed the clasp knife in the younger man's hand. Al's gun lay on the coffee table, several feet away. He swallowed nervously, because of the deal he had made and the ease with which their objective had apparently been achieved. Maybe he had pushed him too far. He held out the bottle for Dave to drink.

'Want some?'

Dave thought he probably needed a drink. Since killing the two in bed his stomach had felt like he'd eaten something disagreeable. Maybe some vodka would fix it. He took the bottle, gulped a mouthful, and handed the bottle back. Then, rolling the man he had tied roughly off the bed, he turned the mattress on top of him and plunged the knife deep into the seam of the divan underneath. He tore away the cover to reveal a six-foot square of something faintly green under a thick polythene sheet. The knife flashed again and the two men stared down at an enormous pallet of cash wrapped in smaller, pillow-sized bundles.

'Didn't I tell you?' grinned Dave.

'You were right.'

'Didn't I fucking tell you?'

'How much do you reckon is there?'

Dave picked up one of the bundles, slit the edge of the polythene with his knife and thumbed through a corner of used notes.

'Hard to say exactly. It's mixed bills. Hundreds, fifties and twenties. Nothing smaller. I don't know. Maybe a couple of million?'

'There're five staterooms on this boat,' breathed Al. 'Do you know how much that is?'

'Five times two? I'm sure you can work it out if you try, Al.'

But the sight of so much cash had made Al impervious to Dave's sarcasm, and instead of cursing him he said, 'That deal we made? Forget it.' The last thing Al wanted now was to have Dave mad at him. Being mad at him might make Dave a little harder to kill when the time came. 'You keep your share. You've earned it.'

'Didn't I tell you?' Dave repeated. Now there was a note of triumph in his voice.

Al said, 'I'll get the bags. You find the rest of the money.'

A few minutes later, Al came back carrying a flat-packed bulk-purchase of Nike sports bags bent across each shoulder. Dave had already ripped apart the four other divans as well as the three-piece leather suite in the *Baby Doc*'s lounge.

Laughing like a crazy man, Al stuffed one of the heavy-duty nylon bags with parcels of cash. Then another. 'Will you look at all this dough?'

Dave zipped up two bags full, hooked a strap over each shoulder and stood up. Being rich couldn't have looked or felt more unwieldy. He was glad of the gloves and the flak-jacket, for the bags weighed close to fifty pounds apiece.

Al was already staggering upstairs, puffing under the weight of the two bags he was carrying. He said, 'Jesus, this is like going to the airport with Madonna and the kids.'

'Now you know what people mean when they talk about the burden of wealth.'

'I sure hope I live to spend it. All this exertion, my heart's beating like Thumper's foot.'

'Make up your mind to be an unfit rich motherfucker, instead of one of those healthy-looking kids always asking for change.'

'I can deal with that.'

Breathing hard, both men came up on deck and dumped the bags gratefully.

Al said, 'Oh man, this is hard work.'

'Got a problem with that?'

'Shit, yeah. I got my *modus vivendi* down man. I didn't ever figure to be no fuckin' hotel porter.'

'Kinda tired myself,' admitted Dave.

'Time is it?'

'There's two more boatloads of money to think about. You've got a lot more bags to carry upstairs before your ass can sit down in the front lobby.'

'I know that. I was just askin' the time. I thought you might be pleased to help me out, you being the proud owner of the Rolls fucking Royce of watches.'

'Be dawn soon.'

'Do I look like a fuckin' vampire? If I want that kind of shit I'll wait for a cock to crow. Numbers. That's what I like to hear. Tick fucking tock. On account of my citified ass and urbane fucking ways.'

'What are you, Stephen Hawking or something? It's nearly 3 a.m. What difference does it make? I'll tell you if we're behind schedule. First thing I do when I get back to Miami, I'm going to buy you a watch, Al. That way you'll know when it's time to shut your mouth. Now let's move before some of these supernumos on their boats start to get curious about what's happening. I've killed enough people for one evening.'

'That shit still bothering you?'

'Oddly enough, yes, it is.'

'Chill out. Like I said before, it was you or them. An accident.'

'That doesn't sound like an accident.'

'Sure it does. An unforeseen contingency. That's all that happened. You want to find your cloudy ass a silver lining damn quick, pal. I don't want you goin' Leonard Cohen on me. Lift your eyes to the good news with which your situation is replete. First, that you are now one rich motherfucker. And second, it could have been them Feds you greased.

The real ones. Think how lower than snake-shit you'd be feeling now if it was that Fed bitch you'd terminated instead of the other one.'

CHAPTER TWENTY-TWO

At Quantico Kate had learned that the secret of escaping from handcuffs, as perfected by the likes of Houdini, was a simple one. You had the keys.

When keys or picks were not required you needed a spring-loaded cuff and a sharp tap in the right place. But mostly Houdini had a key up his ass or a tiny pick inserted in the thick skin on the soles of his feet. Even with a pick, Kate did not think she could have worked all the levers inside the tiny keyhole. That was the kind of skill for which you needed years of practice. Besides, she was particularly careful of her feet. She kept a piece of lava on the side of her bathtub at home, and regularly visited a chiropodist. Health and fitness were important to her. She did yoga to help her relax and keep her body supple. And periodically she was a vegetarian. Howard had said that it made her too thin, but then his idea of what a woman ought to look like was Anna Nicole Smith. It wasn't as if Kate was flat-chested or anything. Just feminine. Finely boned. Not some fantasy fuck built by Goodyear. Once Howard had said that finely boned was just another way of saying scrawny. This was not long after she had confronted him with the evidence of his adultery. Why had he needed to have other women? Didn't he find her attractive? Was there something wrong with the way she looked? It was her own fault for asking. She was slim. Graceful. Willowy. Rangy, even. The only time Kate felt scrawny was when Howard, looking for a quick fuck, tried to squeeze into the shower cabinet alongside her. The hell with him, the fat bastard. Slim and slender was what she was. But not so slim that the cuffs were about to be squeezed off like a tight bangle.

Once, when she was a kid back in T'ville, she had got her head stuck between some railings and her mother had called the fire department. For half an hour her older brother had teased her that they would have to cut through the railings with an oxy-acetylene torch, which might also burn through her neck. But in the event, they had simply covered her head with thick industrial soap-liquid and slid her out. And now, sitting on the floor of the head, staring at the waste-pipe under the basin, she thought she might try something similar. In the closet were several bottles of shampoo and shower gel that Kate was able to pick up with her feet and then place in her manacled hands. It wasn't long before her hands and wrists were covered in a thick oleaginous green treacle of mixed soaps. Kate's hands weren't much wider than her wrists; at least not when the metacarpal bones of the thumb and little finger were squeezed together; and Dave had been too ashamed of himself to have made the cuffs uncomfortably tight on her wrists. Behind the surgical tape stretched across her mouth, Kate cursed him and, determined to ignore the pain, began to pull at the glutinous cuffs as if her life depended upon it.

Dave threw the last bag of money onto the deck of the *Britannia* and returned to the *Juarista* to fetch the scuba equipment. Back on board the chosen getaway boat, he stripped and climbed into a wet-suit under Al's grim and increasingly bleary gaze.

Al shook his head and shivering, said, 'Rather you than me with that Lloyd Bridges shit.' He looked circumspectly over the side of the boat and then spat into the water. 'Water don't look so clean.'

Dave thought of saying something about the bottle of vodka in Al's hairy paw and a possible reaction with the two Scopoderm plasters he was still wearing on his forearms, but thought better of it. Al's job was finished. From here on in, more or less everything was down to Dave.

'What does that shit mean, anyway? Scuba. I never did know.'

'Means Self-Contained Underwater Breathing Apparatus,' Dave explained. 'It's an acronym.' He hauled what looked like a life-vest made of black rubber over his head: attached to the front of the rubber were some tubes, a mouthpiece and a green cylinder about the size of a household fire extinguisher.

Al frowned. He said, 'That's it? That's your tank? I got a bigger tank than that on my fuckin' soda siphon.'

Dave nodded. 'This is a Draeger closed circuit system,' he said. 'A rebreather. It catches the exhaled breath, producing no bubbles. It's comfortable and very light.' He passed the straps under his crotch and then around his waist. 'Pure oxygen, no mixture, makes it ideal for shallow work. And it's very small, as you can see.'

Al looked over the side once again. He said, 'How deep is it down there anyway?'

Dave was watching the sky. The sun was coming up now. They were running a little behind schedule but he was glad of that. He hadn't particularly cared for the idea of making this dive in the water of the *Duke*'s floating harbor in darkness. He said, 'Bout twenty feet,' and tested the supply from the mouthpiece. He hoped twenty feet was right. Oxygen was toxic at anything below thirty-three feet.

'Well,' said Al, and took another drink. 'Rather you than me. That's all I can say.'

Dave spat into his face mask and rubbed the spittle around the glass. He laughed and said, 'Al, I'm gonna take a wild guess here. You can't swim, can you?'

'Lots of people can't swim.'

'Sure. And lots of people drown every year.'

Al grinned back. 'Not if they don't ever go swimming. You ask me, it's mostly people who can swim and who go swimming who get their asses drowned. Let me ask you a question. Which of the two of us is more likely to get himself drowned at this particular moment in time? You or me?'

'You've got a point.'

'Absolutamente. On account of you're the dumb mother-fucker who knows how to swim and how to use a self-contained underwater breathing apparatus. Right?'

'Comforting thought,' admitted Dave, and collected up his searchlight and his knife.

'QED,' shrugged Al.

Dave grinned. 'QED?'

'Yeah, that's another of them acronomes. Means the kind of shit that speaks for itself.'

'I know what it means,' said Dave, retiring to the stern of the boat and climbing onto the ladder. 'I just wondered if you knew what the letters stood for?'

'Sure I do. I may not read books, but I ain't exactly ignorant. Stands for Quite Easily Done. Just like the way even motherfuckers who know what the fuck they're doin' in the water and think maybe they're James Bond or something, can get their land-dwelling selves as drowned as the lost city of Atlantis. You hear what I'm saying? Be careful down there. Your ass gets in a puddle of trouble, don't expect me to jump in and help you out. And don't expect no Pamela Anderson either. Only Baywatch round these parts is that fuckin' clam on your wrist.'

Dave looked at his watch. 'If I drown it's yours.'

'Yeah. Like I'm goin' to come and get it. That thing waterproof?'

'Of course. It's a real tachymeter.'

'You said it, guy. Tackiest lookin' timepiece I ever saw.' Al laughed. 'Naw, you keep it. I got enough shit already.'

Still smiling, Dave slipped into the water. It was a lot colder than he had expected and he was glad for the wet-suit. He paused for a moment, glancing up at the high walls of the ship and the crowd of vessels around him. It wasn't just the daylight he was glad of. It was the calmer sea too. Going into the *Duke*'s floating dock during that storm would have been a lot more dangerous. He switched on the flashlight, adjusted the mask on his face, secured the mouthpiece between his teeth, and then dropped beneath the oily surface.

As Dave swam down underneath the barnacled hull of the boat, a feeling of being enclosed threatened momentarily to give way to panic. It was like being back in Homestead again. Back in his cell, soaked in the cold sweat of his worst nightmare, drowning in the unfathomable depths of his five-year prison sentence. Steeling himself, Dave kicked out toward the underwater support welded to the *Duke*'s dock floor, to which the *Britannia* was securely lashed. He had only to cut through the ropes for the boat to float free from the plinth. But for Al's ignorance of navigation and the workings of a modern motor yacht, this was the stage in the plan when Dave would have been most nervous of being double-crossed by his partner. For once the underwater line was cut, Al had only to let go the port lines mooring the *Britannia* fast to the *Duke*'s dock walls for the ship to float free. A quick burst of reverse engines and the boat would be out in the Atlantic on her own. Al's lack of maritime knowledge had never seemed so reassuring as it did now.

Because the stern of the *Duke* was open to the ocean, there were fish swimming in the dock water. These were mostly mullet and grunt and he paid them little or no attention as he swam strongly underneath the yacht's hull and caught hold of her screw. The rope itself was a thick one and he used his diving knife's serrated edge to cut it. Even so, it was several minutes before the rope was finally severed and he was able to untie the end attached to the screw so that it wouldn't foul the propeller when they were underway. Meanwhile the end tied to the floor support sank down in the water, startling a small school of mullet. Mistaking the rope for some kind of predator, an eel perhaps, the fish turned back on themselves and swam straight past Dave, missing his face by inches, almost as if they intended to use him as cover. He was still marvelling at their speed and beauty and congratulating himself on the ease with which he had completed his task when he saw the real reason for the sudden departure of the mullet. Not the rope at all, but the streamlined, silver-blue shape of a great barracuda. The fright of seeing it made him drop his flashlight.

Swift and powerful, with two well-separated dorsal fins, a jutting lower jaw and a large mouth with lots of sharp teeth, the six-foot barracuda was a fearsome fish and Dave knew its aggressive reputation well enough to be extremely wary of it. Barracudas were responsible for more attacks on Florida swimmers than sharks. And while they didn't ever eat people, they were quite capable of inflicting the severest injuries. Instinctively Dave started to swim gently away, toward the bow of the *Britannia* and, curious, the big fish followed. Barracudas were reportedly attracted to shiny objects and Dave could not decide if the blade in his hand was a source of help or the cause of his continuing danger. He swam on his back, not wanting to take his eyes off the creature in case it decided to attack. It wasn't that he thought the fish might kill him. But the razor-sharp teeth of some barracuda were impregnated with a toxic substance that could poison you. The last thing Dave needed in the middle of the Atlantic was a badly infected bite.

He swam deeper so as not to hit his head on the hulls or rudders of other boats. And the barracuda swam slowly after him, sometimes disappearing in the dark shadow of one boat, only to reappear in a brilliant flash of silver as it entered the sunlit water again. It was, Dave reflected as coolly as he was able, like being followed by a vicious and slightly cowardly dog that was only waiting the right opportunity, such as when his back was turned, to make an attack. And no matter how powerfully Dave kicked his way through the water, the barracuda maintained the same ten feet between them with an effortless flick of its stealth-shaped tail.

Dave risked a glance at his watch. Valuable minutes from

an already tight schedule were ticking by. And finding that he had already swum the entire length of the *Duke* and was now right under the bows of the *Jade* at the front of the floating dock, he sensed that he would have to do something soon, or his small supply of oxygen would give out. Swimming into a pool of sunlight, Dave glanced up and saw the *Jade*'s bow ladder touching the water about ten feet above his head. Paddling into a more vertical position he saw the sun catch his wristwatch and, at the same time, the barracuda turn fractionally toward the small burst of reflected light. There was only thing for it. Reluctantly, Dave unbuckled the watch and transferred it to the hand still holding the knife. For a second or two he let the sun play on the collection of shiny metal in his hand. Only when he was quite sure that the barracuda was watching the two bright objects did he let them go. As they sank toward the floor of the dock, the barracuda flicked its tail and cruised down after them. The creature's man-trap jaws opened and closed on the fish-scale silver of the watch's metal bracelet.

Dave hardly hesitated. He kicked hard for the undulating surface and the ladder above his head.

Even as he reached and then caught the ladder he felt the great barracuda come up after him. Adrenalin shot through his heart and shoulder muscles, launching him up the ladder with such speed that he almost thought it was someone else's arm hauling him out of the water. Inches under the bottom step of the ladder and the heel of Dave's bare foot, the barracuda arced through the oily surface then disappeared into the shallow blue water below.

Dave plucked the rebreather mouthpiece away and gulped a deep, unsteady breath of the open morning air.

'Holy shit,' he gasped. 'That was close.'

Now the fish was gone, so was the strength in his arms and it was a minute or two before he managed to climb up onto the *Jade*'s deck. Standing there, he took another deep breath and tried to gather himself. The next instant he heard a gunshot and something zipped over his head, ricocheting off the *Duke*'s forward bulkhead. He threw himself flat onto the deck, incredulous at this latest turn of lethal events.

'Jesus. What now?'

Lying there, he tried to determine the direction the shot had come from. Who could have fired it? Had he and Al overlooked someone among the crew or the supernumos? Someone with a gun? Or had Kate simply escaped and armed herself with a gun he hadn't known about? He raised his head a few inches to see if he could spot the gunman, then ducked again as another shot clanged into the radio mast above him. Why didn't Al do something about it? Unless this was the double-cross he had feared.

He had to find out. He crawled toward the rail of the boat and shouted, 'Hey Al, it's me, Dave. Who the fuck is doing the shooting?'

There was a brief and, Dave thought, ominous silence. Then Al said, 'Is that you, Dave?'

'Of course it's me, you idiot. Who the hell do you think it is?'

'What the fuck are you doing down there? I thought you was some nosey parker not staying indoors like he was supposed to.'

Dave jumped to his feet. Angrily tearing off his rebreather, he started up and along the wall of the ship.

'You could have killed me, you dumb fucker.'

Dave waited until he was back on board the *Britannia* before saying anything else. Al had put the gun in the galley, out of the way, so as not to irritate Dave any further. Otherwise, he was unapologetic.

'The fuck I was supposed to know that was you?'

'I told you not to drink on top of that medication, didn't I? Jesus, you could have shot me.'

'You go over the side of this boat and you surface at the other end of the fucking ship? What am I? A fucking telepath? Do I look like Mister Spock? Naturally I assumed this would

288

be the boat you'd want to get back on, bein' how it's the one you got off of and how it's supposed to be our getaway vehicle carrying millions of dollars in cash.'

Al pointed to the sports bags, stuffed with money, that now filled the boat's lounge and covered the deck, as if Dave needed reminding. He said, 'My drinking ain't got nuthin' to do with the way your sense of direction is so completely all over the place. With how you end up swimming from one end of this fuckin' marina to the other.' Al frowned and then nodded at Dave's wrist. 'Hey, your watch is gone. And there's blood on your leg.'

Dave glanced down at his bleeding calf. He must have got scratched when he hauled himself up the ladder and out of harm's sabre-toothed way.

'The fuck happened down there anyway?' asked Al.

Dave shook his head as if he couldn't quite believe what had happened himself. He started to throw off the headlines securing the *Britannia* to the *Duke*'s port wall. 'Fucking *Jaws* is what happened. There was a goddamn barracuda down there. At least six, seven feet long.'

Al looked impressed. 'As big as my dick, huh? That's some fuckin' fish.'

'Fish? That was a prehistoric monster. It was just teeth and fins. Scared the shit out of me. I'm lucky to be here with two arms and two legs.' He threw off the springlines and then looked at his empty wrist. 'It ate my watch. Can you believe that?'

'Ain't no accounting for taste.'

'A $5,000 watch.'

'You can buy seven of those when you get home. One for every day of the week.'

'Yeah, that's right. I can, can't I?' Dave waved Al toward the sternlines. 'Cast off at the stern there, will ya? And let's get outta here before something else happens.'

'Told you that swimming was dangerous,' chuckled Al. 'That bitch in *Jaws*? The one who goes skinny-dipping at the start of the movie? Everyone knows her ass is heading for the shark's dinner plate. Man, as soon as I saw that fuckin' film I knew you'd never get my dick in salt water. What we saw in Costa Rica just put that in triplicate. The sea's a bad neighborhood. It's like Overtown at night, and you're some dumb tourist drivin' along in a big white rental with "Sucker" written on the rear window sticker. Radio on, splashin' around, makin' a lot of noise, havin' a good time, not a care in the world. But just askin' to get his ass chewed up by some nigger with a knife. Sharks? Barracudas? Same as.'

Kate could hardly believe it when, yelping with pain and her wrist as raw as a bad case of sunburn, she finally extracted her hand from the cuff. Tearing off the tape that covered her mouth she quickly drank a glass of water, then used the lavatory. She was just about to go up on deck when she heard the gunshots. The sound brought a bitter little smile to her sticky lips. They were still on board. And if they were still on board there was a chance that she could stop them. Stop him. She didn't much care about the other guy. Or even the drugs. It was Dave she was after now.

She crawled upstairs and along to the wheelhouse only to find the radio handset gone. Collecting her binoculars from the control console, she knelt down by the window and searched the ship for some sign of Dave or his partner. Straight away she picked him out, walking quickly along the port wall toward the stern of the ship. He was wearing a wet-suit and he looked pissed, as if something hadn't quite gone according to plan. Then she saw him climb on board the *Britannia* and start arguing with Al.

'Bastard,' she murmured. 'Think you can screw me and my operation and get away with it.'

It was bad enough, she decided, to be a drug smuggler. But to steal someone else's drugs was beneath contempt. Probably they had arranged some mid-Atlantic rendezvous. A large cargo vessel. Well, she could do something about that.

If there was one radio working on the whole ship she could call the French Navy submarine. But the sub was probably already close to the planned underwater rendezvous with the *Duke*. With any luck it would see what was happening and move in to intercept the *Britannia*.

The very least she might do would be to slow the *Britannia* down. But without guns how was it to be done? Maybe she could ram Dave's boat. Perhaps even sink him. And probably sink herself at the same time. Sinking Dave might have been less hazardous if there had been a boat with some sort of gun, like the 25-millimetre rapid fire guns aboard one of the Coast Guard patrol boats that Sam Brockman commanded. Not that he was any help to her now. Nor Kent Bowen. There was simply no time to crack the remainder of the combination to the safe on board the *Juarista* and get the handcuff keys to release the two of them. Bowen would probably be more of a hindrance anyway. The more she thought about it, the more she decided it was better Bowen stayed out of her way. Things couldn't get any worse for her future with the Bureau than they already were. Finding the crew and releasing them looked like a better bet.

Kate crept up on deck, mounted the dock wall, and ran along to the accommodations block. Behind her she heard a sound that made her think she might have a little more time than she had expected. The *Britannia* seemed to be having trouble starting up its engines. They had just backfired and then died. The noise reminded her of Jellicoe's two trophy cannons, and suddenly she thought she saw a way of getting back into the game. Hadn't the captain boasted of firing those cannons once a year to commemorate Nelson's birthday? Jellicoe's eccentricity might provide her with just the edge she needed to stop Dave. Now, if she could only release him and his crew in time.

'Why won't she start?' demanded Al.

Dave winced. 'Damned if I know.' He turned the ignition

key again, listening carefully to the sound it made and then glanced at the fuel gauge. But for the needle registering full tanks, he might have said they were out of gas. Exasperated, Dave shook his head and tried again. Nothing.

'Maybe a stray bullet hit something,' suggested Al. 'Forty-five caliber goes straight through people. Must have ended up somewhere.'

'Maybe. I'm going below to take a look.'

'Well hurry it up.'

The engine room was in the stern of the boat, separated from the full-width master suite where the two bodies lay by a well-insulated watertight bulkhead. Mercifully, Dave did not have to go through the stateroom to get in there. Just climb down a narrow stairwell and open a set of double doors. Once inside the engine room, he knelt by one of the boat's two Detroit diesel engines. A cursory examination of the fuel line entering the engine revealed that it wasn't receiving any fuel at all. Dave opened the tank and shone a flashlight inside. It was full of diesel.

'There must be some kind of blockage in the fuel line,' he said as Al appeared in the doorway. He checked the fuel line to the second engine and frowned. 'Still, they can't both be blocked. Fuel pump must have packed up.'

'Shit.' Al punched the bulkhead wall hard. 'Shit.'

For a moment Dave was haunted by the recollection of something Kate had said at the party. Something about the impellers. If they packed up so did the pump and so did the diesel. Except that there were two engines, two fuel pumps, and two sets of impellers. What were the odds on both impellers packing up at the same time? Two of everything except fuel tanks. There was only one fuel tank. The problem had to be in there.

'I guess we'd better get ourselves another boat,' said Al. 'And here was me thinking I was through fetching and carrying for the rest of my fuckin' life.'

'Wait a minute,' said Dave. 'I've got an idea.'

He went back up on deck, returning moments later with a boat hook.

'It's a long shot,' he explained, inserting the end of the pole into the tank and stirring it around. 'But it could be . . .' Immediately golden diesel filled both clear plastic fuel lines. Dave grinned. 'Son of a bitch.'

'What?'

'There's something stashed in the tanks. I can feel it on the end of this pole. Something soft and squishy. Not hard like the bottom of the tank. It feels like some kind of a rag. Or maybe a bag.' Suddenly it dawned on him what it was he could feel on the end of the boat hook. 'Of course. These tanks must be full of narcotics. That was why they were so nervous, Al. This was the boat the Feds were watching.'

'I thought you said they were watching Captain Jellicoe?'

'He must be in it too,' Dave said, improvising. 'More than likely one of the bags broke free during the storm and blocked the fuel outlet. Look, you'd better stay below deck with the hook in case it happens again. If the engine cuts out just stir it around in there. But not too hard. If the bag bursts the engine will get a hit of whatever shit it is. Coke probably. And that'll be the whole engine OD'd. There ain't no adrenalin shot to remedy that kind of trip.'

'OK,' said Al. 'Now can we get the fuck out of here?'

'We're on our way.'

Kate had never been down to the *Duke*'s engine room, but she figured this was the best place to look for the workshop. Telling her where he had locked up the crew, Dave had saved her some time. If, as he'd said, the crew would be able to break out in only a couple of hours, then he might not have been all that careful about stopping someone from releasing them.

Even before she reached the bottom of the stairwell she heard someone hammering on a door. It had to be the ship's crew. Presenting herself outside the workshop door, she picked up a spanner, hammered back, then yelled, 'Captain Jellicoe? FBI. I'm going to try and break you out of there.'

She listened at the door for a second and heard Jellicoe's voice. When he had finished speaking she threw away the spanner and, laughing, looked at the top and bottom of the steel door.

The door was only bolted.

Back in the *Britannia*'s wheelhouse, Dave turned the ignition. Immediately both engines roared into life. He started up the bow thruster, and, a minute or two later, they were bobbing around in the *Grand Duke*'s wake. He waited another few seconds to let the boat get slowly clear of the ship before engaging engines and steering them to the *Duke*'s starboard side. Then he set the course co-ordinates into the computer and began to radio his position on the agreed frequency. It was easier having Al off the bridge. Not having to explain every single thing he was doing: when they would reach the rendezvous point and shit like that.

As the engines picked up revs and the *Britannia* started to make speed, Dave glanced across at the *Duke*, thinking of the *Carrera* with Kate still aboard and bitterly regretting the way he had been obliged to leave her. So he was a little surprised to see her standing on the foredeck of the ship, alongside Captain Jellicoe and a couple of his officers and men. But he was even more surprised when he saw a cloud of smoke appear in front of one of Jellicoe's brass cannons and heard a loud explosion, followed by the whistling roar of an overhead projectile.

Al came rushing up from the engine room as the cannonball landed harmlessly out to sea. He gasped, 'Did you see that? Crazy motherfucker thinks he's the Crimson fucking Pirate.'

Spinning the wheel in his hands, Dave turned the boat hard to starboard and opened the throttle to full revs, trying to put some distance between the boat and the ship's cannon.

'I think he sees himself more in some kind of law enforcement role,' he yelled.

The cannon fired again. This time the shot came close enough to send a cloud of spray over the bow of the boat.

'Jesus Christ,' said Al. 'That one almost hit us.'

To his surprise Dave found himself laughing.

'What's so funny?' demanded Al.

'They missed, didn't they?'

'One of those lead turds hits us, you won't see any fuckin' comedy in our situation. In case you'd forgotten, paper money ain't waterproof.'

'Chill out, Al. This isn't the Nimitz shooting at your rich-as-fucking-Croesus ass. This is Horatio Lord Nelson gunning for you. This is history, man. Last people those guns fired at worked for Napoleon.'

But Al was looking anything but chilled.

'I'll fix those fuckers,' he snarled and, climbing across some bags of money, he retrieved his submachine gun, racked and aimed it at the figures standing on the bow of the ship.

There was no time for Dave to say anything. The last thing he wanted was anyone else killed, least of all Kate. Not that Al would have been in the mood to listen. All Dave could do was spin the wheel hard to port and then hard back to starboard, sending Al reeling off balance from one side of the aft deck to the other, his nine-mill firing harmlessly into the air above them. When Al finally picked himself off the deck, the *Duke* was well out of range and the third cannon shot was sinking hopelessly short of the *Britannia*'s wide and creamy wake.

'What the fuck did you want to do that for?'

'Evasive action. A zigzag.'

'I was going to shoot that son of a bitch English faggot.'

'Now why would someone with all your obvious advantages want to do a thing like that? Man as wealthy as you are. Guns are no longer a solution. From now on, you want to make your point, you better get out your wallet, not a gun. And remember, it's thickness that counts.'

Al grinned as it began to dawn on him that he was now possessed of an enormous fortune.

'Shit, you're right. I'm rich, aren't I? Hell, maybe I'll let my hair and fingernails grow real long and store my shit in little bottles like that other multi-millionaire guy. The one who invented Jane Russell's tits.'

'Howard Hughes.'

'Right.'

'Al, you can do all kinds of shit now you're rich. But right now I need you back down below, ready to stir that fuel. You hear the engine miss any revs, then make with the teaspoon.'

'Sure thing. How long before we make it to the pick-up?'

Dave glanced down at the console and pressed the Mark button on the computer's GPS. On the screen the waypoint and the interface with the chart plotter appeared, and, above this information, an electronic map. The computer had already set up a range ring to give an indication of how close they were to their next waypoint.

'We've got some cruising to do,' said Dave. 'Storm blew us well ahead of where we were supposed to be. Be about fifty minutes to an hour before we make the rendezvous point.'

'Great,' said Al, and went back inside. There was just enough time for him to have a crap and a beer before he came back up to murder Dave.

When the third and last cannonball had been fired and Jellicoe had finished swearing, Kate said they ought to go and see how Jock was getting on with the combination to the safe aboard the *Juarista*.

They found Bert Ross keying in combinations, watched by Jock.

'I've just calculated how long this is going to take,' said Jock. 'The first number was nine. It takes about ten seconds to try each combination, starting with 9000, then 9001 and so on. That means if we end up checking every one of the 999 combinations, it will take us two hours and forty-six minutes.'

Kate punched the palm of her hand. 'Shit. We need that radio room key,' she said grimly.

'Always supposing it is in there,' said Jellicoe. 'Always supposing that nine is the first of the four numbers on this bloody safe. It could be just a way of wasting our time. It could be he threw the key over the side.'

'I don't think so,' said Kate. 'I know this guy and I don't think he would do that. You'll just have to accept my word on that. May I suggest you persevere with this safe.'

'So what do we do in the meantime?' asked Jock.

'There's only one thing we can do, and that's get after them.'

'Fifteen knots is our maximum speed,' said Jellicoe. 'They're doing a lot more than that.'

'No sir, I meant we should take one of the other boats.'

'In the middle of the Atlantic?'

'They did.'

'Without a radio?'

'Well the fact is, we're not alone,' explained Kate. 'There's a French submarine somewhere in the area. They were supposed to rendezvous with us around now. And there are two guys from the FBI and the United States Coast Guard, handcuffed in the head on my boat. As soon as you find the keys they can radio a message to the sub. There are special frequencies and code words to use. FBI stuff. Meanwhile the *Duke* can hold this position until we find our way back again.'

'Supposing we do catch up with them,' argued Jellicoe. 'What then? They're well armed.'

'As I see it they have two choices,' explained Kate. 'They can make for the Azores and risk being found by local law-enforcement agencies. Or they can sail to a prearranged meeting point with another larger vessel. My guess is that's what they'll do. Transfer the cocaine on board, hide it among whatever cargo the other ship is carrying, and then sink the yacht they're on now, to cover their tracks. If we can get into visual range when that happens, we can at least establish the identity of the other ship and have it boarded by the sub later on.'

Jellicoe nodded. 'Right you are. Bert?'

'9-0-2-3. Nah.' He shook his head and sighing, looked up from the safe. 'Yes, Jack.'

'I want you to hand over the safe-cracking to Jock.'

'Aye sir.'

Jock knelt down in the *Juarista*'s closet and began to key in the next combination of numbers. He said '9-0-2-4.'

'Tell Frank to get his diving gear right away and meet us at the stern of the ship. Whatever boat is nearest the open sea, I want her unlashed in five minutes. As soon as you've got the keys out of the safe, you can sort out these other fellows from the FBI. And then get them on the radio.'

'Aye aye, sir.'

Kate had already left the *Juarista* and climbed up onto the starboard wall of the *Duke*. The *Britannia*, carrying Dave and the drugs, was already 500 yards to starboard and disappearing fast. She turned, looking for Jellicoe.

'Come on,' she yelled. 'The bastard's getting away.'

CHAPTER TWENTY-THREE

'Would you mind telling me exactly what the fuck is going on here? Did the ship hit an iceberg? Are we the only survivors? I hope so, because I've got this thing about people driving my boat, which is partly to do with the small fact that it cost the best part of a million bucks. But mostly it's to do with the fact that to handle not one, not two, but three – three Man diesel engines, each delivering 2,300 revs, and three Arneson surface drives, you generally have to know precisely what the fuck you're doing.'

Kate turned around in the cockpit chair and seeing a red-eyed Calgary Stanford standing there, smiled her most disarming smile.

Coolly she said, 'Nice boat, guy.' Then checking back at the controls, she glanced at the rev counter and saw that they were doing over twenty revs as it was. The movie actor's boat was virtually in flight.

Sitting next to her at the helm position, Jack Jellicoe nodded his nervous agreement. Smiling thinly as the boat surged forward, he said, 'Yes, she's a real thoroughbred. I should think this boat is capable of near competition speeds. Am I right?'

Stanford dropped heavily down in the second co-pilot seat and said, 'Knock it off and just give me the story to date.'

Kate started to tell him about the *Britannia* being used to smuggle cocaine and how she and her FBI colleagues had been working undercover.

'Cut to the chase, will you?' insisted the actor.

'This is it, guy,' Kate told him. 'The FBI has requisitioned your boat and we're now in hot pursuit of the bad guys.'

'No shit. The real cops n'robbers thing?'

'The real thing.'

'So where the hell are they?'

Jellicoe, scanning the horizon with his battered binoculars, said, 'There's no sign of them yet, but we're pretty sure they're on this general bearing.'

Stanford gave Kate an up and down look of appraisal. 'I'll say one thing for you, Mrs J. Edgar Hoover. You sure know how to handle a boat.'

'Thank you.'

'Mind if we have some sounds?'

'Your boat. Your rules,' said Kate.

Stanford flicked a switch on the control panel that turned on the CD player. He grinned and said, 'Rock music for a boat chase, don't you think?' The next second a pair of giant speakers behind the helm position kicked in with a Guns n'Roses track.

'They'll probably hear us before we can see them,' winced Jellicoe.

'Yeah. Sorry it's not Wagner. If you know what I mean Captain Willard.'

'Not really,' admitted Jellicoe. 'And the name's Jellicoe actually.'

'Film reference,' drawled Stanford, shaking his head. 'Scares the hell out of the gooks, n' shit like that.'

'Still not with you, I'm afraid.'

'Forget it, Captain Willard.' Stanford looked at Kate. 'You know, I was kind of blasted last night. I have a vague recollection of a nocturnal visit by someone carrying heat? Was that you guys, or was I outta my mind?'

'That was one of the bad guys,' said Kate. 'They visited all the boats and took away the radio handsets to prevent anyone from calling the Navy.'

'Which disposes of my next question,' said Stanford. He

looked back at Jellicoe and asked, 'How's it comin' there, Willard? Any sign of Mister Christian and those other mutineers?'

'No.'

'Like the music?'

'Music?' Jellicoe snorted.

'Guns n' Roses. How do you like them?'

'Not much.'

'On the subject of guns,' said Stanford. 'Am I going to need to be packin' a piece, or what?'

'Do you mean to tell me you've got a gun?' asked Kate.

'Hindsight is always twenty-twenty,' said Stanford. 'The Hollywood community is full of nervous people and prey to others who make them that way. Being a movie star has some significant bio-hazards. Stalkers. Shit like that. My own life has been threatened on any number of occasions. So yes ma'am, I am licenced to carry firearms. Fact is, there's a gunsafe on this boat. If you're short of a weapon I can probably fix you both up. Highway Patrolman. Glock. Smith & Wesson Sigma. All chambered for cartridges with gravitas. You dig? Easy Andy, I'm not. But when you're on my boat, *mi arma de fuego, su arma de fuego.*'

Kate nodded enthusiastically. She said, 'A gun would be nice.'

'How about you, Captain Willard?'

'No thanks.'

'Please yourself,' said Stanford getting up carefully from the co-pilot's seat. The speed of the boat made the deck difficult to stand on. But clearly Stanford was used to it.

Jellicoe said nothing as the actor went below to fetch the handguns. He was still sweeping the bright blue horizon for some sign of the *Britannia*. From time to time he would glance down at the open-scan radar screen. It was a similar system to the ARPA on board the *Duke*, except that the screen had two displays: the radar image of the general vicinity, and the adjacent chart display – instant confirmation of their position and any hazards that might be in the area. Something on the small screen caught his experienced eye and he touched the instrument's zoom button to take a closer look.

'There,' he said excitedly. 'On the screen. Something to the north-west of us. Less than five miles away.'

Al came out of the head feeling like shit. He had a headache and a bad case of diarrhea and he felt as tired as if he'd missed a whole night's sleep. So tired that it took him a couple of minutes to remember that he really had lost a whole night's sleep. They'd been up all night taking down the score. Then there was the medication. And the alcohol. Tearing the two Scopoderm plasters off his arm he threw them irritably onto the stateroom floor and then sat down on the edge of the bed, paying no more attention to the two dead bodies next to him than he had to the guy in the bath while he'd been taking a crap. They didn't bother him. Dead was dead. He never connected bodies with people who had lived and breathed. But he did wish that he had paid more attention to what Dave had told him about mixing alcohol with the seasickness medication. Not that he had drunk all that much. No more than a few mouthfuls of vodka. A couple of beers. That was just refreshment. But it did seem to have taken its toll on his state of being.

Trying to get his shit together, Al took a deep breath through his nose. He'd killed lots of people before. People he knew well, too. Fact was, it was nearly always people he knew well. The nature of the business he was in demanded it. You came on to a guy you'd done business with, like he was your best friend, and then blew his fucking brains out. Only usually Al had a little more enthusiasm for the job, on account of how he normally felt more like he had some adrenalin coursing through his system. Adrenalin was good for wet work. It kept you sharp and on your toes. Right now, he felt as blunt as a door handle in a padded cell. Gray and sweaty, like it was him who was heading for a Viking funeral, instead of the younger guy up on deck.

Al looked around for inspiration and saw a jade block and a razor blade on the dead girl's bedside table. It had been quite a few years since he'd had a blow of snow. Enjoyable, but expensive, and Madonna was too money oriented to let him turn lots of cash into a handful of dust for snorting up his nose. Besides, Naked Tony wouldn't have liked it. He distrusted people who used dope regularly. But as a now and then thing it was OK. And right now it looked just what he needed to be on top of the hit parade. To give it his best shot. One hit to make another. That was politics.

He leaned across the girl's body, casually inspecting her nakedness, and stroking her titties as he reached for her bedside drawer. Leaving aside the hole in her head and the blood all over her face, she was a nice-looking girl. Still warm too. But for his lethal agenda he might have been tempted to fuck her before she cooled off for good.

The drawer was a regular dessert service tray: shotgun spoons, gold-capped safety razors, gold straws – all the para-phernalia of the regular user, like it was *premier cru* Bordeaux. Even the glass storage bottle containing her supply of coke was wearing a little gold jacket.

'Damn right, babe,' Al told her as he tapped a generous measure onto her jade chopping block. 'It's a luxury, not a lifestyle.'

When Al had finished chopping the coke, he separated the powder into two neat mounds, took the gold straw and snorted one of the piles into his flaring nostrils. His head jerked up from the rush and a big grin spread on his face.

'Now that's what I call vitamin C,' he chuckled and swept the second mound of coke off the jade block with the razor, and into the dead girl's navel. Taking the gold straw, he pressed his face close to her belly and snorted out her navel, licking it clean for good measure. Already he felt invigorated. He said, 'This is good leaf.'

Ever since Dave had found the stash, Al had been wondering if there was a way of getting it out of there and loading the stuff onto the *Ercolano* at the same time as they transferred all the money. Tony might like a windfall like that. It seemed a hell of a waste just to sink the boat with all that dope on board. If it was anything like the stuff tingling through his nose, deep-sixing the motherlode would be nothing short of a fucking tragedy. Al licked the dead girl's belly again, and feeling the boat begin to slow, he stepped out of the main stateroom and shouted up the stairwell.

'We there?'

'I reckon this is about the spot,' shouted Dave.

Snorting happily, Al scratched his nose and went up to the galley where he had left his weapons on the counter. He took the .45 automatic and unscrewed the laser aiming module. He wouldn't need it. Not at the range he was contemplating. The silencer he had already dumped when firing at what he had assumed was the nosey parker. Noise was good when you were trying to persuade someone to stay the fuck out of your way. Ejecting the magazine, he thumbed a few more rounds inside until it was full again and then smacked it back up the handgrip. One round would be all he would need, but Al was too much of a pro to leave anything to chance. Any opportunity you got to reload, you took it. You could never tell what might happen when you had to grease someone. The unexpected. It was always a factor. Especially when it was a guy you knew well. A guy you quite liked, even. Drugs had helped Al to change his mind about blowing Dave away without a word. That no longer seemed such a good idea. He was going to have to talk to Dave. Apologize. Tell him that it was nothing personal. That it was just Naked Tony's fucking paranoia, and what could he, Al, do about it? Except do what the fuck he was told, or end up in a similarly terminated condition. After all he and Dave had been through together, apologizing seemed to be the least he could do for the guy. That and a quick and painless headshot. Back of the cranium probably – SS style. Whatever you thought about their lack of personal morality, those Nazis had known how to off people with a pistol. German efficiency. The ultimate killing machine. BMW with bullets.

The *Britannia*'s original owner had been a keen diver, and the boat was fitted with an Apelco fishfinder. As well as giving the screen viewer the best possible picture of where fish were to be found, the Apelco was also equipped with a dual-frequency transducer, which, scanning forward and downward, could give advance warning of shoals, holes in the seabed or even wrecks to be explored. From the pilot's chair on the bridge, Dave kept one eye on the Apelco and one eye on Al through the skylight window of the galley. There could be only one reason for Al reloading his gun. He meant to use it. On him. This was the moment Dave had been half expecting. Now that Dave had served his useful purpose, it was time for Al's double-cross.

Dave throttled right back so that the engines were just ticking over, picked up the Mossberg shotgun from the control console, and positioned himself immediately over the stairwell that led up from the galley to the bridge.

Al came creeping up the stairs, gun at the ready, and called out, 'Can you see the ship yet?'

Dave pumped a cartridge into the barrel by way of reply and took aim. He said, 'Just the back of your head, Al.'

Recognizing the distinctive sound of a shotgun being readied for business, Al became as still as the boat itself.

'Throw the gun out of there, as far as you can. And better make sure it hits the sea, or I'll get upset.'

'What the fuck is this about?' said Al.

'You tell me.'

'You gone nuts?'

'The gun, Al, or I'll part your hair with buckshot. I've killed two people today already. I don't suppose one more'll make much difference to my immortal soul. But it sure as hell will to yours.'

'OK, OK. I don't need it any more anyway.'

'You said it.'

Al threw the gun. It sailed through the air and plopped into the ocean behind the boat with a scarcely audible splash.

'Come upstairs, real slow, hands on your head,' Dave told him, and backed up to the pilot's chair.

Al did what he was told. But at the very next minute, just as he reached the top of the stairs, the boat began to rock violently, as if the sea had been stirred by some sudden typhoon, or maelstrom. Dave collapsed back into the chair and, glancing down at Apelco, saw the outline of something large on the screen. He knew by the speed of its ascent that this was no shoal of fish or some marine leviathan. He recognized the electronic signature of a submarine when he saw one. But by then the sub was already surfacing, less than fifty yards from the *Britannia*'s bows. And Al was scrambling across the deck toward him, knife at the ready, a murderous expression swiped across his big ugly face.

Dave turned toward Al, the shotgun pointed squarely at his barrel-like body. He could have shot him. Could have blown his head clean off. Al knew that, but he was gambling on Dave's lack of guts, as he saw it, for any more killing. He hardly expected that at the last second Dave would take hold of the gun barrel and swing the Mossberg round like a baseball bat against his head. The stock struck Al's skull with a loud thwack, like someone knocking once and loudly on a wooden door, and Al collapsed onto the deck at Dave's feet.

Most men would have been knocked insensible. Al merely lay there groaning for a minute, time enough for Dave to snatch away his knife and throw it over the side, backing further away as Al sat slowly up. He rubbed his head furiously, focusing on the shotgun and then on the conning tower now looming over them.

'Well, there's no need to take this so personally. Get us out of here for Chrissakes,' he complained. 'Whoever they are, they don't mean to ask for directions. We can still make a run for it.'

'Where do you suggest we go?'

'Anywhere but here.'

Dave turned off the engines.

'What are you, nuts?' demanded Al. 'This little misunderstanding you and I just had. It don't mean that we have to go jail for it. Come on, will ya? They can't chase a motor yacht like this.'

Dave shook his head and said, 'You can't outrun a submarine, Al. Quite apart from the two-inch gun on the conning tower, they have these things called torpedoes. We'd be a sitting duck.'

A figure now appeared on the submarine's conning tower and, speaking English in a thick foreign accent, addressed them through a loud-hailer.

'*Britannia*. Prepare to be boarded. Prepare to be boarded.'

Other figures appeared on the hull and, within a minute, an inflatable carrying several sailors was bobbing its way across the short stretch of water that separated the boat from the sub. Dave threw the shotgun into the sea, just in case Al was tempted to grab it and try something stupid.

It was then that he saw another boat racing toward them. Checking through the binoculars, he saw that it was a some kind of performance yacht. Right away he guessed it must have come from the *Duke*.

'Kate,' he said wearily. 'That's all I need.'

'Now we've got him,' she crowed.

'It looks like Ross must have got into the radio room after all,' yelled Jellicoe.

Kate said, 'Either that, or the French decided to go after them on their own account.'

Calgary Stanford turned down the volume of the boat's CD,

and said, 'I did a movie about a sub once. I was the intuitive sonarman, following a hunch. Course I was just a bit player back then.'

'Or maybe they tried to radio us themselves and, when they got no answer, they figured something was wrong,' Kate continued.

Stanford wasn't listening. 'And it wasn't a real sub at all,' he said. 'Just something they mocked up on the lot at Paramount.'

'The silent service, eh?' remarked Jellicoe. 'Never fancied being in subs, myself. Banged up for all that length of time. A bit like being in prison, I'd have thought.'

'That's exactly where those two shit-heads are headed,' said Kate, and throttled back the Predator's engines. 'A sub will seem like the Plaza Hotel by comparison with where they're going. With twenty million dollars' worth of coke on board, they'll be lucky to get away with twenty years. A million bucks a year.'

Jellicoe and Stanford exchanged a what-a-bitch kind of glance.

'Don't fuck with the FBI,' whistled Stanford. 'I'll try and remember that, ma'am.'

'Absolutely fucking right,' snarled Kate. But even as she said it, she knew she was trying hard to convince herself that she wanted to see Dave locked away for the better part of his adult life. Whatever he had done she loved him and, what was more, she wanted to believe that he loved her. But all that was too late now. There was nothing she could do, except her duty. With Captain Jellicoe on the scene, not to mention the French Navy, she could hardly walk away from this. Her feelings in the matter were of little account here. Dave was going back to prison, and that was where her duty lay. Even so, she half hoped that the captain of the French boat, whose men were already boarding the *Britannia*, would dispute her jurisdiction and lock Dave and Al in his submarine's brig – or whatever it was they called their lock-up. More work for the DA's office when it came to getting them extradited, but a lot easier for her.

Kate steered Stanford's boat alongside the *Britannia* and Jellicoe threw a line to one of the sub's sailors, while Stanford put out fenders to protect his paintwork. Out of the corner of her eye she could see Dave standing beside Al on the aft deck watching her, but she did not look back at him.

'You guys wait here,' she told Jellicoe and Stanford, and trying not to look triumphant, she climbed aboard the *Britannia*, curtly declining the helping hand that was offered to her by one of the sailors.

Dave and Al were covered by a sailor with a machine pistol and, in the absence of her FBI identity card and badge, Kate had brought Stanford's Glock automatic to help establish her authority. From what she had heard of Frenchmen they were notoriously sexist. She figured it would be a lot harder for them to patronize a woman with a gun in her hand. She looked around for someone who seemed like he was in charge. Then, in her halting French, and still avoiding Dave's twinkling eye, she identified herself and requested to speak to the officer in charge.

To her surprise and annoyance, one of the sailors laughed. A swarthy, handsome man, with a thick mustache, and wearing a blue boilersuit, he said, 'Please, there is no need for you to try to speak French. I speak excellent English. Agent Furey, did you say you were called?'

Kate nodded and tried to control her irritation. The French. Even when you tried to speak their language they treated you with contempt. It made you wonder why people bothered to learn it in the first place.

'I lived in New York for many years,' explained the man with the flourishing mustache. 'A dirty city, but also interesting.'

'And you are, sir?'

'I am Captain Lieutenant Eugene Luzhin, the executive

309

officer on board,' he said smoothly, and took a packet of cigarettes out of the breast pocket of his boilersuit. 'Do you mind if I smoke? Only it is forbidden when we're on board the missile boat, and most of us are now desperate to get some fresh nicotine into our lungs. It's been a week or two since we last surfaced.'

He did not wait for an answer, and nodded to his men, who took out their own cigarettes and began to light up. Even the man with the machine pistol. Luzhin did not offer Kate a cigarette, for which she was glad. Diplomacy might have meant she would have had to take it, and French cigarettes were too strong for her. These were as pungent as any she had ever encountered. It was small wonder that Frenchmen sounded so gravelly and sexy.

'Captain Luzhin,' she said.

'Captain Lieutenant,' he said. 'The captain is still on the missile boat.'

'Captain Lieutenant,' she said, acknowledging his grinning correction. Was he still amused by her attempt to speak French? 'I'm sorry sir, but is there something funny here? Something I'm missing?'

He exhaled a cloud of smoke as blue as a car exhaust and shrugged in that Gallic way they had.

'Is that a yes or a no?' she asked.

'It's just that I am not accustomed to a beautiful woman pointing a gun at me,' said the captain lieutenant.

'I'm sorry,' said Kate, glancing awkwardly at the Glock, and wondering where to put it.

'That's all right. As a matter of fact I was rather enjoying it.' Puffing stylishly, with one eye closed against his smoke, he added, 'It is like Humphrey Bogart in the film *Casablanca*, when this beautiful woman — ' He snapped his fingers as he tried to remember the name of the actress who had played Ilse.

It was Dave who supplied the answer.

'Ingrid Bergman,' he said. Catching Kate's eye at last, he

added, in a good imitation of Bogart, 'Go ahead and shoot. You'll be doing me a favor.'

Kate blushed with anger and pushed the Glock under the waistband of her shorts.

'Now then,' she said brusquely, addressing herself to the captain lieutenant. 'These two men are wanted in the United States for piracy and drug smuggling. Hidden on this boat are 100 kilos of cocaine with a street value of twenty million dollars.'

The captain lieutenant whistled.

Even as she was making her explanation, Kate was wondering what could be in all the bulky black sports bags that were piled inside the boat. 'But before we do anything else, I think we have to resolve the question of jurisdiction.'

'A difficult matter,' admitted the captain lieutenant. 'I believe the *Grand Duke* is a British-registered ship. And this boat we are standing on. The *Britannia*. It is registered in the British Virgin Islands. At least that is what is painted on her stern.'

'That's true,' said Kate. 'But both these men are American citizens, and as such they should be tried for their crimes by an American court.'

Dave said, 'You send me back to the States, and I'll be facing a long prison sentence. Like I said before, go ahead and shoot. You'll be doing me a favor.'

'Is this another joke?' she asked him angrily.

'No, it's no joke.'

'Then why in hell are you grinning?'

Dave shrugged and looked for his missing watch.

'We're a long way from American jurisdiction,' said the captain lieutenant. 'May I remind you that these are international waters.'

Kate hardly wanted the two men as her prisoners. But there was something in Luzhin's manner that made her want to win this particular argument. She said, 'Nevertheless I insist that these two men be handed over to my custody. They'll be held on board the *Duke* until we arrive in Mallorca, whereupon they'll be immediately extradited back to the United States.'

'Immediately?' The captain lieutenant laughed again. 'I hardly think so. These things take time.'

Dave said, 'You'd really do that to me, Kate? After all that happened between us?'

'Nothing happened between us. And just keep your mouth shut, unless you want to spend the rest of the voyage in handcuffs.'

'Kate. Be fair. I can hardly stay silent about it, now can I? After all, it's my ass that's maybe going back to jail.'

'You should have thought of that before you pulled this little stunt.'

'And that's your last word on the subject?'

'Last word. Period.' She added below her breath, but just loud enough for Dave to hear, 'How I could have ever fallen for a crummy narcotics thief, I'll never know.'

'This was never about narcotics,' Dave told her, still smiling, as if he didn't have a care in the world.

'S'right,' said Al. 'We was after cash money on them other boats.'

'You keep out of this,' snapped Kate.

Once again Dave looked for his missing watch. Then he leaned toward the captain lieutenant and coolly lifting the executive officer's forearm read the time on his watch. Like they were old buddies. Not that the Frenchman seemed to mind at all. Then Dave said something to Luzhin that Kate didn't quite hear. Or perhaps didn't understand.

'I regret, I cannot accede to your request,' Luzhin told Kate. 'But I tell you what.' He nodded at Al. 'You can have him, the ugly one. And we'll take the other one with us. That's fair, isn't it? Like the judgment of Solomon, yes? Half each, as it were.' He nodded at one of his sailors. Straightaway the man threw away his cigarette, stepped into the cockpit and restarted the *Britannia*'s engines.

'That's the craziest idea I ever heard,' said Kate. 'If this is the way the French Navy does things — '

This time she caught the look that passed between Dave and the captain lieutenant and thought she could smell a rat. As if Dave had cut some private deal of his own. Maybe even bribed the guy.

'Wait a minute,' she said. 'What's going on here? You French — '

'Who said anything about the French?' shrugged the captain lieutenant, and flicked his cigarette across Kate's shoulder into the water. 'Not me.'

'Well, if you're not the French Navy, then whose damn Navy are you, Mister?'

Instinctively she started to reach for the Glock under her waistband. But the captain lieutenant smiled and caught her wrist in his own strong hand. Still smiling politely, he said, '*Pazhalsta*,' and took her gun away.

CHAPTER TWENTY-FOUR

The *Britannia* nudged its way toward the sub, gently towing Calgary Stanford's boat alongside. From the control station on top of the conning tower, another officer shouted down to a sailor standing on the foredeck of the sub. The sailor opened a deck hatch and tossed a line to the *Britannia*. As soon as they were tied off to the sub, the sailors aboard the yacht began to throw the Nike sports bags to the man standing on the foredeck, who dropped them quickly through the hatch.

When Kate turned to look for Jellicoe and Stanford, she saw that another sailor had boarded the *Comanche* and disarmed the two men. By then it was clear that Dave was in league with the men from the sub. He paid close attention to the loading of the bags and from time to time would make some obviously good-humored remark to the other sailors, in Russian.

'Dammit, you're Russian,' Kate told the captain lieutenant.

'Yes, Russian,' he said grinning back at her. 'So, it's true what they say. The FBI finds out everything in the end.'

When the last bag had been dropped down the sub's open deck hatch, another man came up on deck and greeted Dave as if he was his oldest friend. Then he climbed down the short Jacob's ladder that had been hung over the side of the submarine's black hull, and clambered up onto the *Britannia*.

Kate noted that even Al looked surprised when the man from the sub embraced Dave fondly. They looked like they were two characters from Tolstoy, she thought. She could not understand a word of what was said, but it was clear that Al had no knowledge of what was happening. Just as clearly, he was angry. Gritting his teeth, Al moved to take a swing at Dave and then remembered the machine pistol still pointed at the small of his back.

'You double-crossing bastard,' he said. 'We ain't anywhere near the *Ercolano*'s position, are we? You set this up with the Russkies from the very beginning.'

'Now you're getting it,' said Dave.

This time Al hardly cared about the machine pistol. He was strong, but not very quick, and certainly not as quick as Dave, who neatly sidestepped the blow then brought his left hand into Al's side, around the bulletproof vest he was still wearing, and just over the kidney. Al doubled over with pain, leaving Dave a clear shot at his blue jaw, which sent him sprawling onto the deck at Kate's feet.

Dave shook his hand painfully. Looking down at his former partner, he said, 'There's an old Russian saying, that says, roughly translated, you're fucked, pal.'

Einstein Gergiev kissed Dave on the cheek once more and clapped him warmly on the shoulder.

'*Kak pazhitaye ti,*' said Dave grinning widely. '*Pazdrav lya yem.*'

The two men spoke in Russian. Unlike English it is a language in which there are two forms of address: formal and informal. Speaking to the captain lieutenant or any of his men, Dave had used the more formal *vi*; but now, speaking to Gergiev, he used only the informal *ti*, the proper form of address for someone you know very well. Such as a man with whom you had shared a prison cell for four years. Dave's accent was nearly faultless.

'We've done it,' he was saying.

'You mean you've done it, Dave. All I had to do was persuade the Northern Fleet commander to lend me a submarine.'

'Is that all?' laughed Dave. 'You're right, that's not very much. Just the loan of a sub.'

'He was very glad to do it. Things were a lot worse than even I had imagined. The Navy in Murmansk owes the local electricity company almost four million dollars in unpaid bills. Last week, they cut off the power supply to three nuclear submarine bases. I'm no nuclear physicist, Dave, but even I can see that the consequences of what these guys at the electricity stations are doing could be disastrous. The prospect of someone providing the Navy with several million dollars of cash in return for preventing nuclear disaster was an offer he could hardly refuse.'

'It's really that bad?'

'For sure. There are dozens of retired submarines awaiting decommissioning, and quite a few of them are leaking like sieves. They need a constant supply of electricity just to keep the pumps going so that the subs don't sink. It's hard enough to decommission an old reactor on land, let alone at the bottom of the White Sea.' Gergiev laughed loudly. 'Under the circumstances I was able to cut us a very generous deal. A very generous deal.'

'What's the percentage?'

'You won't believe it.'

'Einstein, there must be forty million dollars in those bags.'

'That much, eh?'

'At least. So what's the cut?'

'They settled for 30 percent.'

'Thirty percent. That's only twelve million.' Dave looked delighted.

'It's three times what they owe Kolenergo. That's the power authority.' Gergiev shrugged. 'The Russian Navy's desperate for hard currency. Frankly the commander would probably have settled for 25 percent, but well, I was feeling patriotic. And it's not just the Navy either. Just a few weeks ago, Kolenergo cut the power supply for two whole days to the central command of the Strategic Rocket Forces at Plesetsk. Dave, this is the place that controls our ICBMs. They even cut the power to an air traffic control center when the Prime

Minister's plane was in the air.' Gergiev laughed. 'Twelve million? Believe me, they'll think it's a bargain. After all, they had nothing to lose and everything to gain.'

'Leaves us maybe twenty-eight million dollars,' breathed Dave. 'That's fourteen million each.'

'Any trouble?'

'Plenty. But it's a long story.'

Gergiev was older than Dave. He wore a Lenin-style beard and mustache and, like the captain lieutenant, he was wearing a grimy blue boilersuit. He looked more of an intellectual – a university professor, or a medical man – than someone connected to one of St Petersburg's biggest Mafia gangs. He nodded and said, 'You're right. You can tell me about it later, when we're on our way back to Russia. We'd better be going. The Northern Fleet Sonar Surveillance System reports another submarine in the area.'

'Probably the French one Kate was expecting,' said Dave. 'She's the doll, right?'

'She's the mother of all dolls. A real *matrushka*, my friend. One woman inside another. There was me making love to her, and it turned out she was FBI all along. Not that I ever accepted her at face value. You know me, Einstein. I don't believe in anything.'

'Then we'll make a real Russian of you yet,' grinned Gergiev. 'What was she doing on the ship? Were they onto us, do you think?'

'Not for a minute. Like I said, it's a long story. This boat we're on? As bad luck would have it, the FBI had been keeping it under surveillance. Hard currency isn't the only thing being smuggled across the Atlantic. The fuel tanks of this boat are full of cocaine. She thinks that's what we came after.'

Gergiev looked thoughtful.

'A pity,' he said after a moment.

'What?'

'I was thinking it's a pity we don't have more time. There's a big market for cocaine in Russia these days. Please don't tell me how much there is down there.'

'Not just cocaine. There are three bodies too. I told you. We had some trouble.'

'In that case I'll feel a lot happier when we've sunk this boat.' Gergiev glanced over at Al, who was now restrained by two burly Russian sailors. 'Was the killing down to him?'

'Only partly.' Dave shook his head and said, 'I think he likes shooting people. Ten minutes ago, he was planning to shoot me.'

'So what are you going to do with him?'

'That all depends on whether Kate's still disposed to be the scrupulous federal agent. I was hoping I might be able to persuade her to come along with us.'

Gergiev looked doubtful. 'There are plenty of women in Russia, Dave. With the exception of our politicians' wives, most of them are very beautiful. A little corrupt, maybe, but that shouldn't worry you.'

'This one's special, Einstein. Any objections?'

Gergiev looked at Kate. At a glance he saw what kind of a woman she was. Beautiful, sure. But strong too. And proud. He had seen women like Kate before. Party women, when there was still a Party. KGB women, when there was still a KGB. They might wear a little make-up and dress in an attractive, feminine way; and some of them might also affect an interest in romance; but they were always a lot tougher than the men. Whenever there was a spy scandal and an agent went over from one side to the other, it was always a man who betrayed his country. Never a woman. And certainly never a woman like Kate. It was the same in marriage too. Always the husband who was the traitor, never the wife. Women knew the meaning of loyalty. Men just knew how to spell it. So Gergiev knew her answer would be no, even if Dave hoped it might be something different.

Gergiev said, 'Objections? No, of course not. Bring her

along. I'm sure the missile boat's crew will be delighted to have an attractive woman on board.'

'Thanks Einstein. I'll talk to her.'

'Talk all you like. But, Dave?' Gergiev tapped his watch meaningfully. 'Don't say too much.'

Reluctantly Kate allowed Dave to lead her into the galley where he returned her FBI identity card and badge, and quickly reiterated that he wasn't interested in the drugs aboard the yacht. Then he explained about the money. He said, 'It's drug money. Tony Nudelli thinks the money is Colombian. But actually it belongs to some people in New Jersey. Some friends of Tony, as it happens. Italian friends. They are not going to be pleased when they find out that Tony was behind this. That's my present to Tony. He thinks he's picking up some easy cartel money, on its way to Eastern Europe for laundering. Instead he's going to make some new and powerful enemies.'

Kate looked unimpressed. She said, 'You ask me, it's your personality that needs the laundering.'

'Maybe you'd care to take my list.'

'You're in enough hot water already.'

'Do you poke fun at all men? Or just the ones you know?'

'Don't flatter yourself. I don't know you at all. You're just some guy I once slept with. Most of the time I had my eyes closed, remember?'

Dave smiled uncomfortably. 'You can sell yourself that story if you want, Kate. Who knows? Maybe you can write the report and say that there was a lone gunman and no guys standing on the grassy knoll. Maybe you can even produce a magic bullet. But I've seen the Zapruder film of what happened between you and me, Kate. It wasn't like you described at all.'

Kate shrugged dismissively. 'It's not just the Warren Commission who can cover up. And when it comes to what happened between us, I'm Earl Warren and Richard Nixon and Oliver North all rolled into one. In my head this cine film's already been edited. The scissors have been out. Crucial scenes have been cut. Cut, d'you hear?'

'Snip away, Kate,' said Dave. 'But which of us is the more dishonest? I steal money. You lie to yourself. Not just any lie, mind. But the worst kind of lie. This is the kind of lie that might stop you being happy.'

'Exchange an honest life for a crooked one? That's not even worth ten cents on the dollar. I'll say one thing for you, Van, you're full of surprises. I always thought your kind placed no value on sentiment.'

Dave sighed. 'Well, I had to try. Any law against that, Kate?'

'None that I heard of.' Kate shook her head, and quickly wiped a tear from her eye. 'You know, when I met you, I thought you were the perfect man.'

'You're confusing me with that other guy, in the Bible. The guy you're thinking of got himself nailed.'

'You knew Shakespeare. And Pushkin.'

'When you're in prison, you make all kinds of new friends.'

'It wasn't meant to end like this.'

'You just remember you said that, Kate. When you're back home in Miami. I know I will.'

'And where will you be?'

'Murmansk. St Petersburg. Riga.'

'Sounds cold.'

'They wear a lot of fur in Russia. Don't you like fur, Kate? You'd look good in mink.'

'To tell the truth I sort of hate to think of all those mink going to so much bother.'

'It won't be for very long. I intend to travel.'

'With all the enemies you've made, you'll need to.'

'Maybe even come back to the States, when it's safe.'

'Make sure you let me know in advance, so I can book you a cell in a nice jail.' Kate shook her head. 'Don't even think of it, Dave. I see so much as a homesick dog in the *Miami Herald*'s

Classified and I'll track you down like your name was Doctor Richard Kimball.'

'I'll be looking out for you.'

'Don't bother. You won't see me coming.'

'That I've seen already.'

Kate felt herself blush again. But this time it was not with anger.

Dave smiled and said, 'Did you know blushing is considered to be evidence of a moral sensibility?'

'What would you know about that?'

'Nothing much. I just know I'll always remember that night we spent together. When I'm old and gray it'll keep me occupied just thinking about it.'

'I hear cons have all kinds of ways of getting through a long sentence. But if I were you I'd think of a canary. I believe they can be quite affectionate.'

Dave looked around for inspiration and saw Einstein Gergiev tapping his watch. Sadly he looked back at Kate, her face as implacable as ever. The one tear that had encouraged him had quickly dried. The blush on her smooth cheek had cooled. There seemed to be no way of getting past her sharp tongue. He could see that she'd steeled herself to say some of the things she was saying. None of it came from the heart. He was certain of that anyway. But it was as if she had engaged the services of a smart attorney, like Jimmy Figaro, and the smart attorney was chambered in her mouth. There was no getting past him.

Desperate now, he said, 'Didn't you ever want to take a ride in a submarine?' He took her by the wrist. 'C'mon, Kate. Take a dive with me.'

She retrieved her wrist from his hand.

'Me? Sorry Captain Nemo, but I get claustrophobic taking a shower. No way would you ever get me down in one of those cigar tubes.' She went on glibly. 'So you see, even if I wanted to come with you, I couldn't. I'd be climbing up the walls in less than twenty minutes.'

'Then I guess I'd better be going.'

'It's what I've been telling you,' she said sombrely. 'You should never have done this, you know. You should never have stolen all this money. Maybe you can convince yourself it's just drug money and that it doesn't matter. One thief stealing from another and shit like that. But when you need guns to do it, then you're just as evil as the way the money was made. That's what counts. Nobody can build his happiness on another's pain. Next time you look in a mirror just see if I'm not right.'

'Evil?' He laughed. 'If you ever change your mind . . . Well, it's you I want to see Kate, not the police. I don't look in mirrors very much. Kind of got out of the habit while I was in prison. They don't have them in case you use the glass to make a point on yourself. But the sun. Now that's something I do look at, a lot. What I say is, why look for another light when there's one we already have? Good and evil? Don't be so melodramatic. You know, even the sun, the brightest thing in the solar system, has some black in it. Take a look at a picture of it sometime and see if I'm not right. When you do, you'll realize that those black spots are the sun's most obvious feature. And you know something else? Those spots, they affect everything, more than we'd ever suspected until quite recently. Nobody knows what causes them. Probably nobody ever will. But the next time you look at the sun, just ask yourself if I'm really as black a villain as you say. So long, Kate. It's been fun.'

Dave turned to walk out of the galley, and then remembered about Al. He said, 'By the way, you can take Al with you when you leave. Our partnership is dissolved.'

'No honor among thieves?'

'Just don't turn your back on him.'

Kate waved the handcuffs she had brought with her from the *Carrera*. Her own FBI set. Not the pair she was still wearing on one wrist. She said, 'I was saving these for you.'

'How did you do that anyway?' asked Dave. 'How did you get out of those cuffs?'

Kate smiled. 'Same way I got rid of my husband. I escaped.'

They came out of the galley and stepped back onto the aft deck, where Al was still held between the two Russian sailors.

Seeing Dave again, he said, 'Hey Dave, you're not planning to leave me here?'

'When you're back in Miami, Al, I don't advise you try a career reading people's minds. There isn't any plan. Not any more.'

'After all we've been through?'

'I'll always think fondly of you, Al. Right up until the moment when you were planning to kill me.'

Kate walked back to Al and quickly snapped the cuffs on his wrists. Turning to look at her, Al said, 'I hope you're as tough as you think you are, girlie. Because I'm gonna enjoy tellin' people your sordid little story.'

Kate flashed Dave a narrow-eyed look. He was still in earshot. She said, 'That's what it is, all right. A sordid little story. It'll make a change from all the other sordid stories we get in my line of work.'

'Bitch.'

'You know something, Mister? I've gained a special understanding of the criminal mind. It's my considered opinion that mostly – and this includes you, sport – you're all criminal and not much mind.'

When Kate and Al were back aboard Calgary Stanford's boat, and they had let go the line attached to the *Britannia*, Dave climbed onto the hull of the submarine. As soon as the last sailor had left the boat, he took his own submachine gun and emptied the clip at the *Britannia* just along the waterline. As the boat started to sink, the rest of the sailors climbed down the deck hatch until only Dave and Gergiev were left standing on the foredeck.

'*Zhalost*,' sighed Gergiev. He patted the wallet in his breast pocket, and added, '*Uminya balit zdyes.*'

'Hmmm?'

'I said it's a pity,' repeated Gergiev, in English. 'It give me a pain right here. In my wallet. All that cocaine.'

When Dave answered, his eyes were not on the yacht sinking into the sea with the cocaine and the three dead bodies, but on the one already cruising slowly away. The one with the real fortune aboard.

'You'll get over it,' said Dave, and waved to Kate.

She did not wave back.

'Given enough time, you can get over anything.'

JAVA SPIDER

Geoffrey Archer

A British minister is taken hostage in the South Pacific. The kidnappers' grim video of him is relayed to London by satellite TV. His captors say that if the minister is to live Britain must stop its lucrative weapons sales to Indonesia's repressive armed forces.

Islanders thrown off their island by Indonesian troops to make way for a multinational operation seem to be behind the kidnap. But when undercover investigator Lew Randall is sent to Indonesia, he's aware that in a land of masks, nothing is what it seems.

Peeling back the deception layer by layer, he uncovers an international intrigue of nightmare proportions, and a web of corruption that spreads to the top of his own government.

Randall is not alone. Working beside him, but with an agenda sharply at odds with his own, is TV reporter Charlotte Cavendish. Her aim is to expose injustice, his to find and free the politician. Together they penetrate a world where torture is a tool of power and life is cheap.

THE PARTNER

John Grisham

'A narrative triumph and a stylish joy, this novel has me gasping for more of the new, satirical Grisham'
Gerald Kaufman, *Daily Telegraph*

They kidnapped him in a small town in Brazil. He had changed his name and his appearance, but they were sure they had their man. The search had cost their clients three and a half million dollars.

Four years before, he had been called Patrick S. Lanigan. He had died in a car crash in February 1992. His gravestone lay in a cemetery in Biloxi, Mississippi. He had been a partner at an up and coming law firm, had a pretty wife, a new daughter, and a bright future. Six weeks after his death, $90 million had disappeared from the law firm. It was then that his partners knew he was still alive, and the long pursuit had begun . . .

'All the ingredients of suspense, drama and meticulous attention to detail that have made Grisham's novels bestsellers . . . A terrific read'
Sally Morris, *Daily Telegraph*

'Excellent'
David Pannick, QC, *The Times*

OTHER TITLES AVAILABLE